THE *four Seasons* OF GOLDA MIREL

{ A NOVEL }

THE *four Seasons* OF GOLDA MIREL

{ A NOVEL }

BY EVA VOGIEL

THE JUDAICA PRESS, INC.

The Four Seasons of Golda Mirel
© 2006 by Eva Vogiel

ISBN-13: 978-1-932443-45-5
ISBN-10: 1-932443-45-2

Editor: Toby Cohen
Proofreader: Hadassa Goldsmith
Cover design: RK Design

Also by this author:
Invisible Chains
Friend or Foe
Facing the Music
Distant Cousins and other stories

THE JUDAICA PRESS, INC.
123 Ditmas Avenue / Brooklyn, NY 11218
718-972-6200 / 800-972-6201
info@judaicapress.com
www.judaicapress.com

Manufactured in the United States of America

Acknowledgements

With gratitude to the *Ribono shel Olam* for His *chessed*, I give special thanks for the extra *siyata d'Shmaya* I needed in writing, for the first time, a book for adult readers.

As in the past, there are a number of people who have given me help and support, and I would like to express my gratitude to them:

My husband Nachman, for giving me so much encouragement. My daughter-in-law Ruchi, for being my number one sounding-board and such a constructive advisor (and for persuading me to write this book in the first place!).

My sisters: Rebbitzen Ruth Padwa, for her invaluable advice and knowledge; Mrs. Esther Spitzer, for her total involvement (I really can't thank her enough for all her help!); and Mrs. Suri Kornbluh, for her interest and support.

In spite of his busy work schedule, Dayan Osher Westheim, *shlita*, once again took the time to check the manuscript, for which I am truly grateful.

Many thanks to a good friend, Dr. Bleema (Carol) Harris for her enthusiastic interest and her help with the medical aspects of this book. I am also grateful to Consultant Orthopaedic Surgeon, Mr. Anthony Claysons, FRCS, and his secretary for answering my questions.

Thanks to my close friend and neighbor, Rebbitzen Feigy Kupetz, who read the manuscript chapter by chapter, waiting impatiently for the next one and urging me not to slack and get on with it!

Once again I have enjoyed a good working relationship with Judaica Press, who in their helpful and encouraging way were a pleasure to deal with! Thank you, Mr. Aryeh Mezei, Mr. Nachum Shapiro and, for your superb editing, Mrs. Toby Cohen. Thanks also to Hadassa Goldsmith for your excellent proofreading.

May Hashem bless you all with hatzlochoh and nachas!

Eva Vogiel

PART I:

Spring

Chapter 1

Golda Mirel Wasserbrun's life began *erev Pesach*, 1904, in Lipsk, a small town in Galicia, Poland. Outdoors, a cold, blustery wind whistled at the windows, but in the little room where her mother lay, a warming log fire crackled busily.

"*Mazel tov! A meidel!*" cried Frau Waldschatz the midwife. She raised her hot face and smiled at the weary mother.

Pessel Wasserbrun's heart leaped in joy. She had waited five long years for this! At last, a child of her own! She was a mother—something she had feared would never happen!

She lay back against the pillows, reminiscing. At first, she hadn't been concerned; she was too busy learning to run a household to notice. But as her second year of marriage slid by, worrisome thoughts began to pinch at her. *What if I never have any children?* This cold, unspoken fear reared its head night after night as she tossed in her bed.

As time passed, she grew obsessed about her plight, imagining everyone's pitying eyes on her. She began to avoid public events, and visiting friends. She soon shunned making simple excursions, like going to the market. Finally, she was rescued from falling into depression by a smart, straightforward person who said exactly what had to be said! Pessel smiled, remembering her beloved grandmother, Babbe Golda Mirel. She could almost hear that piercing voice scolding her affectionately. "What is this with you, *mein* Pessele, wallowing in self-pity like this! Your turn will also come, you'll see!"

Yet during the really hard times—when her sister-in-law gave birth to her fourth child, when her younger sister Freidel had a baby boy, and fifteen months later, a second—only the old lady had truly understood, and been able to comfort her. "*Nu, nu,* Pessele," were Babbe Golda Mirel's loving words, "*Der Ribono shel Olam* takes good care of you; don't worry—your *kindt* is coming soon."

And now, her prediction was realized! Pessel sighed wistfully. Babbe Golda Mirel was no longer here to share this joy. She had been taken from them almost a year ago, and could not do what she had always promised: "Pessele, for your *simcha* I'll make the biggest, sweetest strudel roll of all!"

Pessel smiled again at the memory. It suddenly struck her that her grandmother had surely been involved—putting in a good word for her in *Olam Habah*!

"*Baruch Hashem!*" she whispered in a rush of gratitude.

She relaxed, listening to the rustling sounds of the midwife.

"Is the baby all right?" she asked. "She isn't crying …."

She heard a slap and the baby began to wail loudly.

"There!" the midwife exclaimed. "Listen to that! A good pair of lungs!"

"But you slapped her!" Pessel said indignantly, raising herself to glare at the midwife.

"Well, sometimes they need a good slap to make them cry," Frau Waldschatz explained kindly. "Don't worry," she chuckled. "There'll be plenty of times *you* slap her and make her cry!"

Laughing weakly, Pessel watched the midwife place the baby on a folded blanket on the table near the fire, where she had prepared a bowl of warm water. Dipping her elbow into the bowl, she frowned and added some cool water from a pitcher nearby. Then, repeating the elbow test, she nodded with approval.

"Good. It's just right. I'll just make the baby nice and clean and wrap her up and then you can hold her."

Behind the closed door, muffled sounds of *erev Yom Tov* hustle and bustle drifted toward Pessel. How busy everyone was! With all the preparations for a *seder*, who could keep track of what Pessel was up to! No doubt her mother would remember soon, and pop her head in, but now Pessel was glad of a few moments alone to savor the wonder of motherhood.

Anshel, her husband, was also not here, having gone to bake *erev Pesach matzos*, as she had urged him.

"What use will you be, pacing up and down outside?" she had argued. "Of course, Tatte and the others can give you some of their *matzos*, but you know you'd rather have your own. Go and bake. By the time you come back, who knows?"—she felt a stab of excitement—"… there might be some good news!"

Pessel leaned back in drowsy contentment, imagining the pleasure on Anshel's face when he arrived home! She listened, thrilled, to the baby's delicious protests at the treatment she was receiving. Frau Waldschatz deftly swabbed her with lukewarm water and rubbed her dry with a soft, white towel, clucking and scolding all the while.

It took Pessel a few moments to realize that the midwife's chatter had suddenly come to an abrupt halt. She froze, though why the silence should fill her with dread she couldn't say.

"Frau Waldschatz!" she called out instinctively. "Is something the matter? Is my baby all right?"

"Yes, certainly," the midwife replied vaguely. She swaddled the baby tightly and wrapped her in the beautiful crocheted shawl Pessel's mother had used for her own children.

"Here, you can hold her now." She gently placed the warm little bundle into her mother's arms. "Isn't she a little beauty, *k'ein eiyin hora*!"

The child was indeed beautiful. Pessel gazed tenderly at the soft, pink face.

"Hullo, little one," she said softly. *Hullo, Golda Mirel.* There was no doubt in her mind what her daughter would be named.

Her eye caught Frau Waldschatz gazing worriedly at the child, and at once, the alarm bells rang again.

"What is it? Please!" she insisted, her heart beating wildly. "I know something is wrong."

"No, no! Nothing serious," Frau Waldschatz replied airily. "She's perfectly healthy. Just ... well ... one of her legs is shorter than the other."

"Oh." Pessel was relieved. Was that all? She nuzzled her cheek against her baby's downy one, her mind playing pictures of the future little Golda Mirel. There she was, a curly-topped precious darling, prancing in dresses and pink ribbons; here she was pushing a little doll buggy; now she was running to meet her Tatte. Suddenly, the picture changed. Golda Mirel sat on the side, while other little girls hopped and skipped in the courtyard. Cold shivers crawled up Pessel's neck. *My beautiful baby!* What *would* she be like when she grew up? Would she have to walk with crutches? Would she be able to walk at all? Tears welled up in Pessel's eyes.

"H-how much shorter?" she asked tentatively.

"Well, now, I'd say enough to be noticeable," the midwife sighed, shaking her head sympathetically. "But try not to worry. Maybe they will level themselves out as she grows." She took the baby back from Pessel. "I'll put her in her crib now so you can rest."

She plumped up Pessel's pillows and tucked the blankets firmly round her. "You need a nice warm drink," she said. "I'll go to the kitchen and get one for you ... and tell your mother the news. She must be getting anxious already."

"Yes, but please don't tell her about the … her leg …," Pessel begged. "I don't want her to know just yet. It's *erev Yom Tov* and she's so busy. Besides, I ought to tell my husband first …" her voice choked as a lump came to her throat at the thought of telling Anshel. How would he take it?

"I understand," Frau Waldschatz replied, concern on her kindly face. Suddenly, she leaned forward and kissed Pessel on the forehead. "I'm sure she will bring you a lot of *nachas*!" she said with feeling.

She had just reached the door when Pessel's mother burst into the room.

"Pessele, Pessele! *Mazel tov!*" she cried as soon as she heard the news. She leaned down and gathered her daughter in a warm embrace. "Oh, it's wonderful!" She turned and bent over the crib. "*K'ein eiyin hora!*" she exclaimed. "She's beautiful! Oh, I can't wait to start sewing pretty dresses for her!"

Oh, Mamme, Mamme! Pessel's heart cried. *If only I could tell you and have a good cry on your shoulder!* She forced a laugh and said, "Wait, not so fast! She'll be in nightgowns for a long time still!"

"They grow up quicker than you think!" her mother retorted smiling. "I wish I could stay with you for a while, but the chicken soup is just coming to a boil, and I still have to make *charoses*, so I'd better get back. Try to get some rest. The men should be back from baking *matzos* soon and Anshel will rush straight here!" She kissed Pessel once more. "*Mazel tov*, again, *mein tochter*. Have a lot of *nachas*!"

"You too, Mamme," Pessel said, fighting back tears.

Alone with her thoughts, Pessel's mind was in turmoil. *After such a long wait, the child wasn't even perfect?* Then she felt ashamed of herself. Hashem had given her a beautiful gift, and here she was complaining! She should have more gratitude! Guilt and shame overcame her, and the tears began to flow.

If only Babbe Golda Mirel were here! She would make me feel better, even though she would surely scold me for my self-pity. She wished she could be like her grandmother! Babbe Golda Mirel had always been one to take troubles with fortitude. Even during her last illness, while racked with pain, she presented a cheerful face, and had a glad word for everyone.

All at once, Pessel had a strange sensation. It seemed her grandmother was in the room. She stared about her, longing to reach out and be comforted. *Where are you, Babbe! Help me! And, oh, Babbe, will you mind having your name passed on to a—a cripple!*

Fresh tears sprang to her eyes, but she swallowed and dried them. Looking over at her peacefully sleeping baby, she sensed her grandmother's presence hovering protectively over the child.

"Babbe!" she whispered. "If you can grant my baby one gift, please pass on to her your strength of character … your stamina and stoicism. Help her cope with all the difficulties she is bound to come across."

The strange fantasy vanished, and Pessel wasn't sure if she had been dreaming or not. No doubt her anxiety and the trauma of becoming a mother had done it. But she had calmed down. Gazing through the slats at her baby, she felt a surge of love and protectiveness. *I will look after her*, she resolved, *and help her have a happy, fulfilled life.*

Men's voices sounded behind the door, and from the excited shouts it was clear her mother had given them the good news!

Footsteps hurried toward the room. The door flew open and Anshel strode in, beaming from ear to ear.

"*Mazel tov! Mazel tov!*" he cried heartily.

"*Mazel tov*, Anshel!" Pessel replied, smiling in spite of the tears streaming down her cheeks.

Chapter 2

Golda Mirel plodded slowly along the lane, resentfully watching little Reisel up ahead hurrying along, holding the hand of her mother's young sister Sheindel. Their figures receded into the distance, and Golda Mirel's eyes smoldered. It wasn't fair. *She* was Reisel's older sister, and it should be *her* responsibility to bring her safely to school, not her aunt's!

She shook herself and held her breath a moment, releasing it slowly. *Now, don't get angry at Sheindel,* she thought. She's doing Mamme a favor. Who says she wants to be schlepping her big sister's children to school with her? It's not her fault. Golda Mirel knew the situation couldn't be helped. She couldn't expect anyone to be late to school because of her disability. Having lived with this handicap for eight years, she generally accepted it as part of her life. She hadn't walked till age four, when she was finally fitted with a special built-up shoe. This gave her mobility, albeit with restricted speed and a pronounced limp. She knew the shoe was expensive, and was grateful for her parents' sacrifice, but she couldn't help grumbling now and then. Her mother, determined not to let her feel different, tried to treat her the same as the rest of her siblings. The oldest of six children, she was given household chores like everyone else. She had a fair amount of responsibility for her younger siblings. That is ... except for taking her little sister to school!

She heard scampering footsteps and derisive hooting behind her, and recognized some of her Polish classmates. As they caught up, she braced herself for their slurs.

"Hey, Shortleg!" taunted Janek, the biggest and meanest of them. "Hurry or you'll be late!"

Shrieking with laughter, they all began mimicking her walk for a few moments before running off.

Golda Mirel bit her lip and shrugged. She was used to them by now. They viewed all their Jewish classmates with scorn, but with her limp, she bore the brunt of their jibes. Thank goodness, her Jewish classmates, far from mocking her, tried to protect her from the others' cruelty.

Still, the gentile children at school were the least of her problems. The teachers bothered her even more. She knew exactly what would happen this morning when she walked into the classroom. Pana Slawoska would coldly demand the reason for her lateness. She would mumble her excuse, at which the teacher would sneer maliciously, "When you know it takes you such a *long* time to walk, you need to leave home at least a *few* hours early!" She'd then sniff and look back at the class with a satisfied smirk as they tittered appreciatively.

Golda Mirel sighed miserably. Why did she have to go to school? She couldn't help envying her two grandmothers. In their day, most Jewish girls stayed home to help their mothers, learning to cook and bake at an early age. But now it was 1912 and compulsory schooling had already been law in Poland for quite a while. Actually, Golda Mirel enjoyed learning, especially arithmetic at which she excelled, but it was very hard to sit all day amongst *goyim* who despised their Jewish classmates.

Most of the teachers, too, barely tolerated the Jewish children because of their religious beliefs. One such teacher was Roman Padzynski.

If Pana Slawoska's sarcastic remarks were hard to take, they were nothing compared to the experience she had had with Pan Padzynski a few weeks ago. The memory of that incident still made her shudder!

He had seemed quite kind at first. Short and thickset, with shaggy gray hair, his bushy eyebrows and handlebar moustache gave him a fatherly appearance. He always treated Golda Mirel with consideration, making allowances for her disability.

On that afternoon, when he dismissed the class, there had been the usual stampede as pupils eagerly grabbed their belongings and rushed to the door. Golda Mirel usually walked partway home with her friend Rifka Grossbaum, but Rifka was not in school that day, being in bed with a fever. The other Jewish girls hurried out, no one noticing she had no company. Consequently, Golda Mirel was the last one left in the classroom. As she laboriously hobbled to the door, Pan Padzynski called her name. She stopped in her tracks and looked at him inquiringly.

"Golda," he said, "have you ever seen a doctor about your ... er ... problem?"

Warily, Golda Mirel replied, "Y-yes, a few years ago. That's how I came to have this special shoe."

"That's all you were offered?" There was surprise in the teacher's tone.

"I suppose so," Golda Mirel replied vaguely. "I don't really know."

She had been a small child at the time, and hardly remembered the incident, much less any discussion that might have taken place. Her parents never told her how the specialist had urgently advised an operation—a proposal they had rejected immediately. Apart from their inability to afford it, the thought of subjecting their child to the risks of anesthesia had filled them with horror and dread.

Pan Padzynski smiled kindly at his young pupil. "I know someone who can cure you," he said softly. "Come, let me take you to him."

Golda Mirel was touched by his concern. She gazed up at him, a thrill running through her at this dream come true! Could she ever really run and jump like everyone else? She must do this! But she shook her head, and said regretfully "Thank you, but I must ask my parents first."

"Oh, I'm sure they won't object," he said persuasively. "After all, they want you to be cured, don't they?"

"Yes … but … ," Golda Mirel was beginning to feel out of her depth. "I don't know if my father can afford it …."

"Oh, don't worry about that! This man is prepared to treat you free of charge. Look," the teacher said, still smiling encouragingly at her, "you have to decide quickly. There's no time to go and ask your parents and come back. He's a very busy man and he'll fit you in today as a special favor to me. If you miss this chance, you might have to wait a long time for another one."

"I really want to … but they will worry if I don't come home soon," Golda Mirel argued, convinced it would be wrong to go without her parents' consent.

"Oh, come now!" Padzynski's lip curled slightly. "You know very well they can't expect you home '*soon*' … at the pace *you* walk!" He cleared his throat. "Um, well," he said, catching himself. "Look, this doctor is right nearby, on your homeward route, in fact, so you won't get home much later than usual." He opened the door wide, and gave her a reassuring nod.

Golda Mirel was torn in two. She would never do anything behind her parents' back … but on the other hand they might be annoyed if she threw away such a chance—a cure, free of charge!

And, oh how she longed to be rid of this handicap! Surely her parents would approve.

"I guess ... I-I can come," she said hesitantly.

"Good!" Padzynski grinned widely, showing strong yellow teeth. "Well, come on then, let's go. We'd better hurry. We're late as it is."

Golda Mirel struggled to follow her teacher down the road. She was aware that he kept slowing down, stopping from time to time so she could catch up. This made her uncomfortable, and she stumbled often, trying to keep pace with him. By the time they were halfway down the lane, she was exhausted from the effort.

"Is ... it ... much further?" she panted.

"No, no. We take the next turning and then we're nearly there."

Golda Mirel was relieved when Padzynski finally stopped before two large wrought-iron gates. Behind them wound a cobble-stoned drive, flanked by a high, thick hedge.

"Here we are!" he said, waving his hand with a flourish.

Golda Mirel looked up at the gates, impressed. They were certainly very grand! She peered through, but could not see behind the dense foliage. Obviously, whoever lived here must be extremely wealthy to live on such extensive grounds!

Padzynski opened the gates and beckoned to her to follow him in. Golda Mirel suddenly felt a sense of foreboding. Something was wrong! Some instinct told her this was not a doctor's residence. She craned her neck and squinted, trying to see the residence. At last, she glimpsed something rising behind the trees—a tall spire!

Warning bells rang in her head. *No, no! Don't go in there!* a voice cried within her. She had heard horrifying stories of young Jewish girls being spirited away into convents, their parents powerless to retrieve them. Would she, too, be torn away from her family, never to see them again?

Breaking out in a cold sweat, she shrank back, turned and tried to flee. But Padzynski caught her in a vice-like grip and dragged her back. As he propelled her toward the gates, she kicked and clawed at him, screaming "Help! Help!" The road was deserted, and her shouts fell on empty air. In despair, she realized she could never win this battle. Padzynski wrenched her off her feet, pulling her inexorably closer to the gate. She shut her eyes and began to pray fervently as she had never prayed before, begging Hashem to save her from this terrible fate!

The scrape of carriage wheels sounded on the road. Golda Mirel's eyes flew open in shock. She let out one last resounding shout, flailing her arms and legs so the driver would see her. To her immense relief, the carriage stopped and a voice boomed out, "What are you doing in the road?"

"*Baruch Hashem!*" she whispered. She fell to the ground with a thump, and realized her teacher no longer held her. In fact, he seemed to have vanished!

She staggered to her feet, trembling.

A middle-aged, well-dressed man leaned out, looking down at her inquiringly. Golda Mirel stared back mutely, too exhausted to speak. The elegant gentleman raised his brows in amusement, and said affably, "Well, young lady? Are you trying to cause an accident?" He paused, and looked searchingly at her. He had a vaguely familiar look, but of course she must be mistaken ....

"Who are you?" he asked abruptly. "Don't I know you from somewhere?"

She could only shake her head dumbly.

The man snapped his fingers triumphantly. "Of course! You're Wasserbrun's daughter, aren't you?"

Golda Mirel nodded, dumbfounded. Who was this man? And how did he know her father?

"What are you doing here, so far from home?" he asked.

Golda Mirel knew she could not tell him the truth. She hated lying, but this was one occasion she would have to.

"I was on my way home from school," she said, "and I seem to have lost my way."

"I see. Well, we can't leave you wandering about here on your own, can we? Climb up and I'll take you home." He eyed her foot in its built-up shoe. "Do you think you can manage?"

"Of course I can," Golda Mirel assured him, not bothering to explain that her only difficulty was walking. She clambered into the carriage and sat down, feeling a little uneasy. Normally, she would never accept a ride from a strange gentile, but now she had no choice. It was definitely the lesser of the two evils! And, after all, he did know her father.

"So … how is your father?" the gentleman asked, settling in his seat after instructing his coachman where to go. "My name is Karolski, by the way. I own land and fields not far away from here, and your father used to purchase a lot of grain from me. Haven't seen him for a while, though. I believe he's cut down quite a bit on his work. Wants more time to study, or something. Pity. I could still do business with him if he'd be prepared to purchase a large amount." He drew a silver snuffbox out of his pocket and took a pinch of snuff. "And how are you, young lady?" he asked, smiling at her. "Last time I was at your house your father was quite worried about you."

Like a flash, the memory came to her. Yes, she did remember this wealthy landowner sitting at the table with her father working out some figures, after which her father would hand him a wad of money. She also remembered the name "Karolski." Sometimes Tatte would hire a wagon and go to the "Karolski Estate," returning with sacks of grain, which she sold to farmers to feed their cattle. Golda

Mirel remembered the large basket he would bring into the house, laden with fruit from the landowner's orchards.

"I'm glad to see you are getting about," Graf Karolski continued. "Your father was afraid you might never walk."

They traveled along at a gentle trot, Karolski doing most of the talking. Golda Mirel, still shaken by her unnerving experience and lucky escape, sat quietly, only speaking when asked a question. Having resolved not to tell her parents what had occurred, she hoped she would be able to slip unobtrusively into the house and behave as though nothing unusual had happened.

"Please, let me off here," she said when they were near her home. "I can walk the rest of the way."

"Oh, no!" Karolski protested, with an indulgent laugh. "I've brought you this far, I might as well see you safely to your door!"

Golda Mirel could not argue. She sat tight, praying no one would be outside to witness her arrival by carriage!

This time, however, she was out of luck. Her mother, having heard a carriage draw up, came out to see who it was. Her eyebrows shot up in amazement to see Golda Mirel alighting.

"Good afternoon, Frau Wasserbrun," Karolski called out from the carriage.

"Oh!" Pessel's surprise and curiosity deepened. "Good afternoon, Graf Karolski. What—"

"Your daughter lost her way," Karolski interrupted, "and I happened to be passing so I brought her home."

"Thank you so much! How kind of you," Pessel said. She regarded her daughter with a puzzled frown. It was not like Golda Mirel to lose her way.

"How is your husband?" the landowner asked. "Is he at home?"

"No, he's out just now."

"Hmm. Studying, I suppose." There was a note of disapproval

in Karolski's voice. "He won't get rich that way, you know. Well, give him my regards and tell him to pay me a call. I might be able to put some business in his way. Goodbye, young lady," he said, raising his hat to Golda Mirel. "Watch where you're going in the future. I can't guarantee I'll be riding past if you get lost again!"

Pessel and Golda Mirel thanked him again profusely and watched him drive away. Pessel turned to her daughter, about to reprimand her, but thought better of it. The girl looked extremely upset, obviously ashamed of herself for having lost her way.

All she said was, "What a bit of luck that he happened to be passing just at the right time!"

Golda Mirel agreed with her. *You don't even know*, she thought, *just how lucky it was!*

Since that day, Golda Mirel had dreaded going to school. Having to face Pan Padzynski was a nightmare. She was terrified that he might take revenge on her for thwarting his plan. She waited apprehensively for the blow to fall. Would he detain her on some pretext and try to force her to go with him again? Her heart pounded in trepidation as she recalled her first meeting with him when he walked into the classroom that next morning. Yet he merely gave her a brief glance as he passed her. However, there was so much hatred and contempt in that look that it made her quake. After that he simply ignored her. If she asked a question, he appeared not to have heard; if she raised her hand to answer a question, he did not seem to see it, even though she was sometimes the only one with her hand up. In a way the situation was a relief to her, but it was disconcerting nonetheless, particularly as the rest of the class regarded her with curiosity, wondering what she had done to earn the teacher's displeasure.

Golda Mirel reached the school building at last but did not quicken her pace, though she knew she was late. There was nothing for her to look forward to in there. The playground looked empty and bleak. The gray stone building, with its barred windows and corrugated iron roof, was particularly uninviting. Golda Mirel pushed the door open tentatively, afraid she might encounter the headmaster or a teacher. Luckily, the corridor was deserted. Golda Mirel passed various classrooms, from which the strident voices of teachers rose above the pupils' subdued murmuring. She opened her classroom door hesitantly, hoping to slip in unnoticed. But it creaked on its old hinges, and all heads turned to look as she came in.

Today, instead of her usual "why are you late again?" Pana Slawoska changed her tactics.

"Well, well!" she called out shrilly, her voice dripping with scorn. "Golda has arrived! Isn't that remarkable! Well done, Golda! Students! Everyone, rise! Let us give her a round of applause!"

She began to clap her hands, and her students stood up and followed her lead, hooting derisively. The only ones who stayed put were her Jewish friends, whose faces bore expressions of outrage and compassion.

Golda Mirel stumbled to her seat, her face crimson.

Pana Slawoska smirked at her students and continued the lesson. Golda Mirel threw herself into her work, trying to calm her agitated mind as she concentrated on her sums.

But Pana Slawoska wasn't finished with her yet. Apparently, her success had gone to her head. She turned from the blackboard on which she had been writing and sweetly said, "As you can see, I have written the answer to this sum, but some of the numbers are missing. Whoever can work out those numbers, put up your hand and I shall choose someone to write them on the board."

Quite a few hands went up after a few moments, but Golda Mirel, though she had the answers, refrained from raising hers. The last thing she wanted was to hike up to the blackboard from the back row.

"Golda," Pana Slawoska inquired in a falsely solicitous voice, "don't you have the answer?"

"Y-yes," admitted Golda Mirel honestly.

"Well, come on then. Come up here and write them on the board."

Blushing again, Golda Mirel rose and slowly made her way to the front, aware that all eyes were on her. She wrote the required numbers, and waited as the teacher scanned them.

"Correct," Pana Slawoska announced. "Now go and sit down."

As Golda Mirel plodded back to her seat she heard titters, which soon turned into uproarious laughter. *What was so funny?* she wondered, overcome with embarrassment. Glancing furiously about, she saw her fellow pupils watching something behind her. She didn't have to look back to see. She knew. Pana Slawoska was mimicking her limp!

Seething with anger, she finally reached her seat.

"What *are* they all laughing about, Golda?" Pana Slawoska asked, in mock innocence.

This was too much for Golda Mirel! She had been about to sit down, but instead she gathered up her books and walked toward the door.

"Golda! Where are you going?" The teacher called out sharply. Golda Mirel ignored her and continued on her way.

"Golda! Stop being stupid and sit down at once!" There was a note of alarm in Pana Slawoska's voice. She was obviously afraid Golda Mirel would report her. "I don't know why you are offended. I only asked if you knew why they were laughing …."

By now Golda Mirel had reached the door. She turned and eyed the woman, who couldn't mask her obvious discomfort.

"They are laughing," she said, in a tone surprisingly adult for her eight years, "because they think I have one leg shorter than the other. But they're wrong. I have one leg *longer* than the other!"

There was a stunned silence in the classroom as she limped out through the door, closing it firmly behind her.

Chapter 3

t home, Pessel was peeling potatoes when the baby began to cry. Moving her chair near the cradle, she began rocking it with her foot as she continued her work. She groaned in irritation. Why had he woken up just now? He normally took quite a long morning nap, and she was really relying on it today. Her two-year-old, Ettele, was at her aunt's house playing with her cousin, and Pessel had planned to put up the potatoes, then get to work on a gown for a customer who had a fitting that evening.

Her hands and foot working rhythmically, she had little Leibele back asleep before the potatoes were in the pot. She sighed, relieved. Peering at his small, angelic face she felt ashamed of her irritation. Where was her gratitude? Had she not been blessed with a family after five childless years? *Well, that's just because I have that dress to finish*, she reasoned in justification. This, however, brought on another battle with her conscience. Now she was complaining because she was obliged to take on sewing work? No, no! Of course not! When Anshel had worried that the business took up too much of his time, hindering his learning, it was *she* who had encouraged him to spend his afternoons at the *beis hamedrash*, insisting that she could earn a fair amount doing dressmaking. *So don't grumble now*, she thought, setting the pot of potatoes on the stove.

She crossed to her sewing corner and spread out the silken material, enjoying the softness under her fingers.

As she pinned and stitched, she reflected on her life. She really had a lot to be thankful for. She was certainly busy, with very little time to relax, but six adorable children and a good husband who was a *talmid chochom* made it all worthwhile. Even her precious Golda Mirel, whose disability had not developed into a real issue, *baruch Hashem*, was growing up a sensible, well-balanced girl. She was a reliable little thing, always ready to give a hand with the younger children. Pessel smiled, thinking of how much she depended on Golda Mirel every morning, but her help was really invaluable. Pessel was not sure she could cope without her. And even if it did mean Golda Mirel was late for school, surely the teachers made allowances for her.

The back door opened suddenly, and Pessel nearly jumped out of her skin as the object of her thoughts limped into the kitchen!

"Golda Mirel!" she cried. "What's happened? Why have you come home? Are you not well?"

Receiving no reply, she eyed her daughter, noting the girl's red eyes and tear-stained cheeks. Before she could question her further, Golda Mirel sank into a chair at the table and dropped her head on her arms, sobbing bitterly. Alarmed, Pessel put aside her work and sat down next to her. She gathered the little girl to her and rubbed her back, whispering soothing words as Golda Mirel cried herself out.

"Shh, *zeesele*," Pessel whispered softly. "Tell Mamme why you are crying."

Golda Mirel looked up and, wiping her eyes with the back of her hand, declared with a vehemence that surprised her mother, "I am never going back to school! *NEVER EVER!!*"

Pessel almost laughed out loud in relief. *Is that all?* she thought.

Many children make that announcement at some time during their school life and this daughter of hers had more reason than most. Still, it *was* rather out of character for Golda Mirel. Perhaps it wasn't just a mere triviality. And even if it was, she had better appear to take her seriously.

"What's happened, *mammele*?" she asked gently. "Who's upset you?"

Between sobs, Golda Mirel poured out her story. Although the account was somewhat incoherent, Pessel got a clear picture of Pana Slawoska's sadistic behavior. She bridled with anger. This was intolerable! Then she took a breath, controlling herself with an effort. After all, she must not allow the child to indulge in self-pity. Golda Mirel was capable of doing just about everything anyone else could do, *baruch Hashem.*

Pessel was deeply grateful that Golda Mirel's short leg had not developed into a truly crippling issue. She was fully aware that it could have been much worse. The doctor they had consulted had warned that in many instances such children eventually needed crutches to get around, or in severe cases, were confined to a wheelchair by the time they had reached their early teens. Golda Mirel was one of the lucky ones whose legs had continued to grow at the same rate, maintaining the same minor difference in length. Although she would always walk with a pronounced limp, she might lead a reasonably active life.

"Golda Mirele, you must not let these things upset you," she said in a steady voice. "After all, it's only one nasty teacher and a few silly children ...."

"If it *were* only the one teacher!" replied Golda Mirel despondently.

"What? What else has happened?" Pessel asked sharply, in sudden awareness that her daughter had endured more than she revealed.

Despite her pledge never to disclose the incident with Pan Padzynski, the entire story came tumbling out.

Her mother listened, aghast.

"But why didn't you tell us at the time?" she demanded when Golda Mirel's voice finally trailed off into weary sniffles.

Golda Mirel shrugged, unable to explain.

The back door opened, and Anshel strode in. He stopped at the sight of his daughter sitting at the table, her face streaked with tears. His eyebrows shot up.

"What are you doing home, Golda Mirel?" he asked, concerned.

Golda Mirel looked imploringly at Pessel, silently begging her to explain. She was too exhausted to go through the whole rigmarole again.

"Golda Mirel, *zeesele*, run along and wash your face," her mother said, going to the stove to prick the potatoes with a fork. "Dinner will soon be ready."

"Yes, Mamme," Golda Mirel rose obediently and left the room, resolving to stay out long enough for her parents to discuss the matter.

As Pessel recounted Golda Mirel's experiences at school, she watched her husband's face reflect her feelings at the thought of the humiliation his daughter had been subjected to. At the tale of Pan Padzynski, his expression changed to one of horror.

"What a *mazel* Karolski came along when he did!" he exclaimed, shuddering at what might have happened. "I must thank him when I see him again."

"But what are we going to do now?" asked Pessel. "How can we send her back to school?"

Anshel frowned. "That's a problem," he said, looking worried. "I hear the authorities are quite strict about it lately. If a child is absent for more than two weeks they come to investigate."

"So what do we do? Maybe you should speak to the head-master ...."

"Hah!" Anshel gave a short laugh. "A lot of good that will do! Have you ever known them to take the side of a *Yid* against one of their teachers?"

Pessel moved the meat stew off the fire and checked the pota-toes again. "You're right," she sighed, shaking her head in despair. "It's always hard for the *yiddishe* children. But for Golda Mirel it's even harder than for the others." She drained the potatoes at the sink, shook them into a bowl and sprinkled them with salt and pep-per. She looked around the room. "Golda Mirel's not back yet? I hope she isn't lying on her bed crying again. I'd better call her to come and eat." She moved to the door. "I think we'll let her stay at home for the rest of the week. It'll give us time to decide what we're going to do."

Two mornings later, battling a cold wind, Pessel made her short way to her mother's house. As she pulled her coat more tightly around her, she felt a guilty pang of relief that Golda Mirel was at home minding the children, making it so easy for her to run this quick errand. Normally, she had to stuff the two little ones into hats, coats and mittens, and strap Leibele in the baby carriage, just to run over to her mother to borrow some blue thread.

Gittel Danziger's eyebrows rose in surprise at the sight of her daughter standing on her doorstep alone. "Where are the children?" she asked, alarmed. "You haven't left them on their own, have you?"

"Of course not!" Pessel responded, holding up a small piece of material. "I've just run out of this shade of blue thread," she explained quickly. "Golda Mirel is with them."

Her mother nearly dropped the workbasket she had been carrying to the kitchen table. "Golda Mirel? Why isn't she at school? Isn't she well?" Gittel looked at her daughter searchingly.

"She's perfectly well, *baruch Hashem*," Pessel reassured her. She lifted the basket lid and began to rummage through the spools, thinking quickly. She hadn't planned to discuss this problem, but decided she had better do so. Mamme would only worry if she didn't know the truth. "The fact is, Mamme, Golda Mirel has been home for two days already. We don't know whether to send her back to school at all."

"Not send her to school? Why ever not? School is compulsory these days, whether we like it or not."

Pessel sighed. "I know ... and we're in quite a quandary. Listen to what happened and tell me what you think."

She recounted Golda Mirel's story, watching her mother's expressions go from indignation over Pana Slawoska's cruelty to disbelief and horror at her granddaughter's ordeal with Pan Padzynski.

"But this is terrible!" Gittel cried when Pessel had finished. "Of course you can't send her back to school! Though I don't know what will happen when the authorities find out ...."

"When the authorities find out what?" a raucous voice rang out from the back door as the Danzigers' neighbor, Kreindel Traubner, shuffled in, wearing her apron and slippers. A large shawl trailed from her shoulders and her headscarf was wound around her head in a turban, its ends straggling down her back. Tall and angular, her wrinkled skin and rather tired-looking eyes made her seem older than her sixty years.

Gittel looked irritated at first, but then smiled a greeting and placed a chair for the visitor. Despite her neighbor's inquisitive nature and annoying habit of bursting in uninvited, Gittel was fond of her. She was a good soul, who would go out of her way to do someone a favor.

"*Nu?*" Frau Traubner wanted to know, "what's all this about? Who's done something the authorities shouldn't know about?"

"Oh, it's nothing … nothing," Gittel shook her head dismissively. But Frau Traubner would not be put off.

"Oh, now," she persisted. "You can't just leave me in the dark. I'm bursting with curiosity!"

Gittel and Pessel exchanged glances, and Pessel gave a slight shrug. She knew if the woman weren't told, her lively imagination would conjure up the most outrageous calamities.

"We're considering keeping Golda Mirel home from school," Pessel explained.

"What! How can you dare do that? And why?"

"She's been badly persecuted," Gittel said, hoping that would end the discussion.

"Well, all the *yiddishe* children are. What's so new about that? You have to teach her to ignore them!" She peered shrewdly at the two uncomfortable women who couldn't meet her eyes. "There's something mo-ore," she sang out, wagging a finger. "Tell me the whole story."

She continued to badger them until the whole awful tale was repeated, no detail omitted. Heaving a deep sigh, Pessel waited as Frau Traubner thought it over.

"I don't blame you," she said at last. "I would do the same in your shoes. And, do you know, you could even get away with it! You can inform the authorities that Golda Mirel can't walk all the way to school anymore. Since you can't afford a carriage to take her, you have no choice!"

"What an interesting idea!" Pessel said in a bemused tone. "I never thought of that."

"You see, Golda Mirel has the perfect excuse! I wish my *einikel*, Dinele, had such an excuse not to go to school! *Chas v'sholom!*" she added hastily, realizing what she had said.

Pessel stood up holding her swatch and the matching thread. "I'd better go now. I'll talk it over with Anshel and see what he says. Thank you, Frau Traubner. It's certainly worth a try. I just hope it works."

"*Zorg nisht*, it will," Frau Traubner said confidently, "though they might insist you get someone to learn with her at home."

"Oh, no! Do you think so?" Pessel asked, worried. "I wouldn't want a *goyishe* teacher coming to my house, even if I could afford it. I doubt we could find a Jewish *limudei chol* teacher."

"That's true," Frau Traubner agreed. "I don't know of anyone ..." She looked thoughtful for a moment. Then, suddenly, her eyes lit up. "Wait a minute!" she cried enthusiastically, "I think I do! The very person!" She tugged at her shawl and moved toward the door. "Just leave it to me. I'll see what I can arrange!"

Chapter 4

*S*onja Herbst surveyed the skirt she was hemming, sighing deeply as she compared the part already completed to the part still left to do. She had been working for hours, and the garment seemed to grow larger with every stitch! A rueful smile lit her eyes. Who could have imagined the spoiled and pampered only daughter of "Dr. Alexander Herbst, renowned surgeon" shortening her own hem! And—even more shocking—fixing a gown handed down from some unknown charitable lady!

She shook her head vigorously. Surely she wasn't falling into self-pity! Of course not! She didn't regret her situation. After all, she had chosen this life, and she intended to see it through to the end. Her only regret was that her parents refused to understand, forcing her to be completely estranged from them.

She stitched mechanically, her mind straying from her work, reminiscing about her childhood and the incident that changed her life.

Her father, who had followed *his* father into the medical profession, dreamed of having a son who would continue the family tradition. When Sonja was born, Dr. Herbst was disappointed, especially when the doctors informed him that his wife would be unable to bear another child. However, he came to adore his little daughter, who was very bright and full of charm. When she finished school, her father, aware that it was unacceptable for a girl to study medicine, encouraged her to pursue a teaching career. She had enrolled at the Teachers' Training College, and at the end of her first year, decided to fill in the long summer holidays with some teaching experience. It was during this period, when she student-taught at a school near her home in Warsaw, that the pivotal episode occurred.

One Friday morning she noticed a little girl sitting at her desk looking miserable and shivering slightly.

Sonja stopped in front of the child and asked, "What is your name?"

"M-Miriam Elkowitz," the child stammered, shrinking back in fear.

Sonja had already noted how the Jewish children cowered whenever addressed, as if afraid something unpleasant was about to happen. They were plainly subjected to some harassment, and it annoyed her. Although not religious herself, Sonja felt an affinity with her fellow Jews.

"Are you not feeling well?" she asked the child gently.

Miriam shook her head in reply. Scrutinizing her, Sonja noticed a rash spreading over her face and arms.

She's got measles! Sonja thought in consternation. *I'd better get her away from the other children.*

Having had measles as a child, she was not afraid of infection, and she took the little girl's hand and ushered her out the door.

"I shall be back in a moment," she told the class. "Nobody is to *dare* make a sound while I'm out!"

She hurried Miriam to the headmaster's office.

The stern-looking man looked disgustedly at the little girl when he heard what they had come about.

"Hmm. She had better be taken home at once!" he said briskly. "Would you take her, please, Fraulein Herbst? I shall take charge of your class meanwhile." He took a thick ledger off a shelf and thumbed through the pages. "Elkowitz … Elkowitz … ah, here we are." He leaned forward over the desk and cleared his throat. "Ahem … I hope you don't mind," he said, dropping his voice in a conspiratorial manner, "but it is in the Jewish quarter …." His nose curled contemptuously.

"I don't mind at all," declared Sonja, raising her brows. "Why should I mind?" Her voice shook with suppressed anger. She turned on her heel and left the office. Buttoning up Miriam's coat, she took the child's hand again and led her out of the schoolhouse.

As soon as they arrived at the Jewish quarter, Sonja was struck by the unusual atmosphere of the place. The few people in the streets bustled about as if time were precious. There were bearded men with shopping bags, even one with a live fish wriggling about in a string bag. A woman carrying two slaughtered chickens went hastily up the street into a house with an open door, slamming it shut behind her.

At the street bearing the name the headmaster had given her, Sonia allowed Miriam to lead the way to her house.

Sonja knocked, and a slightly built woman of about thirty opened the door. Her apron was covered in flour, and little clumps of dough stuck to her floury hands. Sonja inhaled the warm smell of baking bread wafting out the door.

A look of alarm crossed the woman's face at the sight of a strange young woman with her daughter.

"Frau Elkowitz?" Sonja began.

"Yes. W-what's happened?"

"I've brought Miriam home because she seems to have measles."

Frau Elkowitz gasped and beckoned Sonja to follow her indoors. She led the way to the kitchen, where she quickly washed the dough off her hands. Sonja watched in fascination. This kitchen was a hive of activity. A cradle with a sleeping baby stood in a corner, and a toddler sat on the floor playing with blocks. On the table, three beautifully plaited loaves waited their turn to go into the oven, while a fourth, half-plaited, lay on a floured wooden board. A pot of chicken soup bubbled on the stove, its aroma mingling with the smell of baking bread. A strange feeling came over Sonja. There was something familiar about this mixture of odors. It reminded her of something, but the feeling was so intangible and elusive she could not place it.

Frau Elkowitz, having dried her hands, now bent over Miriam who had begun whimpering. She felt the little girl's forehead with her cheek.

"You're burning hot!" she exclaimed. "You must have a high fever! My poor *sheifele*! We'd better get you to bed and call the doctor."

She turned toward a large double door in the center of one wall and called, "Yankele! Yankele, come here a minute."

The door opened and a boy of about nine emerged. Sonja caught a glimpse of the adjoining room and started. A peculiar feeling came over her again. Something about the white tablecloth and silver candelabra on the table, and the bookcase stretching across one entire wall, struck a chord in her memory. Where had she seen this before?

"Yankele," Frau Elkowitz addressed her son, "run to Doctor Melsky's quickly and ask him to come. Mirele's got measles and she has a high fever."

"Yes, Mamme." Yankele ran out the door.

There was an awkward pause.

"Well, I'd better get back to school," Sonja said backing guiltily away from the double doorway. She did not want them to think she was prying. "I hope Miriam gets better soon. Goodbye, Miriam," she called, "get well quickly!"

"Thank you so much for bringing her home," Frau Elkowitz said, escorting her to the door. "Please excuse the mess in the kitchen," she added. "Friday is a very busy day for us, you see ...."

"Of course. I quite understand," Sonja replied, stepping into the street, "and your bread smells delicious!"

As she made her way back to school, she mused over her puzzling behavior. Something about the house ... why, she almost felt she had been there before! She laughed to herself. That was ridiculous. Yes ... but there was something familiar ... she couldn't put her finger on it. *Oh, well, it's really not that important*, she thought, and hurried back to work.

But surprisingly, that very evening, the recollection did return, triggered by a seemingly insignificant remark.

Sonja's maternal grandmother, Malya Ravitz, lived in an apartment nearby and joined her daughter's family for the evening meal a few times a week. Sonja was fond of her grandmother. She was an intelligent old lady and one could have an interesting conversation with her. Sometimes she displayed bitterness in stating her opinions, and lately had become rather cantankerous, but Sonja assumed this was due to loneliness and old age.

Tonight, as usual, Frau Ravitz handed Sonja her coat and made straight for the kitchen, where she proceeded to peer into every pot on the stove, a habit that annoyed the cook, who pursed her lips but refrained from expressing her displeasure.

"What's this, Elena?" Frau Ravitz asked her daughter, lifting the lid off a pan from which a delicious smell emanated.

"Liver stew, Mama," Elena Herbst explained.

"Liver—shmiver!" the old lady grumbled scornfully. "You know I like chicken soup on Friday night!"

"Yes, I know you do," her daughter replied, "but I can't understand why."

"Because that's what I'm used to!"

Sonja only half heard her mother's repetitive argument about the absurdity of keeping one tradition if one did not follow any of the other ones. The strange sensation had suddenly crept over her again. It was as if a bubble in her head was rising and about to burst. And then, like a flash, she remembered.

Afraid the recollection might disappear again, she made some excuse and hurried up to her room. Sitting on her bed, she turned her mind back eleven years to when she had been a child of six.

She saw her grandmother coming to their house, a yellow slip of paper in her hand and tears in her eyes. She showed them a telegram she had received, saying that her mother had passed away. Sonja remembered her surprise. She'd had no notion that Grandmama *had* a mother!

"I must go to the funeral!" Frau Ravitz had cried.

"But why, Mama?" her daughter had demanded. "You haven't spoken a word to her for over thirty years!"

"I know …," Frau Ravitz's voice was choked, "and now I can't even beg her forgiveness! That's why I've got to go!"

"Very well." Sonja's mother had given a long-suffering sigh. "I'll come with you. I'd better tell Franczek to get the carriage ready."

Half-an-hour later mother and daughter had set off on their journey. Standing at the gate with her father, Sonja had watched them depart.

"Where are they going?" she asked. "Is it a long way?"

"Yes, about a two hours' drive," her father replied. He told her the name of the village, but she could not call it to memory.

"Papa, why has Grandmama not spoken to her mother for thirty years?" Sonja asked, perplexed.

"Oh, it's a long story …." The vague reply was the only answer Sonja could get out of her father.

When Elena returned, several hours later, she was alone.

"Where is your mother?" her husband inquired.

"She decided to stay for the *shiva*," his wife informed him. "Though don't ask me why. Her sisters and brothers hardly said a word to her. But she insisted it was the least she could do."

"What's a *shiva*, Mama?" Sonja had asked.

"Oh, it's a week of mourning," her mother replied in an off-hand manner. "The family sits on low chairs and people come to visit them. I suppose I'll have to go, too," she added, addressing her husband.

"Can I come with you?" Sonja pleaded.

"Nonsense! Why should—" her mother began, but Dr. Herbst interrupted her.

"I don't see why she shouldn't go. It will probably do your mother good to see her."

"Yes, maybe you're right," his wife agreed. "I'm rather busy this week, though. I don't think I can go till Friday. Very well, we'll go on Friday."

They had set off after breakfast on Friday morning and arrived at their destination around midday.

The first thing Sonja was aware of as they entered the house was the smell of cooking and baking that filled the air.

A woman opened the door for them and said something in Yiddish. Seeing their blank expressions, she translated into Polish. "The women are sitting in the kitchen," she said, waving her hand in the direction of a white painted door. Sonja followed her mother into the kitchen and was immediately enchanted. On a large table in the center of the room sat a number of glossy brown plaited loaves, cooling on a wire tray. Various saucepans of different sizes bubbled on the kitchen range, and two women, who Sonja later learned were the wives of her grandmother's brothers, were bustling about, attending to numerous chores. Seated on low chairs near the fireplace were four women. One of them, Sonja realized with a start, was Grandmama! She hardly recognized her with a black headscarf covering most of her hair. Grandmama sat a little apart from the others and didn't take part in the Yiddish conversation her sisters were having with two ladies, who sat opposite them, wearing hats and coats.

As she sat reminiscing, Sonja was amazed at the clarity with which she recalled these events. She remembered following one of her great-aunts into the dining room. There was a long table in the center of the room and a beautiful oak bookcase across one wall, completely filled with books. Near the window, three bearded men sat on low chairs. The man in the middle looked quite old, with a curly white beard down his front. Sonja's aunt had drawn her over to him and mumbled something in Yiddish. Now, Sonja realized this was her great-grandfather, and his daughter-in-law had been explaining who she was.

The old man had taken her hand in his, and, gazing at her, shook his head sadly, tears in his eyes. The other two men also shook their heads, with mournful expressions.

The other aunt came in with a white tablecloth over her arm, which the two women together spread out over the table. One of them took a gleaming silver candelabrum from a cabinet and placed it on a silver tray in the center of the table, filling it with candles. A second candelabrum containing small glass bowls was also placed on the table, and the bowls filled with oil. Sonja's visit to the Elkowitzes, with its cooking aromas and the room set the same way, had conjured up this scene.

Sonja stood up, glad she had gotten to the bottom of it all. Or had she? She remembered the tension in the room when her mother had announced she was leaving.

"I'm coming with you," her grandmother had said, standing up.

Elena had stared at her mother, puzzled, "I thought—"

"The *shiva* officially ends tomorrow morning," Frau Ravitz had explained in a low voice interrupting her, "but since it's Shabbos tomorrow, we get up now, an hour before Shabbos. I don't want to stay here longer than necessary."

"But you can't go now!" one of the sisters protested. "You won't get home in time for Shabbos!"

Frau Ravitz had shrugged and walked to the door. "I'm getting my things," she said going out.

The sisters and sisters-in-law had looked at one another in exasperation and hopelessness, but had remained silent, looking resigned.

Sonja realized there was a story behind her grandmother's estrangement from her family, and she had to know it. That night, after Grandmama Ravitz had gone home, still complaining about the absence of chicken soup, she asked her mother about it.

"Your grandmother comes from a religious family," her mother told her. "She was always a bit of a rebel. She wanted to go to university but her parents wouldn't hear of it. I really don't know all the details. All I know is she made friends with some irreligious Jewish students and started going to their group meetings and lectures. Finally, there was an enormous row at home, and she ran away and moved in with some of her girlfriends. Her family tracked her down and tried to force her to come home, but they made too many conditions and she refused. Two years later, she married a young history teacher named Markus Ravitz—your grandfather—who, as you know, was not religious. When she brought him to meet her family, her father was terribly angry and ordered them out of the house. She never saw them again—until the day her mother died—and even then, her father could not forgive her."

Sonja listened thoughtfully. Her heart was wrung as she recalled her great-grandfather regarding her with tears in his eyes.

Afterward, she often found herself brooding over her lost relatives. She was confused at her strange sense of longing, especially when she'd pass a bakery in the early morning, when the smell of baking bread assailed her. What was the matter with her?

Four weeks went by and Miriam Elkowitz still had not returned to school. Surely, she should be over the measles by now. Sonja resolved to pay a call on the Elkowitz family.

The next day, she found her way to the Elkowitz's street in the Jewish quarter and knocked at the door. As Frau Elkowitz opened the door, Sonja noticed how tired and strained she looked.

"Frau Elkowitz, is Miriam all right?" she asked with concern. "She's been out a long time."

"Yes, I know," Frau Elkowitz replied, ushering her in. "She's really been very ill. The other children all caught the measles from her but they're over it now—thank the L-rd. Miriam had it so badly, though, she developed pneumonia from it, but she's doing better now," she said, adding "*baruch Hashem*" under her breath.

At the strange words, Sonja pricked up her ears, her curiosity aroused.

"What was that you said quietly?" she queried.

"Oh … er … nothing …," Frau Elkowitz replied, looking acutely embarrassed. "It's just something we Jews say in Hebrew. It's our way of saying 'thank G-d.'"

"Oh, I see …. I'm Jewish, too," she blurted out suddenly, surprising herself as much as Frau Elkowitz, who eyed her in disbelief and not a little disapproval. "I don't know anything about the Jewish religion!" Sonja continued. "Maybe you could teach me!"

The woman's expression softened immediately. "I'm not really much good at teaching," Frau Elkowitz said, "but I know quite a few people who are. I could introduce you to some of them, if you wish. All the same, maybe you would like to come and eat with us on Shabbos, Saturday, that is, and see what a Shabbos meal is like."

Sonja was delighted to accept the invitation. That first Shabbos meal set her on the road toward her commitment to *Yiddishkeit*. She began to spend much of her time in the Jewish quarter of Warsaw, speaking to various people who invited her into their homes and taught her whatever they could. After a few weeks had passed, she felt ready to embark wholeheartedly upon a Torah way of life.

Sonja realized she would have to speak to her parents. She could not possibly remain in their home if she wished to follow her newly chosen path. She fervently prayed she would win their support and understanding.

Her hopes, however, were quickly dashed. Her parents were shocked and hurt. At first, they cajoled and pleaded with her, trying their utmost to make her abandon the idea. Her mother wept and her father tried calm reasoning, but hard as it was for her, Sonja stood firm. If they could not accept her new lifestyle, she explained, she could not continue to live under their roof. At that, her father had exploded. If she would not see sense, he shouted, she could go— and he did not wish to see or speak to her again!

Tears streaming down her face, Sonja had left home, taking none of her belongings. She'd gone straight to one of the Jewish families who had befriended her, and they kindly helped her get settled. Her earnings from the summer's teaching job helped her support herself and purchase some basic needs.

Before the summer holidays began, Elena Herbst visited Sonja at school. She told her daughter how mush she missed her. She begged Sonja to reconsider and come back home. Sonja ached to see her mother's distress, but it was very clear that her mother would never become reconciled to her religion, and her father—she could not begin to imagine his reactions. Giving up her new way of life was inconceivable! Sadly, she had to refuse. She realized one thing, however. She could not stay here in Warsaw. To be so near her parents and yet so distant was too painful for her.

Then someone told her about Rebbitzen Reisbard.

The widow of the former *Rov* of Lipsk, Rebbitzen Reisbard was the personification of *chessed*. While her husband was alive, she had been a great support to him, involving herself in many aspects of community work. Now that she lived alone, she had established a home for girls who were orphaned and destitute. She tirelessly collected money and clothing to keep them fed and clothed, and very often helped to marry them off.

Although strictly speaking Sonja was not an orphan, she *was* alone and destitute and needed a home, as well as further Torah guidance. Someone arranged an interview for her, and, to her relief, the Rebbitzen willingly took her in.

Now, several months later, here she was, sitting in the room she shared with another of the Rebbitzen's protégés, shortening the hem of a dress. The former owner must have been quite tall and well-to-do, judging by the elegant cut and the expensive material. Even handed down, it still looked beautiful and Sonja was extremely grateful. Still, she could not help wishing the skirt were not so wide!

"Sonja, the Rebbitzen wants to speak to you." Sonja's roommate, a thirteen-year-old orphan named Lieba, poked her head around the door, interrupting her thoughts. "She asked if you could come down to the livingroom."

Only too glad to put down her sewing for a while, Sonja went down, wondering what the Rebbitzen wanted to talk to her about.

As she entered the room, she saw the Rebbitzen was not alone. A tall, angular woman in a faded brown coat and slightly battered hat was at the table, fiddling with a pair of beige gloves. Sonja was sure she had seen her around a few times, in shul possibly, or on the street, but didn't really know who she was.

"Sonja," Rebbitzen Reisbard said, "this is Frau Traubner. She's come here with a proposition for you. Come sit down and she'll tell you about it."

Sonja shook hands with Frau Traubner and sat down, with a look of polite inquiry.

"My neighbor has a granddaughter with a bit of a problem," Frau Traubner explained. "She has a slight … er … deformity, I suppose you could call it … and has difficulty walking, *nebach*. Well, till now she'd been going to school … though it was hard for her to walk there … but there has been some sort of trouble, and her parents don't want to send her any more. I can't say I blame them under the circumstances. But I'm not able tell you what the trouble was. All I can say is I would have done the same, and of course, they have the added excuse of her walking difficulty …."

She paused and began rummaging in her shabby purse, then finally shut it without removing anything. Sonja waited patiently. At last, Frau Traubner cleared her throat and continued.

"Anyway, to cut a long story short, they are worried the authorities will make trouble … they can, you know. I know someone who had a load of *tzorres*, just because—"

"Frau Traubner was wondering," the Rebbitzen cut in, realizing it was necessary to interrupt, "if you'd be willing to teach this girl at home."

"It might satisfy the authorities," Frau Traubner went on, "you being a qualified teacher …."

"I'm not fully qualified," Sonja told her. "I only did one year at university ...."

"Well, that's good enough!" Frau Traubner declared. "So, are you going to do it?"

Sonja looked at her, amazed. "I haven't had a moment to consider," she said with an amused smile.

"Well, make up your mind, so I can let them know I've solved their problem! *Nu, nu,* already. Are you willing?"

Chapter 5

$\mathcal{P}$essel scrutinized the young girl sitting in front of her and liked what she saw. The girl's appearance was neat, her clothes modest and demure and her honey-colored hair was swept tidily back and secured with a small black velvet bow. Her face bore a pleasant expression and her blue eyes looked candid and sincere. Though her whole bearing was gentle and somewhat fragile-looking, Pessel could detect an air of strong determination in her manner.

"We won't be able to pay you much," Pessel explained in her usual forthright way.

"That's all right," Sonja assured her. "I'll be glad to have something to do. As long as I can give Rebbitzen Reisbard something toward my keep, I'll be quite happy with whatever you can manage."

Pessel smiled, relieved, and stood up. "Maybe you'd like to meet your pupil now. I'll call her in." She went to the door, calling, "Golda Mirel, can you come here, please?" She returned to her seat at the table. "She'll be here in a moment," she smiled.

Sonja heard strange, irregular footsteps outside the door and soon Golda Mirel appeared in the doorway. She approached the table, ducking her head and peeping from behind her dark curls.

Sonja liked her immediately and extended her hand, which

Golda Mirel took shyly, her soft gray-green eyes lighting up as they met the teacher's twinkling blue ones. It was obvious that they would get on famously. Pessel sent a silent prayer of gratitude upward.

"Are you going to be my teacher?" asked Golda Mirel.

"I shall enjoy teaching you," Sonja assured her with a smile.

"I'm glad. I don't miss school, but I do miss learning, especially arithmetic."

"Well, that's excellent, because I love arithmetic, too."

"We don't want her to turn into a scholar," Pessel interrupted this exchange hastily. "One does not want that for a *yiddishe* girl. We only need to satisfy the authorities if they come to check. Just teach her the basics …."

"Yes, I understand," Sonja replied calmly. She wondered what this woman thought of her … a Jewish girl who was obviously educated. She knew the Wasserbruns had been informed of her circumstances, but could they accept her as one of them?

The lessons began the next day. Sonja enjoyed teaching her avid pupil, and was hard put to curb the child's enthusiasm. There was so much she could teach this intelligent little girl, who was enthralled with every new piece of information she discovered. But Sonja respected the parents' wishes not to over-educate her, and broke the study sessions with other activities.

Sometimes they took walks to a nearby park to help Golda Mirel strengthen her leg muscles. She was soon taking longer strides and developing better speed, and could swing into the rhythm of her limp with less faltering. The sunshine, too, gave her more stamina, and she began to stand more easily for longer periods, helping her mother with various household tasks without losing her balance or growing tired.

Since Golda Mirel grasped new material almost faster than Sonja could present it, half the daily lesson was spent in study, while the second often diverged into discussions and personal accounts. Golda Mirel revealed her hidden frustrations and her struggle to be just like other children. When she divulged the shameful incidents that had led to her leaving school, Sonja responded with sympathy and reassurance. Slowly, Golda Mirel's self-respect and confidence in her abilities revived.

Sonja loved listening to Golda Mirel's descriptions of her family life, especially tales of the extended family of aunts and cousins, and the *yomim tovim* treats and activities. She eventually confided the details of her own peculiar history to this quick-witted child, filling Golda Mirel with awe and admiration. A bond deepened between teacher and pupil as their respect and trust for each other strengthened.

Pessel's heart warmed to the new sparkle in her daughter's eyes. The money she paid to Sonja was not easily come by, but was certainly worth it! However, she waited anxiously for repercussions. Would the authorities be satisfied? Every morning her heart pounded at the sight of an unfamiliar figure in their street, and every evening she breathed again. For it was certain that an official would be visiting.

Weeks went by, but no one showed up. Pessel stopped wondering and began to relax a little. Perhaps no one would come after all. Maybe the whole matter would be overlooked and they could actually get away with it. This meant, of course, that it had not been necessary to hire Sonja, but Pessel was not sorry to have done so. Not only was it doing Golda Mirel a world of good, but they were obviously helping Sonja, too. She often came for the Shabbos meals, and these glimpses of a proper Jewish family contributed greatly to the strides she was making in *Yiddishkeit*.

Lulled to a false sense of security, Pessel was startled one morning to hear loud rapping at the door. The sound filled her with foreboding. Opening the door a crack, she saw a strange man on the doorstep and knew instinctively who he was and why he had come.

Stout and broad, his unruly hair falling down his forehead, he glared at her with bloodshot eyes. Pessel noted his reddened nose and the purple veins on his face, and recognized him for a man who indulged in too much alcohol. A fleeting thought crossed her mind to try bribing him with some wine, but she immediately discarded the idea. If it was the wrong thing to do, it could well tip the scales against them.

"Wasserbrun?" the man barked. Pessel's heart sank, hopes of a favorable interview quickly fading.

"Y-yes?" she replied tentatively.

"Stefan Wlotski," the man introduced himself curtly. "School inspector! Your daughter Golda has not attended school for five weeks!"

"Yes, I know ...."

"Why not?" Wlotski demanded sternly.

"My daughter has a severe disability," Pessel explained. "She can hardly walk and it is too difficult for her to go to school."

"Nevertheless, she did attend till recently," Wlotski pointed out. "Why did she stop?"

"The walk there and back was too exhausting for her. It was beginning to affect her general health ...."

"Humph!" He gave a snort of skepticism and disapproval. "Is that just the opinion of over-anxious parents—or has a doctor so decreed?"

"Naturally, we are concerned about our daughter!" Pessel replied with indignation. "But I can get a letter from the doctor, if necessary." She was confident Doctor Friedsohn would be happy to oblige.

"Surely the problem would be solved if you hired a carriage to take her there and back …."

"Unfortunately, we cannot afford such luxuries."

"So you are prepared to let your daughter grow up ignorant and uneducated," Wlotski sneered, "because of a physical disability?"

"Not at all," Pessel told him calmly. "We have engaged a private teacher."

"Oh, so you can afford that," the man pounced on her words, "but not a carriage to take her to school!"

Taken aback, Pessel struggled to steady her nerves.

"The teacher costs us much less than a hired carriage would," she said desperately.

"Can't be much of a teacher then," Wlotski said disdainfully.

"Perhaps you would like to meet her?" Pessel suggested, not sure she was acting with wisdom. "She is here now, teaching my daughter."

Wlotski nodded and Pessel led him to the room where Sonja and Golda Mirel were sitting. Introducing him, she caught the look of anxiety that crossed both their faces and hoped their visitor hadn't noticed it, too.

Blushing slightly, Sonja rose with dignity. "I am the girl's teacher," she told him.

"I see. Hardly out of school yourself, aren't you?" Wlotski said condescendingly.

"I attended the Warsaw Teachers' Training College and also taught in a primary school in Warsaw," responded Sonja coolly.

Afraid the inspector would question Sonja more intently, Pessel interrupted quickly. "Would you like to see some of Golda's work?" she offered.

Wlotski shot her a withering look as if to say, "What do *you* know about it?" but nodded.

"Have you something to show him, Fraulein Herbst?" Pessel asked anxiously.

Wlotski took the page of sums Sonja handed him but did not even glance at it. Instead, he stared at Sonja curiously.

"Herbst? Is your name *Herbst*?"

"Y-yes, it is," Sonja replied a little hesitantly, wondering what this was leading to.

"Any relation to *Doctor* Herbst? Doctor Alexander Herbst?"

Sonja's inclination was to deny any connection, but she told the truth. "Yes," she said quietly, "he is my father."

The man's hitherto stern face was suddenly wreathed in smiles.

"Well, well," he exclaimed, "would you believe it? So you're Dr. Herbst's daughter! A brilliant surgeon, your father! He saved my father's life a few years ago. Well, well!" He looked down at the paper in his hand. "And his daughter is a brilliant teacher! All the sums are correct." Turning to Pessel he said, "Your daughter is in good hands. There is no reason why she should not carry on in this way. I shall not keep you any longer. I have a lot to attend to. Good day to you." Then he added, giving a slight bow in Sonja's direction, "And good day, Fraulein Herbst. When you speak to your father, tell him Stanislaw Wlotski is doing very well, thanks to him!"

"Certainly," Sonja replied, wondering what he would say if he knew that she was unlikely to pass on his message.

Pessel saw him out, closed the door behind him and leaned against it. She heaved a huge sigh of relief.

"*Baruch Hashem!*" she exclaimed. "I was so worried! But it's turned out all right, thanks to you ... or rather, to your father ..."

"I know," Sonja's tone was rueful. "Though it's ironic that my father saved the day!" she added, not really amused.

"Yes, I understand," Pessel was sympathetic, "but it was obviously *bashert* to happen this way. We don't always understand the *Eibershter*'s ways."

"Yes, you're right," Sonja said, brightening up at once. Impulsively, she threw her arm across Golda Mirel's shoulders and hugged her. "I'm so glad for you!" she cried. Then turning to Pessel she said hesitantly, "Perhaps you don't need my services any more now."

"Oh, no!" Pessel protested hastily, seeing the woebegone expression on Golda Mirel's face. "Of course we still need you! You never know, he might come back to check. Besides, we would miss you!"

"Thank you," Sonja said, blushing. "I'll be happy to stay. There is still quite a lot Golda Mirel can learn," she patted the girl's head affectionately, "without becoming too educated!"

Pessel had to wait until evening to tell Anshel the good news, since he went straight to the *beis hamedrash* after work, learning there until after *maariv*, then coming home for dinner. At last, he was home, and as she served him his meal Pessel gave him the full account.

"Well, that *is* good news!" he exclaimed.

"It was a miracle!" Pessel said jubilantly. "The way his attitude changed from one minute to the next! Sonja was a little uncomfortable because it involved her father, but I told her it must be *bashert*."

Anshel nodded. "*Nistorim darkei Hashem,*" he quoted, "the ways of Hashem are hidden from us."

"Exactly!" Pessel declared triumphantly. "Well, *baruch Hashem,* our problem is solved!"

"It's nice to know something is going right," sighed Anshel. "I wish everyone's problems could be solved that easily!"

Pessel eyed her husband doubtfully. There *had* been a worried look on his face when he came in, but, excited about her news, she had paid no attention.

"What is the matter, Anshel?" she asked now.

"I stopped at my parents on the way home," he replied. "They are all upset about Berel again. This last *shidduch* fell through, too."

"Oh, no! What happened?"

"The usual story. The girl's father was over this afternoon to *farherr* Berel ...." Anshel threw up his hands in resigned dejection.

"Oy, vey ..." Pessel shook her head sadly.

She felt desperately sorry for her parents-in-law. Their youngest son, Berel, an exceptionally bright young man of nineteen, had been unhappy at yeshiva for some time already. His yeshiva was located in a nearby town, allowing him to come home every week for Shabbos. Recently, his parents had begun to sense that something was not right. He would sit at the Shabbos table with a faraway look, almost ignoring his father during the discussions on the weekly *sedrah*.

Things came to a head when the *Rosh haYeshiva* summoned the Wasserbruns to the yeshiva for an interview. Reb Yankel Wasserbrun and his wife arrived for their appointment with heavy hearts. Reb Yankel faced his dear friend, Reb Elya Grossheim, across the table, and waited for the blow to fall.

Reb Elya gazed at him in silence for a few moments, his head swaying rhythmically from side to side. "So, you are concerned about your son, too," he said.

Reb Yankel looked down, his color rising. "W-what is he doing?" he almost whispered.

"He is not in the yeshiva most of the time. I don't know where he goes, but I'm very much afraid he is mixing with bad company."

Yankel Wasserbrun stared at him, aghast. "Why wasn't I told about this before?" he asked, horrified.

The *Rosh haYeshiva* sighed. "You are an old friend. I did not want to worry you over a mere suspicion," he said. "I have a high regard for you—and, indeed, for your other sons, who are *talmidei chachomim*. I was sure it was in the early stages, and I could be *mekarev* the boy, but I spoke to him several times with no result." He looked squarely at Reb Yankel. "I cannot get through to him at all."

"I see ...," Reb Yankel's voice trembled and he ran a shaking hand across his forehead.

Mindel Wasserbrun looked down at her hands lying in her lap. She felt a stab of guilt, but was not going to say anything here. Her husband was not in the best of health, and she avoided anything that might upset him. She had never told him of that incident with Berel over some medical books she had found in his room. When confronted, he had shrugged and said, "You don't let me go to university to study medicine, but you can't stop me from learning what I want to know. You know I plan to become a doctor someday."

She had lectured him sharply, telling him that what they planned for their children was to advance in their *Torah* learning. He had turned away, saying disgustedly, "Well, I *am* in yeshiva, aren't I?"

Frightened, but hoping it was a phase he would outgrow, she had said nothing to her husband then. Now, she realized she would have to do so, but she'd wait until later ... not sitting in front of the *Rosh haYeshiva*!

"Are you going to send him home?" Reb Yankel asked nervously.

"I should, really," Reb Elya replied, "and if I thought he was influencing other *bochurim*, I would. But it won't help him improve. Also, it will make *shidduchim* very difficult. I value our old friendship too much to inflict such a worry on you unnecessarily. Maybe, between us, we can still make a *mensch* of him. He has such a good head. It's a pity to let it go to waste!" He shook his head in sorrow.

A very dejected pair made their way back to Lipsk, talking of nothing else all the way. Reb Yankel was shocked that his son had seriously contemplated attending university. He remembered the boy's interest in medicine as a child, when occasionally he'd accompanied his parents on doctor's visits with Golda Mirel. He had always been curious about what was in the medicine bottles and what the doctor was doing. But to want to enter that unholy place and learn from *goyim*—! It didn't bear thinking about! They had enlisted their married children's help in the matter, and everyone tried to spend time with Berel and find him a nice girl to settle down with, hoping that would distract him from "the nonsense," as they called it. And now, again, they were faced with a disappointment.

"I can't help feeling guilty," Pessel said.

"Guilty? About what?" Anshel looked puzzled.

"We're the ones who persuaded your parents to marry off Berel as quickly as possible. And look at the *agmas nefesh* they are having because of it."

"But I still think we were right," Anshel insisted. "The best thing would be for him to settle down with a good, *ehrliche* girl who will make sure he doesn't stray from the *Torah*. The trouble is that their fathers want someone who is worthy of them, and as soon as they *farherr* Berel, that's the end of that!"

"Perhaps we should look for a girl who hasn't got a father," Pessel said thoughtfully, hoping she didn't sound callous.

"Then there's usually a brother, or an uncle, or someone …."

"True. Besides, a girl with no family is enough of a *rachmonus* without adding Berel to cope with," Pessel agreed, "like Rebbitzen Reisbard's orphans—" She broke off suddenly, a curious expression on her face. "Of course," she cried, "it's obvious! Why didn't I think of it sooner?"

"Think of what?" Anshel stared.

"Sonja!" Pessel cried triumphantly.

"Sonja who?" Anshel began, but then her meaning dawned on him. "Oh," he said in a flat voice.

"You don't think it's a good idea?"

"I don't know," he said skeptically. "*My* parents would never agree to it."

"But it's so ideal!" Pessel persisted. "She's clever; she's *ehrliche*; she's got a strong mind of her own, so she'll keep him on the right path … *and* her father isn't going to come *farherr* him!"

"That is all true," agreed Anshel, "but it's not the kind of *shidduch* my parents are looking for. Nothing like the rest of us married …"

"I know—but Berel is not like the rest of you, is he?" explained Pessel. "They must know they have to look away a bit. And they'd have to search far and wide to find someone like Sonja. She's such a special girl!"

Anshel was quiet and thoughtful for a few moments. Then he said, "Maybe someone *should* suggest it to them. I wouldn't like to be the one, though. They might get hurt."

"Talk it over with your brother Yidel," Pessel suggested. "See what he thinks."

Anshel shook his head. "You've forgotten Yidel is visiting his in-laws in Krakow and won't be back till after Shabbos."

"Fine. You can talk to him as soon as he's back. And I think you should also discuss it with Chanah Bleema. She might be the best one to speak to your parents. She is their only daughter, after all, and your mother listens to her a lot."

Anshel agreed and called on his sister the next day. Both she and her husband treated the proposal with misgivings, doubtful of its outcome. In any case, they declared, *they* would certainly never present such an idea to their parents.

Yidel reacted similarly at first. However, after thinking it over carefully for a while, he finally agreed there was something to be said for the idea. But suggest it to Tatte and Mamme? Not he!

There was nothing else for it then, Pessel realized. After all, it was her idea, and she did know Sonja well. *She* would have to be the one.

Chapter 6

Frau Wasserbrun reacted exactly as they had all expected. She was shocked; she was hurt; she was angry. Pessel felt like an absolute worm, treating her mother-in-law that way, but it had to be done. She sang Sonja's praises while subtly alluding to Berel's problems, and slowly saw the older woman's defenses weaken a little.

"Why don't you pop in tomorrow morning," she suggested, "while she's teaching Golda Mirel? Then you can have a peep at her without it being obvious."

"I might," Mindel Wasserbrun replied non-committally. "I'll have to talk all this over with Reb Yankel before I decide anything. I hope I don't upset him too much. He's had so much *agmas nefesh* lately and it really isn't good for him." She sighed deeply. "Oh, why is everything so difficult!"

Pessel put her arms around her mother-in-law, who unconsciously leaned against the younger woman, drawing comfort from the gesture. Whispering a fervent wish that Hashem guide them to do the right thing, Pessel took her leave and hurried home, feeling as though she had been through a mangle.

To Pessel's joy, Frau Wasserbrun turned up on her doorstep the next morning, and after chatting over coffee and cake, they entered the room where Sonja and her diligent pupil sat engrossed in their work.

Golda Mirel leaped from her stool and greeted her grandmother excitedly.

"Babbe Wasserbrun!" she cried. "What a wonderful surprise! Have you met my teacher, Fraulein Herbst? She is the most brilliant teacher ever! Fraulein Herbst, this is my darling Babbe!" She babbled on about her beloved teacher's qualities, until Sonja, blushing furiously, interrupted.

"Golda Mirel, that will do. You're embarrassing me! Now, hush, and come sit down again," she requested with dignity.

"Yes, we had better leave so they can get on with the lesson," Pessel said wisely. "Babbe just popped her head in to say 'hullo' to you," she told her daughter, hoping they had not aroused Sonja's suspicions.

"Well? What do you think of her, *Shvigger*?" Pessel asked when she was sure they were out of earshot.

"She seems very nice," Frau Wasserbrun conceded grudgingly. She would not admit it, but she was disappointed. She had been certain she'd easily find something disparaging about the young woman to use as an excuse to reject the *shidduch*. But there was nothing she could put her finger on. In fact, she had been rather impressed by the girl, by her intelligence, dignity and modesty. Logical reasoning argued with her to stop resisting the notion and let her daughter-in-law get on with it. But her pride balked at the possibility.

Meanwhile, Pessel decided to enlist the aid of the local *shadchan*, Reb Lazer Meisner, who had suggested the family's other *shidduchim*. To her dismay, Reb Lazer refused the offer, saying this was not the type of *shidduch* he usually dealt with.

"We'll have to find someone else," Pessel said, discussing it with Anshel. *But who?* She searched her mind, trying to come up with someone bold enough, yet worthy, too. The idea came to her quite suddenly, and as soon as she thought of it, she knew she had hit upon the ideal person!

Rebbitzen Reisbard listened to Frau Traubner without interrupting. Then she leaned forward, compelling Frau Traubner to look her in the eye.

"What is wrong with this young man?" she asked directly.

"Wrong? Why should there be anything wrong?" demurred Frau Traubner, growing flustered.

"Come now, Frau Traubner ... I know the Wasserbruns! They are a highly respected family, with *yichus* going back to some great *rabbonim*. If they are interested in this *shidduch*, there must be some problem with the son."

Admittedly, the same thought had crossed Frau Traubner's mind when Pessel approached her, but she had refrained from comment. Flattered to be entrusted with this mission, she was determined to carry it out properly.

"Oh, no," she disclaimed such a notion. "I'm sure it's not like that! He's a very presentable boy, and from what I hear, quite clever, too."

"Then why?"

"The Wasserbruns hold Sonja in such esteem! Well, you know better than anyone what a special girl she is! They obviously think it's worth looking away a bit to get such a jewel!"

The Rebbitzen was unconvinced. She remained silent a few moments, weighing the pros and cons. After all, she argued with herself, Sonja could not be too choosy, in spite of her good qualities. It would be ideal for her to be a member of a good *Torahdik* family, a fact that might outweigh some small disadvantage. On the other hand, if there was some major health problem, her life might become very difficult, and Rebbitzen Reisbard certainly did not want that for her Sonja!

"Are you aware of any health issue?" she inquired cautiously.

"There's certainly nothing *I* know of!" declared Frau Traubner emphatically. "I can make some enquiries, if you like, and let you know."

"Thank you. I will be most grateful," Rebbitzen Reisbard said. "I will wait to hear from you."

Two days later Frau Traubner was back. "It's all right!" she gushed, charging straight in. "I asked my neighbor, Gittel Danziger—you know, Pessel Wasserbrun's mother. She assured me there is absolutely nothing to worry about—and she should know, being a *mechuteniste*. She says there are no health problems in the family … except for Golda Mirel's limp, poor thing … but that's nothing to do with bad health, really. It's just one of those things that can happen. Actually, the boy's father has some heart trouble, but he's not a young man any more. The *bochur* himself is perfectly well, *baruch Hashem*. I've seen him myself, once or twice, and he looks the picture of health to me!"

"Good. I'm glad to hear it," the Rebbitzen cut the conversation quickly, depriving Frau Traubner of any more elaboration.

"Well, there then! All we have to do now is arrange a meeting!"

"Well, certainly," Rebbitzen Reisbard agreed. "But I must discuss this first with Sonja and see if she is interested."

"But why wouldn't she be interested?" asked Frau Traubner, implying there was nothing to discuss.

"First of all, she may not be ready for a *shidduch* yet. Second, how can we assume she would marry into a *chassidishe* family? It's not what she is used to, after all."

Frau Traubner opened her mouth to point out that any *frum* family was "not what she was used to," but snapped it shut quickly, leaving the tactless remark unsaid. *To be a shadchan, one must be clever!* she thought, pleased with herself.

"Oh, certainly, I understand," she said politely, getting up. "When shall I return for your answer?"

"Come the day after tomorrow," the Rebbitzen told her. "I will speak to her tonight, but she may need some time to think it over."

Sonja did indeed need time for the proposition to take shape in her mind. The idea of getting engaged at this time was quite unnerving. She could not envision herself taking charge of a proper Jewish home alone, and was certain she was not ready for marriage. However, her discussions with the Rebbitzen that night and again the next day were reassuring, and she realized that, since marrying a *Ben Torah* was her ultimate aim, she would be wise to recognize this as a G-d-given opportunity. Besides, what could be better than a *Ben Torah* who was the brother of Golda Mirel's father, a man for whom she had the highest regard?

After Frau Traubner's second visit, things moved quickly.

Reb Yankel Wasserbrun and his wife called on Rebbitzen Reisbard that afternoon, and after some conversation with her, Sonja was called in. Shaking hands with Frau Wasserbrun, Sonja recognized the woman who had popped her head in recently to "say hullo to Golda Mirel." Obviously, her motive had been to have a peep at her! *Well,* she decided, *it was understandable.*

They made polite conversation, albeit with some difficulty. Frau Wasserbrun spoke mostly Yiddish, having a rather broken Polish, and Sonja's Yiddish was still poor. Their main topic was Golda Mirel, about whom Sonja spoke with affection. Frau Wasserbrun grew even more impressed by Sonja than the first time she had seen her. Presently, she looked searchingly at the earnest young woman. "Do you think you would feel comfortable marrying a *chossid*?" she asked gently. "Our way of life is a bit different. It would take some getting used to."

"I know, but I admire that way of life," Sonja replied. "Your son—Golda Mirel's father—is a *talmid chochom*, and that is what I want my husband to be, too. I want to marry a man whose life revolves mostly around his *Torah* learning!"

Involuntarily, Mindel winced, the girl's words stabbing at her heart. Sonja, shyly avoiding eye contact, missed the telltale gesture.

She was still looking down bashfully, tracing the lacy pattern of the tablecloth, when Reb Yankel looked at his wife. His eyes asked the all-important question, and his wife responded with a vigorous nod.

He turned and addressed the Rebbitzen.

"I think we should make arrangements for a meeting between the couple," he said. "Our son is in yeshiva, but we can get a message to him to be home by tomorrow night."

"Very well," agreed the Rebbitzen, "though I don't think it should be here. There are other girls, you understand."

"Certainly," he bowed his head. "If it's all right with you, we can arrange to have it at the home of our *mechutonim*, the Danzigers. Shall we say tomorrow evening at eight o'clock?"

The Rebbitzen turned to Sonja and asked, "Is that acceptable to you, Sonja?"

Sonja nodded calmly, managing to conceal the butterflies fluttering about inside her.

Having arranged everything satisfactorily, the Wasserbruns stood up to go. At the door, Frau Wasserbrun turned and smiled tentatively at Sonja, an expression in her eyes that Sonja could not make out.

When Berel was told of the arrangements he gave a long-suffering sigh. *Not again,* he thought, hardly listening to his brother Anshel, who had come to the yeshiva to give him instructions. This was the umpteenth time he'd been summoned home for a *shidduch.* Although he had never actually met any of the girls concerned—only their fathers—he was fed up with the whole thing. He wished they would leave him alone!

As Anshel gave him some details of this prospective choice, his attention was suddenly caught. This *shidduch* sounded different. *Well, well,* he thought sardonically, *they must be growing desperate!* At Anshel's next statement Berel sat up straight. Her father was a *doctor?* Now that *was* something to take notice of! A father-in-law in the medical profession could be very useful to him. So what if the girl had no contact with him anymore, as Anshel was telling him. Once they were married, he could always persuade her to pick up the threads again and then ... who knows? Yes, this *shidduch* sounded promising!

"*Mazel tov! Mazel tov!*" There was a general air of excitement in the room, with much hugging and kissing amongst the women, and handshakes and backslapping between the men. Everyone, including the *chosson,* was beaming, and Sonja looked radiant. She could hardly believe she had been able to make up her mind so quickly. Before they had set out, Rebbitzen Reisbard had briefed her on the usual procedure.

"Normally, amongst *Chassidim,* there is only one meeting. The young man and woman would make their decisions after talking to each other for a little while. But you won't have to decide so quickly.

If you are not sure, you can ask for another meeting, so don't be embarrassed to say so. It's better to be sure before you commit yourself. Another thing you should know is that once you become engaged, you and your *chosson* do not see each other again until the *chassunah*. Do you feel you can agree to that?"

"If that's the *minhag* of *Chassidim*, of course I do," Sonja assured her, accepting the constant changes in her lifestyle.

She had been pleased with Berel's manner and appearance, and had felt quite at ease in his company. When the Rebbitzen asked for her decision, she had given an immediate "yes."

After that, the room suddenly became full of people. Pessel and Anshel came rushing over, as well as Yidel with his wife, and Chana Bleema and her husband. Everyone seemed to be talking at once. Frau Wasserbrun placed a gold necklace around Sonja's neck, after which they all drank "*Lechayim*" and made plans for the *vort* to take place the next night at the Wasserbrun home.

For a fleeting moment Sonja was overcome by a desire to contact her parents and share the good news with them. But she realized immediately that they would not consider it "good news," and could possibly spoil things for her. Maybe she would let them know after the wedding. *How ironic*, she thought. *Here I am, doing exactly what my grandmother did all those years ago, though the situation is quite reversed!* Once again, the image of her great-grandfather regarding her with tears in his eyes sprang to her mind, and she reflected how pleased he would be if he knew!

Judging by the lavish preparations and the general air of festivity at the *vort*, it was obvious the family was delighted with the match, but no one was more overjoyed than Golda Mirel. She was ecstatic!

Her beloved teacher was going to be her aunt! Nothing quite as exciting had ever happened to her before! She couldn't wait for tomorrow, when she would have Sonja to herself and they could talk about it.

To her disappointment, however, her mother informed her that she had told Sonja to take off a few days.

"You can't expect her to apply her mind to teaching so soon after getting engaged," Pessel explained to her crestfallen daughter. "But never mind, she's coming to us for the Shabbos meals so you'll see her then."

That isn't quite the same, Golda Mirel thought. *I'll have to share her with the whole family then!*

When Sonja came to teach Golda Mirel on Monday morning, it was obvious they wouldn't get much learning done. *Well, what does it matter*, she thought contentedly, sitting back and listening to her pupil's incessant chatter. *She doesn't really* have *to learn.*

"Where are you going to live?" Golda Mirel asked her eagerly.

"I don't know yet. It will have to be near Berel's yeshiva, so he can learn as much as possible."

"Yes, that's good," Golda Mirel nodded sagely. "It will make him forget about wanting to be a doctor."

Her words gave Sonja a jolt. She sat bolt upright and stared at Golda Mirel.

"A *doctor!*" she gasped. "Did you say he wants to become a *doctor?*"

"Oh, yes, he always talked about it. He used to say to me lots of times, 'One day I'll be a doctor and I'll find some way to cure you!'"

"W-when did he used to say that?" Sonja asked, her voice shaking.

"Oh, ages ago," Golda Mirel said calmly, unaware of the havoc she was creating.

"Oh," Sonja breathed a sigh of relief. "Lots of young boys

dream of becoming doctors. It was only a childish whim!"

But, even as she spoke, she wondered. Boys who grew up in the environment Berel was raised in did *not* ordinarily indulge in such dreams!

"I heard Mamme tell Tatte the other day that if anyone can get all that nonsense out of Uncle Berel's head, you can!"

Golda Mirel glanced at Sonja, expecting her to look pleased at the compliment, but was surprised to see her looking pale and distracted. What was wrong? Was Sonja feeling ill, or something? She held her breath, waiting to see if the strange look would pass, but Sonja just sat and stared, unseeing, her lips pressed together. Then she came to herself, and said abruptly, "Come! Let's get on with the lesson!"

She can't be very ill, Golda Mirel thought, relieved, *if she wants to teach*.

However, after only a short while, Sonja closed her book, saying, "That's enough for today," and stood up.

It was so unlike Sonja to finish a lesson before time was up. Golda Mirel looked up, worried again. Sonja left quickly, without so much as a "goodbye," and didn't call out to Pessel on her way out! Golda Mirel scrambled up and limped hurriedly to the kitchen.

"Has Sonja gone?" Pessel asked, surprised at her daughter's sudden appearance.

"Yes, I think she's not feeling well, Mamme. She seemed very strange. Do you think it's anything to worry about?"

"No, don't worry. It's just the excitement, I imagine," Pessel replied calmly. "It takes time to adjust to being a *kallah*."

Reassured, Golda Mirel forgot her worry instantly, as any child would.

However, her anxiety returned the next day when Sonja failed to turn up for the lesson. Even Pessel seemed concerned.

"It's surprising she hasn't sent a message," Pessel observed. "I wonder what's the matter. If she doesn't come tomorrow, I'll go around and enquire."

But they did not have to wait for the next day. By that afternoon, Sonja's absence was explained.

A loud rapping on the front door sent Pessel running in alarm to open it. There stood her mother-in-law, ashen-faced, holding an envelope in a hand that shook violently.

"*Shvigger!* What's wrong? Come inside!"

"What's wrong? You ask me what's wrong?" Frau Wasserbrun's voice trembled as she stumbled through the doorway. "You and your good ideas! 'A wonderful girl!' you said, 'the best in the world!' A *nechdige tug*!" Her voice broke, and bitter tears choked her.

Pessel was baffled. This could not be her Sonja! "You must sit down, *Shvigger*, and tell me what's happened."

Pessel drew the distraught woman to the kitchen and sat her down, pouring her a cup of tea. She set it down on the table, and pushed over a plate of nut cakes. Then she joined her on the other side, propping her chin on her hands. Frau Wasserbrun took some rasping breaths, and lifted the cup. Her teeth chattered on the rim, but she managed to gulp some down. Slowly, she grew calmer. Then, noticing the envelope at the side of her saucer, Frau Wasserbrun groaned loudly. Golda Mirel, who had been sitting in the corner with little Leibel on her lap, looked up in trepidation.

"What's happened? What's happened? This is what's happened!" She pulled up the flap of the envelope and shook out the gold necklace and the ring she had purchased for the *vort*. Stabbing at them with a trembling finger, she cried, "She's broken the engagement, is what!"

Pessel gasped, speechless, while Golda Mirel could only gape.

Pessel finally found her voice. "But did she say why?"

"There's a letter. Here, you'd better read it. My Polish isn't so good." She handed Pessel the letter, muttering through clenched teeth, "Who does she think she is!"

Pessel read the letter aloud.

Dear Family Wasserbrun, it said,

> *I don't know how to write this because I know you will be very hurt by it and, believe me, that is the last thing I want! All I can do is beg you to forgive me!*

> *When I became engaged, I was happy, thinking I was marrying someone dedicated to learning Torah. But I have since learned that he has dreams of becoming a doctor and that I am expected to drive the notion out of his head.*

She was suddenly interrupted by an anguished cry from Golda Mirel. Depositing the baby in his cradle, she limped hurriedly from the room.

"What's got into her?" Frau Wasserbrun demanded.

"She's obviously upset," Pessel explained. "She adores Sonja and she was so excited about the engagement."

"Hmm! So were we all!" Frau Wasserbrun said bitterly.

Taking the baby, who had begun to cry, Pessel resumed her reading.

> *… Apart from the fact that I cannot undertake so great a responsibility, I can't bear the thought of being committed to someone who hankers for the life I have torn myself away from so painfully.*

> *Please try to understand and release me from my promise! I'm sure Berel will one day find the right girl and be happy, but I know I am not the one. Please, please forgive me!*

> *Wishing you all the best, and much nachas from all your children.*

> *Sonja*

> *Please give my love to Golda Mirel. I shall miss her terribly!*

Pessel handed the letter back, and moved closer to her mother-in-law whose eyes spilled over with tears. She hugged the grieving woman, trying to find the right words.

"*Shvigger*," she said, "don't be so upset. You were against the *shidduch* at first, remember?"

"I know, but I really took a liking to her. And Berel seemed so happy. What am I going to tell him? And what am I going to say to everybody? People keep wishing me *mazel tov*! Oh, I'm so ashamed! It's such a disgrace for the family!" The tears coursed down her cheeks unchecked.

"I wonder where she heard about Berel wanting to be a doctor," Pessel mused. "Not many people know about it …."

"I don't know," Frau Wasserbrun wiped her eyes, her mood switching from sorrow to anger, "but I know what I would like to do to that person, whoever it is!"

Golda Mirel, crouching in the foyer, overheard her grandmother's words and fled to her bed, where she lay sobbing her heart out. It was bad enough that Sonja had broken the engagement and the wedding she had so eagerly anticipated would not take place, but the knowledge that *she* had brought it all about cut into her like a knife! What had she done? Why hadn't she kept her mouth shut? She had only wanted Sonja to know how impressed everyone was by her … and now look what had happened! A vision of her grandmother's sickly white face rose up in front of her, filling her with remorse. Babbe would be so angry with her! And her parents, too! How could she face them all?

She realized they must never know. This would have to be her guilty secret … something she would keep to herself and never tell a soul! The knowledge bore down on her like a great burden, almost crushing her with its weight.

Pessel was extremely concerned about Golda Mirel. Two weeks had passed since the broken engagement, yet Golda Mirel still had a long face. She picked at her food, wouldn't play at anything and couldn't be coaxed into the slightest smile. Pessel knew how this had upset her daughter's life, but children, generally more resilient than adults, normally got over disappointments quickly.

Everyone else had come to terms with the situation by now. Mindel Wasserbrun, still hoping to bring Sonja around, had sent Pessel to Rebbitzen Reisbard's house, convinced her daughter-in-law could persuade the girl. But Pessel had returned, still smarting from the Rebbitzen's severe rebuke at misleading the poor girl, and imparted the information that Sonja had left the premises. At this news, Frau Wasserbrun at last accepted the fact that there was nothing to be done.

How long would Golda Mirel take to get back to normal? Pessel wondered. She resolved to give it a little more time, but after a third week with no change, she could stand it no longer. It was time, she decided, for a sharp reprimand.

"Golda Mirel," she announced one morning at breakfast, "this has got to stop!" She pointed at the girl's plate with most of the food left on it. "I know how fond you were of Sonja and how disappointed you are, but this *shidduch* was obviously not *bashert* ...." She realized this philosophy was small comfort to an eight-year-old, but it had to be said, all the same. "We've all accepted that, even Babbe Wasserbrun ...."

"Isn't she still angry?" Golda Mirel asked, in a small voice.

"Angry?" Pessel was surprised at the child's choice of adjective. "Well, I don't think she'll ever forgive the blabbermouth who told Sonja, but—"

She was interrupted by Golda Mirel rising from her seat and flinging herself into her mother's arms, weeping uncontrollably.

"*Sheffela!*" Pessel murmured, hugging her tightly. "Don't take it so to heart!"

"But Mamme," Golda Mirel cried, unable to bear her heavy yoke of guilt any longer, "it was *me*! I was the one …" She slid to the floor and went into another fit of sobbing.

"*What* was you?" Pessel asked, baffled.

"I … told Sonja … about … Uncle Berel …" The words were out, and Golda Mirel buried her head between her knees, still convulsed in tears.

"*YOU!!*" Pessel was incredulous. "But, *sheffela*, why? Whatever for?"

In a choked voice, Golda Mirel tried to explain her motives to her mother.

Chagrin rose in Pessel's chest. Her own daughter! She opened her mouth to deliver a serious scolding, when her eyes fell again on the anguished little girl. She bit back the harsh words. The poor child had suffered enough, keeping it to herself all this time. And she was only a child, after all. She swallowed her displeasure and pulled the child back onto her lap.

"It was a bit thoughtless," she said, giving her daughter a tight squeeze, "but, as I said, it's probably better that it happened now rather than after the *chassunah*. Now, we are not going to speak about it anymore. I don't know how Babbe Wasserbrun will feel about it, so it's better if she doesn't know … or anyone else for that matter. It will have to be our secret. Just you and me. All right?"

Golda Mirel looked up and nodded gratefully, her tear-stained face peaceful once again. Her heavy burden of guilt, now shared with someone else, had become so much easier to bear!

Mindel Wasserbrun's heart sank as she gazed at the young man on her doorstep. Incredible, but this was her own son! For a fleeting moment, she saw the Berel he had once been … dressed in *Chassidic* garb, his long, dark, neatly curled *peyos* framing a handsome face on which the beginnings of a beard were visible. But the image quickly vanished, leaving reality in its place. Before her stood a person with his shock of dark, wavy hair uncovered, his face clean-shaven and his attire consisting of an open-necked shirt and the sort of trousers only worn by the modern youth of the time. Of the beautiful long *peyos*, there was not a sign. And yet, he was still her Berel—her youngest child, for whom she still felt a love and tenderness beyond the anguish she was suffering at the sight of him.

A year had gone by since the broken engagement, and although it had been the talk of the town at the time, it had long ceased to be a nine-day's wonder. The people of Lipsk went about their everyday lives, evincing no interest in the doings of the youngest Wasserbrun boy.

Most of them were unaware of the trouble brewing in Europe and the impending war.

In the Wasserbrun family, however, the atmosphere was far from peaceful. When Berel was informed that Sonja had broken the engagement, he had been furious, blaming his parents—and Anshel and Pessel—for getting him into this embarrassing situation.

"Why can't you all leave me in peace!" he had stormed. "I didn't want to get engaged in the first place! And that girl is as narrow-minded as the rest of you! Well, since now you all know how useless I am, I might as well live my life the way *I* want to! I've had enough of yeshiva and the *Rosh haYeshiva*'s disapproving looks. I'm getting out of here!"

He had marched out of the house and no one had any idea where he was. Occasionally, he made brief visits to his parents, but he refused to tell them where he was living. Each time he came, there was some noticeable change in his appearance, causing the Wasserbruns a great deal of *agmas nefesh*. His father was ready to throw him out when he came to visit, but Mindel had persuaded her husband not to alienate their youngest.

"We'll *chas v'sholom* lose him completely," she had pleaded. "If we welcome him when he comes to visit, he might come back for good one day."

"*Halevai!!*" Reb Yankel had cried fervently, convinced by his wife's argument. However, the aggravation was taking its toll on the elderly man's health. His chest pains were more frequent and he grew increasingly short of breath. Mindel did her best to protect him from becoming agitated.

Facing Berel now, she was of two minds whether to let him in. Yankel was resting now, but if he were to wake up and see the way his son looked, there was no knowing what might happen.

She wondered if she had been right in dissuading her husband from throwing him out. There seemed to be no sign of Berel returning to the fold. On the contrary, he appeared to be moving further away from *Yiddishkeit*.

Fighting an inner battle, her maternal instinct prevented her from slamming the door in Berel's face.

"W-why have you come?" she asked hesitantly.

"Well, there's a nice welcome!" Berel remarked sarcastically. "Aren't you going to ask me in?"

His mother stepped back irresolutely, opening the door a little wider.

"Don't worry, I'm not staying long," Berel said, stepping inside. "I've just come to pack some of my things ... and then it's 'goodbye'!"

"Goodbye? What do you mean? Where are you going?" his mother gaped at him.

"I'm joining the army," her son told her coolly.

This bombshell sent his mother reeling backwards. "*The army!*" she cried, groping the wall for something to hold onto. Then, remembering her sleeping husband, she dropped her voice to a whisper. "What for?"

Berel laughed. "Mamme! Don't you know what's going on in the outside world at all? Haven't you heard of the trouble brewing all over Europe?"

"Trouble? Europe? What are you talking about?" Frau Wasserbrun regarded her son in bewilderment.

Berel sighed condescendingly. *What a bunch of ostriches they were in this town! Their heads were buried in the sand, oblivious of the danger soon to be upon them.* Squelching his sneers, he patiently gave his mother a rough outline of the situation.

"Germany and Austria have joined forces and are preparing to fight Russia, who is threatening a full-scale invasion—"

"But what have we got to do with Germany and Austria—or Russia?" his mother interrupted, puzzled.

"Mamme! You know very well that this part of Poland—all of

Galicia—*belongs* to Austria!" Berel's tone was patronizing. "And part of Poland belongs to Russia. Do you think they'll leave us out? They'll be here in no time! We'll be involved whether we like it or not! The Russian army is very powerful!"

His mother turned pale, beginning to understand what her son was telling her, but all she could think of was the threat to his safety.

"You might be killed … *chas v'sholom*! Please, Berel, I beg you … don't do it! Don't join the army!"

"Mamme! Be realistic!" Berel gave a short laugh. "If there's a war, we will all be forced into the army, anyway. They'll come and drag us off! Those who volunteer beforehand will be in a much better position than the others and probably have more privileges … so why shouldn't I go now instead of waiting?"

His mother just stood shaking her head in distress. Unable to meet her gaze, Berel shrugged and went off to his little room at the back of the house. His mother watched him helplessly, fear clutching at her heart. Dreadful pictures swam before her eyes; she imagined her son, his face grubby and bloodstained, wielding some cumbersome weapon; she saw him lying on the ground, wounded … or even … no, no! She must not think that! The paralysis that had overcome her suddenly vanished! She must do something! She could not let him go!

She reached out a trembling hand and took down a bunch of keys from a hook on the wall. Selecting the one to Berel's room, she crept stealthily toward the door. She would lock him in and refuse to release him until he promised to give up his plan.

As she inserted the key in the lock, the door rattled, alerting Berel. In two big strides, he was at the door, wrenching it open furiously. His mother stared up at him, open-mouthed.

"Mamme!" he cried, exasperated. "What are you doing? Trying to lock me in?" He shook his head at her, his eyes softening ruefully at her pained expression. "It wouldn't have helped, you know," he said gently, smiling sadly down at her. "I would have climbed out the window."

His mother raised her hand to brush away a tear, and Berel grabbed his opportunity. He pulled out the key and pocketed it.

"I'll keep this, if you don't mind," he said. "Now, please, Mamme," he begged, "don't make it so difficult for me. I've *got* to go!"

He turned away to avoid meeting her eyes. His mother gave up in despair and moved away from the door. As she plodded down the corridor, she heard a movement at the other end. Reb Yankel must have woken from his sleep and left the bedroom. She hurried desperately toward the sound, determined to keep Berel's visit from him until he'd had left the house and was well away.

She helped her husband to the kitchen and fussed around him for the best part of an hour, making him a glass of tea and chatting nervously about this and that, when they were startled by a loud bang. *Trust Berel to slam the door*, she thought, irritated. *Why couldn't he have slipped out quietly? He wasn't planning to see his father, anyway!* Reb Yankel looked up, alarmed at the sound.

"What was that?" he asked tremulously.

Mindel saw she had better tell him, if only to dispel his fear. *Please*, she prayed silently, *don't let him go running out after Berel.* Who knew what the exertion might do to him!

To her relief, her husband showed no desire to follow his son. He grew white around the lips, but only said, "Let him go. There's nothing we can do. He never listened to us."

"But the danger! What will become of him?" his wife pressed her palms to her temples.

Reb Yankel lifted his hands in a gesture of resignation.

They sat in silence for a while, the silence only broken by the clink of Reb Yankel's spoon as he stirred his tea—which he made no attempt to drink. Presently, he spoke in a grim voice. "I probably should have thrown him out, right at the start. He might have come to his senses then. You claimed he might come back if we were kind to him … but he never did! He's just gone further away!"

Mindel was stung by the accusation, but said nothing in her defense. If putting the blame on someone made her husband feel better, it was worth keeping the peace. His well-being, after all, was her main concern.

"Perhaps the army will show him how wrong he is," she suggested tentatively, not really believing it herself. "He told me some *bubbe meiseh* about there being a war," she went on. "I don't know where he gets his *meshugene* ideas from!"

Reb Yankel gave a sigh and said, "I'm not so sure it *is* a *bubbe meiseh*. I've heard snatches of conversation in shul and in the *mikveh*. From what people are saying, I don't know if there isn't some truth in what Berel told you!"

Berel's departure went unnoticed by most of the townspeople. But among the Wasserbruns, it was the main topic of conversation. Anshel and Pessel felt it keenly, having been so personally involved.

"I feel as if it's our fault," Anshel commented to his wife. "If we hadn't pushed him to get engaged, he might have settled down after a while …."

"I doubt it," Pessel said. "The *Rosh haYeshiva* only let him stay out of respect for your father. He would have sent him away eventually." She lapsed into silence for a moment. "I wonder if he'd have changed if Sonja *had* married him," she mused.

"Well, that's something we'll never find out," Anshel said. "I wonder what became of her. Does anyone know?"

"I'm sure the Rebbitzen does … but *I'm* certainly not going to ask her!" Pessel declared with feeling.

She thought about Sonja often but avoided mentioning her, knowing how Golda Mirel missed her. Indeed, she missed the young teacher, too. She was such a pleasant girl and they had enjoyed many interesting conversations. Also, since Sonja had left, Pessel lived in constant fear that the red-faced government inspector would turn up again.

"If Golda Mirel hasn't heard about Berel yet, it's better if we don't tell her," Pessel told her husband now.

"Why not?" Anshel asked, surprised. "It's no secret."

"Well, it might bring up her guilt feelings all over again," Pessel said heedlessly.

Anshel looked at his wife, confused. "What has *she* got to feel guilty about?"

Pessel had to do some quick thinking. She had promised to keep her daughter's guilty secret and had kept her word until now, but she decided to share her knowledge with her husband. Briefly, she told him of the girl's anguish after the broken engagement and her guilty confession.

Anshel was stunned. "You mean *she's* the culprit!" he exclaimed. A sad smile crossed his face. "Well, I suppose you could say it was *gam zu letoivoh*!" he said. "She certainly did Sonja a favor. All the same, my mother must never find out. Now, more than ever!"

Two weeks after Berel departed, Anshel received a letter from him. It had been pushed under the door early one morning, and he found it as he was leaving for *shacharis*.

Mystified, he opened it and began to read:

My dear brother Anshel,

I am sending you this letter via a soldier in my unit, who is home on leave. I can't write Tatte and Mamme since I know how they feel about me, and they might tear up the letter without reading it. But please let them know I am well and happy here. Because I was studying medicine for the past year, I have the position of assistant to the army doctor of our unit. It is very interesting and I am learning many things that will be useful to me later on for the career I am determined to pursue!

Hoping you are keeping well and are preparing for the war, which you must now know is imminent.

Regards to all,
Berel

Pessel entered the room while he was still reading.

"W-what is it?" she asked, alarmed at his pale, worried face. "Who is that from? How did it get here?"

"I found it under the door. Someone must have posted it in the night. Here," Anshel said, handing it to her with a shaking hand, "read it!"

Pessel perused the letter, folded it and returned it to her husband. "He must have planned it all along," exclaimed Anshel. "He probably volunteered in the hope that he would be assigned to this doctor!"

"Well, he certainly was lucky," Pessel remarked. "You'd better not tell your parents. In fact, it would be better not to tell them you got a letter. They might ask to see it."

"You're right," Anshel agreed. "They've had enough *agmas*

nefesh already. But I have to let them know he is well. I'll just say we got a message from him through another soldier."

Pessel nodded, her mind elsewhere. "Tell me, Anshel, what does he mean about a war being imminent? Is that true?"

Anshel's expression was grave. "I'm afraid it is. We will have to prepare ourselves for it. *Der Eibershter zoll uphitten!* Who knows what is going to happen to us!"

Chapter 8

Shortly after daybreak, Pessel rose, dressed quickly and slipped into her dimly lit kitchen. She had barely an hour to prepare for her family's needs before the carriage would arrive to carry her off to work.

Moving about noiselessly, she placed a pot of beans on the stove to cook, eyeing it ruefully. If only she had something more substantial to feed her children! But, with the war on, food had become terribly scarce. There was no meat or fish to be had, and even vegetables were hard to come by. Once again, it would be just beans and potatoes. Deftly, she peeled the potatoes and put them in a pot with water and salt for Golda Mirel to cook later.

She had already wakened Golda Mirel, and it was not long before her sleepy-eyed eldest daughter appeared in the doorway.

Poor child, thought Pessel, *only ten years old, much too young to be looking after five younger siblings all day!* But what could she do? This war had turned everyone's world upside down! Lipsk, like other *shtetls* in the vicinity, was a ghost town. There was hardly a man in sight, most having gone into hiding. Those who had not managed to do so in time had been snatched into the army. Only the elderly and the infirm remained.

Anshel was one of the fortunate ones. He and his brother Yidel had slipped away one night to a larger town further away, where they hoped to remain undetected. Although Pessel and Tzirel knew their husbands whereabouts, they were not to contact them except in an emergency. Poor Chana Bleema's husband had been one of the unlucky ones. He had been arrested one night just as he was setting out, and was taken to the army.

"Good morning, *zeesele*," Pessel greeted her daughter. "Sorry to wake you so early, but I've got to give you all the instructions for today."

Golda Mirel stifled a yawn and shook herself, determined to give her mother her full attention.

"The beans need another hour of cooking. Just check that there's enough water in the pot. Cook the potatoes for the boys when they come home for dinner, and reheat the beans. Mash them up well for Ettele and Leibele."

"I did that yesterday," Golda Mirel said defensively, "but they still didn't eat."

Pessel sighed, her brow creased. "I know," she said sadly, "they just don't like it. But what can I do? There isn't anything else … and at least beans are nourishing. Try your best. Perhaps Sheindel will find some way to coax them."

Golda Mirel winced. *Oh, certainly, "Tante" Sheindel is so much older and smarter than me, surely she will know just what to do,* she thought resentfully, but kept quiet. Obviously, Mamme worried less knowing someone was giving her daughter a helping hand, but Golda Mirel didn't see why she needed her mother's young sister's help at all. Having just turned *bas mitzvah*, Sheindel tended to take charge, and Golda Mirel did not enjoy being bossed around.

A carriage rumbled up, stopping at their door. Pessel hurried to peep through the curtain.

"It's here already!" she cried in a panic. She rushed about, grabbed her belongings and flung on her coat. "I hope you'll be all right, Golda Mirel. Wake the boys soon and make sure they *daven*. I hope the little ones behave! That pile of laundry in the basket has to be folded and put away. If any socks need darning, give them to Sheindel to take to Babbe Danziger when she goes home ...."

She hurried breathlessly out to the waiting carriage and climbed in with a heavy heart. She hated leaving her family all day to work, but she had no choice if they were not all to starve. She had been fortunate to find a position as housekeeper to the wife of a wealthy, high-ranking government official. Also, she was grateful for the carriage that came for her every day, saving her the hardship of trudging through the dark, trying to avoid the odd soldier who might be roaming the streets.

All the same, leaving at six o'clock in the morning, and busy until ten o'clock at night when she returned home, left her utterly exhausted. Every day she prayed fervently for this war to end and Anshel to be home again, so life could return to an even keel.

"Oh, Sheindel! They're refusing to eat again!" Golda Mirel wailed in frustration. She scooped up the blob of mashed beans two-year-old Leibele had rudely smushed on the table. "Mamme will be so worried!"

"Let's try telling them a story," Sheindel suggested as she grabbed hold of Ettele, who had scrambled down from her seat. She firmly sat the little four-year-old back down at the table.

"A story?" Golda Mirel asked, surprised. "That's not going to make them eat something they don't like!"

"It might," Sheindel replied confidently. "If it's interesting enough they might not notice what they're eating. Here, let me try."

She held her hand out for the spoon and Golda Mirel reluctantly handed it over, looking skeptical. She was torn between her desire for her little sister and brother to eat, and her hope that Sheindel would not succeed.

Fascinated by Sheindel's tale, Ettele and Leibele at first allowed their young aunt to shovel a few spoonfuls into them, but they soon began to spit out the food, refusing to open their mouths for more.

"It's no use!" Golda Mirel cried triumphantly, yet disappointed, too. "We'll have to tell Mamme we tried our best. Maybe they'll—"

Her words were interrupted by a commotion at the back door. A moment later it was flung open, and Hershele and Mottele burst in in a state of great excitement. Golda Mirel stared at them. They were not meant to be home just yet.

Since the war had begun, the Wasserbrun children had stopped going to school. True, school was still officially compulsory, but with the country in chaos nobody paid attention, and Pessel preferred having her children close by, in the community where they lived. As their *melamed* had unfortunately been dragged away to the army, Reb Yankel Wasserbrun offered to teach all his young grandsons.

"Why are you home already?" Golda Mirel asked anxiously. "Is Zeide all right?"

"No! He's not!" Hershele declared. "You'll never guess what happened!"

"A soldier came knocking at the door," Mottele took up the tale, "and Zeide started shouting at him to go away!"

"He wouldn't, at first, and he called Zeide '*Tatte*'!" Hershele continued. "Then Zeide slammed the door shut in his face!"

"And then Zeide sort of fell onto a chair—like this …," Mottele began to reenact the scene by throwing himself onto the nearest chair, panting breathlessly and clutching his chest. "Babbe was in a terrible state! She sent Moishe Boruch to call the doctor quickly and then she sent us all home!"

"What's happened to Zeide?" Golda Mirel cried, her face white. "I must go and see!" She turned to Sheindel, glad for once that she was there. "Do you mind if I leave you? I must go and see how my Zeide is!"

Sheindel assured her she would manage, and giving instructions to the older girl about the boys' dinner, Golda Mirel grabbed her coat and rushed out.

She ran as quickly as she could all the way to her grandparents' house, afraid of what she would find. *Please*, she prayed, *let Zeide Wasserbrun be all right*!

Golda Mirel realized who the mysterious soldier was. She had heard how Uncle Berel had joined the army causing his parents added *agmas nefesh*. She sometimes felt guilt when she recalled her part in the affair, but the feeling had eased considerably over the last two years.

Suddenly, it burst upon her again in full force, almost stopping her in her tracks. Whatever had happened to Zeide Wasserbrun was *her* fault! If she hadn't stopped Sonja from marrying Uncle Berel, things would have been different. Maybe he wouldn't have been the *talmid chochom* Sonja hankered for, but he would certainly not have joined the army!

Golda Mirel was overcome by a sudden desire to turn around and run back home. How could she face her grandparents? But her anxiety over her grandfather's welfare drove her on.

Her aunt Chana Bleema was already there, and greeted her at the door, her face pale and drawn, her eyes moist.

"Your Zeide's had a heart attack," she told her niece. Golda Mirel followed her into the room where her grandmother sat, looking shriveled and frail in the easy chair.

"The doctor's just left," Chana Bleema continued, her voice quavering. "He says he doesn't know if ..." Unable to continue, she broke into heartrending sobs.

"Oh, Babbe!" Golda Mirel cried, putting her arms around her grandmother and bursting into tears herself. She wanted to say words of comfort and hope but was unable to speak.

After weeping together with her daughter and granddaughter for a few moments, Mindel Wasserbrun pulled herself together, sat up and looked around. She stared at her granddaughter in consternation.

"Golda Mirel," she said hoarsely, "where are the children? Have you left them alone?"

"No, Mamme's sister Sheindel is with them," Golda Mirel assured her.

"Well, go home to them, *sheffela*. There's nothing you can do here. Say some *Tehillim* when you get home, if you can."

"Yes, I will, Babbe," Golda Mirel promised. "But what should I do about Mamme? We ought to let her know ... but how can we?"

Her grandmother sighed. "Yes, I know," she said sadly. "There's no way you can get to her now. You will have to tell her when she comes home tonight. If she's not too tired, perhaps she can still come over."

Who knows what will be by tonight, Mindel thought to herself, refraining from voicing her feelings out loud.

For three days, Yankel Wasserbrun lay unconscious, hovering between life and death. His loyal wife never left his bedside, resisting all attempts to persuading her to rest. Occasionally, she would doze off a little in the chair, but never for long. She knew there was very little hope, and wished her sons Anshel and Yidel could be at her side. However, she had forbidden her daughters-in-law to contact their husbands, knowing they would insist on coming home despite the grave risks.

Pessel and Tzirel, and other family members and friends, came and went continuously. Chana Bleema had made arrangements for her children to be cared for, and was constantly with her mother. Mindel was alone with her husband only during the short visits Chana Bleema made to sort out the essentials at home. During those moments, she would speak softly to him, imploring him to wake up and come back to her.

But it was not to be.

One late afternoon, she observed a different expression on her husband's face. He looked so peaceful and serene. All signs of strain and *agmas nefesh* that had been so evident these past few years were gone, erased as if they had never been there at all! She groped for his hand, murmuring, "Yankel?"

At the touch of his icy cold fingers, she gasped, her hand flying to her throat. "Yankel! Yankel, *mein man!*" she shrieked, and then collapsed in her chair. She was found there by Chana Bleema on her return.

A solemn crowd gathered to accompany Reb Yankel Wasserbrun to his final resting place. Due to the absence of many townspeople, the turnout was small, but all who had remained turned out to pay their respects to this much-loved member of their community.

Reb Yankel's good friend, the *Rosh haYeshiva* Reb Elya Grossheim, delivered a moving *hesped*, praising the *niftar's* wonderful *midos* and his exemplary *yiras Shomayim*.

The procession had begun to move forward when a handful of soldiers came around the bend, demanding an explanation for this illegal gathering. As soon as they heard the reason, they moved away respectfully, to the relief of the crowd. Suddenly, another soldier, not part of the first group, darted into the crowd and began marching with the procession. The first group of soldiers noticed him and pulled him aside for questioning. No one could hear what was said, but they saw him produce a pass that seemed to satisfy the soldiers, who nodded and allowed him to return.

A cluster of women on the opposite side of the street noticed the disturbance. One of them was Chana Bleema, who recognized the young soldier immediately and was struck by the irony of the situation. Neither Anshel nor Yidel could attend the *levayah*, yet Berel, who had brought on his father's heart attack, managed to obtain leave and come!

Her pent-up grief and anxiety suddenly exploded into one great burst of fury. Unmindful of the consequences, she sprang across the road, pushing her way up to confront her younger brother.

"How could you?" she cried. "You—who have killed him! Have you no shame?"

Amid gasps from the crowd, she was quickly hustled away by some well-meaning women back to her mother's side.

Berel turned a fiery red in shame. Then, his brows snapped together, and he swung out of the crowd, glaring wrathfully around him. He strode away, shouting over his shoulder, "Don't expect to ever see me around here again! And you can keep your holy religion!"

The crowd rocked back on its heels in shock at the boy's blasphemy—and at his father's funeral, too! Her anger spent, Chana Bleema was overcome with remorse at her erratic and un-*tzniusdik* reaction. She knew she had incited her brother. It was her fault there had been such a scene of disrespect to her dear father's *neshomoh*.

And worst of all, she regretted adding additional pain to her mother in her time of grief!

Mindel was seething over her daughter's unwarranted behavior. Besides the shame of it, there was her youngest son, who had actually come to pay last respects to his father! She had not even had a second to speak to him. Now, who knew if she ever would get another chance? *She's ruined the one chance to bring Berel back,* Mindel thought sadly.

When they returned to the house and sat down on their low stools, not a word passed between them. Chana Bleema could not look her mother in the eye and Mindel could not bring herself to speak to her daughter. But after a few days into the *shiva,* neither could bear the silence any longer. Chana Bleema begged her mother's forgiveness.

Mindel tried to explain how she felt.

"You've pushed him away completely," she said sorrowfully. "Now he'll never come back to *Yiddishkeit.*"

"Mamme, I really don't think he would have anyway," Chana Bleema argued. "He doesn't want anyone to stop him from becoming a doctor ... ."

Mindel disagreed. "I'm sure he'll come back to see me," she said, "and if he does, please, promise me you won't push him away ...."

"Yes, Mamme, I promise." *But I don't think he will come back,* Chana Bleema thought.

Mindel, however, waited hopefully, but by the time the *shiva* and *shloshim* had passed, there had been no sign of Berel. She began to fear that Chana Bleema had been right.

Chapter 9

"Tatte! Mamme! I beg you! Please don't wait for me any longer!" Golda Mirel stood regarding her parents with imploring eyes. "It might be ages till I find a *shidduch*, and it's holding the others up. It's not fair to them! Please look for *a shidduch* for Hershel. He's already twenty-one! Why should he wait just because—"

"No, Golda Mirel!" Anshel interrupted her. "We will never consider it!" His tone was resolute.

"But …," Golda Mirel began to protest.

"I'm sure we'll hear of somebody soon," Pessel put in quickly. "Just be patient …"

Golda Mirel sighed in exasperation. How could she get her parents to understand that it wasn't herself she was concerned about? She knew her problem. She had lived with it all her life, and coped with it all through her childhood. At twenty-three, she had no illusions about finding an ideal *shidduch*. But she felt discomfort at knowing she was holding up her siblings.

They never showed resentment, but Golda Mirel knew they must be frustrated. If only Tatte and Mamme would ignore the tradition of not marrying off a younger child before an older one!

Mostly, she worried about her parents. The war had taken its toll on them.

Golda Mirel would never forget how her father had looked when he returned home. Pale and thin from lack of nourishment and uncomfortable living conditions, he was only a shadow of the robust, energetic man she remembered, appearing stooped and bent.

Her mother, too, was different. Completely exhausted from her hard work and the struggle to keep her children clothed and fed, she had aged considerably. Caring for her bereaved mother-in-law had sapped her of her spirit, and she was no longer the lively, positive person she had once been.

This new worry of finding a *shidduch* for their oldest daughter was adding another strain on them!

Golda Mirel had almost consented to some most unsuitable suggestions, just to remove the worried lines from her parents' faces. But when it came to the crunch she just couldn't push herself to do it. On one occasion, it was someone who was extremely deaf, with whom she could barely make eye contact, much less conduct any sort of conversation. Another had been a boorish young man of poor intellect, who sat picking his teeth all through their meeting. She could not face watching that for the rest of her life!

In truth, Anshel and Pessel had been relieved when their daughter rejected these suggestions, which were certainly not what they wanted for their bright, intelligent, levelheaded daughter! They knew her pronounced limp was a disadvantage and that they couldn't be too choosy, but they couldn't help wishing that *something* more presentable would come up!

Eventually, a *shidduch* was proposed that seemed promising. The *shadchan* had suggested it hesitantly, certain Anshel would reject it outright. And in different circumstances, that is precisely what he would have done! This young *bochur*, who lived in a nearby town, was from a *Chassidic* family that had been highly respected—until a few years ago, when his mother had suddenly left home. Apparently, she had harbored a secret desire to become an actress, and, encouraged by some disreputable people, she had abandoned her family and her *Yiddishkeit*. Her husband had divorced her and remarried, but the slur on his family had remained.

Pessel persuaded Anshel to consider the match. "Golda Mirel isn't getting any younger," she pointed out, "and neither are Hershel and Reisel. At least go meet the *bochur*. If you think he would be suitable for Golda Mirel, I think we should look away …."

Taking her advice, Anshel went to interview and *farherr* the young man. When he returned, he looked pleased, and told his wife he was highly impressed.

"He certainly knows his gemara," he declared, "and he is presentable and intelligent. I also spoke to his *Rosh Yeshiva* who gave me a glowing report! You were quite right. I really think we should consider this *shidduch*!"

Feeling hopeful for the first time, they contacted the *shadchan*, who set about arranging a meeting. Even Golda Mirel began to feel excited. If he really matched her father's description, perhaps she would put them out of their misery at last! Her single worry was the possibility that the young man would not want a cripple. However, she adamantly refused her mother's advice to remain seated when he came with his parents.

"If he doesn't like the way I walk," she insisted, "it's better if he says so at once."

"Golda Mirel, meet Herr and Frau Holtzer," Anshel said, as his ʾter entered the room, "and this is Gavriel."

Golda Mirel smiled shyly at the three strangers and moved to the table, averting her eyes as she walked. If any of them winced at her limp, she would rather not see it!

Once seated beside her parents, she allowed herself to glance at their visitors. Herr Holtzer was in his late forties, his black beard streaked with gray. His face looked somewhat strained, and as they conversed, he twirled his long *peyos* nervously. Frau Holtzer, a round-faced matron, threw an occasional anxious glance in her step-son's direction.

The two sets of parents chatted amicably for a while. Then, at a sign from Herr Holtzer, Anshel nodded and stood up. The two men made their way to the door, followed by their wives, leaving Golda Mirel and Gavriel alone.

Golda Mirel did not have to wait for Gavriel to break the ice. As they conversed, she could see why her father had been so impressed. His conversation was lively and interesting. They talked about this and that, and then Gavriel asked her how she spent her day. He looked surprised when she told him that she worked.

"Girls generally stay home and help their mothers with the household chores," he said, "learning to be good Jewish *baal habostas*, don't they?"

Golda Mirel refrained from pointing out that most girls were married by the time they were twenty!

"Mornings, I help my grandmother, who is quite old and frail and needs a bit of looking after," she explained, "but in the afternoon I have a job, looking after another old lady who is completely dependent. Her daughter runs a busy shop and cannot care for her mother herself."

"Do you enjoy that?" Gavriel asked.

"Oh, yes! She's a darling, and we've become quite attached to one another!"

"Then it will be difficult for both of you when you have to give it up."

"But why should I have to give it up?" Golda Mirel asked, surprised.

"Well, for one thing, I don't believe in married women working—they are meant to stay at home and run the house. And for another, we won't even be living here. I want to stay on in my present yeshiva after we are married, which is in—"

"One minute, please!" Golda Mirel interrupted, somewhat put out by the strange way this conversation was going. "Aren't you taking things for granted?"

"What do you mean?" he asked.

"What makes you so sure I am going to say 'yes'?"

"Well, of course you are!" Gavriel's tone was arrogant. "Why shouldn't you? *I* haven't got anything wrong with me! It's just because of something that happened in my family ..."

"I see!" Golda Mirel said icily, suppressing her indignation. "That is why you are prepared to take someone with a limp, I suppose?"

"Of course! I've got the sense to know that I can't be choosy ...."

Her face crimson, Golda Mirel stood up. "Thank you," she said unsteadily. "I think you had better go!"

"I certainly will," Gavriel answered, looking annoyed as he stood up, too. "But I think you are making a foolish mistake!"

He marched toward the door just as Anshel and Herr Holtzer entered. It was clear to both that something was wrong. Gavriel reached the door, his face dark with anger, and turned to face Golda Mirel.

"A very stupid mistake!" he threw at her, and left the room with his father.

Anshel just stood there, nonplussed, until Pessel joined them, an equally stupefied expression on her face.

"What happened?" she asked quietly.

Golda Mirel, about to declare that she wouldn't marry him if he were the last person on earth, was stopped by the sight of her parents' crestfallen faces. Feeling as if a knife had turned in her heart, she sank into her chair and buried her face in her hands.

Pessel sat next to her daughter, putting her arm round the girl's shoulders. The gesture released the tears that Golda Mirel had been bottling up, and she sobbed bitterly for a few moments, while her parents looked on helplessly.

"*Sheffela*," Pessel said presently, "don't take it so much to heart—and don't give up hope. He might still change his mind."

Golda Mirel stopped weeping abruptly and stared at her mother in amazement. So that's what they thought! Well, she had better put them in the picture at once.

"Mamme, you've got it wrong! It's *I* who refused! I could never marry him. He's so arrogant and conceited!"

"Oh, come Golda Mirel," Anshel said, "you can't judge from a few minutes' conversation. Maybe you should see him again ..."

"No, Tatte!" Golda Mirel cried vehemently. "Never!"

Her parents looked exasperated. Golda Mirel was about to tell them exactly what he had said, but it suddenly occurred to her that it would hurt them, too, possibly more than it had hurt her. She could not do it!

"I'm sorry, Tatte and Mamme," she said tearfully. "I know it's hard for you both, but please—don't try and persuade me!"

She stood up and limped out, leaving her parents staring at each other.

"I just can't understand it," Anshel said, utterly perplexed. "I thought I was quite a good judge of character and this boy seemed just right for Golda Mirel. What's made her so choosy all of a sudden?"

Pessel nodded in agreement. "I, too, thought our troubles were over at last," she said ruefully. "It seems we don't even know our own daughter!"

She pondered over her daughter's temperament, wondering if there was some sort of rebellious streak in the Wasserbrun family. After all, look at Berel. He had got his way in the end. He had gone off to Germany, and become a doctor there. Except for an occasional letter to his mother, he had cut off all ties with his family One of these bits of correspondence had informed her of his marriage to a nurse from the hospital where he worked. He assured her the girl was Jewish, but the family gathered from the gist of his letter that she was not observant.

Is it possible, Pessel thought with a sinking feeling, that this trait is inherent in our daughter, too?

She naturally said nothing of her idea to Anshel. He would be horrified to think she harbored such thoughts about his family!

However, the next day, when Anshel casually mentioned a different sort of discussion he'd had with a *shadchan*, she wondered whether a similar notion had not occurred to him, too.

"A *shidduch* was suggested the other day for Hershel," he said. "A very good family from Krakow. I think we should follow it up."

Chapter 10

Leaning heavily on his walking stick, Reb Elya Grossheim stood in the doorway of the *beis hamedrash*, surveying the scene with satisfaction. *Baruch Hashem*, the yeshiva was full of students again, as it had been in the days when he was *Rosh haYeshiva*. It had been pathetically empty during the war years, and indeed for some time afterwards, but now, twelve years after the war, it was packed to capacity once more, and the sounds of Torah reverberated through the building.

Reb Elya's oldest son Simcha was *Rosh haYeshiva* now, but Reb Elya still took an active interest in his beloved yeshiva, and though in his eighties visited often to observe the *bochurim* at study. It gave him such pleasure to watch them learning all through the day and often quite late into the night. Occasionally, they went out for short breaks, but Reb Elya didn't mind. They were only young, after all, and it was good for them to relax a little and converse together.

Lately, one student had caught his attention. Although he learned with a *chavrusa* most of the time, he never socialized with the others, and sometimes sat learning alone. The full, beard framing his thin face proclaimed him to be older than the rest, and Reb Elya wondered whether he was married.

His interest aroused, Reb Elya decided to ask his son about the young man.

"His name is Moshe Leib Steiner," Reb Simcha told his father. "He's from Vienna and no … he is not married, although he's about thirty."

"Is that so?" Reb Elya raised his eyebrows. "Is there a problem with him? I notice he doesn't mix with the others at all."

"That is simply because of the age difference between them. I wouldn't call him unsociable. He's actually a very pleasant person."

"Well, then …?" Reb Elya eyed his son quizzically.

"I had a long talk with him some time ago," Reb Simcha explained. "Let me put you in the picture. His family sent him to learn in a yeshiva here in Poland. One day, he and a friend went to a Rebbe's *tisch*, just to see what it was like, and he was so impressed that he was drawn to the *chassidishe* way of life. He has become a fully-fledged *chossid*, much to his family's disapproval, as they are not *chassidish*. Apparently, there was some friction between them although he speaks of them with great *derech eretz*. They had no objection to his learning for several years, but they decided it was time for him to come home and learn a trade—or join his father's business. Moshe Leib, however, wants to go on learning."

"I see …" Reb Elya was thoughtful as he digested this information. "So why is it difficult for him to find a *shidduch*? Most fathers want their daughters to marry someone who wants to stay in learning."

"True," Reb Simcha agreed, "but those fathers who are prepared to offer support prefer to go about things in the usual way, through the *bochur's* parents. Moshe Leib would be glad to involve his parents, but whenever *shadchanim* write to the Steiners in Vienna, they ignore the letters. They don't want a *chassidishe shidduch*, for one thing, and they also believe he must have a *parnossoh* before he gets married."

"Hmm … it's quite a problem," Reb Elya mused. "He looks like a fine *bochur*. Do his parents *have* to be involved? Can he be persuaded to find a *shidduch* on his own?"

"He could, by now," Reb Simcha reflected, "but any prospective father-in-law would be worried about that kind of situation. And now that he's older, it's even harder …."

Reb Elya brooded over the problem for a long time after that conversation with his son, and presently he sought an opportunity to talk to Moshe Leib himself.

Finding him alone in the *beis hamedrash* one evening, bent over a gemara, Reb Elya went over and sat down beside him. They discussed the *sugya* for a while, until Moshe Leib leaned back in satisfaction.

"Thank you," he said, "I've been puzzling over that *shtickel* for quite a while. The *Rosh haYeshiva* has made it really clear to me!"

"You're welcome," Reb Elya smiled at him. "I'm ready to help anyone who needs it. Now tell me. How long have you been in this yeshiva?"

In that way he drew the young man out, asking him about himself. Moshe Leib answered all his leading questions in an honest, forthright way.

"Tell me …," Reb Elya said, in his most fatherly tone, "have you not spoken to your Rebbe about your problem?"

"Yes, I have. Several times,"

"And … ?" Reb Elya prompted.

"The Rebbe gave me a *brochoh*," Moshe Leib replied simply.

"And have you thought of asking the Rebbe if you could look for a *shidduch* by yourself, without consulting your parents?" Reb Elya asked.

"Yes, I did," Moshe Leib told him.

"*Nu* … what did the Rebbe say?"

"That I should ... but I should ask my parents' permission first."

"And have you asked them?" Reb Elya probed.

"Yes, I wrote them recently," Moshe Leib replied, a look of sadness crossing his face, "and my mother wrote back saying I should go ahead. They aren't happy about it, but they've accepted it."

"Well then ... what's holding you up?"

"I think," Moshe Leib responded candidly, with a rueful smile, "I am too late!"

Reb Elya couldn't get Moshe Leib out of his mind. If only he could think of a *shidduch* for him. But how would an old man know someone who might consider a thirty-year-old *bochur*?

And yet ... he had a strange feeling about it. There was an idea lurking at the back of his mind. What was it? It was so vague and intangible, he was convinced he would never put his finger on it. But he refused to give up. Sitting in his armchair, sipping a glass of tea, he tried to prod that elusive thought to the forefront of his brain. At last, through a simple incident, he was rewarded.

One afternoon, his wife came in holding an invitation from Anshel Wasserbrun, asking him to the *chassunah* of his daughter Reisel.

"Oh, they're marrying off a daughter this time," his wife remarked. "Last year it was their son ..."

At her words, Reb Elya sat up straight. He could almost hear his daughter-in-law Tzirel's voice when they had received the last invitation.

"What a shame about their oldest daughter," Tzirel had said. "They've jumped over her. I wonder how she feels about it."

"Is Reb Anshel's oldest girl still single?" Reb Elya now asked his wife.

"I believe she is, " she replied. "I suppose they didn't have any choice. She must be about twenty-six or twenty-seven by now. And with a problem like hers …" She shook her head and gave a sympathetic sigh.

Reb Elya's ears pricked up immediately. What was this? Was there another problem in the Wasserbrun family? His mind went back to the time he'd had to break the news to his old friend Reb Yankel about their son. What *agmas nefesh* they had had. And now their son Anshel seemed to have some trouble as well.

"What's wrong with this daughter?"

"Oh, it's something to do with her legs," his wife informed him. "I don't know what, exactly, but it makes her walk with a distinct limp!

It's such a pity," she continued. "She is such a special girl! Except for that, she's got *alle maalos*! Clever … sensible … good *midos* … the lot! But her walk puts people off."

"I see …" Reb Elya said musingly, relieved that the problem was only a physical one. All the same, he sympathized with Reb Anshel. It must be very hard for him. A pity he did not feel strong enough to attend the *chassunah*. He *had* made the effort to go to Hershel's *chassunah*—the *chosson* having been his *talmid*—and he hadn't been aware that this was not Anshel's oldest child!

Now he wondered whether Reb Anshel might consider this young man from Vienna; and also whether Moshe Leib would consider a girl with a limp.

There's only one way to find out, he told himself, and if I don't do something about it, no one will!

Golda Mirel gave her hair another quick sweep of her brush and regarded herself in the mirror with a wry smile. Here she was, at it again, and it was probably just a waste of time!

It was a few years since any *shidduch* had been suggested for her.

Once her parents had begun marrying off their other children, the *shadchanim* gave up on her.

So, when the strange man had called on them, explaining that he was a *maggid shiur* at the yeshiva and had come on behalf of Reb Elya Grossheim, they had assumed he had a suggestion for Mottel, who was already twenty-two. They could hardly conceal their surprise when he explained it was for Golda Mirel! When he heard the boy's age, Anshel had been skeptical, convinced there must be some severe disadvantage, but out of respect for his old *Rosh haYeshiva* he had agreed to meet the *bochur*.

When he returned, they waited to hear the problem, but Anshel looked pleased. "I found nothing the matter," he said. "The young man seems pleasant and well-mannered, and he can certainly learn!"

"Then why ... ?" Pessel began.

"Oh, it's something to do with his family coming from Vienna," Anshel interrupted, understanding her unspoken question, "and their not being *chassidish*. Apparently, it caused problems."

Her parents seemed satisfied with the explanation, but Golda Mirel had reservations. *There must be more to it than that*, she told herself. That he impressed her father did not mean much, she thought, the painful memory of the incident with Gavriel springing to mind. And if he was as good as the *Rosh haYeshiva* and everyone else made out, then he certainly wouldn't want *her*!

Determined to keep an open mind, Golda Mirel waited for her mother to call her. She had heard them arrive, the *bochur* and Reb Yisroel Kahn, the *maggid shiur* who had come with the suggestion. There were no parents to meet. Golda Mirel didn't know whether she was glad about that or not.

Soon there was a gentle tap at the door, and Pessel looked in.

"Are you ready?" she asked. "Come along, then. He seems very nice," she added, a hopeful gleam in her eye.

As she stood up to follow her mother, Golda Mirel realized that Pessel planned to play down her limp a little by walking in front of her.

"Mamme," she whispered urgently, "I beg you. Please let me walk in by myself. We can't hide the truth!"

Aware that Golda Mirel had guessed her intentions, Pessel's heart sank. However, she respected her daughter's wishes, and when they got to the dining room, she pushed open the door and waited for Golda Mirel to enter before her.

"Go ahead," she said softly. "I'll follow you in a minute."

Three pairs of eyes watched as Golda Mirel walked toward the table. She noticed the young man did not look at her directly—only out of the corner of his eye—and that a slight flush was creeping up his face.

He seems shy, she noted with satisfaction. She reflected that one couldn't be shy *and* arrogant at the same time.

She sat down at the table and Anshel and Reb Yisroel Kahn stood up. Since there were no parents for her to get acquainted with, there was no point in them staying.

Left alone in the room, each was reluctant to start the conversation, and there was an awkward silence. At last, Moshe Leib took the plunge.

"Your father says he went to the yeshiva where I'm learning," he remarked.

"Yes, he did. And so did my brother Hershel. My other brother, Mottel, is there now. Do you know him?"

Flushing, Moshe Leib hesitated. "I-I'm not sure. There are so many *bochurim* …."

And of course, he is so much younger than you, Golda Mirel thought. *How tactless of me!*

"Reb Elya was a good friend of my Zeide, *alav hasholom*," she put in quickly, to cover her embarrassment.

"Yes, he told me that," Moshe Leib replied, relieved that the conversation was warming up a little. They continued making small talk, and eventually came to the subject of her work.

"It must be very rewarding," Moshe Leib observed, "and very useful. I remember my own grandmother. Unfortunately, there was no one who could care for her like that and she had to end her days in a home. My parents were terribly upset about that, but they had no choice."

At least he's not talking about me giving it up, Golda Mirel thought, impressed. But perhaps that's because he has already decided that the *shidduch* isn't relevant, she wondered with a sinking feeling.

Despite her anxiety, she was enjoying the conversation, and was actually disappointed when her father returned. She realized that this time his assessment had been correct. However, she did not allow herself to think beyond this point. She had to protect herself from being hurt!

Anshel nodded to Moshe Leib, who stood up, and with a polite "good evening" and a shy smile at Golda Mirel, followed her father out of the room.

Left alone at the table, Golda Mirel had a feeling of anti-climax. *Was that it?* she wondered. She heard the front door close and, surprisingly, felt overcome with hopelessness. Her eyes smarted with sudden tears. Fighting them, she told herself that she hadn't expected anything, anyway.

Pessel and Anshel came in, eyeing their daughter expectantly.

"Well?" Pessel asked her. "What do you think?"

"What does it matter what *I* think!" she responded in despair. "It's what *he* thinks that counts. And that was pretty obvious, wasn't it? He's gone away!"

"Well, of course he has!" Anshel said in a matter-of-fact tone. "That's what was arranged. He's going back with Rabbi Kahn to discuss the matter. Then, if he's interested, Rabbi Kahn will call here again to see if you are, too … and we'll take it from there."

"Well, I don't count on him coming back," Golda Mirel said despondently, trying to sound as if she didn't care.

However, her pessimism was unfounded. Less than two hours later, Rabbi Kahn returned. "The *bochur* is interested! What about your daughter?" he asked.

Golda Mirel was so surprised when her father came to ask how she felt that all she could do was nod.

Everything went quickly after that. Rabbi Kahn left, returning shortly with Moshe Leib. Then Golda Mirel and Moshe Leib were left alone again to have another brief conversation. This time they discussed the things in life that affected them, and were both pleased that they agreed on all the important issues.

The Wasserbrun household suddenly exploded in an atmosphere of excitement. Members of the family came in, and amid cries of "*mazel tov!*" everyone drank "*lechayim.*"

The whole family approved of Moshe Leib, and Golda Mirel began to relax. He seemed genuinely happy—not at all like someone who had only agreed to a *shidduch* because he had no choice!

Discussing a time to hold the *tenaim*, Pessel asked Moshe Leib if he would like his parents to come.

"I will send them a telegram first thing tomorrow, but I'm not sure if they will be able to make the journey from Vienna. It's quite a long way. They'll come for the *chassunah*, of course," he added hastily, making sure they did not have the impression that his parents were totally disinterested.

Later that night, when everyone had left and Pessel and Golda Mirel were clearing up, Pessel kissed her daughter and said, "I've waited a long time for this moment!"

"I didn't made it very easy for you, did I?" Golda Mirel acknowledged with a rueful smile.

"Well, it seems you knew best what was right for you," Pessel agreed. "Though I must admit we didn't always understand you."

"I know ...," Golda Mirel nodded understandingly. She knew exactly what her mother was referring to. All at once, she felt a strong urge to justify herself over that incident—and now was the best time to do it.

Repeating her conversation with the arrogant Gavriel, she saw Pessel react as she had hoped she would.

"Golda Mirel!" she cried aghast. "Why didn't you tell us at the time?"

"I was afraid you'd be too upset," Golda Mirel explained. "And at any rate," she added, smiling, "it's a good thing I didn't, or you wouldn't have considered accepting *shidduchim* for the others! They'd have had to wait a really long time, since my *bashert* has only just come along!"

Pessel regarded her daughter in admiration. How amazingly perceptive this girl was! There was no denying it. Her Golda Mirel was quite an exceptional girl!

I only hope, she thought with typical motherly pride, *her* chosson *is worthy of her!*

Chapter 11

Golda Mirel wheeled the cumbersome pushchair down the few steps to the basement of the house where she lived. Frau Folgerman, her landlady, had kindly allowed her to leave it there and Golda Mirel was thankful she didn't have to drag it all the way upstairs.

She lifted eight-month-old Yankele out and carried him up the three flights of stairs to her little flat. Unlocking the door with her key, she stood for a moment, viewing the flat with satisfaction. It was neat and tidy, just as she had left it that morning, and, though small and quite sparsely furnished, it looked cozy, and she loved it because it was their own home—hers and Moshe Leib's. And since their little son had arrived, it was even more complete!

After their wedding, Golda Mirel had continued her job until the old lady passed away. Then, still determined to be the breadwinner so her husband could go on learning, she had taken a job in a busy grocery shop. When Yankele was born, Moshe Leib had wanted her to give up work, concerned that it was too much for her. He suggested finding work himself, but Golda Mirel wouldn't hear of it, knowing it was not what he really wanted. In the end, they had compromised, Golda Mirel agreeing to cut down on her working hours and Moshe Leib giving private lessons to supplement their income. Now Golda Mirel worked only in the morning, leaving her baby at her mother's and picking him up on her way home.

Golda Mirel took off her little son's outdoor clothes and sat down to feed him, just as he began to whimper. She felt him relax against her, and she leaned back, indulging in this moment of peace and contentment. Life was certainly treating her well! She had waited quite a long time, but now she was married to a wonderful man, and had an adorable little baby, too!

Money was scarce and they managed with just the bare necessities, but they were happy in their little flat, high up on the third floor. Moshe Leib had found a yeshiva nearby, and Golda Mirel was greatly relieved that they could remain here in Lipsk, near her parents and grandparents.

Many girls were compelled to move near their husbands' families, and Golda Mirel admitted that would have been extremely difficult. Her relationship with her mother-in-law could not exactly be described as warm. Although Frau Steiner was obviously a good, kind person, she was rather stiff, and there was a considerable barrier between them.

Pausing in her reverie, Golda Mirel glanced involuntarily at her wedding pictures displayed on the mantelpiece. One was a photograph of Golda Mirel flanked by the two mothers. Pessel was smiling, but Frau Steiner's face was completely devoid of expression. It was as if she was switched off, determined not to display any emotion!

As her mind went back to the day she had first met her mother-in-law, her feeling of euphoria began to dissipate a little.

Moshe Leib's parents had arrived the day before the *chassunah*, and after settling in the room Pessel had found for them in Frau Lander's guesthouse, they had come to meet the Wasserbruns.

Golda Mirel wondered now whether she had just been over-sensitive, but it seemed to her that Frau Steiner had deliberately stood in the doorway, waiting for the girl to walk toward her. When she had done so, the look of horror on the woman's face had been unmistakable. Golda Mirel wondered whether Moshe Leib had told his parents about her limp. If he had, it was obvious that he hadn't laid very much stress on it. To be *don lekav zechus*, one had to admit that it must have been quite a shock to Frau Steiner.

Forcing her smile to remain on her face, Golda Mirel had shaken hands with Frau Steiner, and studied her future parents-in-law with interest. Herr Steiner was tall and gaunt, with a small, pointed gray beard and a neatly groomed moustache. He was immaculately dressed in a dark suit, a starched white shirt and a somber gray tie. Raising his black Homburg slightly, he smiled kindly, regarding her through thick, horn-rimmed spectacles.

Frau Steiner, slightly below average in height, was also thin. She was dressed in a neat, dark green suit and a cream-colored blouse, a hat of black and green feathers covering most of her pale blonde *sheitel*. Golda Mirel noted her thin lips and pale gray eyes as the woman leaned forward and kissed her future daughter-in-law perfunctorily on both cheeks.

Anshel and Pessel had led their guests to the table and plied them with refreshments while they all made polite conversation with some difficulty, as the Wasserbruns spoke only Yiddish, and the Steiners mainly German. However, the similarity of the two languages helped them make themselves understood.

Frau Steiner soon commented on young couples settling down without a proper *parnossoh*, and Pessel hastened to convince her that their children would manage on Golda Mirel's wages.

"As long as they're happy …," Pessel remarked airily, "that's the main thing."

Still skeptical, Frau Steiner took the conversation to the subject of Golda Mirel's limp. Struggling to look and sound unperturbed, Pessel assured her it was *not* a genetic disease in the family, but merely an accident of birth. To her relief, Frau Steiner's worried expression relaxed a little.

Golda Mirel, however, felt extremely alarmed. *This is it!* she told herself. *I'm going to call off the* chassunah!

The Steiners did not stay very long. Before they left, Pessel reminded Frau Steiner to come at five o'clock the next day for photographs before the *chuppah*.

Promising to be there, the Steiners had left in—what seemed to Golda Mirel—a rather abrupt manner.

Golda Mirel had tossed and turned the whole night, not sleeping a wink! If Pessel noticed that her daughter looked bleary-eyed the next morning, she thought nothing of it. It was not unusual for a *kallah* to be unable to sleep the night before her *chassunah*.

The pre-wedding hustle and bustle was soon underway, but Golda Mirel was strangely detached. She went through the morning on tenterhooks, expecting a messenger to arrive at any moment with the dreaded message!

She had spent the entire time saying *Tehillim* until, half way through the afternoon, her mother came in and suggested she get dressed so that she could *daven mincha* before the photographer arrived. Golda Mirel had nodded half-heartedly, still convinced that the *chassunah* would be called off. Closing her *Tehillim*, she preparing to go to her room. At that moment, there was a loud rapping at the door. Golda Mirel froze and stood stock still as her mother went to the door. Expecting to hear Pessel give an exclamation of dismay, she was surprised at the cheerful way her mother was saying "thank you" to the person at the door. A moment later Pessel came in, an attractive bouquet of white and pink flowers in her hands.

"The *mechuteniste* has sent you a bouquet," she told her astonished daughter. "It's beautiful! Here's a note with it, but it's in German. Can you read it, because I can't!"

Golda Mirel had learned a little German with Sonja—and had brushed up her knowledge a bit once she became engaged to a Viennese. Now, taking the bouquet, she read the note in a voice that matched her shaking hands.

I hope this goes well with your dress, Frau Steiner had written. *I will see you at five o'clock, as we arranged. With all my best wishes, Martha Steiner.*

Overcome with relief, Golda Mirel hadn't at first noticed the impersonal style of the note. Only later, while they waited for Frau Steiner to arrive, did she think of it, and her apprehension rose again.

Golda Mirel laughed a little at these recollections. She realized she had really enjoyed her *chassunah* after all. Frau Steiner had been far less formidable than she seemed. She was even quite friendly, in her own reserved way. And so was Moshe Leib's sister Ilse, who had also seemed disapproving at first. Golda Mirel decided that she *had* been accepted by the family, after all.

However, she definitely knew one thing, she reflected now, as she bounced her little son on her knee. She and her mother-in-law were too different and didn't see things the same way. She was sure she'd never be able to live in the same town with her!

Golda Mirel changed the baby and put him in his cot for a nap, intending to peel some vegetables for the evening meal. But little Yankele had other ideas. He had recently mastered the art of standing up in his cot, but hadn't yet learned to let himself down again, and now, as he stood clinging to the dowels, he registered his frustration in no uncertain terms. He obviously had no intention of going to sleep!

Quite unperturbed, Golda Mirel decided that since Moshe Leib would not be home for another four hours there was plenty of time to cook supper. She would take the baby to visit Babbe Wasserbrun.

Babbe Wasserbrun had a special soft spot for little Yankele, who was the only great-grandchild living nearby named for her late husband. Her granddaughter Reisel had two daughters and her grandson Hershel lived in Krakow and didn't bring *his* Yankele to see her very often.

Her face lit up when Golda Mirel came in with her son. Though she was so frail by now that she could barely move about, she insisted on holding the child on her lap and cuddling him.

Watching them, Golda Mirel was thankful she could give her grandmother some pleasure. The poor woman had had so much trouble in her life! Although she rarely spoke about her youngest son, Golda Mirel knew that Berel was often on her mind. From his occasional letters, as infrequent as they were, Mindel Wasserbrun knew he was a successful orthopedic surgeon, but she also understood that his life was far removed from the *Torahdik* upbringing she and her husband had done their best to give him.

Golda Mirel stayed until she saw the old lady was becoming tired. She had a satisfied feeling as she wheeled her baby home, knowing it has been an afternoon well spent.

With a sleeping Yankele in her arms, she went into the house and was about to climb up to her flat when Frau Folgerman came out of her kitchen, an envelope in her hand.

"This telegram came for your husband while you were out," she said, handing it to her.

Golda Mirel took it from her, somewhat alarmed. It was obviously from Vienna, but what it was about? What could have happened?

Her first reaction was to rip open the envelope, but she stopped herself. *It's addressed to Moshe Leib*, she thought. *I'd better leave it for him to read. He'll be home in an hour. I can surely wait that long.*

She set about preparing supper, eyeing the envelope nervously from time to time, and was relieved when she heard Moshe Leib's key in the door.

"There's a telegram for you," she told him immediately, pointing a floury finger at the table where it lay.

Worried, Moshe Leib picked it up and tore it open hastily. As soon as he read the contents, his face paled.

"W-what is it?" Golda Mirel asked, alarmed.

"I-it's my father," Moshe Leib said in a voice that shook. "He's had a stroke!"

"Oh, no!" Golda Mirel cried, aghast. "How bad is it?"

"He's unconscious. Golda Mirel, I've got to go there at once!"

"Of course you have!" Golda Mirel agreed, though her heart was heavy at the thought. "I hope he'll have a speedy *refuah sheleimah*!"

"*Amein!*" Moshe Leib cried vehemently. "Hopefully, I won't be gone too long. What will you do? I feel bad to leave you on your own. Perhaps you should move in to your parents with Yankele ...."

"No," Golda Mirel said, determined not to leave the home that she loved. "I'd rather stay and wait here for you to come back!"

Utterly weary and somewhat despondent, Golda Mirel climbed the stairs, her little boy in her arms. Almost three months had passed since Moshe Leib had left and it seemed like an eternity, with no sign of the situation coming to an end. Lacking her husband's earnings, Golda Mirel had gone back to working full time after her mother had kindly offered to mind Yankele all day. Pessel had begged Golda Mirel to move in with them, and was a little hurt by her daughter's refusal. Golda Mirel was aware of this, but found it difficult to explain her reluctance to leave her little home.

A week after Moshe Leib's departure, he had sent her a telegram stating that his father had regained consciousness, and Golda Mirel had been sure her husband would be home shortly. But Herr Steiner's progress was very slow and Moshe Leib felt he could not leave him until his condition was more stable.

He wrote often and Golda Mirel wrote back, telling him the news in town and informing him of what his son was up to. Poor Moshe Leib! It must be so hard for him to miss each stage of the little boy's progress. Today, she would write and tell him how Yankele had taken his first steps!

She had stopped by the little table in the hall to pick up her mail, and, riffling through the pile, she found the one she was searching for … a letter from Moshe Leib.

She put it on the table, ready to read as soon as she had put Yankele to bed. Since Pessel had already given him supper, all he needed was a bath and a bottle of milk, and shortly, the lively little boy was tucked up cozily in his cot, fast asleep.

Now Golda Mirel picked up the letter and took it over to the armchair. Settling herself down, she eagerly tore open the envelope. Maybe … maybe this time he was writing to tell her that he was coming home. After all, it was just a few weeks until Purim, and Pesach followed close behind.

She began to read, her hope growing. He told her that, *baruch Hashem*, his father was much better and was beginning to take an interest in his business. That sounds promising, Golda Mirel thought, feeling excited. She read on.

All the same, he is not nearly ready to go back to work, if he ever will be. I don't know how I'm going to write this,

Golda Mirel, but a problem has arisen. Papa begs me to move back to Vienna and run the business for him. Of course I have refused. But the result was that Papa had a setback and had to go back to the hospital. He's home again now, but the doctor says he must have no more aggravation. What shall I do? Mamma is begging me to stay, afraid that Papa's life depends on me!

Of course I can't remain here without you and Yankele, which is why I'm asking if you could consider coming to live here. I know how you feel, and believe me, I ask this of you with a heavy heart. I, too, would be happier with our old life, so you can see what a dilemma it is for me!

If you feel you can't, then of course I will understand and come home. Your wishes come first, after all. But please give it some thought before answering.

Please forgive me for putting this pressure on you.

Give a kiss to little Yankele from me.

Yours ever,

Moshe Leib

No! No! Golda Mirel's whole being cried out in protest! *You can't ask this of me!*

Tightly gripping the arms of the chair, she looked around the room, taking in every detail of the flat she loved so dearly. The hand-embroidered tablecloth on the table—a present from Babbe Wasserbrun; the tapestry on the wall her grandmother Danziger had made; the photos on the mantelpiece; the curtains her mother had sewn so lovingly; in fact, all the furniture in the room that she had so enjoyed choosing. How could she leave it all behind? No, she wouldn't agree!

She re-read the last paragraph: *If you feel you can't, then of course*

I will understand and come home. Your wishes come first, after all. The words eased her conscience a little. If she wrote and explained exactly how she felt, he would understand.

Not giving herself time to think, she sat down and wrote a lengthy letter, putting her point of view as clearly as she could. One of her arguments was the attachment her grandmother Wasserbrun felt for Yankele. How could she take him away from her?

Besides which, she wrote, *I feel I will never settle in a strange country, with different type of people. And what about Yankele? Don't you want him to grow up in a chassidishe environment?*

I don't understand why it has to be you who runs the business. Why can't Ilse's husband Kurt take over? It's not fair of your family to demand this of us!

She ended the letter apologizing if she was unreasonable and hoping Herr Steiner would nevertheless have a complete recovery.

Convinced she was doing the right thing, she addressed the envelope and stamped it.

Then, taking the letter, she went downstairs and knocked on Frau Kalinsky's door in the flat below, asking her to listen for Yankele while she went to post her letter.

As she limped along to the post-box, conflicting thoughts suddenly began to overtake her. Why had Moshe Leib asked her to do something he knew she would resist? It was so unlike him! He must feel strongly about it. After all, it would not be easy for him either to settle back in Vienna. How would he feel when he read her letter? He would understand … of course he would … but wouldn't he be disappointed? Wouldn't he feel that *she* was showing a lack of understanding and consideration?

Suddenly, she didn't feel so sure of herself. Was this the right attitude of a Jewish wife … going against her husband's wishes? Was this called "*oseh retzon ba'alah*"?

By now she had reached the post-box, and she put her hand out to drop the letter in. But, as if her arm had suddenly become paralyzed, she stopped in mid-air, unable to carry on.

Withdrawing her hand, she leaned against the box, thinking. She realized she was wrong. She could not send that letter so quickly. She would go back home and think things over. She would see if she could reconcile herself to the notion of possibly living in Vienna, after all. She hated the idea, but she would be together with Moshe Leib, and that was the main thing.

Her mind in a whirl, she made her way home. Once inside her flat, she tore up the letter and threw it onto the fire, watching the flames destroy her moment of rebellion.

Then she sat down to think it all over. She pictured the reactions of her beloved family on hearing the news, and she could not stop the tears from spilling down her cheeks. She allowed herself to wallow in misery for a while before checking herself.

Stop it! she told herself. *This isn't going to help! It's a* nisayon, *and you'll have to accept the fact that you really have no choice.*

Clinging to this positive attitude for all she was worth, she took out her writing pad once more and sat down to write a new letter to her husband.

PART II:

Summer

Vienna, 1932. Martha Steiner nervously smoothed an invisible crease on the lace tablecloth, and replaced the little porcelain vase of yellow crocuses in the center of the table. She stood back to survey the room one more time. The flat she had chosen was pleasant, and now, with the afternoon sun shining in through the window and a gentle early-spring breeze fluttering the crisp, new curtains, it looked positively inviting.

She had done her best, choosing good quality, serviceable furniture and arranging it in the flat herself. Surely, her daughter-in-law would not find fault with it. Compared to the dingy, third-floor flat they had been crammed in till now in Poland, this was virtually a palace! She felt a wave of annoyance remembering her shock when she had visited them after little Yakob's birth. What had they done with the money the Steiner's had given them to buy furniture? Golda Mirel had shrugged it off, saying they didn't need much furniture and the money was helping to pay the rent, leaving her earnings to cover their living expenses. Ridiculous! If Leo had been sensible enough to find a job, they wouldn't have had to live like paupers. Still, it was their choice and she grudgingly conceded to some admiration for Golda Mirel's attitude.

They would be arriving soon, Leo and his wife and child, and the thought of it filled Frau Steiner with a confusing mixture of feelings.

She was grateful to Golda, of course. (Frau Steiner adamantly refused to call her daughter-in-law by both names. "So unnecessary!" she insisted.) Leo had explained how his wife felt about leaving Poland and what a great sacrifice it would be for her. If she hadn't agreed to come, who knows what would have happened to Heinrich! All the same, she wished it hadn't been necessary. She couldn't say she looked forward to introducing her foreign-looking daughter-in-law to her friends. She had assumed her husband would give up the business and they would manage off their pensions and life insurance.

Pity Kurt wasn't willing to take over, Frau Steiner reflected, not that she blamed him. Why should he give up a successful career as a solicitor? *If only Max were still alive*, she thought, sadness enveloping her at the thought of her eldest son who had died after a climbing accident many years ago. Max would have been in the business already, having expressed his intention to join his father when he finished his time in yeshiva. Furthermore, Frau Steiner thought irrelevantly, he would have been married by now, most likely to a girl who was more their type.

Feeling guilty, she tried to rid herself of her negative thoughts. It wasn't that she disliked Golda. On the contrary, the girl had excellent qualities and a very pleasant manner. Also, she was a good wife to Leo and seemed to be making him very happy. However, having her living here was bound to present problems. For one thing, people in their circle tended to look down somewhat on Polish *Yidden*. Then there was the matter of Golda's limp. She could just hear some of her friends' comments.

"Poor Martha!" she imagined them saying. "It must have been very hard for her Leo to find a *shidduch* if he had to take a Polish girl who's a cripple and has to wear such a dreadful shoe all the time!"

With sudden shock, Frau Steiner realized she was ashamed of her daughter-in-law! It's not right to feel like that, she reprimanded herself sharply. She resolved to be especially nice to Golda Mirel.

Since she had put herself out to arrange this flat, she felt less guilty. *I am already treating her nicely*, she thought. And, although originally she had planned on settling them a little further away, in the *Dritte Bezirk*, perhaps, she had acknowledged that it wasn't kind to expect someone with a limp to have so far to walk if she wanted to visit them on Shabbos. In the *Zweiten Bezirk*, where they lived, there was an *eiruv*, so Golda could even take Yakob in the pushchair. Frau Steiner had considered a flat near one of the *Chassidishe shteiblech* dotting the district, but quickly rejected that idea. *Golda will get too close to these people*, she argued with herself, *and never get used to our way of life*.

She glanced at her watch and saw it was time to go home and see to the meal she had prepared for the new arrivals. She had gone to great lengths, cooking some of Leo's favorite dishes, and she hoped Golda Mirel would enjoy them, too. Their train arrived in an hour's time, and Ilse and Kurt, who owned a car, had offered to meet them at the station. They would take them to the flat to unload their belongings, then bring them to her house for supper.

Hurrying home to relieve Ilse, who was minding her father while her mother was out, Martha Steiner struggled to control the apprehension playing havoc with her nervous system!

Moshe Leib was at work, and little Yankele was still napping, so Golda Mirel hurried to her favorite spot at the kitchen window, looking down on the street. Soon the postman would come along with his bursting leather bag. Would there be a letter today? *Please! Please, I'm so lonely!* came the unbidden thought.

Over two months had passed since she had moved to Vienna, but she was not acclimating as well as she had hoped. Everything was strange and different, but that was not the real problem. She was an adaptable person and was prepared to make changes in her lifestyle. Her main obstacle was the feeling that Moshe Leib's family did not accept her. Coming from a warm, close-knit family, she found their aloofness bewildering. Though she was sure they didn't mean to treat her as an outsider, their manner was distant, almost unfriendly! Her mother-in-law seemed to bend over backward to please her, but her actions seemed cold and calculated. Even the way she kissed Yankele seemed somehow mechanical.

Then there was the discomfort she felt with the local populace. She wasn't bothered by people staring at her heavy, built-up shoe, and reacting to her limp What disturbed her was the obvious embarrassment it caused her mother-in-law.

Frau Steiner had kindly taken her around the district, showing her the shops and other places of importance, but she appeared to avoid introducing Golda Mirel to many of her friends and acquaintances. If anyone she knew entered a shop they were in, she would suddenly hustle them out of there in a hurry. Occasionally, some woman would come bustling up to them before they could escape, with a remark such as "Oh, Martha! Is *this* Leo's wife? *Sholom aleichem!*" and then proceed to look her up and down. Golda Mirel, determined to be friendly, would converse politely, but noticed that her broken German also made her mother-in-law cringe.

How often Golda Mirel felt tempted to throw in the towel and beg Moshe Leib to take her back home! But she could not add more strain to her husband. She knew he wasn't happy either, running a business when all he wanted was to spend his life learning. He would come home tired after a hard day's work and try to put his mind to learning, but it just wasn't the same.

Golda Mirel understood that only his concern for his father kept him here. She couldn't forget her shock at her first sight of her father-in-law. He looked nothing like the erect and dignified gentleman she had met at her *chassunah*, and later at Yankele's *bris*. Now he sat, a tragic figure propped in a wheelchair, hardly able to move, his speech slurred. He had spoken to her during her visit, and she could barely catch his inarticulate words. When she'd understood that he was thanking her for coming, she had tried to smile encouragingly, but her eyes shone with unshed tears. However desperate she felt sometimes, she knew one thing. She would never do anything to cause her poor father-in-law *agmas nefesh*!

She heard a clang. There was the post! Golda Mirel quickly peeked in at her son, still curled up in deep, dreamless sleep, and plodded down the steps to the front door. Eagerly, she removed the Steiner letters and riffled through them as she climbed back up. There it was—a Polish postmark! She went hot and cold in excitement. Discarding the rest of the mail on the table, she settled down to read her mother's letter. It was full of news. *Shidduchim* were already being suggested for Leibel, who was doing well in yeshiva. Reisel had given birth to a boy after three girls! The baby had been named Yankel, much to Babbe Wasserbrun's delight. Golda Mirel's youngest sister, Ettel, had also had a baby—after waiting three years. It was a little girl and she was named Golda Mirel …. *Babbe Danziger is thrilled*, her mother wrote, *and hopes she will grow up to be like her mother, aleha hasholom … just like you are (a nice compliment for you!)* …

The rest of the letter was full of gossipy bits of news. Frau

Traubner had turned eighty and she didn't want anyone to know, but the secret was out since her children and grandchildren had made an enormous party for her! A large new grocery shop had opened and Herr Telzer—Golda Mirel's former boss—was complaining that it was taking away his business ... and so on ...

Golda Mirel felt pangs of homesickness increasing as she read, and suddenly, without warning, she began to cry, her tears soaking the letter.

For ten minutes she sat and sobbed her heart out, releasing the pent up emotions of these past two months. As she calmed down, she heard Yankele calling from his cot. She pulled herself together and got up, dashing cold water on her face and patting it dry before going to pick him up. She brought him into the kitchen and sat him in his chair, smiling at his babbling almost-words as she mashed his food. As she sat down to feed him, her eye fell on the letter she had dropped on the table. It was dimpled from her wet tears, and some of the writing was smudged. Oh, no. How could she show it to Moshe Leib in that condition? What would he think? She had been so careful till now to hide her homesickness. He had enough to put up with without that!

When the letter had dried out, she placed it between some books and set a heavy wooden box on top of the stack, hoping it would straighten out.

When Moshe Leib came home, she gave him the letter, which still showed telltale signs of wetness. Certainly, the smudged words could not have rewritten themselves! Moshe Leib scrutinized it for a moment, then gazed at his wife with concern.

"Why does it have such a bumpy texture?" he asked searchingly. "And do you know how these words became smudged like that?"

He's guessed! Golda Mirel thought in panic. *I must put his mind to rest! What shall I say?*

A sudden idea flew into her mind. She remembered once hearing a *shiur* that explained one reason *Rochel Imeinu* had been glad of Yosef's birth. Now she had a child on whom she could blame any breakages that occurred! The memory gave her inspiration.

"Oh," she said mendaciously, "Yankele spilled his drink all over it! I hope you can still manage to read it."

The relief on his face told her that the lie was justified. But, still, it was a lie.

At that moment she realized she had better stop feeling sorry for herself and make up her mind to settle. She was here to stay and nothing would change that. She might just as well make the best of it!

Chapter 13

*H*aving made a decision, Golda Mirel was not one to fall back on it, and while still missing her family she began to adjust. What she lacked mostly was the *chassidishe* environment of the *shtetl* in Galicia where she had been raised, but as Moshe Leib adhered to the way of life they had chosen, she gradually stopped feeling like a fish out of water. He davened in one of the *chassidishe shteiblech*, instead of the Shiff shul his family attended, and he promised Golda Mirel that Yankele would attend a *chassidishe cheder* when he was ready.

Golda Mirel's relationship with Moshe Leib's family was also improving. Frau Steiner's attitude toward her daughter-in-law grew more relaxed. She seemed fond of her little grandson, and though she rarely kissed or cuddled him, she gave him treats from the kitchen and sometimes bought him little presents.

Strangely enough, little Yankele struck a bond with his Zeide, Herr Steiner. Not having known him before his stroke, he accepted his grandfather's strange appearance and would sit beside him for hours, stroking his hand and talking incessantly in his own brand of baby language. The old man obviously derived great pleasure from the child and gave him a crooked smile whenever he came in. For that alone, Golda Mirel told herself, it was probably a good thing they had come!

Moshe Leib's sister, Ilse, became friendlier, too. The two sisters-in-law actually got on quite well, despite the patronizing way Ilse hovered over Golda Mirel to prevent Golda Mirel from making a *faux pas* and earn her mother-in-law's disapproval.

Although she did not know it, there was still one hurdle ahead for Golda Mirel. She had not yet met Tante Fanny!

She had not previously even *heard* of Tante Fanny. No one had bothered to mention her and the first Golda Mirel knew of her existence was on a visit to her in-laws. She was sitting with Yankele and her father-in-law one afternoon when they were suddenly startled by a loud, impatient rapping at the front door.

Ilse came flying down the hallway to the door, calling in to them as she passed, "That can only be Tante Fanny!"

"Who is Tante Fanny?" Golda Mirel asked as Frau Steiner entered the sitting room.

"She's my husband's older sister," Frau Steiner said primly. "She has been away. She goes to the Tyrol every year for her summer holidays."

"With her whole family?" Golda Mirel asked.

"She hasn't any family," her mother-in-law informed her. "She's been a widow for ten years and never had children." She lowered her voice. "Before she comes in, I'd better warn you. She's rather ..."

Whatever the warning was about remained unsaid as the subject of their conversation came marching into the room, Ilse following sedately behind.

She strode purposefully up to her brother in his wheelchair, a tall, angular person in a suit of gray tweed, with a black and purple turban wound imperiously around her head. A large, black leather bag hung from her shoulder.

"Heinrich, how are you?" she asked in her strident voice, shaking a black-gloved finger at him. "You don't look well. Does he get enough fresh air, Martha?" she glared at her sister-in-law.

"Of course!" Frau Steiner protested defensively. "Fritz takes him out every day!"

"Oh, that *goy*!" Tante Fanny's tone was scornful. "I don't know what you pay him for! He probably takes him to the nearest beer-hall and leaves him sitting while he has a drink." She peered at her brother solicitously. "He looks pale. Someone from the family must take him out every day!"

Frau Steiner timidly opened her mouth to speak, but the forceful old lady didn't give her a chance. "Well, *I'm* back now, so I shall do it!" she announced decisively.

"Tante Fanny, you know you can't!" Ilse protested. "That wheelchair is much too heavy for you!"

"Perhaps," Tante Fanny conceded, "but someone has to. And have you taken my advice and changed the physiotherapist? That Herr Grimler doesn't seem to be doing him much good! I can't see—"

She was interrupted by Herr Steiner, who mumbled something incoherently, his manner agitated.

"What's that?" Tante Fanny asked in bewilderment.

Frau Steiner bent close to her husband.

"He says he doesn't *want* another physiotherapist. He prefers Herr Grimler!" Frau Steiner explained, a note of triumph in her voice. "He gets on very well with him."

Aware that she had lost that argument, Tante Fanny shrugged and abruptly turned her attention to Golda Mirel and Yankele, who was clinging to his mother, having scrambled onto her lap as soon as the strange woman came marching in.

"And this, I presume, is Leo's wife!" Tante Fanny declared.

"Why, yes, Fanny," Frau Steiner said, hurrying to make the introductions. "This is Golda and her son Yakob …."

"Pleased to meet you," Tante Fanny said, grasping Golda Mirel's hand firmly and patting the frightened Yankele on the head. Then, without warning, she fixed her eye on Golda Mirel's bad leg. "I hear you have a limp," she said in her forthright way. Golda Mirel felt her cheeks grow warm as Martha and Ilse both stiffened in embarrassment.

"What is the trouble? From the shoe you are wearing, I'll guess you have one leg shorter than the other. Am I right?"

A long forgotten memory suddenly sprang up in Golda Mirel's mind, and before she could stop herself she repeated her parting words to Pana Slawoska years ago.

"Not really," she said mischievously, ignoring the horrified faces of her mother- and sister-in-law. "I've actually got one leg *longer* than the other!"

There was a loaded silence in the room for a minute, then Tante Fanny flung back her head and roared with laughter.

"Very good!" she said between chuckles. "Yes, very good! But tell me," she said, suddenly serious, "how long have you worn one of those shoes?"

"Ever since I started walking," Golda Mirel told her simply. "As my foot grew longer, the same cobbler would refit me. Luckily, the gap didn't widen, so for many years he has used the same mold."

"Well, how do you know you'll find a shoemaker here in Vienna?" frowned the scandalized woman. "I don't know what your parents were thinking of! You should have had an operation while you were young! Now it will be much more complicated!"

"Exactly," Golda Mirel agreed. "That's why I'm not having one."

"Nonsense! It's not too late! *I'll* see you find a good specialist …."

"No thank you!" Golda Mirel said firmly. "I don't need an operation! I'm quite happy as I am!"

"Rubbish!" Tante Fanny snapped. She was not used to anyone contradicting her. "Surely you would prefer to walk normally and look like everybody else!"

"Not particularly," Golda Mirel told her. "I've been like this all my life, so I'm used to it. And anyway, as people say in Poland, *ess wert nisht shatten zum shidduch*. It didn't stop Moshe Leib from marrying me, did it?"

"Moshe Leib? Oh, you mean Leo! Do you always call him by his Jewish name? How nice! I think I'll call him that, too!"

Golda Mirel found herself warming to this old lady! She certainly had character ... and quite a sense of humor, too—unlike some other members of the family, she reflected glumly.

Tante Fanny did not stay very long. She made no more reference to Golda Mirel's leg, but regaled them all with a detailed account of her holiday in the Austrian Tyrol.

Then, brusquely, she stood up, pulling on her gloves and sliding her purse up her arm.

"I'd better go," she announced. "I haven't finished unpacking yet. Goodbye, Heinrich. I'll come again tomorrow. I hope you look better by then!"

Herr Steiner nodded and gave his crooked smile.

"Well, goodbye, Golda. It's been nice meeting you and little ... er ... what's his name again?"

"Yankele," Golda Mirel said hastily, before Frau Steiner could reply.

"It's been nice meeting you, too, Tante Fanny." She stood up and walked Moshe Leib's aunt to the door, expecting another comment about her limp. Tante Fanny, however, did not mention it.

"You must come for a meal sometime," Golda Mirel said.

"I will, if you invite me!" Tante Fanny replied. "Give yourself time to settle first, and when you're ready send Leo ... I mean Moshe

Leib ... around with an invitation. He knows where I live. No. 29 Neubaugasse."

With another wave of her black-gloved hand, she was gone.

Golda Mirel went back into the room, bracing herself for some criticism from her in-laws. But her mother-in-law just nodded at her dazedly.

Ilse, however, jumped up and took both her hands, squeezing them between her own. "My goodness, Golda!" she exclaimed admiringly. "You actually answered her back! None of us ever dare do that!"

"Why not?" Golda Mirel laughed. "She doesn't bite! She's a bit domineering, perhaps, and meddlesome, but I rather like her!"

Neither Frau Steiner nor her daughter contradicted her, but while they were more than a little impressed, they secretly decided they would never get used to Leo's wife and her different ways!

Golda Mirel's life developed into a daily routine. She busied herself about the house, keeping things running smoothly so Moshe Leib could spend his free time learning undisturbed. She visited her parents-in-law every day, knowing that Yankele's presence gave his grandfather pleasure. She sometimes sat down with her father-in-law, holding a somewhat one-sided conversation with him. Once she offered to take him out, but the suggestion was icily refused by Frau Steiner, insinuating that it would hardly be appropriate for someone with a limp to push a wheelchair in the street.

At times Golda Mirel was bored, and those were the times when homesickness for Poland overcame her. She tried to combat this by making friends with people in her neighborhood, but since she and her husband were *chassidim*, it set them apart, even though Moshe

Leib never wore his *shtreimel* in the street. Occasionally she sought company in the *chassidishe* areas, where she was made very welcome, but there were very few young women amongst them with whom she could socialize.

During her first Viennese winter, Golda Mirel had already lit the oil lamp as she busily prepared the evening meal. It was growing dark earlier every day, and there were just a few weeks to *Chanukah*. Suddenly, there was a frantic knocking at her door. *Who could be coming at this hour?* she thought as she hurried to open it. There stood a young woman, whom she recognized as the neighbor from the flat across the corridor. She had seen her a few times, and though they always smiled a cordial "good morning" or "good Shabbos" to each other, they had not become friendly.

The woman, in a pale brown *sheitel* above a slightly freckled face, looked at Golda Mirel with pleading blue eyes. She had always seemed very calm and collected with her children, but she looked positively distraught.

"Oh, good afternoon!" she said breathlessly. "I'm so sorry to trouble you! I feel so bad to come for a favor when I've never been in to welcome you ... my name is Tirtza Gradman, by the way."

"And I am Golda Mirel Steiner ...." She gave an inquiring smile.

"Pleased to meet you," Frau Gradman said distractedly. "The truth is, I wasn't sure you spoke German ... I believe you're from Poland ... but I can see you do ...."

"Well, a little ...," Golda Mirel said, modestly. "But what is the favor you need? I can see something is the matter."

"My daughter, Naomi, slipped on the ice coming home from school and I think she's broken her arm!"

"Oh dear! Poor thing!" Golda Mirel exclaimed. "How old is she?"

"She's eight. She is in a lot of pain and I have to take her to the hospital. My husband is not yet home from work, and I don't know what to do with my two little ones ...."

"Bring them in here," Golda Mirel said spontaneously. "I'll look after them."

"Oh, how kind of you!" Frau Gradman cried, relaxing a little. "I'll bring them right in."

She hurried across to her flat and emerged a few moments later with a little boy of about two and a curly-haired baby tucked under her arm. Following behind was a white-faced little girl who clutched her left arm in obvious pain.

"Here we are!" Frau Gradman said, trying to sound cheerful. "This is Danny ...," she pushed the little boy forward a little, "and this ...," she placed the baby into Golda Mirel's outstretched arms, "is Esty. She's six months old. I hope they'll be good ... I don't want you to have any trouble."

"Oh, don't worry!" Golda Mirel was reassuring. "I'm used to babies. I'm the oldest child in my family!"

Frau Gradman looked relieved. "I'll bring a bottle over for Esty, in case she cries," she said, pulling little Danny into the flat. "My husband should be home in about an hour and a half. I'll leave him a note explaining what's happened and telling him to fetch them from you."

She thanked Golda Mirel profusely and hurried out, her arm protectively around her injured daughter's shoulders.

Golda Mirel had no idea what a hectic hour she had let herself in for! Little Danny, realizing he had been "abandoned" by his mother, began to wail loudly and refused to move away from the door. After quite a long while, when Golda Mirel managed to entice him away by offering him one of Yankele's toys, a fight ensued between the two boys. The baby added to the chaos by joining in the chorus, rejecting her bottle. Eventually, she succeeded in quieting everyone down, about ten minutes before Herr Gradman came to collect his children.

"Yes, they've been very good," she answered to his question, allowing herself the white lie.

As soon as they were gone, she flopped onto a chair, utterly exhausted. Nevertheless, she was glad she had been able to help her neighbor. *At least we're not strangers any more,* she thought. She liked the look of the woman and hoped they would become friends.

Indeed, only a few hours later, Tirtza Gradman knocked on her door again, looking drained.

"I just wanted to let you know that we're back home ... *at last!*" she added with feeling. "I was right. It *was* broken and they've set it in plaster-of-Paris. Whew! It took ages! Poor Naomi! She was so brave!"

"Yes, poor dear," Golda Mirel agreed. "I wish her a *refuah sheleimah!* I hope it heals quickly."

"Thank you," Tirtza said, "and thanks again for looking after the children. Were they *really* good?" There was incredulity in her voice.

"Well, they both cried a bit, but they soon settled down," Golda Mirel admitted, laughing. "But *you* look worn out!" she continued sympathetically. "Why don't you come in for a cup of coffee and relax a bit?"

Tirtza's face broke into a sudden smile. "I really shouldn't—I've got loads to do, but it sounds too tempting! David's put the children to bed, so I may as well."

They spent a pleasant half-hour exchanging information about each other, and by the time Tirtza got up to go a bond had formed between them. It was the beginning of a lasting friendship!

Life was really improving for Golda Mirel. Besides making a friend, she had quite a relationship with Tante Fanny, who often came for the Shabbos meal or just dropped in to visit. Golda Mirel enjoyed her company. She was interesting and had a delightful sense of humor. Golda Mirel soon found Tante Fanny wasn't nearly as intimidating as she seemed. Although she still tried to force her opinions on her nephew's wife, Golda Mirel would tactfully put her in her place, and the old lady respected her for it.

Gradually, Golda Mirel began to enjoy the letters she received from Poland without pangs of homesickness– until the letter telling her that Leibel had become engaged!

The best part of it is that it's a girl from Lipsk! her mother had written. *You remember the Felbers, who live a few doors away from Babbe Wasserbrun? Well, their sweet little daughter Rifkele has grown up into a lovely girl! We're delighted with the shidduch! I wish you could be here to join in the simcha! ...*

Well, I wish I could, too! Golda Mirel thought, hardly able to read the rest of the letter as tears blinded her vision.

When Moshe Leib came home that night, she handed him the letter, and forgetting her intention to avoid upsetting him, she blurted out in obvious despair, "I can't believe I won't be at my baby brother's *chassunah*!"

"Who says you won't be there?" Moshe Leib asked, looking up from reading the letter. "I don't see any reason why you shouldn't go!"

Golda Mirel stared. "What? You mean go all the way to Poland?"

"Why not? It's not all that far. And it's quite a while since your parents have seen you and Yankele. I wish I could come, too, but I can't get away ...."

Golda Mirel was still gaping in disbelief. "B-but it's so expensive," she stammered, feeling a little guilty, "and you told me the other day that the business isn't going so well."

"Well, it isn't, but it's not so bad that we can't afford a train ticket once in a while. And especially for a *simcha*!" He smiled warmly at her. "As soon as we know the date of the *chassunah*, I'll book your ticket!"

The *chassunah* and *sheva brochos* were over. Leibel and Rifkele, the happy young couple, were settled in their little home near the yeshiva, as Reb Yoine Felber, Rifkele's father, had promised to support them for a few years. The Wasserbrun family were settling back to normal life again. Golda Mirel packed her things in preparation for her return home the next day, feeling a little sad, although she would be glad to see Moshe Leib again.

She had had a marvelous time. The family had made a great fuss of her and Yankele, maybe even more than they'd made of the *chosson* and *kallah*! It had been wonderful to see all her siblings, complete with their offspring—especially Ettel and her little Goldie, who bore an amazing resemblance to Golda Mirel herself! Seeing her parents "*shepping nachas*" gave her great pleasure, too. She had taken Yankele to visit Babbe Wasserbrun, who was delighted to see her little great-grandson again.

Her mother came into the room while she was packing, looking mournful.

"I'm going to miss you both like mad!" she said, sighing.

"Mamme, I'll miss you, too!" There was a sob in Golda Mirel's voice. "In some ways I wish I hadn't come. It's made me all unsettled!"

"I know how you feel. It's the same for me, in a way. But I'm sure you'll settle down again. You *are* happy, aren't you?" Her mother regarded her solemnly.

"Yes, of course! I can't wait to see Moshe Leib. I've missed him.

But life in Vienna is so different …." She paused for a moment, then burst out impulsively, "Mamme, why don't you come and visit me there?"

"Golda Mirel!" her mother cried. "I can't see myself traveling all that way! I've never been further away than Krakow!"

"It's not such a long journey," Golda Mirel persisted. "I wish …" She stopped abruptly as an idea occurred to her. "If there was a special reason, would you come?"

"What kind of special reason?" Pessel asked, suddenly understanding and eyeing her daughter searchingly.

Golda Mirel smiled inwardly and made a decision. It was early days yet, but she would let her mother in on her secret. That would give her time to get used to the idea of traveling to Vienna!

Chapter 14

Golda Mirel's daughter was born in February 1934, three weeks before Purim. Though not the easiest time of year for Pessel to leave home, she kept her promise and came to care for her daughter.

Relaxing under her mother's loving care, Golda Mirel was glad she had not agreed to her mother-in-law's advice that she should book in at the local hospital for the birth. Frau Steiner had been appalled when her daughter-in-law announced she would have her child at home, using the services of the local midwife, Frau Speigel.

"Nobody does that nowadays!" she had sniffed. That primitive method, she felt, was more for the poorer people who could not afford the hospital fees. She did not actually say so in so many words, but Golda Mirel knew she was thinking, "*What will everybody say?*"

However, Golda Mirel had stuck to her guns and now, as Frau Steiner saw how warm and cozy her *mechuteniste* had made the flat, serving the new mother nourishing, delicious meals, she admitted it had not been such a bad idea after all!

The baby was adorable, resting snugly in her mother's arms. Golda Mirel held her out to her mother-in-law.

"Here," she said, "would you like to hold her?"

Frau Steiner took the child and looked down at her tenderly.

"She's beautiful!" she whispered, stroking the soft cheeks with the tip of a finger. Looking at the old-fashioned way the midwife had swaddled her in her blanket, she was gripped by a sudden feeling of alarm. "Why is she wrapped up like that?" she demanded.

Golda Mirel realized what her mother-in-law was worried about. It occurred to her that it was probably why she had wanted the child to be born in the hospital. Should the baby have inherited her mother's problem, *chas v'sholom*, the doctors there would surely have done something about it.

"Oh, that's just how they do it at home!" Golda Mirel responded airily. "Frau Speigel follows the old custom, too. But I'm going to take off the blanket soon and make her more comfortable. And then you'll see she's *baruch Hashem* quite perfect!"

Frau Steiner's color rose, and Golda Mirel guiltily changed the subject. Taking the baby back, she smiled, "*Mazel tov*, Shwieger-Mama! Have a lot of *nachas*!"

"And you, too, Golda!" Frau Steiner said, surprising herself, as well as Golda Mirel, by leaning forward and kissing her daughter-in-law.

Golda Mirel rested well those first few days as a mother of two, since Yankele was across the hall at the Gradmans. Frau Speigel came every day to check the baby and bathe her, and Pessel pampered her daughter with the best of her dishes.

On the third day, Tante Fanny came to visit with Frau Steiner and Ilse.

"And what are you going to call the baby?" Tante Fanny called out suddenly in her resonant voice.

There was a sudden hush in the room as everyone looked at Golda Mirel expectantly. Golda Mirel suppressed her annoyance.

She wanted to discuss it privately with her husband.

"We haven't decided yet," she replied reservedly, "and even if we had, we mustn't tell anyone until Moshe Leib gives the name on Shabbos in shul."

"Well, with Heinrich being so ill, it would only be right to name her after his mother—our mother," Tante Fanny asserted, defying anyone to disagree.

To her surprise, no one protested.

"That's a nice idea!" Pessel said, addressing Golda Mirel. "Yankele's name is from our side of the family, so now it's Moshe Leib's family's turn."

"Yes," Golda Mirel agreed. "What was her name, Tante Fanny?"

"Gertrude," Frau Steiner cut in quickly before Tante Fanny could reply.

"Gertrude!" Tante Fanny snorted derisively. "Martha, you know very well Golda Mirel wants to know her Jewish name!" She turned to Golda Mirel. "It was Gittel!"

"That's right!" Ilse added. "My Gita is called after her."

"Oh, dear, then it's out of the question!" Pessel objected. "Gittel is my mother's name."

"Oh," Tante Fanny said flatly. There was no argument against *that*! "So, what about your mother, Martha?"

"Oh ... er ... I don't know ...," Frau Steiner murmured reluctantly.

"What do you mean, you don't know?" Tante Fanny took charge again. "Whoever heard of not wanting to give a grandchild your mother's name? What was it?"

"Er ... it was Helena," Frau Steiner stammered, looking embarrassed. "Everyone called her Leni."

"But her Jewish name!" Tante Fanny persisted. "What was her Jewish name?"

"I can't say," Frau Steiner's color deepened. "She didn't like the name and didn't want anyone to know it. She wouldn't tell us, and only after she died Papa told us what it was."

"Well, tell us then!" Tante Fanny commanded, unperturbed by her sister-in-law's discomfort.

"I'd rather not! Mama would have hated it," Frau Steiner protested.

Just then, Moshe Leib walked into the room. Nobody had heard him come in, Tante Fanny's loud voice drowning the sound of the key turning in the lock.

"Ah, Moshe Leib!" Tante Fanny said immediately. "Do you know your maternal grandmother's Jewish name?"

"Yes, I do. It was Elke," Moshe Leib replied.

"H-how do you know?" his mother exclaimed, gaping. "I never told you!"

"I know you didn't. But years ago, when you were in the hospital, Papa told me to say some *Tehillim* for you … Mattel *bas* Elke …"

Everyone broke into exclamations at this, till Golda Mirel called out authoritatively, "I think we should stop discussing this now! Moshe Leib and I will decide on the baby's name, and you'll all hear about it on Shabbos!"

Life became busy for Golda Mirel and she was glad. There was certainly no time to be bored, with her days occupied with feeding and changing little Elkie, as well as coping with Yankele's occasional bouts of jealousy in which he found all sorts of ways to gain her attention.

Her mother left after two weeks, and life became even busier for Golda Mirel with preparations for Purim and Pesach. Their parting had been tearful, but Golda Mirel had very little time to brood once her mother had gone home.

Purim came and went without too much fuss. Last year, she had been so homesick, having barely settled in, that Purim in Vienna had been extremely disappointing compared to the lively festivities she was used to in the *shtetl*.

This year, knowing what to expect, she had adapted to her surroundings. She dressed Yankele as a clown, in a costume she had made before Elkie's birth, and sent *mishloach manos* to the Gradmans, her parents-in-law, Tante Fanny and Kurt and Ilse. She went to the *chassidishe* area for a bit, where the activities felt more like home, but the Purim *seudah* at her in-laws was more sedate. The only difference from the previous year was the addition of one little person, whom Frau Steiner insisted on calling "Leni."

Golda Mirel would have liked to make Pesach at home this year, but Moshe Leib was needed at her in-laws to conduct the *Seder*—Herr Steiner being unable to do it.

As it turned out, she was glad they had that last week in her father-in-law's company.

Shortly after Pesach, Herr Steiner suffered another stroke. Once again he was rushed to hospital, where he lay unconscious.

The distraught family took turns at his bedside, except a frustrated Golda Mirel who could not leave such a young baby to support her mother-in-law.

"What you *can* do," Moshe Leib told her when he came home briefly, "is say *Tehillim*. Say as much as you can, in particular *kuf yud tess* ... his name is Elchonon *ben* Gittel."

Glad she could do *something*, Golda Mirel left the dishes in the sink, settled Yankele down with some toys and, rocking Elkie in her pram, sat and prayed with a full heart that Elchonon *ben* Gittel should wake from his coma as he had done before. But three days later, his *neshomoh* quietly departed from the world.

The week that followed was painful for everyone. Incredibly

saddened herself, Golda Mirel found it hard to watch the grief of the Steiner family. Moshe Leib seemed a different person, bowed under the weight of his anguish and guilt. When he returned home at night, he poured his tortured thoughts out to his wife. Perhaps he hadn't done enough for his father … perhaps he hadn't concealed his desire to return to his beloved yeshiva, learning his precious Torah, or perhaps his father guessed he felt closer to his Rebbe. His father must have realized all this and had a lot of *agmas nefesh* because of it … and so on. Golda Mirel tried to reassure him, but her words had very little effect.

Never one to show her feelings, Frau Steiner did not weep visibly but seemed to have withdrawn behind a shell, sitting the entire day in frozen silence.

Ilse, on the other hand, cried often and unrestrainedly, greeting all who came to be *menachem oveil* with red-rimmed eyes. Tante Fanny coped with her feelings by reminiscing about her dear brother in her resonant voice.

Since Golda Mirel was the only female member of the family not sitting *shiva*, it was her responsibility to bring ready-cooked meals to the house every day. This was an exhausting task. If not for her good friend Tirtza Gradman, who rallied around to help, she wondered if she would have survived it. Her friendship with Tirtza was the one bright spot in an otherwise sad and depressing time!

As the Steiner family adjusted to their situation, Frau Steiner, who had insisted on remaining in her large house, seemed, somehow, more attached to Golda Mirel and the children, visiting them quite often and begging Golda Mirel to bring them to see her. Golda Mirel went as often as she could, pleased to find the withdrawn woman warming to her *einiklach*.

Gradually, they all became accustomed to the new rhythm of their life. Moshe Leib threw himself into his work, but also made more time to learn. Mrs. Steiner actually joined her son's family for occasional Shabbos meals, which often included Tante Fanny, and even Ilse's family grew closer to them.

Spring turned to summer, and before they knew it the *Yomim Noraim* were almost upon them. Golda Mirel realized Yankele's third birthday was coming up right after that, on *Rosh Chodesh Cheshvan*.

She began to plan. She knew she could not make a grand affair, with Moshe Leib still in the year of *aveilus*, but she would bake a honey cake and decorate it with all the letters of the *aleph-beis* to send when Moshe Leib would carry his son wrapped in a *tallis* to *cheder* for the first time. She would also prepare a tray of fancy cakes and invite the family over to drink "*lechayim.*"

The only person she told of her plans was her friend Tirtza, who gave her a recipe for honey cake and offered to help with the baking.

Then, the day after *Simchas Torah*, Moshe Leib dropped his bombshell. He planned to take Yankele to the Rebbe for his *upsheren*.

"What? To Poland?" Golda Mirel stared at her husband, dumbfounded.

"Yes. I was thinking of leaving early tomorrow morning so that we arrive in time to see the Rebbe on Friday for the *upsheren*. Then we'll come home after Shabbos and be back in time for his birthday, which is on Wednesday."

"Moshe Leib! How can we do that?" Golda Mirel gasped. "Elkie's only eight months old! I'm not taking a baby of under one year on a draughty, smoky train for hours and hours! It's dangerous! The Silbersteins down the road took their baby on a train some time ago and the smoke got into his chest. He was terribly ill after that!"

Moshe Leib was astonished at his wife's outburst. "I-I didn't mean … I wasn't thinking …," he stammered. "You're quiet right, of course … it wouldn't be good for Elkie …"

"Well, what did you have in mind?" Golda Mirel demanded.

Moshe Leib looked down in embarrassment and replied in a barely audible voice, "I thought … perhaps … I should take Yankele by myself …"

"I won't be there for my son's *upsheren*?" Golda Mirel stared, incredulous.

"You're right. I can't do that to you!" Moshe Leib said, immediately contrite. "Forget I ever suggested it!"

He turned and went into the sitting room, a strange expression on his face, and bent over his gemara again.

Somewhat shaken but relieved, Golda Mirel turned to her baking, albeit with a little less enthusiasm. She dropped an egg absently into the bowl, mulling over the incident. Suddenly, it occurred to her that her husband's odd expression had indicated disappointment!

Now it was her turn to feel contrite. Yet, she felt she was in the right. He couldn't expect her to miss such an important occasion! But, then again, it meant so much to him. How could she deprive him of it … especially now, when he was still in mourning?

At once, she knew what she must do! Wiping her hands clean, she marched straight into the room, waiting patiently for her husband to look up.

"Moshe Leib," she said softly, when at last he turned his eyes on her. "It's I who am wrong. Of course Yankele should have the Rebbe preside over his *upsheren*. I'll be glad to stay at home with Elkie and prepare his birthday celebration."

The gratitude in her husband's eyes was worth the sacrifice, she thought, as he thanked her joyously.

"Just make sure the Rebbe gives you a *brochoh* for all of us!" she said, and went off to pack for their journey.

Golda Mirel felt a little lonely after her husband and son had left, but pushing the feeling away, she began to prepare for her visitors. Besides the Steiner relatives, she had invited the Gradmans.

Tante Fanny arrived early as usual, and was there when young Naomi Gradman entered with a tray of attractive fancy cakes. "Mama sent this for you," Naomi said, "and said to tell you that she and Papa will be over soon."

"Oh, how kind of her!" Golda Mirel exclaimed. "Would you mind putting them on the table for me? I've just picked up Elkie."

Naomi walked carefully to the table and gently set down the tray.

"Tante Fanny, this is Naomi Gradman ... my good friend Tirtza's daughter. Look at the gorgeous cakes Tirtza has baked!"

"Mm! They're beautiful!" Tante Fanny said, smiling at Naomi. But, as the girl walked out, Golda Mirel noticed her aunt's narrowed eyes following her. No sooner was Naomi out of the flat when Tante Fanny asked, "What's wrong with her arm?"

"Her arm?" Golda Mirel looked puzzled. Then her face cleared. "Oh, yes! She broke it some time ago. But it's almost two years ago. It was set in plaster for six weeks and they told Tirtza it had healed well."

"Well, it hasn't!" Tante Fanny declared firmly. "You mark my words! There is something wrong with that arm. It doesn't look straight to me!"

Her pronouncement filled Golda Mirel with alarm. Tante Fanny was usually right when she was that emphatic. Making a mental note to observe Naomi closely next time she saw her, Golda Mirel prayed that this time Tante Fanny had made a mistake!

Chapter 15

With so much happening over the next few days, Golda Mirel forgot about Naomi's arm—and since she did not see the girl very often, she did not remember it for quite a long time afterwards.

Moshe Leib and Yankele had returned home on Monday, exhausted but definitely exhilarated!

Seeing her little son for the first time after his haircut, Golda Mirel regarded him with mixed feelings. His two little curly *peyos* hadn't yet grown long enough to hang down. A round little yarmulke perched on his closely cropped head, and as Golda Mirel grew accustomed to him, she found he looked quite adorable. From a lovable toddler he was transformed into a sweet miniature person!

Winter set in, and the days grew short and dark again. People didn't get out as much, and it was Chanukah before Golda Mirel had occasion to think about her friend Tirtza's daughter. She had fried a large batch of doughnuts and brought some over to the Gradmans. While Yankele and Elkie played with Danny and Esty, she chatted with Tirtza. She was idly watching Naomi play *dreidel* with her two brothers when suddenly Tante Fanny's words came back to her. She observed the girl carefully and realized that there was, indeed, something odd about her left arm.

She said nothing to Tirtza then, because she didn't want the children to overhear, and because she was of two minds whether to mention it at all. She was not sure how her friend would take it.

She decided she would discuss it with Moshe Leib.

That evening, after dinner, she brought up the issue. "I see your dilemma," her husband agreed, "but I think you have to tell her. She wouldn't thank you if she found out later that you hadn't said anything when she still could have done something about it."

Golda Mirel assented, and eagerly sought an opportunity to broach the subject.

To her dismay, Tirtza disagreed with her. "That's ridiculous! She's perfectly all right now!" she insisted. "They checked her at the hospital and told us everything was fine."

The hurt in her friend's eyes touched Golda Mirel to the quick, and she wished she could take back her words. Yet, at least she had a clear conscience and would not have to say anything about it again.

Several months later, Golda Mirel was returning home from a shopping trip when she met Tirtza in the corridor, just coming out of her own flat.

"Oh, Golda Mirel!" she cried. "I was just coming in to you! Have you got a moment, please?"

"Of course, come in! What's the matter? You look really worried." Golda Mirel unlocked her door, pushed her laden pushchair into the flat and beckoned Tirtza to follow.

As soon as she was inside, Tirtza blurted out, "Golda Mirel, I should have listened to you! You were right about Naomi!"

"Why? What's happened?" Golda Mirel asked, completely taken by surprise. She lifted Elkie out of the pushchair and set her down on the floor. Then she pulled a chair out for Tirtza to sit down on.

"Oh, I can't stay long," Tirtza said nervously. "I have to give the children supper. I'll just tell you quickly. Yesterday, I got a note from Naomi's teacher, asking me to come and see her. I was really worried, hoping my daughter wasn't in trouble at school. Well, she asked me about Naomi's broken arm! She told me she had noticed that Naomi had trouble catching a ball in her left hand but was fine with her right, and it was not because of the ordinary right/left hand strengths. She felt there was an odd clumsiness and advised me to see my doctor about it. I told her the doctor at the hospital had said it was fine! But, since you, too, had mentioned it, I'm really worried! I'm going to take her to Doctor Fisher as soon as David comes home! Hopefully, he'll check it out properly and find the problem."

"Oh, Tirtza, I hope it's nothing serious!" Golda Mirel cried sympathetically. "Let me know what the doctor says."

When Tirtza knocked on her door later that evening, Golda Mirel noticed that she seemed less tense, although she still had lines of worry on her face.

"Doctor Fisher gave Naomi's arm a thorough check," Tirtza told her, "and he came to the conclusion that it hadn't been set right. He's really angry with the hospital and he's going to write them a letter of complaint! All the same, he advised me not to go back there. He thinks I should see a specialist ...."

"Quite right!" Golda Mirel agreed. "You can't take risks ..."

"Yes, but the only ortho—whatever it is ... I can't get the name right .... Well, anyway, the only specialist for that here in Vienna works in the same hospital. So he recommended another very good one, but he's in Germany ...."

"So?" Golda Mirel pushed. "Germany is not so inaccessible! Whereabouts is it?"

"In Munich," Tirtza told her. "How can I go off and leave the children like that?"

"Why, you can leave them with me!" Golda Mirel volunteered eagerly. "The little ones will be excellent company for my two."

The appointment was made, and several weeks later Tirtza took Naomi to Munich. On their return, she naturally came to discuss the results with Golda Mirel.

Apparently, the specialist had agreed that the bone had been improperly set and advised surgery.

"He says they have to break the bone and reset it," explained Tirtza.

"Ugh!" Golda Mirel shuddered. "Poor thing! It sounds frightening!"

"Yes, that was my reaction, too," Tirtza agreed. "But the doctor said it's not as bad as it sounds. Anyway, he has a long waiting list, so we have plenty of time. He seems to be a very good doctor and he was very nice." She scrutinized Golda Mirel for a moment. "You know, it was funny," she said, "but the way he talked reminded me of you!"

"Well, thank you very much!" Golda Mirel exclaimed in mock indignation. "I can't say I enjoy being compared to a male *goyishe* doctor!"

"Oh, I meant nothing—I mean, only his accent, maybe!" Tirtza protested. "His German was similar to yours. Besides, who says he's a *goy*?"

"You think he could be a *Yid*?" Golda Mirel asked curiously.

"I don't know. He might be, though he doesn't seem *frum*." Tirtza screwed up her eyes for a moment, trying to visualize the doctor's face. "Then, there were his eyes … ," she mused. "He took his glasses off for a moment and his eyes reminded me of your eyes …."

"Oh, yes? Perhaps he's a long lost relative or something!" she joked sarcastically. "What's his name, anyway?"

"Dr. Wasser."

"Well, he may be half a relative!" Golda Mirel quipped, still mocking. "My maiden name was Wasser*brun*."

A sudden suspicion crossed her mind and her face turned still and solemn.

"W-what is his first name?" she asked, a tremor in her voice.

"I've got his card here somewhere." Tirtza pushed her hand into her pocket and felt around. "Here it is. Dr. Berthold Wasser," she read.

Berthold! It had to be! Berthold Wasser … Berel Wasserbrun! It was too much of a coincidence to be anything else!

Hardly able to contain her excitement, she said, "Tirtza, tell me … was there anything else interesting about his face?"

Tirtza stared at her friend. What was the big deal?

"Oh, forget it!" she said dismissively. "I'm not even sure what I noticed. Don't let it worry you!"

But Golda Mirel would not be put off. "Did you notice his teeth?" she persisted. "Was there anything unusual about them?"

"Golda Mirel, I'm not a dentist! I don't go round looking at people's teeth! Why are you so interested? Do you think it's someone you know?"

"I don't know," Golda Mirel replied evasively.

She decided to drop the subject, but when she met Naomi in the corridor that afternoon she couldn't resist putting the question to the girl.

"Dr. Wasser *does* have funny front teeth," giggled Naomi. "They sort of cross each other."

"I knew it!" Golda Mirel cried, excitement getting the better of her.

That evening Tirtza knocked at her door, asking as soon as Golda Mirel opened it, "Golda Mirel, who is this person? You obviously know him! Maybe you can get him to put Naomi at the top of his waiting list."

Golda Mirel would have preferred not to divulge the relationship, of which she was hardly proud, but at her friend's plea she felt she had to try to help. "He's my uncle," she said quietly.

Tirtza stared, open-mouthed. "How?" she asked.

Golda Mirel told her Berel's history. "He finally went away," she said, "and we haven't seen him for years. We didn't even know where he was."

"Then I doubt you can be of any help," sighed Tirtza. "What a pity."

Golda Mirel agreed regretfully.

For a few days Golda Mirel brooded, wondering whether to write home and let the family know. At last she concluded that she had no right to withhold such important information from them, and she sent a detailed letter home.

Certain her amazing discovery would elicit a quick response, she was surprised to have to wait three weeks before hearing anything. When at last her mother's letter came, she understood the reason for the delay. The letter filled her with sadness. Her beloved grandmother, Babbe Wasserbrun, had passed away.

> ... *We never told her your news about Berel, as we didn't want to risk upsetting her. All the same it was good you let us know. Once we knew his name and where he was living, Uncle Yidel made some enquiries and found out his address. We sent him a telegram straight after the petirah so he could come to the levayah or, perhaps, sit shiva with the family, though we weren't surprised that he didn't come ...*

Golda Mirel read the letter, her vision blurred with tears. For a long time she sat, letting her memories of her grandmother pass through her mind.

She remembered her special smile with little Yankele; her

bouncing him on her lap when he was a baby and when they had gone back to Lipsk and visited; her happiness when she saw him.

Other memories came flooding back, especially how happy she had been when Uncle Berel became engaged to Sonja, and her bitterness when it broke.

Golda Mirel felt a sudden pang of guilt. Babbe Wasserbrun had been so angry at the person who had caused it. And it had been *she*—Golda Mirel!

She never ever found out it was me, Golda Mirel thought, *so I couldn't even ask her* mechilah. *And now it's too late!*

"Oh, Babbe!" she whispered, her heart heavy. "If you can hear me up there in *shomayim*, please forgive me for the *agmas nefesh* I caused you."

Chapter 16

The look of strain on Moshe Leib's face was a constant source of worry for Golda Mirel. He obviously wasn't happy with his lifestyle. His mornings began happily enough, learning with his *chavrusa* before davening with the early *minyan*. But she couldn't bear watching him leave for work after breakfast, his shoulders drooping as he left the house. *Why doesn't he give up the business?* she wondered. *He says it's not doing so well, anyway. What's the use of keeping it going if all it gives him is stress, and it's stopping him from doing what he really wants to do?*

Until now, she had kept her opinions to herself, not wanting to be a nagging wife. But since the arrival of little Elchonon, the air of being weighed down by a burden had grown so strong in her husband that she felt she must say something.

An opportunity to broach the subject arose one night when Golda Mirel took a cup of hot cocoa in to her husband, who was learning in the living room. He sat in his usual position at the table, but the gemara lay closed at his side as he bent over a ledger, frowning in concentration and making scribbles in it with a pencil.

"What's the matter?" Golda Mirel asked, her voice full of

concern. "What is that you are studying?" She put the cup down next to him and squinted at the pages full of figures.

"Oh, it's just the business accounts," he said. "I shouldn't be doing this now but something is puzzling me, so I decided to glance through them … and believe me, I wish I hadn't!"

"Why, what's the problem?"

"They're not very good … and that's why I'm puzzled." He went on to explain. "Someone made me an offer for the business … quite a good offer … which he hasn't withdrawn, even after seeing these figures …."

"You mean you're going to sell the business?" Golda Mirel exclaimed with unmistakable eagerness.

"No, of course not!" Moshe Leib replied emphatically. "How can I do that? It's just surprising that anyone wants it. It's not the same as it used to be. In Papa's day, he was the leading leather merchant in this part of Austria, but now, although leather is still in demand, some new kind of man-made imitation has come on the market. This man who made the offer is one of our competitors and I think he wants to deal in this new material, too. It must be worth it for him to pay us a substantial sum so that we, his rival firm, are not standing in his way."

"Well, I think you should accept!" Golda Mirel declared positively. "You may never get such an offer again! And you're always complaining how the business doesn't allow you time to learn!"

"I wish it was that simple!" Moshe Leib's tone was rueful. "For one thing, the business doesn't belong only to me. My mother has a share in it, as well as Kurt and Ilse. They all have to agree. Secondly—what are we going to live on? We've got three children now, *k'ein eiyin hora*, who need to be fed and clothed. And we had just decided to look for a larger flat, and that means higher rent …."

"But those things are not important!" Golda Mirel cried. "Surely, you feel that way, too?"

"Of course *I* do," Moshe Leib reassured her, "but I don't want to inflict hardships on *you*."

"I wouldn't care!" Golda Mirel protested vehemently. "We can manage in this flat much longer, and I could find some way to earn some money at home ... maybe do sewing ... or something ... just as long as you could do what you really want!"

"Thank you," Moshe Leib said sincerely, his eyes lighting up in admiration. "But the main reason I can't sell the business is that Papa would never have allowed it! He started it when he was young and built it up with toil and trouble. He always said he wanted it to stay in the family. How can I do this to his memory? It would have broken his heart!"

Golda Mirel sat down purposefully across the table and regarded her husband intently.

"Moshe Leib, listen to me!" she said earnestly. "I understood why you had to come and take over when your father was taken ill. But now he has gone to a better place ... a place where material things are not important. Don't you think his *neshomoh* will rejoice much more if you devote as much time as you can to learning Torah?"

For the first time that evening, Moshe Leib smiled ... a real smile that lit up his entire face.

"Bless you, Golda Mirel!" he exclaimed. "You've certainly got a knack of putting things into perspective!" He closed the ledger and reached for his gemara. "I'll think about what you said ... and talk it over with the others. Whatever I decide, let's hope it's the right decision!"

There were different reactions from the family when Moshe Leib discussed the matter with them. Ilse dissolved into a flood of tears and accused her brother of betraying their father's memory to even think of doing such a thing! Kurt, however, declared that Moshe Leib would be mad not to accept such an offer, and he managed to persuade his wife to change her tune.

Frau Steiner, who had always secretly resented her husband's preoccupation with the business, shrugged indifferently and commented that she hoped her son was aware that he had a family to support and had considered an alternative way of earning a living.

Once the wheels were set in motion, it did not take long for the business to change hands. There were palpable signs of relief in Moshe Leib, and Golda Mirel was glad she had persuaded him to take this step.

Their share of the proceeds from the sale was placed in the bank—apart from a small amount they used to purchase Golda Mirel a sewing machine so that she could embark on her career as a dressmaker.

She did not meet with much success, however. Whereas in Poland in the early part of the century, women rarely bought ready-made gowns, Vienna had many exclusive dress-shops. There were already two Jewish dressmakers in the neighborhood to serve those who did want to have something made.

So, despite Golda Mirel's determination to make do on a meager income, she soon found it very difficult to manage.

Realizing they could not go on like that, Moshe Leib decided to find work, even if it was only for a few hours a day. It was not long before a chance presented itself. With no Jewish school for boys in Vienna and secular education compulsory, the Jewish boys attended a *cheder* after school hours. It was here that a vacancy for a teacher was advertised, and Moshe Leib applied. To both his and Golda Mirel's delight, he was readily accepted.

"At least I can learn all morning," he said happily, "and I will be teaching Torah, which has a lot of *tachlis*."

Golda Mirel agreed, adding, "I wish *I* could find something *tachlisdik* to do as well!"

"You run the house and look after the children," her husband declared. "If that isn't *tachlisdik*, I don't know what is!"

But, while Moshe Leib enjoyed the job, it did not pay very well, and only just helped them keep their heads above water.

"Where are all the teaspoons?" Golda Mirel demanded one morning, irritated, as she searched in the cutlery drawer for one to feed Chuni (as she and her husband had taken to calling little Elchonon) his cereal. It was strange how teaspoons always seemed to disappear in their household, she reflected. Yankele and Elkie both looked innocent, although Golda Mirel suspected they had most likely carted them off to the garden or thrown them accidentally into the dustbin,

"I'll have to buy some new ones," she said with a sigh.

Breakfast over, she dressed the children and set out for Yankele's *cheder* and Elkie's kindergarten. Then she wheeled the baby in the direction of the shops.

The bell on the door of Herr Spangler's Household Store gave a friendly chime as she pushed it open. Golda Mirel loved this shop. It was full of attractive crockery and shiny saucepans and, though she could ill afford most of them, she enjoyed looking at them and was glad of any excuse to go inside.

"Good morning, Frau Steiner!" Herr Spangler said, cheerfully smiling. An over-sized black yarmulke covered most of his balding head, and though his attire was neat and clean, Golda Mirel noticed that once again, a button was missing on his waistcoat. The man lived all alone, she knew, his wife having passed away some years ago.

He brought out a variety of spoons for Golda Mirel to choose from, and when she made her selection, he asked, "Would you like me to *toivel* them for you?"

"Oh, yes, please!" Golda Mirel said gratefully. The small *keilim mikveh* Herr Spangler had installed some time ago at the back of his shop had been a novel idea, and had been the talk of the town for a while.

"It's such a boon to be able to come home and use things straight away," Golda Mirel commented now.

To her surprise, Herr Spangler gave a small sigh. "I don't know what will happen if a *goy* buys my shop," he said sadly.

"What!" Golda Mirel cried in disbelief. "You're selling the shop? But why?"

"I've decided to move away ...."

"Oh, don't say that!" Golda Mirel protested spontaneously. "Where to?"

"To Eretz Yisroel," Herr Spangler said simply.

Golda Mirel stared at him. She could not imagine just picking up and moving to Eretz Yisroel.

"Why would you want to go there?" she asked. "It's governed by the British and it's full of Arabs who make the lives of the *Yidden* a misery! You have a good life here. Why move away?"

"The *kedusha* is there and not here," Herr Spangler said. "And besides, there is plenty of *rishus* here and it could even get worse ..."

"Why do you say that?" Golda Mirel could not help but feel a sense of alarm at his words. "People seem quite pleasant here."

Herr Spangler sighed again. "Maybe I'm just pessimistic," he said, "but I know that *Yidden* in Germany are beginning to feel nervous. The new Fuehrer there is known to be an anti-Semite. Who knows what effect it could have on the people ... and whether it could rub off onto the Austrian people, too!"

"Well, let's hope it doesn't!" Golda Mirel exclaimed. "And let's hope you will be happy in Eretz Yisroel! Have you any relatives there?"

"Yes, I have a cousin who promised to help me settle down. My daughter wants me to join her in America, but I don't think the life there is for me!"

He went to the back to *toivel* the spoons. Golda Mirel heard him say the *brochoh* and she called out *"Amein."* When Herr Spangler returned, he was his usual cheerful self again.

Paying for the spoons, Golda Mirel left the shop in a thoughtful mood. She pondered fleetingly over Herr Spangler's gloomy predictions, then dismissed them from her mind. *What's the use in worrying about something that might never happen,* she thought. But the possible closure of the shop—that was something to be upset about! She could not imagine the neighborhood without Spangler's Household Store!

That night, at dinner, she told her husband about it. She brought two bowls of soup to the table and, putting them down, sat down across from him. "Herr Spangler told me today that he's selling his shop and moving to Eretz Yisroel! I wonder who will buy it. I hope it's a ..." She stopped in mid-sentence and sat down abruptly, a dazed look on her face.

"What's the matter?" Moshe Leib asked, alarmed.

"Why don't we buy it?" Golda Mirel cried excitedly. "It's the ideal solution!"

Moshe Leib stared at her for a moment and then burst out laughing. "Oh, really?" he said teasingly. "Do you see me as another Herr Spangler—serving a lot of dithering ladies with a cheerful smile on my face? I might just as well have kept Papa's business ...."

"No, not you," Golda Mirel interrupted earnestly, without a trace of a smile on her face. "My idea is to serve in the shop myself!"

"You're serious!" Moshe Leib declared incredulously. "And what are we going to buy it with? A week's pay from my *cheder* wages?"

"No, of course not. I thought we could use the money from the sale of the business …."

"Absolutely not!" Moshe Leib was emphatic. "That money is for the future, when it comes to marrying off the children and so on …"

"But what about the present?" Golda Mirel persisted, almost in tears. "It's a good investment," she pressed on, "and I don't mind working hard if it helps our *parnossoh.*"

She was so earnest and sincere that Moshe Leib softened. "I appreciate it," he said, "but how can you go out every day to a shop? You can't leave the children alone at home."

"But that's just it!" Golda Mirel cried brightening. "They *would* be with me, because we'd be living in the shop! There's plenty of room for living, there—much more than we have here! We'd be solving two problems in one!"

Somehow, her eagerness and her practical arguments convinced Moshe Leib, and he agreed to go with her to discuss the matter with Herr Spangler.

Within months, the shop was theirs! Herr Spangler had been so delighted that it would remain in *Yidden*'s hands that he quoted a price far below his original sum, and threw in the stock for next to nothing.

"I can't take a lot of money with me," he said, "but I *can* take the *mitzvah* of helping a *Ben Torah* with *parnossoh*!"

Kurt acted as their solicitor in the transaction and was professionally obliged to keep it a secret, but as soon as it was final, they made haste to tell the rest of the family before it was common knowledge among the whole *kehillah.*

Frau Steiner was appalled! "You can't do this!" she cried. "I won't allow it!"

"It's too late to change our minds now, Mama," Moshe Leib smiled, trying to keep her calm. "It's all signed and settled."

"Well, resell it to someone else!" his mother demanded. "I shall die of shame when the news gets out! I'm surprised at you, Leo, allowing your wife to be a shop-owner! Women don't do that sort of thing around here!"

"I'm sorry, Mama," Moshe Leib said, wishing he could soften the blow, "but it's done now. I wish you could accept it."

"Never!" Frau Steiner declared. "Don't imagine that I'll ever come in to buy something there! And I hope you won't either, Ilse!" she said to her daughter.

Ilse was not sure how she felt about the whole affair, but knew she had to support her mother, and so she declared that she, too, would never frequent the shop. Tante Fanny, however, was delighted and offered to come in and help Golda Mirel serve in the shop.

"But I can't afford to pay you!" Golda Mirel said.

"Oh, I don't want payment! I'll just enjoy seeing what people are buying," Tante Fanny said. "You know what I'm like!"

Yes, I do! Golda Mirel thought affectionately. *You're an incorrigible nosey parker and busybody!* "I'll let you help me," she said with a twinkle in her eye, "if you promise you won't put my customers off by telling them what to buy!"

The one person who greeted Golda Mirel's news with mixed feelings was Tirtza. While she was pleased for her friend, she was sad to be losing a neighbor.

"But I'm not far away," Golda Mirel assured her. "I hope we'll see each other a lot, all the same!"

The shop gave Golda Mirel a new lease on life. The flat above it was quite spacious, and besides the stock-room, there was another room downstairs that they used as a sort of living-room, where the children could play and Golda Mirel could keep an eye on them, even while she was busy with customers.

At long last she really began to feel part of the community. The women who came in often stayed for a little chat, and she soon got to know people who, till now, had just been nodding acquaintances. Occasionally her customers were complete strangers, usually from a different district or town, adding a bit of variety to Golda Mirel's everyday life. One morning a woman from England came in to buy a gift. She spoke a perfect German and explained to Golda Mirel that she had been born in Vienna, but had lived in London since her marriage several years ago. She came from time to time to visit the cemetery, where both her parents were buried. They chatted for a while, and Golda Mirel was fascinated by the woman's description of life in Stamford Hill, so different from Vienna. Before she left, the woman took a notepad out of her handbag and wrote down her name and address, tearing it out and handing it to Golda Mirel.

"If you ever come to London," she said, "pay me a call and I'll take you around a bit."

After she left, Golda Mirel pushed the note to the back of a drawer beneath the counter, thinking wryly, *England is a place I'm hardly likely ever to go and visit!*

Although the shop was doing well and Golda Mirel was happy, the one fly in the ointment was her mother-in-law. They had been getting on so much better lately, but a distinct coldness had crept back into their relationship after they had purchased the shop.

Frau Steiner hardly spoke to her daughter-in-law, and refused to visit their new home. Finally, Golda Mirel decided to take the bull by the horns. She made up her mind to visit and confront her mother-in-law outright. When Moshe-Leib came home, after the shop was closed for the day, she slipped down to Frau Steiner's.

"Shwieger-Mama," she said, "what have I done to upset you?"

"You know very well what you've done!" Frau Steiner said

sharply, and turned her back on her. A moment later, she swung around again and regarded Golda Mirel with angry eyes. "How could you do it?" she cried. "You don't care how much embarrassment you caused me! I've never felt so ashamed in my life!"

Golda Mirel opened her mouth to explain that she did it for her husband's sake, so he could sit and learn without worries, but Frau Steiner had turned away again, and the unyielding set of her shoulders bespoke a terrible implacability.

Golda Mirel sighed, and quietly left the room.

I've tried, she told herself as she trudged home, *and if she refuses to understand, it's just too bad! As long as Moshe Leib is behind me, I'm going to live my life the way I want to live it!*

*L*eaving Tante Fanny to mind the shop—and little Chuni—Golda Mirel dashed out to post the "get-well" card Yankele and Elkie had made for Naomi Gradman. At last she had been summoned back to Munich for the operation. Golda Mirel had offered, again, to take the children, but Tirtza had refused since now Golda Mirel had a shop to run, and they would be away for two weeks. Tirtza had sent the younger children to her sister in Switzerland and the two older boys had gone to friends.

As soon as a telegram with the words "OPERATION SUCCESSFUL. NAOMI DOING WELL." had arrived, she had sat her two older children down to make the card.

So it was a quite a shock when, just a couple of days later, Tirtza appeared at the shop.

"Tirtza!" she cried. "You're back already! Naomi, too? I thought she had to stay in the hospital for two weeks!"

"No, she's home, too," Tirtza said, sounding mournful.

"Why? Is something wrong? You look rather upset," Golda Mirel asked, looking worried. "Didn't my uncle do a good job, after all?"

"No!" Tirtza replied. "I mean … he didn't do any job at all! He wasn't there! Another doctor did the operation."

"What? You waited a whole year and then he went off on holiday just when it was your turn?" There was incredulity in Golda Mirel's tone.

"No, it wasn't his fault. I'm quire sure he *wanted* to do the operation. The hospital sacked him a few months ago .…."

"*Sacked him!!*" Golda Mirel almost shrieked in her surprise. "I thought he was so good!"

"Oh, he was!" Tirtza assured her. "It had nothing to do with that. He was sacked because they found out he was Jewish. Golda Mirel, you have no idea what's going on in Germany! It's terrible!"

"What do you mean?" Golda Mirel paled. Suddenly, Herr Spangler's ugly talk about Germany leaped into her mind. "Tirtza," she said with foreboding, "tell me what happened."

"Well, I didn't even know that Dr. Wasser … your uncle … hadn't done the operation till yesterday morning," her friend said. "The nurse came in to tell us that the specialist was on his way to examine his patient, and a different doctor showed up! He totally ignored us … just checked Naomi's arm, mumbled something to the nurse and marched out! When he'd gone, I asked the nurse why the doctor who performed the operation hadn't come, and she said, 'He *is* the doctor!' 'But where's Dr. Wasser?' I asked. And she said in this starchy voice, 'Dr. Wasser is no longer with us. The hospital has dispensed with his services.'

"I was flabbergasted. I said I thought he had a top reputation. And, Golda Mirel, she gave me *such* a look—I get shivers down my spine even now! Full of hate! And then she said, '*Weil er ist eine Jude!*'"

Golda Mirel stared, aghast.

"I was so shocked, I couldn't utter a word! But I knew I was getting my daughter out of that hospital—at once! As soon as she left the ward, David and I gathered her things together and slipped her out through a door that led to a small balcony with a fire escape. We made it down the steps, which wasn't easy for Naomi with her arm in a sling. We hailed a taxi, and just stopping to fetch our things from the guest-house where we were staying, we made straight for the station."

"What an ordeal! How is Naomi feeling after all this?" Golda Mirel asked.

Tirtza sighed. "She is in quite a lot of pain. But what could we do?" She threw up her hands. "Dr. Fisher has just been to see her. He assures me that it hasn't done her much harm, really. He says we can look after her just as well at home and he'll go on treating her himself."

"Oh, *baruch Hashem*," Golda Mirel said. "But does he know what treatment she needs?"

"Well, he *is* a doctor, so he knows what she ought to have. But in any case, *I* solved that problem for him!" There was a wicked gleam in Tirtza's eye.

"Why? What did you do?"

"As we left, I grabbed Naomi's notes off the clipboard at the end of her bed!" Tirtza said triumphantly.

"Whew! That was risky!" Golda Mirel looked at her friend with admiration.

"I know," Tirtza shrugged. "Dr. Fisher said I could be prosecuted if they chased it up. But he was pleased. He wrote everything down and told me to destroy the original paper. No one will ever be able to prove I'd had it!"

"Brilliant!" Golda Mirel chuckled. "Now, how about a cup of coffee?"

"No, I can't leave Naomi alone for too long," Tirtza said, making for the door. "By the way, she loved the card! Elkie's drawing of Naomi half hanging out of the hospital bed really made us laugh!"

After Tirtza had gone, Golda Mirel sat, lost in thought. *So there was something in Herr Spangler's pessimistic predictions after all*, she reflected gloomily. How dreadful if, *chas v'sholom*, the anti-Semitism raging in Germany were to spill over into Austria! How would they take it? *Oh, nonsense*, she reassured herself. Germany and Austria were two separate countries. Why should one country be affected by the doctrines of another? Feeling more positive, she pushed her fears out of her mind.

Yet, as the months went by, Golda Mirel found it difficult to ignore the disquieting thoughts gnawing at her. Stories were filtering across the border of the fiery, hate-filled speeches of the German leader, Adolf Hitler. There were reports of Jews in important positions losing their jobs, and of people packing up and leaving the country because of ugly anti-Semitic incidents.

The hearts of the Austrian *Yidden* bled for their neighboring brethren, wishing they could help ease their plight, but there was little they could do. In Vienna, the atmosphere was calm, although many people found themselves looking warily over their shoulders for any signs of anti-Semitism amongst their own countrymen. There were rumors that Hitler was planning to annex Austria with Germany, but most people were confident the Austrian Chancellor would resist.

Golda Mirel could not shake off her apprehension. For months she suppressed her anxiety, but finally, one day, she blurted it all out to Moshe Leib, begging him to consider leaving Austria.

"It is not that I lack *bitochon!*" she explained hastily, before he could lecture her. "I know everything is *bashert* and I *daven* to the *Eibershter* to protect us, but I think we *are* obliged to do whatever we can, aren't we?"

To her relieved surprise, Moshe Leib raised no argument, simply saying, "Yes, you are right. I have been secretly keeping my feelings about this from you. But where can we go?"

"I don't know," Golda Mirel said. "We really don't know where it's safe. But I think it makes sense to return to Poland. After all, we originally intended to live there."

Moshe Leib considered this for a few moments, nodding thoughtfully. "I think I should write to the Rebbe first."

Golda Mirel was relieved. At last, things were beginning to move! *B'ezras Hashem, we'll soon be away from danger,* she told herself. And, what was more, she would be reunited with her family again! The thought filled her with pleasure and excitement.

But the Rebbe's reply sent her daydreams crashing to the ground!

She had watched eagerly as Moshe Leib scanned the answer to their request, but as he read, and reread, she grew anxious.

"W-what does it say?"

He looked up from the letter with a dazed expression.

"The Rebbe says if we feel we are in danger and must get away, Poland is not the right place. We must go farther away."

"Farther away?" Golda Mirel cried, tears of disappointment in her eyes. "But where?"

"I wish I knew!" Moshe Leib looked frustrated. "I hear the Kalmans are planning to go to America. Maybe we should go there, too."

"America!" Golda Mirel exclaimed. "As far as that! It'll be like going to another world!" The thought of being such a great distance from her family was too much to bear. There must be somewhere closer. But where?

Golda Mirel sat looking out the train window, her mind still in turmoil. The last few weeks had been such a whirlwind, she hadn't really had time to think. Now, on her way to Paris from where she would travel to Calais to catch a ship to England, she reviewed the events that had put her into these odd circumstances.

She had been rummaging in a drawer for a particular invoice when she came across a note that mystified her. Printed across the top was the name ROSA MITTELSTEIN, with a London address scribbled below.

"Where did this come from?" she wondered, quite sure she had never seen it before. Then, suddenly, she remembered her interesting customer that first year in the shop—the woman from London. About to crumple up the paper, she paused in sudden excitement.

The very thing! England! That wasn't too far away, but it was separated from the rest of Europe by a stretch of water! Surely, that was protection from Hitler and his despicable Nazi Party!

Moshe Leib listened in agreement to her proposal, but was doubtful they could manage it.

"We can't pick ourselves up and walk into England, just like that, you know" he said. "We need visas to gain entry." He paced thoughtfully. "I'd ask Kurt, but I think it's better if the family knows nothing of our plans just yet. Let me speak to Reb Shimon Silber. He has helped some people."

Herr Silber had, indeed, organized visas for some people who had some relative in England to vouch for them. The Steiners were at a loss. Golda Mirel didn't even *know* this Frau Mittelstein .... However, she would not be put off. She decided the only solution was to visit Frau Mittelstein in London and ask her for help.

Golda Mirel had sent an express letter saying she would be in London on such and such a date, asking to stay with her for a week. Preferring to be cautious, she didn't explain the situation clearly.

A telegram had arrived in response from Rosa Mittelstein: DELIGHTED. MEET YOU AT LONDON STATION. Golda

Mirel, though extremely grateful for the kind offer, couldn't help wish that someone would meet her at Dover and help her get to London. Of course, that was too much to ask! Yet, unable to speak a word of English, she had no idea how she was going to do it. Even getting to Calais from Paris to catch the boat was a problem, since she didn't speak French either!

What am I doing? she found herself thinking. *I must be crazy!*

It had been decided that Golda Mirel must be the one to go, though racing around with her weak leg would be exhausting. However, Mrs. Mittelstein did not know her husband, and the situation was awkward enough! She had had no time to worry about how she would manage, and had simply purchased German/French and German/English dictionaries. She had been so busy seeing to her passport, purchasing tickets for boats and trains and making arrangements for the shop that she had laughed away Moshe Leib's worries about her going alone. She was more concerned with leaving Moshe Leib and the children, with only Tante Fanny to help.

Now, as the train pulled into Paris, Golda Mirel did not feel sure of herself at all. She got out and stood on the platform, looking around uncertainly. She hesitantly approached a guard, hoping he understood German. She asked him where to catch the train to Calais. He stared at her and then, recognizing the word "Calais," smiled and nodded, pointing and gesticulating in what seemed like several directions to Golda Mirel, who grew more bewildered as she tried to catch his garbled instructions in French. She thanked him and trudged down the platform, wondering what she was going to do.

"*Entshuldigt*," a voice behind her said, and she felt a light tap on her shoulder. Turning, she came face to face with a pleasant-looking woman of about thirty, in a brown fur-trimmed coat with a small fur hat perched on her blonde *sheitel*. She pulled a trolley laden with suitcases behind her, and was accompanied by two little girls of about eight and ten.

"Do you need help?" the woman asked in Yiddish. "I see you don't speak French, and you look as if you don't know where to go."

"Oh, thank you so much!" Golda Mirel cried profoundly relieved. "I need the train to Calais, where I'm catching a boat to England."

"We're going to England, too!" the woman exclaimed enthusiastically. "Put your suitcase on the trolley and come with us. I'm Shulamis Levy from Manchester."

Offering a silent prayer of thanks to Hashem, Golda Mirel joined the Levys on the Calais-bound train, relieved that her journey would now be smooth sailing.

As they disembarked at the English port of Dover, Golda Mirel looked around the busy port, thankful again that she was not alone. Mrs. Levy had promised to put her on the London train before continuing on to Manchester. She could never have coped alone, she admitted ruefully to herself.

As she boarded the last train of her journey, she relaxed, secure in the knowledge that someone from the Mittelstein family was meeting her at her last stop!

However, when she stepped off the train in London, she saw no one who looked Jewish, and panicked for a moment. What would she do if no one came? It was already dark outside, making this unfamiliar world seem quite daunting. All at once, a man with an uncovered head walked toward her saying, "Mrs. Steiner?"

"Y-yes?" Golda Mirel said, staring at him apprehensively. He lifted her suitcase and mumbled something she did not understand. But hearing the name "Mrs. Mittelstein," she felt reassured enough to allow him to take her case. She followed him along the platform, soon catching sight of Rosa Mittelstein among a crowd of people, waving and smiling. Golda Mirel went toward her, her hand outstretched.

"Mrs. Steiner! *Sholom Aleichem!*" Mrs. Mittelstein cried, embracing her warmly.

As they went to the car, Mrs. Mittelstein explained that the man was her husband's driver. "I suppose his Cockney accent was a bit hard for you to understand," she said, laughingly.

"I don't understand English at all!" Golda Mirel declared.

"Well, don't worry. I'll help you."

As they rode along, her hostess told her a little about their area.

"The *kehillah* in Stamford Hill is still fairly small," she said, "but it's growing all the time. We moved here from Liverpool ten years ago because my husband felt there was more opportunity for his business in London. At that time most *Yidden* lived in the East End, but they have gradually been moving up our way. Also, there has been quite an influx of people from Germany lately. The stories they tell are quite horrifying! Is it like that in Vienna, too?"

"Not yet, *baruch Hashem*," Golda Mirel replied, "but we can't help being afraid ...."

"I see ...," Mrs. Mittelstein said, beginning to understand, but she refrained from questioning her visitor. No doubt she would tell her in her own time.

The car turned from a busy main road into a residential street.

"Here we are," Mrs. Mittelstein said. "Lordship Park."

They stopped before a double-fronted house, and Mrs. Mittelstein opened the car door and got out. "Welcome to our home!" she said with a flourish.

The rest of the evening was rather hazy in Golda Mirel's mind. Mr. Mittelstein came out of the dining room to wish her "*Sholom Aleichem.*" After that, she was taken up to her bedroom where, as soon as her head touched the pillow, she sank into oblivion and slept soundly through the night.

In the morning, she woke refreshed and got up quickly, dressed and *davened*, then went downstairs in search of her hostess. Mrs. Mittelstein was in the morning-room, collecting a pile of used breakfast dishes.

"Good morning, Mrs. Steiner," she said. "Did you sleep well?"

"Yes, thank you. Very well, indeed! But please call me Golda Mirel."

"Of course. And you must call me Rosa. Now, come and have some breakfast. Everyone else has left already, so you've just got me for company!"

She brought some fresh toast to the table and filled two bowls with porridge. There was a companionable atmosphere as they ate breakfast together. After they had bentched, Mrs. Mittelstein took the plates into the kitchen. "I'll wash these later," she said. "Let's sit down in the dining room and chat a bit."

"Yes, I've got something important to discuss with you," Golda Mirel said.

"I thought so," Rosa Mittelstein nodded. "Do you need to speak with Reuven, too? He should be home any minute."

As if on cue, a key was heard turning in the front door, and a moment later Mr. Mittelstein strode in.

They sat down together at the table, and Golda Mirel told them her story.

"… so I was wondering if you could put me in touch with the right people, who can help me to get visas for my family," she finished.

"Most certainly!" Mr. Mittelstein declared. "I have quite a lot to do with them. You need someone to vouch for you, and I will be happy to do that for you. In fact, if your husband agrees, I can offer him a genuine job!"

Golda Mirel's heart sank. How could she decline his offer without sounding ungrateful? "I'm afraid Moshe Leib would want to …"

"Wait, wait …," Mr. Mittelstein interrupted hastily. "I didn't mean a job in my business. You say he is a *melamed?* I happen to be looking for someone to give the twins some extra tuition. They're bright, but they don't learn enough *limudei kodesh* for my liking. I would pay a regular wage, and I would also like to help with the rent for a flat."

"But why would you do all this for us?" Golda Mirel cried, stunned at his generosity.

"*Baruch Hashem*, my business is doing well," her host explained. "Who knows, perhaps the *Ribono Shel Olam* has sent me *hatzlochoh* so that I can help my fellow *Yidden* in trouble. When my wife returned from Vienna a few years ago, she told me about you. She was full of admiration for the enterprising way you took over a shop, in spite of people's obvious disapproval. That is the kind of person I am glad to help. Now, let us take care of the important business first. Give me the names of all your family members and their dates of birth, and I hope to have the visas ready for you within a few days."

Reuven Mittelstein arranged everything and obtained the visas for her with ease. There had been a slight wait when she couldn't supply the dates of birth of her mother-in-law and Tante Fanny, but a few telegrams soon sorted that out.

Golda Mirel was immensely grateful to the Mittelsteins, thanking them profusely over and over as they settled her down in the train to Dover.

Leaning back in her seat, she hugged her shoulder-bag tightly, knowing it contained the precious papers that ensured her family's entry into England and escape, with Hashem's help, from the threat of a Nazi invasion into Austria!

Chapter 18

"No! Most definitely not!" Frau Steiner, who rarely raised her voice, was almost shouting in her vehemence. "I absolutely *refuse* to uproot myself, at my age, from the place where I have lived all my life!"

She glared in revulsion at the sheet of paper Golda Mirel held out to her. Why was Leo's wife always doing this to her? Since their disagreement over the shop, they had hardly spoken, their relationship practically bordering on animosity. And now, just when she was trying to be friendlier, her unpredictable daughter-in-law came up with another absurd idea, no doubt bent on upsetting her!

To be fair, she admitted, that wasn't really Golda's way. She wasn't a spiteful person. But why did she have to be so unconventional and so ... different? Once again, Martha Steiner found herself indulging in one of her occasional bouts of regret. Why couldn't her son have married a regular, nice Austrian!

"Please, Shwieger-Mama," Golda Mirel coaxed, "don't reject the idea outright! It's not safe to stay here! Can't you see that?"

Frau Steiner sighed and shook her head. She wasn't interested in discussing the dangers. To her, there was more to fear in a foreign country she knew nothing about! How could anyone expect her to go and live in a place where she couldn't speak the language and didn't know a soul? The notion was ridiculous!

"I think you are over-exaggerating the situation, Golda," she said. "Who says the Nazis *will* come here? And even if, G-d forbid, they do—they wouldn't bother to harm an old woman like me!"

Golda Mirel, seeing she was getting nowhere, eventually gave up trying to persuade her mother-in-law. Someone would have to talk her around, though. They couldn't just move and leave her to fend for herself. Perhaps Moshe Leib would have more success.

She replaced the form, unsigned, in her bag and left. Her next stop was Tante Fanny, and she braced herself for a similar reaction from that old lady, too.

Tante Fanny, however, reacted with delight!

"Golda Mirel! You are brilliant!" she exclaimed, her face wreathed in smiles.

"How did you manage to arrange all this? When do we go?"

"Not so fast!" Golda Mirel said, laughingly. "There's a lot to be arranged. For one thing I have to sell the shop …."

"Oh, of course … the shop …," a sad look crossed Tante Fanny's face. "What a shame. But which *Yid* would buy it now?"

"I know," Golda Mirel agreed. "I think I will have to sell it to a *goy*. Pity about the *keilim mikveh*, though. I wonder what will happen to it." Changing the subject, she hugged her aunt, exclaiming warmly, "Tante Fanny, I'm so glad *you're* willing to come with us!"

"Aha!" Tante Fanny said astutely. "Don't tell me! Martha's protesting, isn't she?"

"Yes. She can't face the idea of uprooting herself." Golda Mirel sounded exasperated.

"I thought as much! Well, leave it to me. I'll have a word with that sister-in-law of mine! *I'll* make her see sense!"

"Oh, Tante Fanny, don't!" Golda Mirel cried "Moshe Leib will talk to her. I'm sure he'll manage to persuade her." She feared her aunt's domineering way would likely make her mother-in-law dig her heels in even more.

Moshe Leib and Golda Mirel kept their impending departure quiet for the time being, since it would take a month or two before they were ready to go.

Tirtza, of course, was one of the people Golda Mirel confided in. The look of dismay on her friend's face gave Golda Mirel a pang of regret. How would she ever find such a friend in London, she wondered.

"Why don't you come to England, too?" she said impulsively. "I'm sure you would easily get a visa …."

"I'm not so sure," Tirtza said doubtfully. "David is a qualified architect. He's got a good job here. We can't just pick ourselves up and go away, not sure of *parnossoh*!"

"An architect can get a job anywhere," Golda Mirel argued. "And here you are in danger!"

"Who says so? How do we know what's going to happen. It might just calm down …."

"You think I'm over-reacting," Golda Mirel said, her eyes meeting her friend's challengingly.

"No, I don't." Tirtza tried to appease her friend, not wishing to offend. "You might be right …. Who knows? But David isn't ready to move just yet. He'd rather wait."

"But by then it might be too late!"

"Well, we won't wait *that* long!" Tirtza reassured her. "As soon as there is any sign of danger, we'll go straight to Switzerland. Don't forget David has a Swiss passport, so he'll have no trouble bringing his family in."

What she said made sense, and Golda Mirel was relieved to know that they had somewhere to go.

Meanwhile, Moshe Leib kept "storming the ramparts," trying to get his mother to back down, but his pleas fell on deaf ears. He called on her practically every day, begging her for all he was worth. Each time, she repeated *her* argument, until one day, unable to bear it any longer, she burst into tears.

Moshe Leib, near to tears himself, felt terrible, but knew he had to persevere for the sake of her safety.

In the middle of these histrionics Kurt and Ilse walked in, assessing the situation immediately.

"Leo! Give it a rest!" Kurt exclaimed in exasperation. "Can't you see she's had enough? She doesn't want to go ... full stop!"

Moshe Leib's voice shook. "But how can I leave her here—in possible danger?"

Ilse, who had put her arm around her mother trying to comfort her, looked up at Moshe Leib, her eyes flashing. "*Pah!* Danger!" she said scornfully. "It's just typical of Golda to overdramatize things! I don't know why you let her talk you into her mad notions, Leo!"

Moshe Leib was shocked that she would criticize Golda Mirel!

"My wife deserves nothing but applause for the way she has handled everything!" he cried. "Do you think it was easy for her to travel all the way to England on her own? And getting those papers was no small achievement, either! We're lucky to have them! And now Mama wants to throw away a golden opportunity! If you know what's good for her, Ilse, *you* will try to persuade her. I can't understand why you and Kurt don't make the effort to secure papers for your family, too ...."

"*We* have every confidence that things will soon quiet down," Kurt replied patronizingly. "Only nervous, high-strung people think of running away."

Recognizing that he was facing a brick wall, Moshe Leib felt defeated, and desired only to get home. Muttering a few soothing words to his mother, he bade them "good night" and left.

Of all the arrangements Golda Mirel had to make, one of the hardest was organizing the sale of the shop. She had grown attached to her dear little establishment, and would miss it sorely. Steeling herself for the inevitable, she contacted an agent to find her a buyer, realizing she could not put up a notice or even announce that the shop was for sale. Knowing it would probably be bought by a non-Jew made her feel almost as if she were betraying the members of the community. On the other hand, if a *Yid* were to make an offer, she would feel just as guilty, taking their money when the shop might be taken away from them in the end. She knew such things were already happening in Germany.

The would-be buyers who came to view the shop were few and far between. Then one day a large, pompous man calling himself Konrad Schmidt came along and, after looking around, appeared interested.

"The agent has told me how much you are asking, Frau Steiner …," he said with a sneer.

"Yes," she replied politely, "and that includes the entire stock. It's quite a bargain!"

Herr Schmidt gave a short, mirthless laugh. "A bargain? Well, let *me* make you an offer, Frau Steiner." He named a sum that was about half the asking price.

"What?" Golda Mirel was astounded. "That's ludicrous! My price is already low because I want to sell it quickly."

"Frau Steiner, you're Jewish, aren't you?"

Golda Mirel stared at him, nonplussed. "What has that to do with anything?" she asked.

"Everything!" He pointed a fat finger at her. "You should be glad that I'm paying you *something*! When Hitler and his army take over this country, you Jews will lose your shops. They will just be taken from you!"

"And who says that is going to happen?" Golda Mirel asked, refusing to display fear before this awful person.

He smirked nastily, snorting, "Leave it to Hitler!" He made a peculiar saluting gesture as he said the name.

This man has Nazi sympathies! Golda Mirel hoped he could not see the goosebumps creeping over her.

"Herr Schmidt," she declared heroically, "I would not sell this shop to you if you offered me a *hundred* times the amount I'm asking!"

A scowl crossed Herr Schmidt's face.

"Is that so?" he said angrily. "Well, you'll regret it then! Good day, Frau Steiner!" And he stamped furiously out of the shop.

Shattered by the experience, as soon as she got home she declared to Moshe Leib that she wasn't interested in selling the shop any more.

"I don't care if I leave it *hefker*!" she cried. "I just want to get away from here as soon as possible!"

Moshe Leib knew better than to argue with her, convinced that she would think differently once she was over the shock. Sure enough, when Tante Fanny came in a few days later informing them that she had found some prospective buyers, she found her interest suddenly reviving.

The people concerned were Tante Fanny's neighbors, an elderly gentile couple named Piller. For many years, Herr Piller and his wife had been putting away money for their old age. Now that he had retired, they were looking for something to invest in that would keep them occupied. A household shop would be ideal for that purpose.

Golda Mirel liked the Pillers immediately, and was happy to negotiate with them. Before long, a contract was drawn up and a time set for the elderly pair to take possession. They were willing to allow the Steiners to remain on the premises till they were ready to travel.

At last, they could focus on their journey. Their passage was booked, and packing begun. Since they could only take the barest necessities, many treasured items were either thrown away or given away, and some of the better furniture was put into storage in the slim hope that they would come back and reclaim it someday.

How is Tante Fanny doing this? Golda Mirel wondered. *It's harder for an old woman like her.* But Tante Fanny, it seemed, was more practical and down-to-earth than she was!

"I've gotten rid of everything except a few clothes," she told her niece, "so you won't be stuck with a lot of luggage from *me*!"

There was still the enormous problem of Frau Steiner's dogmatic refusal to accompany them. Golda Mirel felt she must make one last attempt.

"Please, Shwieger-Mama," she begged, "change your mind and come with us! We don't want to leave you here!"

"Then why are you going?" her mother-in-law snapped.

"Because we don't feel it's safe here. And we don't want you to be in danger, either."

"You're not really concerned about me!" Martha Steiner shot at her. "You only want me to come with you to ease your own conscience!"

"You know that's not true," Golda Mirel said quietly, hiding how hurt she was.

"Maybe not," Frau Steiner murmured, relenting a little, "but you should understand how hard it is for me to go away. Of course it's easier for you. Your roots aren't here, like mine are!"

"But I've lived here most of my married life," Golda Mirel objected, surprised at this new argument, "so I do feel this is my home."

Frau Steiner shook her head. "No," she said sadly, "you never really fitted in. You still stick to your strange way of life ... and because of that Leo does, too!"

"That's not fair!" Golda Mirel cried, unable to maintain her calm. "He took it on before I ever met him!"

"But he would have eventually come back," her mother-in-law insisted. "It was you who built up the barrier between us. And now you're taking him away from me!"

Tears sprang to her eyes as she spoke, and all at once Golda Mirel felt her resentment dissipating. The poor woman looked so pathetic and defenseless that she felt only pity for her.

There was no point in persisting, she decided. Placing the entry papers on the table, she said, "Keep these papers in a safe place, and if, *chas v'sholom*, worst comes to worst, hopefully you can still follow us to England."

Frau Steiner took them up impatiently. "What do I need these for?" she said. "I'll never leave, don't you understand? Even life under the Nazis is preferable to that. We're in *golus* in any case, and if these papers are found on me, I might be in worse trouble!"

She turned quickly toward the coal fire and flung the papers under the grate before her daughter-in-law could stop her. Golda Mirel gasped in shock, watching helplessly as the flames began to lick the edges, then flare up into a full blaze, reducing the precious papers to ashes!

Too stunned to speak, she just stared accusingly at her mother-in-law and was amazed at the strange calmness on Martha Steiner's face. Still at a loss for words, Golda Mirel turned and left the house in a daze. What were they going to do now? Reuven Mittelstein could never provide her with another visa! If only she had managed to prevent this from happening!

The day they departed, friends and other well-wishers stood around the van as it was loaded when a car drove up with Kurt in the driver's seat. A moment later, Frau Steiner alighted, Ilse holding her protectively. The older woman's face was an inscrutable mask. She embraced the children, pressing a small package of sweets and biscuits into each one's hand. She turned to Golda Mirel and planted a dutiful kiss on her cheek. On impulse, Golda Mirel gave her a tight squeeze, clinging to her for a few moments. She could feel Frau Steiner quiver a little and then, to her surprise, her mother-in-law returned her hug.

Moshe Leib placed a hand on his mother's arm and wished her well, expressing a fervent hope that they would see each other again very soon.

The moving scene was interrupted by the impatient sound of the driver's horn. They all piled into the van, on their way to a foreign land and an uncertain future.

Chapter 19

*I*t was a weary, somewhat bedraggled Family Steiner who stepped off the Dover-to-London train, completing the last lap of a harrowing journey. The adults looked ready to drop, and the children were whiny and disgruntled.

Crossing the Channel had been rough. Elkie was violently sick, Yankele was unable to settle down and Chuni cried non-stop, refusing all food and drink.

In Dover, they had spent a grueling two hours, waiting in queues and then being interrogated by Immigration officers.

At one point, Golda Mirel was so harried that she forgot to keep the children cluttered around her to distract the officials from noticing her limp. Hobbling toward the door she heard, "One moment, Mrs. Steiner. Come back here, please," and was then subjected to a barrage of questions until they were convinced that the limp did not affect her life at all.

By the time they received official stamps on their visas and were directed toward the station for the London train, only Tante Fanny still had a gleam in her eye, in obvious enjoyment of this unexpected adventure at her time of life!

Mercifully, the children slept through the ride to London. As they debarked and collected their belongings, trying not to wake the children until the last moment, Tante Fanny offered to fetch a taxi. Marching up to a guard on the platform, she posed her question in heavily accented, stiff English.

The guard, realizing she was "one o' them foreign refugees," was eager to help.

"'Course, Luvvy!" he said affably in his strong Cockney dialect. "Gow dahn t'end of the platform, turn roight, gow stright ahead till yer comes ter the undergrahnd station, and yer'll see the taxi rank on the left. Owkay?"

"Y-yeh, senk you," Tante Fanny stammered and turned back to the others, shrugging her shoulders and looking perplexed.

"I couldn't understand a word he said!" she declared in a frustrated tone.

"I thought you learned English at school," Moshe Leib said.

"I did," Tante Fanny insisted, "but that wasn't English!"

"Well, never mind," Golda Mirel said quickly, seeing her aunt was upset, "we'll find it ourselves."

When they did find a taxi, having no idea what arrangements had been made for them, they decided that they would have to give the Mittelsteins' address, where Rosa would, no doubt, direct them further.

But as they reached the barrier and handed in their tickets, Golda Mirel spotted a familiar face. It was Reuven Mittelstein's driver!

Rosa must be waiting in the car, she thought with relief.

However, when the driver coming up to them said something about "Mrs. Mittelstein" and handed her a note, she realized she was wrong. She opened the note and read it.

Dear Golda Mirel,
Sholom Aleichem to you and your family! Baruch Hashem, you made it! I would have come to the station to

meet you, but I would be taking up space in a car that will be hard enough for you all to squeeze into. Pete, our driver, will take you to your house where I will be waiting for you.

Looking forward to seeing you!

Rosa

The livingroom of the rented house in Allerton Road, North London, was beginning to look more like home at last, Golda Mirel's personal belongings in place. The tablecloth her grandmother, Babbe Wasserbrun, had embroidered so lovingly covered the bulky mahogany table, and the tapestry stitched by her other grandmother, Babbe Danziger, hung on the wall. Four colorful cushions, a gift from her mother, were scattered on the shabby black leather sofa, and a variety of photographs and pictures from Vienna were placed strategically on the walls and the sideboard.

Golda Mirel tried to avoid comparing this flat with its ill-matched second-hand furniture to her cozy little flat above the shop in Vienna. It struck her as ironic, remembering how she had missed her humble little flat in Poland when she had first come to Vienna. But this time, *she* had chosen to come here, and she was convinced it had been the right decision. Looking around at her comfortable new home, second-hand and all, she was grateful to Hashem for sending Rosa Mittelstein into her shop all those years ago!

As the months went by, Golda Mirel grew used to her surroundings, but didn't feel she was really settling down. Her whole existence in London seemed unreal. Shut off from everything and everyone she had always known, it was as if she was in some sort of bubble, with no idea of what was going on outside it. When she expressed her feelings to Moshe Leib, he understood exactly what she meant.

He, too, felt like someone who was floating in mid-air, with nothing to hold him down. The *Chassidim* in London were few and far between, and since his Rebbe was not accessible, he feared he was in danger of losing his grip on the *chassidishe* way of life. Afraid to go out with his *shtreimel*, he sometimes forgot to put it on when he came home on Shabbos, which greatly upset Golda Mirel.

Yankele, too, found it hard to adjust. He was sent to a Jewish Primary school in the neighborhood, but it was a far cry from the *cheder* he had been used to. It served pupils from families of various degrees of *Yiddishkeit*, and his long, curly *peyos* set him apart from his classmates, especially since he spoke only Yiddish.

On top of these difficulties, Golda Mirel was worried about her parents and her mother-in-law, whose letters seemed to take a long time getting to her. Not owning a wireless, and unable to read the English papers, she and Moshe Leib remained comparatively ignorant of the goings on in the world. They just went about their everyday duties, struggling to make ends meet and doing their best to keep the children happy.

And then, one day, the bubble suddenly burst! It was the day after *Pesach*, 1938, and as Golda Mirel stood in the queue at the local kosher bakery waiting to buy her first loaves of *chometz*, she overheard a piece of news that shook her to the core!

Two women were discussing how Hitler had marched into Austria a few months earlier.

Golda Mirel began to tremble. The dreaded *"Anschluss"* had already taken place! Hardly able to contain her impatience, she hurried out of the shop as soon as she had made her purchase and rushed home. Fortunately, Moshe Leib was at home when she burst in, and when she blurted out the news he, too, turned pale.

"I can't believe I haven't heard about it!" he exclaimed. "Why did no one tell me?"

"Maybe they didn't want to worry you, knowing that you're from Vienna," Golda Mirel suggested, "or perhaps everyone thought you knew. But, Moshe Leib, we must try to get your mother out!"

"I know," Moshe Leib agreed, his voice shaking, "but how? If only she hadn't destroyed her visa!"

"Wishing won't get her another one!" Golda Mirel commented practically. "I was too ashamed to tell Rosa about it, but now we'd better pocket our pride and ask Mr. Mittelstein for help."

"Yes, you're right," Moshe Leib said, trying to sound hopeful. "I'm on my way there now, to learn with his boys. As soon as Reuven comes home, I'll speak to him."

As Reuven Mittelstein listened to Moshe Leib, a dubious expression crossed his face. "I'm not sure if anything can still be done," he said with concern, "but I'll try my best. There might possibly be a copy of your mother's papers in the Agudah office, in which case we could print out another one with the original date …. I'll go there first thing tomorrow morning and see."

In spite of his reservations, Reuven met Moshe Leib the next afternoon with a smile, and handed him a document.

"Here you are!" he said triumphantly. "It worked! Send this off as soon as you can! We must have hope, but we can't be too optimistic. Who knows whether those fiends in charge now will pass it?"

"We can only try," Moshe Leib remarked philosophically. Thanking Reuven profusely, he took the document and hurried home.

For the next few weeks, they pounced eagerly on the post as soon as it arrived, praying for the letter that would tell them Frau Steiner was on her way. Golda Mirel made promises to herself to forge a new relationship with her mother-in-law. Tante Fanny decided to give up her little room on the half-landing, and move. At Golda Mirel's protests, she made the excuse—in which there was a certain amount of truth—that she wanted her independence. She found a tiny, two-roomed flat nearby and took on the job of dinner-lady in Yankele's school. She was appreciated there, since she spoke German and could communicate with the new refugee children.

"I'll be able to keep an eye on Yankele and see that he eats properly," she told her niece laughingly.

Although Golda Mirel was sorry she was moving out, it certainly solved the problem of how to accommodate Moshe Leib's mother when she came. But the weeks turned into months, and they had no word from Frau Steiner. They were frantic with worry and frustration and there was nothing they could do!

"Can she still be refusing to come?" Golda Mirel cried, the old exasperation creeping back into her voice.

"How do we know the visa ever reached her?" Moshe Leib asked in despair. "And even if it did, who says those beasts would let her out?" The idea of his mother forcibly held back made him shudder.

As 1938 turned to 1939 with still no news, the Steiners felt utterly helpless, trying not to imagine the dreadful things that might be happening to Frau Steiner, or to Kurt and Ilse and their children. They prayed fervently that their family was safe. Many more families had found their way to England from Germany and Austria ... even some from Vienna. The stories they told of the treatment of Jews at the hands of the Nazis were too horrific to bear—particularly by those who had left loved ones behind. Moshe Leib and Golda Mirel realized that they must keep up with the news. Everyone was now aware of Hitler's intention to conquer all of Europe, and when they heard of the advance into Czechoslovakia, Golda Mirel began to panic over her family in Poland. Somehow, they must get them out, too!

She confided her worry one day to Rosa Mittelstein.

"How I wish we could help," Rosa sighed sympathetically, "but it's much harder now than two years ago. I don't suppose your parents have any English relatives who can vouch for them ...." It was more of a statement than a question.

"Hardly likely," Golda Mirel answered dully. Then she looked up, an expression of utter surprise on her face. "Wait ...," she began, then shook her head. "No, no! It could never happen!"

"What?" Rosa asked anxiously. "You look as if you've seen a ghost!"

"I'm not sure if I'm right," Golda Mirel said, "but my father may have a brother here ...."

"*A brother!*" Rosa shrieked. "And you're not sure? I don't understand!"

Golda Mirel began to explain about Berel, starting from when he had become engaged to Sonja. Rosa listened, amazed.

"What a story!" she exclaimed when Golda Mirel's narrative came to an end. "Golda Mirel, you must try to find him! It could save your parents!"

"Maybe you're right," Golda Mirel said, a hopeful look in her eyes. "But I wouldn't even know where to look for him."

"You say he's a doctor? Well, that should make it easier. What's his name?"

"Originally it was Wasserbrun, but in Germany he called himself Wasser ... Berthold Wasser ..."

"Right!" Rosa began to sound business-like. "Leave it to me! I'll find this Doctor Wasser by hook or by crook!"

However, after two days of searching in telephone directories and reference books, Rosa Mittelstein had to admit defeat.

"There's no Doctor Wasser anywhere," she told Golda Mirel despondently. "The nearest I got was a specialist with the same initials ... Barry Waters ..."

"Hmm," Golda Mirel was thoughtful. "It could even be. He changed his name once. He could do it again. Which field does he specialize in?"

"He's an orthopedic surgeon ...."

"Just like Uncle Berel!" Golda Mirel cried excitedly. "Do you think it might be him?"

"Who knows. Let me make a few inquiries. Perhaps I can find out more."

"Oh, Rosa, I don't know how to thank you! Where would I be without you?"

"You know I'm only too happy to help you!" Rosa said kindly. "But don't count on it. It might all come to nothing in the end."

However, two days later an excited Rosa knocked on Golda Mirel's door. "I've been digging and delving," she said enthusiastically, "and it looks as if you're a winner! This Mr. Waters practiced as an orthopedic specialist in Munich and came over to England in 1935. He worked as a house doctor in the London Hospital, then was promoted to Registrar, after which he worked himself up to become a Harley Street specialist. Quite an achievement in such a short time! He must be a brilliant doctor—unless they are just short of orthopedic specialists!"

"Well, he had a terrific name in Germany ... until they found out he was Jewish! Still, it wasn't what my grandparents wanted for him," she added sadly.

"Well, I think you should go and see him," Rosa suggested. "Make an appointment as if you want to consult with him ...."

"Yes, I could get away with that once anyone sees me!" Golda Mirel commented with a laugh.

"You might have to pay for the consultation. Do you think you can manage that?" Rosa asked in concern.

"Yes, we have some money put away, and anything's worth saving my parents!"

"I can phone to make the appointment for you," Rosa offered, "though your English has improved a lot."

"I'd be grateful if you would," Golda Mirel said appreciatively.

An appointment was made for the following Tuesday afternoon, and Golda Mirel felt very nervous as the taxi took her to Harley Street. She wondered what would happen when she came face to face with her Uncle Berel after so long!

Chapter 20

"Mr. Waters will see you now," announced the receptionist, a thin, slight woman with graying hair pulled tightly into a bun.

Golda Mirel still found it strange to hear a doctor referred to simply as "Mister," though Rosa had explained that in England this title was given only to Consultant surgeons, who, she said smiling, would be most insulted if you called them "Doctor." Apprehensively, Golda Mirel followed the receptionist to a door bearing a plaque with "Mr. B. Waters" inscribed on it.

"Mrs. Steiner is here, Mr. Waters," the receptionist said, ushering her into the room. She placed a patient form on the doctor's desk before withdrawing.

Golda Mirel's first reaction was shock. The man behind the desk was so utterly unlike her uncle, she was sure she had made a mistake. In her mind's eye she had pictured Uncle Berel as a tall, thin young man with dark, curly *peyos* framing his face and the beginnings of a beard. This man, bareheaded and clean-shaven, was thick-set, and his hair was tinged with gray. A pair of dark-rimmed spectacles rested on his slightly hooked nose.

What should she do now? How could she pretend that she was

consulting him about her limp? She had no interested in treatment for it, and could not afford it, in any case.

"Good afternoon, Mrs. Steiner. Please sit down," he said somewhat vaguely, removing his glasses to glance at the sheet of paper in front of him.

To Golda Mirel's surprise, he pronounced her name "Shteiner" and not "Steener" as the receptionist had done. She sat down gingerly on the edge of the chair, searching for some sign of recognition. After scanning the form, Mr. Waters looked up at his patient, his spectacles still in his hand.

A second shock-wave passed through Golda Mirel! In that moment before he replaced his glasses, Golda Mirel thought she saw her father looking at her! There was no mistaking those eyes! She knew now what Tirtza Gradman had meant. She had always known her eyes were like her father's, but she had never realized that Anshel Wasserbrun's younger brother's eyes resembled his, too.

"Well, now, Mrs. Steiner ...," the doctor began, smiling at her. "What seems to be the problem?"

Golda Mirel hardly heard him. She almost fell off the chair in her excitement. The smile revealed his teeth and, exactly as she remembered, the two front teeth crossed over each other. Now that she was certain, she found the courage to charge straight in. Obviously, he had no idea who she was, but she would make sure that he did!

"Hullo, Uncle Berel," she said, speaking in Yiddish, "don't you recognize me?"

Mr. Waters—formerly Berel Wasserbrun—paled, then turned crimson. After a moment he cleared his throat, and Golda Mirel sensed that he had intended to bluff it before realizing that it would be a futile attempt. He just stared at her for a while. Then, in an awed whisper, he said, "Golda Mirel! I don't believe it!"

"I've changed a bit, haven't I?" Golda Mirel asked. "But then, so have you."

"True," he agreed. "And one of the things that has changed," he added, "is that my Yiddish is not very fluent any more. Can you speak English?"

"Not very well ... but I can speak German, and as you lived and worked in Germany, you must be able to, as well."

"You seem to know a lot about me," Berel remarked in German. "How do you know all this? And how did you find me?"

"Oh, it's a long story," Golda Mirel replied, not willing to go into lengthy details.

"Well, I'm glad you've decided to consult me at last. I can see you've got more sense than your parents ...."

"I haven't come to consult you," Golda Mirel assured him hastily. "I've lived with this limp all my life and I'm not interested in correcting it ... and I couldn't afford your price anyway!"

"Then why have you come?" Berel asked defensively. "Don't say *you* want to get at me, too ... like some other members of the family!" There was marked bitterness in his tone. Clearly, the incident at his father's *levayah* still rankled.

"I'm not trying to get at you," Golda Mirel declared. She certainly disapproved of his way of life, but she was not going to antagonize him when she had come with a request. "I'm here because I need a favor from you!"

"A favor?" He looked suspicious, but his curiosity was aroused. "What kind?"

Golda Mirel began to describe the plight of his relatives in Poland under threat of a Nazi invasion and unable to escape because they had nowhere to go.

"Well, why did you run away yourself and leave them stranded there?" Berel challenged her.

Golda Mirel explained how she had lived in Vienna since her marriage, and had fled, thinking only Austria was in danger. "But now it looks as if Poland is next, and who knows what will happen to them!" she cried, her voice full of anguish.

"So what do you want *me* to do?"

"I need your help to bring them over to England," Golda Mirel said beseechingly. "*I* can't vouch for them. I'm a refugee myself. But you have an important position here. If you give a guarantee for your brother and his wife, they'll have no problem coming."

"No, Golda Mirel!" Berel interrupted her, holding up his hands and shaking his head. "You're asking the impossible!"

"The *impossible*?" Golda Mirel cried, in disbelief. "How can you say that when your brother's life is in danger?"

"Golda Mirel, please! Keep your voice down!" Berel hissed. "I don't want Mrs. Bradley rushing in to see what's going on!"

"Sorry," Golda Mirel dropped her voice a few degrees, "but I can't believe you wouldn't do a simple thing to help a member of your own family! Are you still holding a grudge after all these years?"

Berel sighed. "No, it's not that—though there are some things that I can't forgive ...." His face darkened for a moment. "But I had nothing against your father. I had great respect for Anshel ...."

"Well, then ... ?"

"You don't understand, do you, Golda Mirel?" He looked at her sadly. "You have no idea what I suffered in Germany. Let me tell you about it." He continued in a low voice. "As you seem to know, I had become a prominent specialist in Germany. I had a good position and was treated with respect by my colleagues. But, as soon as Hitler came to power, everything changed! It wasn't obvious at first, but after a while I noticed I was hardly ever asked to perform important operations ... they were usually given to surgeons who had worked under me. That hurt! One day, through a mistake, a patient died on the operating table, and though I hadn't even been present at the operation they tried to throw the blame onto me! I somehow managed to prove my innocence, but the stigma still clung. Eventually I was asked, in a very unpleasant manner, to leave. As I walked out, I heard the Chief say, in a nasty tone of voice, 'Good riddance, Jew!'

"I wasn't really surprised, though I wondered how they knew I was Jewish. By then, I had heard of many similar happenings in Germany and had seen a few bricks thrown through the windows of Jewish shops. I knew then that I could not stay in the country! I decided to go to England, but I was aware that without credentials all my achievements in Germany would get me nowhere. Luckily, I was friendly with another specialist at the hospital, and he took a great risk and wrote a recommendation for me on hospital paper, apologizing because he couldn't do more. That helped me get a foot into the profession here, and I worked my way up from there. Can you understand …," he looked at his niece searchingly, "that I can't risk jeopardizing my career again? Giving a guarantee for a brother would bring my Jewish origin out in the open. I couldn't take the persecution all over again!"

"But why should you? It won't happen here!" Golda Mirel protested.

Her uncle sighed again. "I thought the same about Germany," he said sadly. "How can one be sure? So please, Golda Mirel, don't ask me to do this!"

Not one to give up easily, Golda Mirel argued, cajoled and pleaded for a while, appealing to his conscience, but to no avail. Eventually, in defeat, she stood up and began to limp toward the door.

"Er … Golda Mirel … wait a minute!" Berel called out. Thinking he had changed his mind, Golda Mirel turned hopefully.

"I would like to do something for *you*, though," he said. "I'm willing to do the operation you obviously need, free of charge!"

"No thank you," Golda Mirel said, her hand on the doorknob. "One amputation is enough for me!"

"Amputation?" the surgeon asked, puzzled. "I wasn't thinking of an amputation. What gave you that idea?"

"As much as my leg is part of me," Golda Mirel replied tartly, "my parents are part of me, too!"

Without waiting for his reaction, she wrenched open the door and limped out.

Tears of disappointment and frustration stung her eyelids. She blinked them away as she approached Mrs. Bradley's desk. A young girl stood beside the receptionist, and Golda Mirel was sure that this slim girl, with dark curly hair, was without a doubt his daughter!

"You can go in to your father now," Mrs. Bradley was saying. "His next patient hasn't arrived yet."

Aware that they were both staring at her, Golda Mirel knew that her eyes were reddened. Embarrassed, she was forced to stand and wait to be told how much she owed for her unsuccessful mission. The door of the consulting room opened suddenly and the doctor called out, "Mrs. Bradley … no charge." Then, seeing his daughter, he exclaimed, "Heidi! What are you doing here?"

"Oh, Daddy, I need help with my Latin!" the girl said. "Have you got time?"

"Not much. I've got another patient coming. But you can come in till he's here," her father replied indulgently.

As soon as the door closed behind father and daughter, Mrs. Bradley turned her attention to Golda Mirel, a look of surprise on her face. She had never known her employer to waive a fee before!

"Mr. Waters says there is no charge," she said primly, but still had a quizzical look on her face.

Her embarrassment heightened, Golda Mirel didn't know what

to say. All she could do was stammer, "W-would you mind calling a taxi for me?"

"Certainly," the receptionist replied, her voice impassive. "If you take a seat in the waiting room, I'll let you know when it comes."

"Oh, thank you, but I'll wait outside," Golda Mirel said, anxious to leave that place as quickly as possible.

Once she was out in the street, Golda Mirel allowed her tears to flow freely. A taxi soon drew up and the driver, noting her tearstained face, looked away. He was used to picking up weeping passengers from Harley Street, and assuming she had been given some bad news, he knew better than to ask questions.

Golda Mirel's mind was in a whirl through her long ride home. Her last bid to save her parents had failed! What would become of them? Her pain at the thought of them was unbearable! And what would she tell Moshe Leib? *And* Rosa Mittelstein, for that matter? What would they think of someone who refused to help his own relatives? She could not avoid telling them, nor even cushion the truth. She was filled with mortification! Remembering her uncle's insecurity and the lameness of his explanation, she felt contemptuous. He needed respect in the *goyim*'s eyes? What about in the *Yidden*'s? … *And in* Hashem's, she thought, sighing.

Suddenly, she pitied him, trapped in the lifestyle he had chosen and living in constant fear of losing it. And his poor lovely daughter! What kind of a future did she have with a father who had no confidence in who he was, and who had given her nothing spiritual to hold onto?

Her pity gave way to anger once again. Her uncle had thrown away an opportunity to do a *mitzvah* that was very unlikely to cost him anything! How low had he sunk that he could put his material desires before the life of a brother he had cared for?

Thinking of her parents brought on another fit of weeping.

What hope was there for them now? *If only she could do something,* she thought in utter frustration.

The taxi pulled up and Golda Mirel paid the driver. Getting out, she saw Moshe Leib standing in the doorway, no doubt waiting to hear how she had fared. One look at her red eyes and tear-streaked face gave him all the answer he needed.

The menacing rumblings of war grew louder and uglier every day, but in England people went on with their lives as usual. Golda Mirel, however, though she kept occupied with her household chores, dragged through the days with a leaden weight on her heart. Moshe Leib had bought a wireless, but Golda Mirel often had to steel herself to switch it on. She went numb any time there was news about Poland, and her *Tehillim* was never far from her hand.

One afternoon, a week or so after her visit to her uncle, she was chopping up some vegetables for dinner when there was a ring at the doorbell. Wondering whom it could be, she put down the paring knife and went to open the door.

The young girl standing there was no stranger to her. She immediately recognized her as the girl she had seen on Harley Street—Uncle Berel's daughter Heidi! The girl who had seemed young and carefree in her father's office looked serious, and even anxious.

"Mrs. Steiner?" she said, timidly. "May I come in?"

"Of course," Golda Mirel said, suddenly thinking, *this girl is my first cousin!*

Leading her into the kitchen, she waved her to a chair and poured her a cup of tea, placing it on the table with a plate of biscuits. Then Golda Mirel asked, "What can I do for you?"

"I don't know if you remember me, but I saw you at my father's surgery …."

"Yes, I do remember," Golda Mirel told her.

"There's something I have to know," Heidi blurted out with sudden vehemence, "and I hope you will tell me!"

"If I can, I will," Golda Mirel promised. "Tell me what all this is about."

Heidi took a deep breath. "I don't often disturb Daddy at his surgery, though my school is nearby, but that day we had a free period with a Latin exam straight after so I came by to see if Daddy had a minute to explain something to me. He did help me, but he was acting so peculiar and seemed pretty shaken up. I was scared to ask him about it, but I suspected it was something to do with you, because, um …" Blushing furiously, she broke off. "I-I'm sorry …"

"I know," Golda Mirel smiled at her, "I was crying. You needn't be embarrassed."

Heidi smiled gratefully and continued. "While Daddy went to the bookshelf to look up a Latin term for me, I spotted your form, with your name and address, lying on his desk. Luckily, I've a good memory so I remembered it. When Daddy came home that night, he still acted like he had something on his mind. My mother and my older sister, Laura, noticed it, too, but we didn't dare ask him about it. Later that night, wondering if he was telling Mummy about it, I crept downstairs … and … well … I know it was wrong, but I listened at the door." She flushed again and looked down at her teacup, stirring it unconsciously with her spoon.

Golda Mirel merely tut-tutted and said, "Go on."

"They weren't even talking quietly—they thought I was upstairs. Besides, they were speaking German, which they hardly ever do. Daddy is very strict about it. He won't allow us to speak German, and he thinks I don't remember it anymore. I had missed the beginning, but the first thing I heard Daddy say was, 'She had no right to come and ask me such a thing, even if I *am* her uncle! Bringing my brother and his wife over here might put my whole career in danger again! People will find out that we're Jewish and who knows what that might lead to!'"

Golda Mirel sighed deeply but made no comment.

"Mrs. Steiner, please tell me!" Heidi stared at her with imploring eyes. "Are we truly Jewish?"

"You mean you didn't *know*?" Golda Mirel asked, shocked.

"No! I had no idea!" Heidi declared. "I don't even know any Jewish people. There aren't any where we live and I don't think there are any at school." She paused. "So, it is true, then."

"Yes, Heidi, it is," Golda Mirel said gently. "But why didn't you ask your father about it?"

"Oh, I couldn't!" Heidi exclaimed. "He'd be furious if he knew I'd been eavesdropping!"

"Well, he'd be quite right!" Golda Mirel laughed.

Heidi ducked her head. "It *was* wrong of me, but I was so curious! Mrs. Steiner—is Daddy really your uncle?"

"Yes, he is," Golda Mirel said. "My father is his older brother …." A lump came to her throat as she mentioned her father. She swallowed it, and forced a smile. "Which makes us first cousins," she said heartily.

Heidi gave a half smile at that, but she sat very still, a dazed look on her face. Golda Mirel would have liked to talk about what being Jewish meant, but she saw this was not the right time. The girl was obviously in a state of shock and needed time to digest this new discovery.

Presently, Heidi stood up. "I must go," she said. "Thank you for telling me. I just had to know the truth!"

Golda Mirel smiled kindly at her, saying, "I'm always here if there's anything else you want to know." She walked her guest to the door and they shook hands. As she watched her young cousin walk away, a slight droop in her shoulders, Golda Mirel hoped she had not seen the last of her.

August 1939 brought a fresh influx of refugees to England. An air of doom hung over the country. On the first of September, Hitler invaded Poland. This news plunged Golda Mirel to the depths of despair. She longed to hear that her parents had managed to get to somewhere safe, but she knew how slim that chance was. If, *chas v'sholom*, they were still in Poland, there would be no escape for them now!

Neville Chamberlain, the British Prime Minister, announced on the wireless that he would put pressure on Hitler to withdraw, giving her a small glimmer of hope, but only two days later, his second announcement dashed it all away. That morning, the third of September, all the family—Golda Mirel, Tante Fanny and Moshe Leib—huddled over the small wireless set to listen to the ominous message:

"I am speaking to you from the Cabinet Room at 10 Downing Street.

"This morning the British Ambassador in Berlin handed the German Government a final note stating that unless we heard from them by 11.00 a.m. that they were prepared at once to withdraw their troops from Poland, a state of war would exist between us.

"I have to tell you," he went on somberly, "that no such undertaking has been received, and consequently this country is at war with Germany!"

PART III:

Autumn

Chapter 21

*L*ondon, 1950. It was five years since the war had ended, yet signs of the devastation were still evident in many places. The remains of bombed houses could be seen here and there, and many official buildings, such as Town Halls and hospitals, were still painted the camouflage colors of gray and black that they had worn to protect them from enemy planes flying overhead.

Golda Mirel sat darning socks in a melancholy mood. She still could not accept England as her permanent home. It was as if her earlier life had just been blotted out. All she had left of her childhood in Poland were memories. There was just no going back.

Tears welled up in her eyes. What had become of her parents, her siblings and her maternal grandparents …. Would she ever know? Moshe Leib, at least, had learned of his family's tragic fate. The Nazis, *yemach shemom*, ever methodical, had kept records of all the people they sent to the gas chambers. The names of Martha Steiner, Kurt and Ilse Hoffler and their children were on those dreaded lists. Tante Fanny and Moshe Leib—and herself—had been distraught over the news, but they had been able to grieve and mourn for their loved ones. They had a *yahrzeit* every year and could light candles for their *neshomos*. But all she had was a gaping void.

Golda Mirel tried to cheer herself up by realizing how fortunate she was, not only because her family had been able to settle in England, surrounded by a fine *frum kehillah*, but also because of the *nissim* Hashem had granted her family during the Blitz. On one such occasion, Hashem had openly revealed His boundless *Hashgochoh Protis* to the Steiners.

Early one evening, as Golda Mirel was clearing away the supper dishes, the ominous screech of the air-raid siren rang out—a sound they never grew accustomed to. Grabbing their coats, the children rushed to the door, followed by their mother who stopped to snatch up her handbag. Moshe Leib did not accompany them, preferring to stay at home with his gemara rather than sit among the rowdy crowd gathered there, the men sometimes the worse for drink, using obscene language, and the women improperly clad.

After huddling together for about a quarter of an hour, they saw a shadow of someone at the entrance. Golda Mirel, busily reading from her small *Tehillim*, looked in surprise. It was Moshe Leib! She hurried over to him.

"What's happened?" she asked anxiously.

"Nothing! Nothing at all," her husband reassured her. "It's just that the money has run out in the gas-meter, and I haven't any change. Have you got a shilling or two?"

"Of course," said Golda Mirel, delving into her bag for her purse and extracting the necessary coins. He took them and opened the shelter door.

"Please be careful, Moshe Leib!" she begged. "It's not safe to be in the street during an air-raid!"

"Don't worry!" Moshe Leib replied cheerfully. "The *Eibershter* looks after me!"

At that moment, a mighty explosion rocked the very ground they were standing on! Ashen-faced, Moshe Leib spun around and retreated in shock, shutting the door and leaning against it. In the shelter, pandemonium broke loose! People screamed and moaned in fear and worry over their possessions, but no one could leave before the "all clear" signal. When it came, there was a frantic scramble as people rushed to check up on their own houses.

When the Steiners reached Allerton Road, they saw the bomb had completely demolished the house two doors away from theirs! Their house was mercifully still standing, but most of the windows were shattered and slates had fallen from the roof.

Ordering the children to wait outside, Moshe Leib and Golda Mirel crept cautiously into the house to inspect the damage. The sight was devastating. Bits of plaster had come off the walls and lay crumbled up, mixed with fragments of glass from the windows.

But when they got to the livingroom, they had the fright of their lives. Exactly over the spot where Moshe Leib had been learning gaped an enormous hole, revealing bare wooden beams and joists. Moshe Leib gave a cry, pointing aghast at a huge chunk of plaster that lay sprawled across the table, covering his gemara and the chair on which he had been sitting. He tried to raise it a bit to release his *sefer*, but it was far too heavy to lift. He turned to his wife who gazed back, too numb to speak. Tears started in her eyes, and he gave her a tremulous smile.

"*Geloibt is der Eibershter,*" he whispered in utter shock. His voice choked with emotion, stretching his hands up and gazing skyward he added, "*Chasdei Hashem ki loi somnu, ki loi cholu rachamov!*"

Golda Mirel knew she would never forget that poignant moment.

Indeed, the war years in England had been fraught with hardships, such as Moshe Leib being interned for a while on the Isle of Man as an "enemy alien," or their temporary move to Chesham, Buckinghamshire, to be safe from the constant bombing. This picturesque country village had been pleasant, but naturally lacked a *heimishe* environment. The gentiles had been kind and friendly, but having never seen Jewish people before, they regarded them as invaders from another planet! Then there was the rationing of food and clothing, which was difficult with three growing children!

Golda Mirel looked around at her cozy little home, and, remembering how she'd gotten there, suddenly snapped out of her gloom. The bomb that had hit an empty house had truly been *gam zu letovah*. But the condition of *their* house had left the Steiners virtually homeless. Some Jewish neighbors, who had hitherto just been nodding acquaintances, rescued them. Without a blink, they had immediately taken in the five of them, giving them food and shelter until another house could be found. Their kindness warmed Golda Mirel's heart and made her feel thankful again to be part of such a fine community.

Now, all those years later, here they were, still in the house in Fairholt Road that they had moved into shortly afterwards. At first, they had shared it with another family, but the other tenants had moved out after the war, and now they had the large, comfortable house to themselves, which was a *brochoh* considering the size of their family! Furthermore, they hoped to become its owners very soon!

During the war, a *heimishe* Jewish school had opened, and Moshe Leib had secured a teaching position there. He had worked his way up to become vice-headmaster of *limudei kodesh*, and earned a steady wage. Golda Mirel still supplemented the family income by doing dressmaking, and the demand for her services grew with the expanding community. Thus, they had managed to save for a deposit on the house, and since they had recently acquired British citizenship, they likely would have no problem obtaining a mortgage.

Golda Mirel placed the last sock, neatly darned, into her work-basket on the table. Then she began on eight-year-old Menachem Dovid's trousers. Examining them, she marveled at the small hole at the knee. When Chuni was this age, she'd had to sew patches on his trousers, the holes were so big! But Menachem Dovid was a quiet, serious boy, hardly ever getting into scrapes or playing rowdy games with the other boys. He was born in a small cottage hospital in Buckinghamshire, and she and Moshe Leib had sat in the quaint little hospital ward, discussing a name for him. Hoping against hope that her father was still alive, she refused to consider giving the baby his name. Moshe Leib suggested calling him Menachem, after his brother Max, who had left the world so tragically.

"But we can't name him after someone who died so young," Golda Mirel had protested. "And an unmarried *bochur* at that."

"We'll add a name, naturally," Moshe Leib said. He pondered for a moment. "How about Dovid?"

"Why Dovid?"

"For *Dovid Hamelech*, who is with us every day now through his *Tehillim*."

This notion appealed to Golda Mirel, and after turning the two names over in her mind, she agreed. Menachem Dovid it was. He was a good child, never causing trouble, but Golda Mirel sometimes wished he were more assertive. However, that was not a *midah* one tried to instill in a child!

In contrast, Mindy, born two years later, had more than her share of assertiveness! She was an outgoing little live wire who tended to wield her charms to get her way.

What a strange collection of children I've got! Golda Mirel reflected. Yankel, now a nineteen-year-old yeshiva *bochur*, took his learning seriously, yet still had a light-hearted outlook on life. Elkie, at sixteen, was quite grown-up for her age. Reliable and far from frivolous, she

217

had a delicious sense of humor. Chuni, like Mindy, was lively and carefree, yet without the self-centeredness. He would give away his last penny to someone who needed it and he went out of his way to help people whenever he could. *A truly perfect blend of personalities,* she thought, *who would have brought much* nachas *to their grandparents!* ... And they were almost the only known offspring left to carry on the traditions of her family .... *At least our entire family was not wiped out like some others,* she thought, ending her musings on a happier note of thanks for her good fortune.

Her ears pricked up at the sound of the post dropping through the letterbox. She went to fetch it, and amongst the bills and circulars was a letter from Heidi, her young cousin. Hindy—as she was now called—lived in Gateshead with her husband, a *Kollel* student, and their baby son, the other *sh'eiris hapleitah* of the Wasserbrun family. Putting the letter on the kitchen table, Golda Mirel cleared away her mending and put the kettle on so she could enjoy a cup of tea while she read it.

Hindy's story was another open example of Hashem's great *Hashgochoh Protis.* Golda Mirel had been disappointed, though hardly surprised, that Heidi's first visit had not been followed by a second, but she had told herself philosophically that it was unnatural for a young girl to probe into the unknown. It was a pity, but in all probability she would never see her again.

Then, shortly before the end of the war, Golda Mirel heard her name being called just as she was about to get on a train one afternoon. She turned to see a young woman with a portfolio under her arm making her way toward her. It took Golda Mirel a moment, but then she connected the face with the youthful schoolgirl who had come to see her just before war had broken out. Undoubtedly, this was Uncle Berel's daughter Heidi!

"Oh, Mrs. Steiner!" the girl said, panting as she reached her.

"I'm so glad I've found you! I've been so worried! I didn't know what happened to you!"

"*You* didn't know what happened to *me*?" Golda Mirel exclaimed. "*I've* been wondering what happened to *you*! You never came back!"

"Oh, but I did! Not straight away, though. I was so busy studying for my exams, and then war was declared and nobody could think of anything else. But after a while, I remembered that I'd wanted to ask you some questions. I came by your house and had an awful shock! I could see that the house two doors away had been bombed, but your place looked damaged, too—with the windows all boarded up and bricks missing from the walls. I thought … well, you know …" She broke off, blushing.

Golda Mirel smiled and told Heidi how lucky they had been, and about her husband's narrow escape, deliberately remarking on the intervention of G-d. She saw with satisfaction that the girl was impressed.

"Oh, Mrs. Steiner, there's so much I want to know about being Jewish … and what you've just said makes me want to know even more! Please, will you tell me everything?"

"Well, not all in one go … and definitely not here in the underground station!" Golda Mirel told her with a laugh. "If you make regular visits to my house, I'll teach you what I can. My address now is No. 18 Fairholt Road, if you'd like to write it down. And please call me Golda Mirel. We are cousins, after all!"

Heidi started visiting often and she avidly soaked up everything Golda Mirel taught her, growing more attracted to the Steiner's way of life with each visit. When she felt ready for a total commitment to Torah observance, she faced the problem of how to tell her parents, but she bravely resolved to confront them at the first opportunity.

A few days later the telephone rang, and when Golda Mirel answered it a gruff voice barked, "Is that Mrs. Golda Steiner?"

"Y-yes," Golda Mirel replied tentatively. Her heart thudded when she heard that voice and she suddenly wished she had not persuaded Moshe Leib to have a telephone installed.

"Golda Mirel!" Berel's voice shouted into her ear. "What do you think you're playing at? Is this your way of taking revenge?"

"Revenge?"

"Yes, revenge! Just because I wouldn't risk *my* life to save your parents, you set about taking my two daughters away from me!"

"Your *two* daughters?" Golda Mirel cut in, surprised. "I haven't even met the older one!"

"Well, Heidi's stuffing Laura's head with the nonsense *you* put into hers! Laura had a brilliant career as a doctor ahead of her, but she's gone off to Palestine to work in some primitive hospital there ... just so that she can work with Jewish people! And Heidi is *absolutely* fanatical! You have a lot to answer for, Golda Mirel! You're worse than all my family put together! At least Chana Bleema came out in the open with her opinions, though she did embarrass me in public. But you chose to get at me in the most underhanded way—"

"Just a minute, Uncle Berel," Golda Mirel broke in on his tirade. "*I* never told Heidi that she was Jewish ... she overheard it from *you*! And once she knew it, the spark of *Yiddishkeit* in her *neshomoh* was ignited. She came to me of her own accord. I certainly could not—and would not—turn her away. *You* may not be pleased that your daughters have picked up the *yiras Shomayim* you dropped, but one thing I know. Your parents in the *Olam Ha-emes* are rejoicing!"

There was a loud click and the dial tone hummed in her ear. Her words had obviously struck home, Golda Mirel thought, as she replaced the receiver in its cradle.

Heidi had left home and moved into her own flat, making great strides in her *Yiddishkeit*. She had kept her job as assistant pharmacist in a hospital, and been granted permission to take off on

Shabbos and *Yom Tov*. Eventually, she married Shimon Moscovsky, an orphaned refugee who had come over from Poland with a *kindertransport* at the beginning of the war. He was a brilliant Torah scholar at the *Kollel* in Gateshead, where the young couple settled after their marriage.

Laura, too, had progressed, marrying a young doctor—also a *baal teshuva*—and was happily settled in Eretz Yisroel, living a true Torah life.

Hindy's letter was full of news about life in Gateshead and the antics of little Zevy. It was the letter of a contented person. Golda Mirel enjoyed reading it, gratified to have been instrumental in bringing all this about.

As she folded up the letter to place on the sideboard, the doorbell rang, and she hurried to the door. The woman on the doorstep was a stranger, yet there was something vaguely familiar about her.

"Golda Mirel?" the woman asked hesitantly. "It is you ... isn't it!"

Golda Mirel felt suddenly weak, as though she were walking in a dream.

"Wh-ho are you?" she asked, a tremor in her voice.

"You don't know me?" the woman asked, a mysterious smile hovering about her lips.

That smile! Of course she knew who it was! Golda Mirel felt her legs turn to jelly and she gripped the door-handle tightly to steady herself.

"*Ettel!!*" she shrieked. "Ettel! Is it really you? Please tell me I'm not dreaming!"

And, without waiting for a reply, she stepped forward and threw her arms around her sister in a tight embrace!

Chapter 22

Still in a daze, Golda Mirel placed coffee and cake in front of her sister and scrutinized her closely. How changed Ettel was! It was difficult to believe that this sober, middle-aged woman was her youngest sister! The Ettel she remembered had been a pretty, happy-go-lucky girl, always dressed in frilly clothes, ribbons dancing among her blonde curls. Her blue eyes had shone in health and the joy of living, and her flashing smile had been magnetic. The last time Golda Mirel had seen her was on her visit to Poland eighteen years ago. Ettel, then a young married woman with a baby, had worn her hat at a jaunty angle, as carefree as ever.

Now, in a turban, her clothes shapeless and demure, she looked older than her forty years. Little lines wreathed her strained eyes. Her smile still broke out unexpectedly, lighting up her face, but it was clear that the suffering she had endured had stolen her sparkle. Plying her with questions, Golda Mirel had to tread carefully, lest the memories were too painful to talk about, yet she just had to know how Ettel had fared during the war, and how she turned up out of the blue, five years later!

Ettel, however, was only too happy to fill her sister in on all the details. She described their escape into Hungary in a van full of cupboards.

"We had to pay the Polish furniture mover a huge sum to smuggle us over the border," she said. "And the journey! It was so nerve-racking. We were wedged between these heavy articles of furniture, constantly afraid something might get loose and crush one of the children! And it was so cramped, we were numb with pain. Eating and drinking was an ordeal, especially with two hungry little children." She sighed, wiping away a stray tear. "Every time the van was stopped by a border guard, I thought my heart would burst through my eardrums, it pounded so loud. The children had, *nebach*, already learned how not to make a sound, knowing discovery meant instant death.

"*Baruch Hashem*, we arrived safely—though I can't say we *felt* very safe while we were there. Having come in illegally, we had to be very careful not to be noticed. At that time, the Hungarian government was in league with the Germans, and if we'd been discovered, they would have handed us over to the Nazis straight away!" There was a haunted look in Ettel's eyes, and Golda Mirel, too, shuddered at the thought of what that would have meant!

"Somehow, we got to Budapest," Ettel continued. "We knew there were *heimishe* families there, and hoped someone would take us in. *Yidden* being *Yidden*, nobody turned us away, though we knew they were frightened. If they were found hiding us, it would mean trouble for them. We felt so bad putting fellow *Yidden* in danger that we didn't stay with any family for long, but moved about from one to another. It was terribly unsettling, especially for the children. Goldie was only ten at the time and Mordchele was six. They didn't know what we wanted of them! But when we finally found a house to stay in, it had its own difficulty."

She explained how, during a brief stay with a couple named Altstein, her nerves had given way, and she had burst into an uncontrollable fit of crying. In the middle of this outburst, the back door had opened, and a gentile Hungarian woman had walked in, a bag of vegetables in her arms! Ettel had jumped in panic, but Rifka Altstein had laid a reassuring hand on her arm.

"Don't worry about Mrs. Koják," she said. "We can trust her."

She explained that this kind-hearted woman often brought her fresh carrots and potatoes from the market garden where she worked, because the Jews were afraid to venture out to do their shopping.

Marika Koják had looked at Ettel with concern, asking what was wrong. Upon hearing of her family's plight she said, "You're right. It is dangerous for everybody for you to move so often. Let me speak to my husband and see if we can suggest something."

That evening, Mrs. Koják's husband Vidor came over. A broad, burly man with a grizzly moustache and bushy eyebrows, the kindness in his eyes contradicted the severity of his appearance. He announced that he could hide them in his house. "But there is one problem," he said, addressing Ettel's husband, Kalman. "A strange man in our house might arouse suspicion and put us all in danger. If we just take your wife and children, we can tell people that your wife is a relative of ours whose husband deserted her."

"But where will my husband go?" Ettel cried, extremely distressed. "It's not possible!"

"I understand how you feel," Vidor Koják spoke gently, "but believe me, it's the only way." He pondered for a few moments, then turned to Kalman and said, "I've just thought of something. I have a cousin who owns a farm, deep in the country. If I give you a letter, he will take you in as a farmhand. He owes me a favor and he'll do it for me. I'd better find you some suitable clothes and tell you how to get there. A train will take you part of the way, but the rest will not be so easy. I hope you will manage to find it …."

"We had no choice but to agree," Ettel told her sister. "Golda Mirel, can you just imagine what it was like for me when Kalman went off! And it got worse! I never received word that he had arrived, and I was worried sick all the time! Right through the war, we had no contact with each other."

"You poor thing!" Golda Mirel exclaimed sympathetically. "How terrible for you! But, is … was … ?" She couldn't say the words, but—Ettel was here on her own! Where *was* her husband?

"Yes, yes, *baruch Hashem!*" Ettel smiled, reading Golda Mirel's thoughts. "He came back as soon as the war was over. He'd had to sleep in a barn, and while Mr. Koják's farmer cousin treated him quite well, he certainly made use of him!" Ettel sighed again, and gave a wry smile. "He was so thin and worn out. I suppose I didn't look much better.

"After the Nazis marched in to Budapest, it was horrific! You can't imagine it, Golda Mirel! I sat tight and prayed I would not be found, but I was terrified! The Nazis were constantly making house-to-house searches. When they came, I was with Marika Koják in her kitchen. My heart was in my mouth, as you can imagine, but luckily they swallowed the story about the children and me being relatives. It's a good thing Goldie is blonde, like me, and Mordchele's a redhead, so they didn't look strikingly Jewish ….

"It was awful, Golda Mirel! They kept rounding up *Yidden* and taking them away! The day after that search the Nazis were rampaging about all over the area. I couldn't bring myself to look out of the window, but I could hear them marching in their hobnail boots, shouting in harsh voices … and the crying and wailing …." She broke off, shivering at the memory, then pulled herself together and continued. "Sometime later, Vidor Koják came hurrying in with something concealed under his coat. He was panting breathlessly and said, 'I hope no one saw me.' He threw off his coat, and in his arms was a small boy, whimpering and struggling to get away. I recognized him immediately. It was Rifka Altstein's little boy, three-year-old Ari!

"My mouth went dry and I began to tremble. 'W-what happened?' I asked.

"'They dragged the Altsteins out and shot Mr. Altstein,' Vidor told me quietly. 'Then they ordered Mrs. Altstein, her baby in her arms, to join a heavily guarded line of women. The little boy was still standing near the house unnoticed, and I managed to grab him just as he began to run toward his mother. I had to put my hand over his mouth to stop him from screaming. I'm not surprised he's terrified of me now.' He smiled sympathetically at Ari, but the little boy ran to me and began crying into my apron.

"'I guess you'll have to look after him from now on, Mrs. Davinsky,' Mr. Koják said. 'I don't know if he'll ever see his mother again.'

"So you see, Golda Mirel," Ettel concluded, "I've got three children now! Ari has been with us ever since. We notified the Agudah after the war, in case Rifka Altstein turned up searching for him, but there has been no news of her, so I'm afraid she and her baby daughter did not survive." There was deep sadness in her voice. "A few months ago, we legally adopted Ari. He's a lovely nine-year-old and he's very attached to us. We love him as if he was our own son."

Golda Mirel was spellbound at Ettel's narrative. She regarded her sister with wonder. She couldn't believe her flighty little sister had turned into such a serious, responsible person. Was it the suffering that had done it—or had she just grown up?

"Where did you go after the war?" Golda Mirel asked. "You obviously didn't stay in Hungary, or you'd still be there now. Since the Communists took over, no one can get out."

"No, of course we didn't stay. We wanted to go home to Poland, and we made our way there as soon as we could …." Her voice trailed away, and her eyes took on a faraway gaze.

"To Poland!" Golda Mirel gripped Ettel's arm intently. "Did you … did you go to Lipsk?"

"Not at first. We went to Breslau, where there were quite a few *Yidden*. Everyone warned us not to go to the small *shtetlach*, as the Poles had murdered some people who had returned. I still felt a strong urge to go. Kalman didn't want to let me, but I persuaded him, saying I had masqueraded as a *goyishe* woman once and could do it again."

"So you went?" Golda Mirel asked breathlessly.

"Yes. I went," Ettel said. Her low, flat tone gave Golda Mirel the answer to her unspoken question. "I went straight to our old house and the first thing I noticed was washing hanging on the line. I was trembling as I knocked on the door, and then I had a big shock! The woman who answered the door was our daily help, Katrina! Remember her?"

Golda Mirel gasped. "Katrina! You mean she just moved into our house?"

"Yes! She recognized me—maybe I reminded her of Mamme—and this dreadful look of hatred crossed her face. I was frightened she was going to kill me! But she just began to scream. 'Why didn't Hitler kill you?' she shouted. 'You're not having this house back! It's mine now! Get away from here!' And she slammed the door in my face.

"I didn't know what to do! And then I noticed old Mrs. Dabrowska next door peeping out. She beckoned me to come in. I was scared, but there was so much I wanted to know, so I went in. She told me everything."

"Tell me!" Golda Mirel cried apprehensively.

Ettel eyed her sister sadly and her eyes smarted. She choked, and said in a voice, thick with tears, "They … they dragged them out into the street and killed them … Tatte … Mamme … and Leibel and his family, who were there …" Ettel put her head on the table and wept. "Oh, Golda Mirel! I didn't want to have to tell you!" she sobbed bitterly.

"I ... had to know ...," Golda Mirel's grief overcame her, and she wept, too. For a long time the two sisters sat, arms around each other, until their tears were spent.

The ringing of the telephone made them both jump. It was Moshe Leib.

"Were you out before?" he asked. "I rang, but you didn't answer."

"No, I wasn't out ...," Golda Mirel replied.

"Golda Mirel, have you come down with a cold? You sound terrible!"

"No, no, I'm all right," Golda Mirel assured her husband. "Moshe Leib, you'll never guess who is visiting me! My sister, Ettel!"

"What? Just like that?" Moshe Leib sounded astonished. "But I don't understand. Why do you sound so upset? You should be delighted!"

"Of course I'm delighted! You can't imagine how much! But ...," her voice faltered, "... she's just told me about ... Tatte ... and Mamme ..." She broke off, unable to say the words.

"Golda Mirel, I'm coming right home!" Moshe Leib declared, understanding immediately.

"You don't have to," Golda Mirel protested, knowing how difficult it was for him to leave a class he was teaching. "I'm all right, really! And Ettel's with me."

"Yes, but I want to come. In any case, you have to *reiss kriyah* and sit *shiva* for half an hour. Don't do anything till I come. I won't be long."

Replacing the receiver, Golda Mirel told Ettel what Moshe Leib had said.

"Yes, he's right," Ettel told her. "I had to do it, too, though I didn't know till I returned to Breslau."

"Did you go anywhere else in Lipsk while you were there?"

"Not really. I was in a hurry to get back. But I asked Mrs.

Dabrowska if she knew what happened to the others. The only ones she was sure about were Zeide and Babbe Danziger. Her husband saw them being led away ….." A sob came into Ettel's voice. "Why are you making me tell you all this bad news?" she cried plaintively.

"I'm sorry, Ettel," Golda Mirel said, tears welling up in her eyes again. "I don't think I can bear to hear any more."

Sitting on the low chair Moshe Leib had brought in, Golda Mirel clutched the photograph of her parents that she had picked up from the sideboard. She and Ettel pored over it tearfully, reminiscing about how wonderful their parents had been.

Suddenly, in walked Tante Fanny. She took in the scene, and turned pale. "W-what's happened?" She gripped the back of the nearest chair for support.

Moshe Leib explained the situation, and the kindly old woman pulled the chair toward Golda Mirel and sat down.

"It's a good thing I came in now," she commented. "At least I can be *menachem oveil.*" She surveyed Ettel shrewdly. "And who is this?"

"This is my sister, Ettel Davinsky." Golda Mirel introduced them. "Ettel, this is Moshe Leib's aunt, Tante Fanny Gerber. She came with us from Vienna."

"Well, how nice, an older sister," Tante Fanny remarked. "I always thought you were the oldest in your family, Golda Mirel."

There was an awkward silence and Golda Mirel, seeing Ettel was upset, answered simply, "I am. Ettel's a bit younger," and quickly changed the subject. Normally, Golda Mirel enjoyed Tante Fanny's company, but now she was impatient for her to go. There was so much still left untold, and she wanted to hear it before the children came home.

However, she had to wait till much later that evening since Tante Fanny stayed for supper. Only after the children had gone to bed and

Tante Fanny had gone home was she able to satisfy her curiosity. The two sisters sat cozily by the open fire, sipping lemon tea, when Golda Mirel said, "Ettel, I still don't know where you have been for the last few years … and what brought you here all of a sudden."

Ettel smiled. "Well, I knew I had a sister in London, didn't I? So why shouldn't I want to see her? That was part of the reason. We're living in Paris at the moment—"

"In Paris?" Golda Mirel interrupted. "What made you go there?"

"Well, we had to go somewhere. There was no point in staying in Breslau. Lots of people were going to Paris, so we joined them. It was nice at first. There was quite a *chassidishe* crowd there, and a large Lubavitch community, and Kalman, being a *shochet*, soon found work. But lately, people are moving away, and as there's no Jewish school, or the right kind of *cheder* for the boys, we've decided to move again. Besides, Goldie is eighteen and there isn't much choice of a *shidduch* there. So, since you are here, London was the first place I thought of. I actually wrote you at the address I had in my notebook, and I couldn't understand why you never answered."

"Oh, Ettel, you don't know what happened …," Golda Mirel began.

"Yes, I do," her sister told her soberly. "When I didn't hear from you, I decided to come and surprise you. I went to the address in … what was it? … Allerton Road … and don't ask what I thought when I saw the house! I think I would have gone straight back to Paris if a nice *Yiddishe* lady hadn't come out of a house and asked whom I was looking for. She told me what happened, and where you live now."

"*Baruch Hashem!* Imagine if we had not met after all!" Golda Mirel exclaimed. "Oh, Ettel!" she continued enthusiastically. "It would be fantastic if you came to live here!"

"Yes, but I don't think it's easy to get into England, just like that," her sister said. "Someone from the *kehillah* would have to give Kalman a job and bring him over."

"I'm sure there's a demand for *shochtim* here!" Golda Mirel declared eagerly. "Moshe Leib will know whom to approach. I'll speak to him the minute he comes in!"

"That would be truly marvelous, Golda Mirel," Ettel said hopefully. "Kalman couldn't come himself while he's still working there, so he sent me to arrange it. I've got a letter of recommendation from the Rabbi there."

Golda Mirel hugged her sister impulsively. She felt like dancing for joy! One of her beloved sisters had suddenly come back to her! She hadn't lost her entire family after all!

Chapter 23

Golda Mirel went inside, having waved off her married daughter and her daughter-in-law for their shopping trip. The house was peaceful and quiet. Tzivia, Yankel's wife, had settled her eighteen-month-old son Anshel upstairs in a cot Golda Mirel kept for that purpose, and Elkie's little daughter, Pessie, just six months, was fast asleep in her pram in the livingroom.

Sighing contentedly, Golda Mirel sat down to write some letters. It was wonderful to have her two married children nearby. Yankel, a fine, upstanding young man, had married Rosa Mittelstein's niece Tzivia, a delightful girl whom Golda Mirel adored. He had been an exemplary *talmid* in yeshiva, but had left at twenty-one to study accountancy so he could earn a *parnossoh*, and had a well-paid job in Reuven Mittelstein's office. He had not adhered to the Chassidic way of life, yet he could not bring himself to cut short his long *peyos* and kept them curled up behind his ears. Elkie, too, had settled down well. Her husband, Ezriel Wohlkind, had come over with his family from Germany just before the war. Seven years Elkie's senior, he had already acquired a name as a *talmid chochom*, as well as an expert in Jewish History, which he taught at a Jewish High school in Golders Green.

Golda Mirel addressed her letter to Chuni, her twenty-one-year-old, who was learning in a *chassidishe* yeshiva. He had announced that he would not follow the example of his older siblings, but would put on a *shtreimel* when he married. Golda Mirel wondered whom he would find. There were not many girls nowadays who wanted that way of life. Chuni, a warm-hearted, generous person, had one other stipulation. His wife must be prepared to lead an open house, taking in guests at short notice. *Hachnosas orchim* was a *mitzvah* he felt strongly about.

She put the letter aside for Moshe Leib to add to it, and began Menachem Dovid's. Her third son, still as earnest and serious as ever, had just enrolled in Gateshead Yeshiva and was doing extremely well. His *maggid shiur*, however, had once or twice expressed his concern to Moshe Leib about the boy's seriousness. Hard as the *maggid shiur* tried to encourage him, Menachem Dovid did not socialize much with the other *bochurim* and did not seem able to let go and enjoy himself at all. *Should I mention the subject?* Golda Mirel wondered as she picked up her pen. *Will it help if I tell him to have a bit of fun from time to time?*

She had just written "*Dear Menachem Dovid ...*" when a ring at the doorbell disturbed her.

"Oh, who is that?" she muttered in irritation. If she didn't get her letters written now, she didn't know when she would finish them! Reluctantly, she went to open the door.

The gaunt, white-haired man who stood on her doorstep seemed strangely familiar. She stared at him for a moment, then gasped.

"Uncle Berel!" she cried, staring. What had happened to him? Was it really seventeen years since she had last seen him? Could time have wrought such a change in him? He was slightly stooped and painfully thin, his clothes hanging loosely on him.

"Golda Mirel, may I come in?" he asked humbly.

"Of course!" Golda Mirel said, opening the door wide and stepping aside. "Uncle Berel, are you all right?" she asked, as she led him into the livingroom. "I hardly recognized you!"

"No, Golda Mirel, I'm *not* all right!" he told her, sounding more like his brusque self as he sank into the easy chair. He tersely informed her that he was very ill and did not have long to live.

"Don't say that!" Golda Mirel cried. "You must have *bitochon* ...."

"Oh, please," Berel interrupted her cynically, "don't give me that! Remember, I'm a doctor. I know my condition. And if you're talking about miracles ... well, I don't think I'm really someone who deserve miracles!" He gave a wry smile.

Golda Mirel wanted to tell him that it was not up to human beings to judge who deserved miracles when a little whimper from the baby's pram distracted her.

Her uncle asked, "Is that your grandchild?"

Golda Mirel nodded. "Yes, my daughter Elkie's baby. She's six months old."

A wistful look came into Berel's eyes. "I don't even know if I've got any grandchildren," he said sadly. "I suppose I must have. You probably know. Have I?"

"You do," Golda Mirel told him, suddenly pitying him. "Hin ... er ... Heidi's got two boys and a girl, and I think your daughter in Eretz Yisroel has a son, too."

"It wouldn't have hurt them to let me know," Berel said bitterly. "Not for my sake ... after all, I did throw Heidi out, and Laura left before I had a chance to do the same to her ... but my wife had a right to know. None of this is her fault."

They were both startled suddenly by a series of loud bumps in the hall and a child's anguished wails.

"Anshele!" Golda Mirel cried panic-stricken as she rushed to the door. "He must have climbed out of the cot!"

She ran to the stairs, where she found her little grandson lying in a heap at the bottom, howling. Scooping him up, she carried him into the room, cuddling him and kissing his tear-soaked cheeks.

"I hope he hasn't done something to himself," she said. "I didn't know he could climb out of the cot ...."

She looked at her uncle, hoping for some professional reassurance, but he was staring as if he had seen a ghost.

"D-did you call him Anshel?" he asked in a hoarse whisper.

"Yes," Golda Mirel said pointedly. "He's named after my father! Chaim Osher Anshel. We had to give him an additional name, due to the circumstances ...."

Golda Mirel nodded toward the pram, and added, "That one is Pessie."

"Pessie?" Berel said in a somewhat stupefied tone. "Your mother, too?"

Golda Mirel nodded.

"What happened to them?" Berel asked, his voice low.

"The Nazis shot them," Golda Mirel told him, looking at him directly.

"How can you possibly know that?" Berel asked desperately. "You didn't witness it! Maybe they escaped ...."

Golda Mirel shook her head sadly. "I heard it from my baby sister, Ettel," she said, and gave him the gist of Ettel's account. He seemed to shrink a little in front of her eyes, and his face, already pale, had turned a kind of translucent gray. Suddenly, he dropped his head into his hands and sat like that for a few moments. When he looked up he spoke in a hushed voice.

"You asked me to try and save them," he whispered, "and I refused. You must understand, I couldn't help it. I was afraid for myself!" He looked at her pleadingly. "Besides, how do we know it would have helped? Not everyone managed to get out ...."

He was clutching at straws and Golda Mirel felt desperately sorry for him. About to say something comforting, she stopped herself suddenly. *No, I probably shouldn't!* It wouldn't do him any good in the end. In the *Beis Din Shel Maalah*, there would be no excuses.

He stood up abruptly. "I'd better go," he said stiffly.

"Oh, please, don't go yet!" Golda Mirel cried, feeling she was losing some sort of opportunity but not quite sure what it was. Perhaps she could still persuade him to return to *Yiddishkeit*.

"You must be wondering why I came," he said. "I came to ask you a favor—two favors, in fact. But now, how can I? You'll probably refuse me outright. I deserve it after I refused *your* request!"

"Uncle Berel, I'm not a vengeful person!" Golda Mirel declared. "If there's anything I can do for you, you only have to ask."

Berel sat down again and clasped his hands on the table. "It's been years since I last saw my daughters," he said. "I want to see them ... before—"

"Of course you do, Uncle Berel!" Golda Mirel said quickly, not letting him finish the sentence. "I'll give you Heidi's phone number, so you can contact her."

"Could—would you mind doing it, Golda Mirel? She might slam the phone down on me."

Golda Mirel didn't argue with this reasoning, and promised to telephone Hindy as soon as she was home from her teaching job. "And I'll tell her to get in touch with Laura, too. But you said you had two requests. What's the other one?"

"The other one is more complicated. You know I haven't lived a Jewish life all these years." Berel avoided his niece's eyes. "I didn't even belong to a shul. Everyone thought we were *goyim*, but I don't want to be buried in a *goyishe* cemetery! Can you arrange something for me, please? I don't know how to go about it."

"Of course I can," Golda Mirel assured him, glad he still felt

Jewish at heart. Suddenly, she felt she must persuade him to do *teshuva* and end his days keeping the Torah again.

"Uncle Berel, it's not too late to start keeping the *mitzvos* again ..." she began.

Her uncle gave a sardonic smile. "Still the same, after all!" he commented. "I wondered how long it would be before you tried to reform me!"

"I'm only trying to help you," Golda Mirel protested.

"I know," Berel replied, immediately contrite. "I appreciate it. But I can't do what you suggest. It's too late for me. Even if I wanted to, it wouldn't really be fair to Thea—my wife. She's got enough to put up with just now, and since she's never been religious herself she wouldn't be able to cope with it."

The note of finality in his voice told Golda Mirel not to persist. He got up to go and Golda Mirel saw him out, repeating her promise to do anything he asked of her.

That afternoon, having reached Hindy, Golda Mirel broke the sad news to her cousin, and listened patiently as the convulsive sobs at the other end of the line subsided. Then she said softly, "Hindy, he wants to see you."

Hindy gulped. "Does he?" she asked, sounding doubtful. "He said he never wanted to see me again as long as he lived!"

"Yes," Golda Mirel said. "That was then. He's had a change of heart ... you can imagine why. Will you go?"

"Of course I will!" Hindy replied, still crying.

"I know it's a long way from Gateshead, but it would be a good idea to take the children. He would dearly love to see them ... and so would your mother, of course."

"Yes, you're right ...," Hindy said, her voice choked with emotion. "Perhaps Shimon will come, too."

"Will you contact your sister?" Golda Mirel asked. "He wants to see her, too."

"Of course, though I don't know how she'll take it. She was even closer to Daddy than I was …." Hindy began to cry again. Between racking sobs she thanked Golda Mirel and hung up.

For the next few weeks, Uncle Berel was seldom out of Golda Mirel's mind. Hindy had promised to keep her informed and, true to her word, she telephoned every time she came home from her trips to London.

"I could tell he was pleased to see me and the children," she reported after her first visit, "but he seems so sad and listless …."

"Well, what do you expect?" Golda Mirel sighed. "We have to keep davening for his *refuah*. I say *Tehillim* for him every day."

"Yes, so do I. And I mention his name when I say '*refaeinu*' … Yissochor Dov *ben* Mindel … as you told me to."

"*Der Eibershter zol helfen*," Golda Mirel said with feeling.

Some weeks later, Golda Mirel answered the telephone to a very agitated Hindy.

"Golda Mirel," she cried, "Daddy's been taken to the hospital! He took a turn for the worse last night!"

"Oh, Hindy! I'm so sorry!" Golda Mirel cried. "What happened? Was it sudden?"

"Yes, though the doctor told me that already a month ago he seemed to have lost the will to fight."

A month ago! That was just about when he had been to see her! Was it the visit that had taken the spirit out of him, or had the news of her parents' fate triggered off this downward spiral? For a moment, Golda Mirel felt terribly guilty. Then she consoled herself, recognizing that she could not have concealed the truth from him. All she could do now was say *Tehillim*.

The next few weeks were fraught with tension. Hindy and Laura had made arrangements for their children and were staying over in London, hardly leaving their father's bedside. Golda Mirel only visited once with Ettel, but although their uncle hardly acknowledged them, Golda Mirel had a feeling her presence was causing him some agitation. She resolved not to go again and stayed near the telephone at home, receiving daily updates from Hindy. At last, the dreaded call from a distraught Hindy came one late afternoon.

"Oh, Golda Mirel!" Hindy managed to say before dissolving in a flood of tears.

Golda Mirel's heart sank. "Hindy," she whispered, "is it … ? Has he … ?"

"Yes," Hindy sobbed, "about an hour ago!"

"Did he suffer very much?"

"It was very bad the last few days," Hindy told her somberly, "but in the end it was peaceful. He was very weak and could hardly speak, but just before … before … the end, he tried to lift his head and, Golda Mirel, the last words he said were *Shema Yisroel*! I couldn't phone you till now because I was having an argument with Mummy …" She broke off, weeping again.

"What about?" Golda Mirel asked.

"She … she … oh, Golda Mirel! She wants to have Daddy cremated!" Hindy cried, hardly managing to get the words out.

"*What!!*" Golda Mirel was aghast. "Why?"

"She says Daddy told her he doesn't want to be buried in a non-Jewish cemetery, so that, according to her, was the only solution …."

"Hindy, you must phone the *chevra kadisha* right away. I gave you the number …."

"Oh, please, Golda Mirel, could you do it?" Hindy pleaded. "Mummy won't let me out of her sight. Laura's distracted her now so I could phone you, but she's calling for me …"

"Yes, of course," Golda Mirel agreed, reaching for her telephone book.

For a long time after Uncle Berel's passing, Golda Mirel could not get the upsetting episode out of her mind. The *levayah* had been most pathetic. The only people present, besides Uncle Berel's wife and two daughters, had been Golda Mirel, Ettel and the men in their family, which, with the members of the *chevra kadisha*, was enough to make a *minyan*.

Hindy and Laura had wept copiously, both saddened as much by his cutting off all ties with them during his lifetime as by his death. Aunt Thea had stood alone in bitter silence. Golda Mirel had tried to speak to her, but she remained rigid and unapproachable. Even during the *shiva*, she avoided Golda Mirel, presumably blaming her for the years of estrangement from her daughters Hopefully, now, that breach would heal.

olda Mirel called out to Mindy, who was in the living room doing her homework—or so she thought. However, her young daughter's reply came from her room upstairs. Mildly surprised, she requested that the girl come down and set the table for supper.

When Mindy appeared in the kitchen, Golda Mirel stared at her, horrified. Her twelve-year-old daughter had changed out of her school uniform into some unfamiliar clothing. A purple and white polka-dotted blouse topped a narrow skirt. She had undone her plaited pigtails, and her long hair hung down loosely, framing her face.

"Mindy!" Golda Mirel cried. "What are you wearing? Where did you get that blouse? *I* never bought it for you!"

"It's Shoshy's," Mindy explained. "She lent it to me. We're all going to Sara Levine's house later to rehearse our choir."

"Well, you're not going in a borrowed blouse!" Golda Mirel declared. "And Tatty will have a fit if he sees your hair. You know he hates it loose. It's un-*tzniusdik* and it makes you look common!"

"But I hate my plaits!" Mindy protested. "They're so babyish!"

"If you don't like plaits, we'll have your hair cut short," her mother told her. "Now go change, and tie up your hair before Tatty comes home!"

Mindy knew she had no choice but to obey. Grumbling, she flounced out of the room, leaving Golda Mirel to set the table herself. As she laid out the plates, she fretted over her youngest child. The others had never behaved like that. Mindy was basically a good girl, but she tended toward rebellion. Golda Mirel remembered when Moshe Leib had discovered her reading a non-Jewish book on Shabbos, something he had forbidden her to do. There had been quite a row about it, with Mindy dissolving in tears, but she believed her daughter didn't break that rule again. Unless, it suddenly occurred to Golda Mirel, Mindy was deceiving them. She fervently hoped that was not the case.

An alarming thought suddenly struck her. Was history repeating itself? Was this Berel defying his parents all over again? If Uncle Berel had not turned up that afternoon, she might never have thought of it, but now that she had she was consumed with worry. She must take care to handle this the right way. But what *was* the right way? Zeide Wasserbrun had been strict and heavy-handed, but only succeeded in turning his son away. She had better not make the same mistake. On the other hand, too much softness would not do either. A young girl like Mindy needed to be disciplined.

I will have to give her much more attention, she thought. *Maybe, if I talk to her a lot and explain all the rights and wrongs, she will see things clearly in the end.*

Golda Mirel resolved to talk this over with Moshe Leib and decide with him how to handle the situation.

Another year passed by, with, *Baruch Hashem*, more *simchos* and *nachas* from Golda Mirel's children. It had also brought a new grandchild to the Steiners. Yankel and Tzivia had presented their family with a darling little girl named Matty, for Moshe Leib's mother.

There were just two things that worried Golda Mirel. One was the unpredictable behavior of Mindy, her youngest. She could be very sweet and pleasant at times, but there were moments when her rebellious streak reared its ugly head, causing scenes and usually ending in tears.

The other problem was the difficulty they were experiencing with a *shidduch* for Chuni. Golda Mirel could not understand it. There was nothing wrong with him and the *shadchanim* were trying their best, but either the girls in question didn't want a *chossid*—or someone without a *parnossoh*, or they didn't meet Chuni's criteria.

In the end, Golda Mirel herself found the right girl. Shopping one afternoon, she entered a local Jewish grocery just behind a young girl who was pushing an old lady in a wheelchair into the shop. There was something about the way the young girl spoke to her elderly charge that charmed Golda Mirel. The girl walked around, choosing things from the shelves and asking the woman in a sweet voice if they were what she wanted, patiently giving her a choice of two or three items.

What a nice girl! she thought, studying her and taking in the neatly pulled back auburn hair, and the heart-shaped face with that pleasant smile.

Their purchases selected, the girl brought the wheelchair up to the counter and helped the old woman select the correct amount of money. Then she wheeled the chair out of the shop, its occupant happily clutching the bag of groceries on her lap.

"Isn't it nice to see young people looking after their old grandparents," Golda Mirel remarked to the woman behind her in the queue.

"That's not her grandmother," the woman told her.

"No?" Golda Mirel was surprised. "Who is she then? And who is that girl, anyway?"

"Oh, that's Roisy Gelkorn. Lovely girl! Always doing *mitzvos*. That old lady is Mrs. Kahn, who lives next door to the Gelkorns. Roisy often takes her out."

Golda Mirel knew the Gelkorns. They were a Hungarian family who had come to England at about the same time as the Steiners, toward the end of 1937.

It suddenly occurred to Golda Mirel that this was just the kind of girl Chuni needed. Not one to waste time once the idea had come to her, she asked Elkie to make a few discreet enquiries and, after receiving a glowing report about the girl, she went straight to Reb Zalman Beckner, the *shadchan*, and asked him to carry out the *shidduch*.

Reb Zalman's face broke into a broad smile. "Do you know," he said, "I was going to suggest this *shidduch* to you myself!"

Oh yes? Golda Mirel thought in amusement. *Whom are you trying to fool?* However, she refrained from voicing the thought. *If he wants to present it as if it was his idea, let him,* she reflected. *What does it matter, as long as he's successful in bringing about the shidduch.*

And successful Reb Zalman certainly was! Within three weeks, the engagement between Elchonon Steiner and Roisy Gelkorn was announced!

Everyone was delighted and Golda Mirel's heart was full of gratitude. *Baruch Hashem*, that was another child settled! The only one fly in the ointment was Chuni's announcement that he planned to continue learning in his present yeshiva in Eretz Yisroel. He had discussed it with Roisy before the engagement was finalized and she had agreed. If Golda Mirel was disappointed that they wouldn't be living nearby, Mrs. Gelkorn was quite beside herself!

"I can't let my daughter go so far away!" she wailed. "When will I see her? And life is so hard there! It's still a fairly new state and you can hardly get anything! Besides, I'll be nervous with all those Arab countries around who could start a war any time!"

"Why look on the black side? They might not," Golda Mirel consoled her, although she herself felt worried. "You can't keep your children tied to your apron strings," she told her *mechuteniste* philosophically. "The important thing is that the young couple should be happy!"

"That's easy for you to say," Mrs. Gelkorn pointed out. "After all, Elchonon's been away from home till now. But my Roisy's always been near me. I'm bound to miss her!"

Golda Mirel had to admit that she had a point.

The *chassunah* and *sheva brochos* over, Chuni and Roisy departed, bag and baggage, to embark upon their new life. There were tears and hugs and expressions of good wishes all around as the two families came to the port to see them off. Then, after a few more waves and promises to write regularly, the ship began to sail, taking them away.

With her *mechuteniste* in such a tearful state, Golda Mirel resolved to visit her often and cheer her up—a resolution she kept, though not quite to the extent she had intended. Her mind—and, indeed, much of her time—was taken up with Mindy.

Hardly a day went by without some crisis arising. Having conferred and planned a strategy with Moshe Leib, Golda Mirel gave the situation her full attention. She spent as much time as she could talking to her daughter, very often just letting Mindy get her own feelings off her chest. However, there were times when she felt she was banging her head against a brick wall. Mindy would complain bitterly that she didn't understand, and that so-and-so's mother let *her* daughter do whatever it was *she* had been forbidden to do.

Occasionally, though, Golda Mirel did feel she was getting through to Mindy, which gave her the courage to persevere. However, she felt she would be more successful if her older daughter would refrain from interfering.

Elkie, in true "older sister" fashion, had an unfortunate way of putting in her oar. She constantly criticized Mindy and didn't stop lecturing her, which only set her younger sister's back up. She also tended to advise Golda Mirel on how *she* thought her mother ought to handle her. This really annoyed Golda Mirel, and one day she suddenly felt she had had enough.

"I wish you'd let me bring up my daughter my own way!" she snapped.

"Why, Mummy," Elkie protested, "I'm only trying to be helpful. I can probably see things more clearly because I'm not with her all the time …."

"I think I'm quite capable of giving my children the right *chinuch*!" Golda Mirel said huffily. "I didn't do such a bad job with you, did I?"

"Well, I hope not!" Elkie said, laughing. "But don't forget, you were younger then."

"Thank you very much!" By now Golda Mirel was really rattled. "So, I'm growing senile, am I?"

"Oh, Mummy! I'm sorry!" Elkie was remorseful at once. "I didn't mean that! On the contrary, you've always been the most understanding mother. It's just that I can't stand the way Mindy leads you and Tatty such a dance!"

"Don't worry about us," Golda Mirel told her, somewhat pacified. "We've worked out together how to deal with her, and hopefully we'll get there in the end."

"I'm sure you will!" Elkie said. "And I'll try not to interfere any more."

As time went by, things improved a little. Elkie tried to keep her opinions to herself, although Golda Mirel suspected that she did sneak in a lecture when her mother wasn't around. She had a feeling Yankel and Tzivia were doing the same. She couldn't confront them because Mindy never complained, but she often came back in a bad mood after babysitting for them.

In the summer of 1960, things really came to a head. Mindy, then sixteen, would graduate shortly and had been scheduled, much to her dissatisfaction, to start attending the local seminary after the holidays.

"Mummy," she said, coming home from school one afternoon looking starry-eyed. "We've had a brilliant idea for the summer holidays!"

"Oh, indeed? What's that?" Golda Mirel asked warily. The "brilliant ideas" thought up by Mindy and her friends often put her on the defensive.

"We want to take a flat at the seaside, Shoshy, Dina, Sara and me! It won't cost much if we share the rent, and Shoshy's father says he can—"

"Stop right there, Mindy!" Golda Mirel interrupted her emphatically. "The answer is NO!"

Mindy's face fell. "But, Mummy, why?"

"Just because!" Golda Mirel answered firmly. Then, realizing that was a mistake, she proceeded to explain to her daughter the dangers of young girls going off on their own, without being chaperoned by a responsible adult.

"Oh, rubbish!" Mindy exclaimed, disbelief on her face. "We're not babies!"

Determined not to lose her patience, Golda Mirel tried to convince Mindy with sensible arguments, but the girl remained resistant to reason.

"Tatty won't allow it!" Golda Mirel finished lamely.

"Tatty's even stricter than you!" Mindy cried bitterly. "Shoshy's father's not like that! He's even offered to find us a flat in Eastbourne!"

"*Your* father's not Shoshy's father!" Golda Mirel remarked. "And it's your father you have to obey!" Then, seeing the explosive expression on Mindy's face, she softened her tone. "Believe me, Mindy," she said, gently, "it's only your good we think about …."

"It's not!" Mindy threw at her. "You're just worried what other people will say! And I know what *my* friends are going to say! They'll make so much fun of me!"

Golda Mirel was about to point out that friends like that are not worth having, but she didn't get the chance. Mindy just burst into hysterical tears and ran out of the room, slamming the door behind her.

After a few days of watching Mindy walk about with a long face, hardly speaking and only picking at her food, Golda Mirel hit upon an idea. She put it to Moshe Leib, who admitted that it was worth a try.

"I'll have to phone Chuni and Roisy, though," Golda Mirel said practically. "If we write and wait for their reply, it'll be too late." Calls to Eretz Yisroel were only made for matters of importance, and since Chuni and Roisy did not have a telephone, they could only reach them through one of their neighbors who had that rare luxury.

Chuni and Roisy, at first alarmed at being summoned to the phone, were delighted with the suggestion that Mindy visit them for the summer holidays. Golda Mirel carefully warning that it might not be an easy time for them.

"It's all right, Mummy," Chuni said laughing. "I know my little sister! Don't worry, we'll cope. I hope she'll enjoy it, though. We don't have much time to take her around …."

"Yes, I realize that. In any case, I'm telling Mindy that we're sending her to help Roisy with the twins … and please make sure that she *does* help! I'll write you a letter explaining what brought all this on, so you'll know what you're up against."

Mindy was thrilled when she heard the news. A trip to Eretz Yisroel! Her friends would be green with envy! *And* she would be going by plane! That was really one-upmanship at its best!

"We will have to send her by plane," Moshe Leib had told his wife when they had discussed her journey. "I know it's madly expensive, but what can we do? We can't send a young girl off by herself on a ship, can we? It's a bit risky. If we take her to the airport and Chuni picks her up at the other end, there's not much she can get up to on the way."

Golda Mirel had been in total agreement, noting that if it did the trick, the expense would certainly be worth it!

The house was unnaturally quiet while Mindy was away. Golda Mirel missed her company, though she enjoyed the respite from arguments and tantrums. She hoped her daughter was having a good time and would come home with a healthier attitude toward life. She knew she couldn't have chosen two better people than her son and daughter-in-law for Mindy to be with, but still she worried. What if the child rebelled against them, too, and managed to sneak out behind their backs and seek different company ... the wrong kind of company ... ? The thought was far-fetched, she knew—Chuni and his wife were responsible, and would keep a proper check on her— but she couldn't entirely relax till Mindy was home again.

The weeks flew by, and today, Mindy's plane was due at four o'clock! Yankel had offered to bring his mother to the airport to fetch her, and as soon as she saw Mindy walking toward her, she knew she needn't have worried. Even Yankel noticed the difference in her.

"She looks really happy," he remarked to his mother. "She must have enjoyed herself."

Mindy had a lot to tell them, talking excitedly all the way home. She raved about her adorable nephew and niece, Shragi and Gitty, the two-year-old twins. She recounted their various antics, bringing a tender smile to Golda Mirel's lips. At home, with both parents an avid audience, Mindy couldn't stop going on and on. She began to describe the delicate beauty of Eretz Yisroel, the subtle tints of the foliage and the misty golden expanses delighting your eye when you came to the top of a steep road. She marveled at the interesting, dedicated way of life led by the inhabitants of Bnei Brak. She was full of praise for Chuni and Roisy, complimenting Roisy enthusiastically.

"I don't know how she does it!" she told them. "She's always got a house full of guests—and you should see what kind of people they are. All sorts of *nebachs* who have nowhere else to go. Roisy puts herself out to make sure they get plenty to eat. Some of them haven't got the best table manners, either, but she and Chuni make them all feel important."

"Yes," Golda Mirel said with satisfaction, "that's just what Chuni wanted."

"But even though she's so busy," Mindy went on, "she's so much fun. Whenever we were busy in the kitchen, we played some hilarious word games. It was great! Do you know what she's organized in Bnei Brak? A group of young women who get together every week, with their housework! They just bring it along. Sometimes she takes all her mending and other times she takes a big bag of vegetables and a peeler and comes home with a whole bowlful of peeled and cut vegetables! Isn't that original?"

Golda Mirel beamed as she listened, proud of her excellent choice of a daughter-in-law. "Did you talk to her a lot?" she probed.

"You know … about this and that, and about life in general? She's quite a deep person, isn't she?"

"Yes, we had lots of serious chats," Mindy said, fortunately not aware that this had been the object of the exercise. "She made me see things in such a different light." She paused and took a long, thoughtful breath, exhaling slowly. She looked straight into her mother's eyes and said, "I've been quite selfish till now, haven't I? But I'm going to try to be more like her!"

Her words warmed Golda Mirel's heart, though she knew they were mostly spoken in the excitement of the moment. No doubt her enthusiasm would wear off after a while. A person doesn't just change overnight. All the same, it was a step in the right direction. Now it was up to her to carry on the good work, and hopefully she would help mold her daughter into a better person.

With Mindy still on a high, the next few days were very pleasant. Golda Mirel felt her tension easing a little, only to have her doubts stirred up again abruptly when Mindy's friend Shoshy stopped in one afternoon.

"Hi, Mindy! *Sholom Aleichem!*" Shoshy cried, stepping into the hall. "How was your trip?" Her voice was exceptionally loud and boisterous, and Golda Mirel, busy in the kitchen, could hear every word she was saying.

"It was fabulous!" Mindy told her friend. "How was your holiday?"

"Oh, we had a whale of a time! Do you know, we never ever went to bed before three in the morning!"

"Wow! What did you do all the time?" Mindy asked, fascinated.

"Oh, you know. Singing, dancing, playing games. Generally acting crazy! It was fun!"

"What was the flat like?" Mindy asked, a feeling of regret creeping in. Maybe she had missed something after all.

"The first one was nice …," Shoshy began.

"The first one? Were there two? I didn't know you'd booked two different flats."

"We didn't!" Shoshy told her, amusement in her voice. "But we were chucked out of the original one. The landlady was a bit of a battleaxe! We were only having fun. It was Dina's birthday so we had a party for her. We were just enjoying ourselves, noshing and singing silly songs. Then, of course, we started dancing and suddenly old Mrs. Crosspatch thumps at the door and asks us what we thought we were doing, making all that noise in the middle of the night. 'It's not the first time,' she said, 'and I've 'ad enough! You'd all better be out of 'ere, first thing in the morning!' We didn't have any choice— she might have called the police—so the next day was spent searching for another flat.

"We found one in the end, but it wasn't very nice. The other tenants were a weird lot. We were a bit scared of them but they left us in peace. They made so much noise themselves that they didn't seem to mind ours. Not like that spoilsport of a landlady in the other flat!"

"You must have made a bit of a *chillul Hashem*," Mindy commented, more out of a "sour grapes" attitude than anything else.

"Hey, since when have you gone so *heilig*?" Shoshy exclaimed. Then she added defensively, "We never meant any harm. We were just having fun! Anyway, how did you get on in Eretz Yisroel? Are you an expert in changing nappies already?" Her tone was condescending.

Stung by her words, Mindy tried to convince her that she had enjoyed herself, but Shoshy didn't seem interested. "I must fly," Shoshy announced suddenly. "I've got to pick up my photos from the chemist before it shuts. I'll bring them in to show you sometime." She hurried out through the door, giving Mindy a cheerful wave from the gate.

With a sinking feeling, Golda Mirel waited for her daughter to come into the kitchen, not sure what she was going to say to her. But Mindy ran straight upstairs to her room, slamming the door loudly. *So that's that!* Golda Mirel thought unhappily. *The whole thing has collapsed, like a pack of cards! There isn't any point in me trying to talk to her. She'll never listen …*

The atmosphere in the house had suddenly turned gloomy. Mindy mooched around the house all day, doing nothing. She wasn't even preparing herself for her start at the seminary, and Golda Mirel feared she would suddenly announce that she wasn't going. *How would I cope with that?* she wondered.

It was a few days later when Mindy came slinking into the kitchen and stood beside her mother at the counter. There was an unfathomable expression on her face. "Thank you, Mummy," she said suddenly in a timid voice.

"Thank me? For what?" Golda Mirel asked, nonplussed.

"For not letting me go to Eastbourne," Mindy replied simply, the look in her deep blue eyes saying more than her words.

Chapter 25

Coming home from Menachem Dovid's *chassunah* in the early hours of the morning, Golda Mirel still felt she had to pinch herself to believe it! She had been sure that her youngest son would be the hardest of all to marry off, yet here he was, just twenty-one and married to the first person suggested!

Wealthy businessman Mechel Fischberg had been determined to find an outstanding *talmid chochom* for his only daughter, and when Menachem Dovid's name came up, he had made enquiries and received an excellent report from the boy's *Rosh haYeshiva*. Later, when he came to *farherr* him, he was even more convinced he had found what he was looking for. Avigayil, his daughter, had been most impressed when, during their meetings, Menachem Dovid told her about the *sefer* he was writing. He became quite animated when he spoke about it, and Avigayil had visions of him becoming famous, picturing herself basking in his reflected glory.

Golda Mirel had been delighted with the engagement. An outgoing, vivacious girl like Avigayil was just what Menachem Dovid needed to bring him out of himself, she declared. The family, in general, agreed with her, with the exception of Tante Fanny, who, in her usual outspoken manner, expressed open disapproval.

"I don't see it working out," she announced pessimistically to Golda Mirel. "She's too lively for him—and, frankly, rather empty within!"

Unwilling to put a damper on her pleasure, Golda Mirel ignored her remark. Old people tended to be overcritical, and Tante Fanny, though remarkably clear-headed for her age, was, after all, already ninety-two!

Once Menachem Dovid's *chassunah* was behind them, Golda Mirel and Moshe Leib found their thoughts turning to Mindy. Golda Mirel argued that she wasn't ready to get married yet, though she had come a long way since the day she had suddenly seen her empty-headed friends in their true light.

"At any rate," Golda Mirel said, "I wouldn't mind a short rest from *shidduchim* for a while. I seem to have been doing nothing else for the last few years!"

"That's what happens when your children grow up!" Moshe Leib told her laughingly. "But you're right about Mindy. We probably should wait a bit longer."

Yet Golda Mirel did not get the relief she had planned from the subject of *shidduchim*. It was not long before she was enmeshed, albeit indirectly, in a drama concerning a *shidduch*.

It started with a phone call from her sister Ettel. Although Ettel lived quite near her, Golda Mirel did not see her very often. Ever since Ettel had opened a milliner's in Stamford Hill, making most of the hats herself, she was so busy they had to be content with visits on Shabbos and a few phone calls during the week. This time, however, Golda Mirel could tell that it was not merely for a sisterly chat that Ettel had telephoned.

"Golda Mirel, can I come around to your house later? There's something I'd like to discuss with you, and I'd rather not do it over the phone."

"Of course," Golda Mirel replied, realizing that if her sister didn't start the conversation talking about her daughter Goldie or her son Mordche, who were both married, it must be something important. "If it's a private matter, the best time to come is after six, when Mindy goes to her typing lesson."

"Good. I'll come in as soon as I've closed the shop. See you then," Ettel said, hanging up.

A minute after six, on the dot, Ettel was ringing the doorbell. The sisters settled comfortably on the sofa, and Ettel launched into her problem without further ado.

"The thing is," she said, setting down her cup of tea, "someone has suggested a *shidduch* for Ari, and I'd like your opinion."

"Certainly, if I'm able to give it," Golda Mirel said. "Tell me who it is."

"You know Mrs. Redner … ?"

"Charna Leah? Of course I do. But she hasn't any children of her own! … only that girl she adopted … Oh, I see!" Golda Mirel stopped short, comprehension dawning.

"Exactly! What do you think of it? I don't really know the girl." Ettel eyed her sister searchingly.

"Well I do, and she's a nice girl. An *exceptionally* nice girl," she added emphatically. "Quiet and refined, with good *midos*. And she seems intelligent, too."

"You sound just like Mrs. Wickler, the *shadchente*!" Ettel laughed.

"So why are you hesitating?" Golda Mirel asked.

"I'm not really," Ettel told her. "It's just that … well … I feel as if she only suggested it because she knows Ari's adopted, too, so—it's a perfect match!"

"So what? She's a nice girl and Ari's a good boy," Golda Mirel's tone was practical. "Isn't that what matters?"

"Yes, that's what Kalman says. He's all for it. I just wanted to hear your opinion."

"Well, I think you should go ahead," Golda Mirel encouraged. "*Ess zoll zein mit mazel!*"

Ettel went to meet the Redners' adopted daughter, Esther, and was captivated. The girl was modest and refined, with a sweet, shy smile and a look of sincerity in her gray-blue eyes. Her attire was attractive yet simple, her soft brown hair held back by a velvet hairband.

The two women had discussed their children's backgrounds before the meeting. Ettel had been able to reassure Mrs. Redner about Ari's identity, telling her how he had been rescued.

Mrs. Redner sighed. "I wish I could be just as informative about Esther," she said forthrightly. "We don't know that much about her. We approached the Agudah after the war about possibly adopting a Jewish orphan They suggested this adorable three-year-old girl from the Jewish orphanage. They were certain she was Jewish. The person who registered her had been told by the woman who was looking after her before being taken ill that her mother had died of starvation in the camp because she couldn't bring herself to eat the *treife* food. Once we heard that, we were happy to take her."

Listening to Mrs. Redner's narrative, Ettel began to have misgivings. Was it right to accept someone with such an obscure background for Ari? Would the Altsteins have wanted this for their son? She had some responsibility to them, after all. But when Esther entered the room, something inside her seemed to melt. She felt instinctively that this girl was the perfect match for her adopted son.

"I just couldn't say 'no'," she told Golda Mirel later. "That girl just stole my heart!"

"I know just what you mean," Golda Mirel agreed. "So? What's next?"

"I've telegrammed to Ari to come home from yeshiva, and I'm waiting for his reply. As soon as I know when he's coming, I'll make arrangements with Mrs. Redner for them to meet." There was suppressed excitement in Ettel's voice.

Upon his meeting Esther, Ari told his parents that he was agreeable, and Esther gave the Redners the same answer. However, both sets of parents unanimously felt it would be prudent to have at least one more meeting, to make absolutely sure. The following evening, after an hour of earnest conversation, the two young people joined their parents in the morning-room, their faces radiating happiness.

"Well?" Mrs. Redner asked. "Is it *mazel tov?*"

"Not just yet," Ari told her.

"You mean you want another meeting?" There was surprise in Mrs. Redner's voice.

"Not at all," Ari explained. "We didn't even need this one! I just need to get my Rebbi's *haskomoh* ...."

"Very well. You should get a *brochoh* from a Rebbe, but why should that hold things up? We can drink '*lechayim*' and announce the engagement, and you can get your *brochoh* afterward." Mrs. Redner sounded annoyed.

"Please forgive me, Mrs. Redner," Ari said apologetically, "but my Rebbi has been my mentor since I was fifteen, and I never make a serious decision without consulting him."

Mr. Redner turned to Ari. "Would you like to send the telegram now? The phone is just behind you, on the wall."

"Thank you." Ari took the phone, and with everyone listening intently he began to dictate the message, transliterating the *loshon kodesh* words into English letters for the operator. "Aharon *ben* Rifka," he said at the end, "v'Esther *bas ... bas ...* ?" He looked around questioningly.

"Charna Leah!" Mrs. Redner prompted immediately.

"No, no! That's not right!" her husband said hastily. There was a loaded silence in the room, everyone looking baffled. Ari quickly turned back to the phone. "That's the message," he said, giving his parents' address for a reply.

The atmosphere in the room was tense and subdued.

"Well! We should get an answer in a few days, and we'll have the '*lechayim*' then," said Ettel to lighten the mood.

"Right!" Mrs. Redner brightened up at once. "That should give me plenty of time to do lots of baking for the *vort*!"

Golda Mirel was piping cream onto a gateau when the telephone rang, as it had a habit of doing when she was busy with both hands! Sighing, she put down the piping-bag and went to answer it.

"Golda Mirel," Ettel's voice over the line sounded almost ominous. "We got the reply from Ari's Rebbi …."

Golda Mirel held her breath. Ettel didn't sound very excited. "Is it *mazel tov*?" she asked tentatively.

"No! It's not!" Ettel sounded near to tears. "It sounds as if it's never going to be."

"The Rebbe wasn't *maskim* to the *shidduch*?"

"No, the telegram doesn't quite say that," Ettel said. "We don't really know what it means."

"Why? What does it say?"

"Let me read it to you …" There was a rustling, then Ettel read. "*M'zoll zich nochfregen wegen ihr mishpocho.* That's all it says! What does he mean, Golda Mirel, 'we should enquire about her family'? Nobody knows who her family was. How can we make enquiries?"

Not knowing how to answer that, Golda Mirel asked, "What does Ari say?"

"He says the Rebbe apparently thinks the *shidduch* is not *bashert,* so as far as he's concerned, that's the end of it. But he's absolutely heartbroken, I can tell!"

"Perhaps you *can* find out who she is," Golda Mirel suggested.

"Maybe …," Ettel didn't sound very hopeful, "but I'm inclined to think that maybe there is something wrong with the family she comes from."

"You might be right," Golda Mirel agreed. "Perhaps she's not even Jewish!"

"Oh, Golda Mirel!" Ettel wailed. "I've got to go break the news to the Redners. I don't know how they're going to take it!"

The Redners certainly were not pleased. "I just don't believe this!" Mrs. Redner's face was scarlet with fury. "How can you do this to a girl? It will break her heart!"

"I know …," Ettel agreed miserably. "Ari feels the same …."

"Oh, I'm sure he does!" Mrs. Redner's tone was loaded with sarcasm. "That's why he'll drop her, just like that, because some Rebbi tells him to!"

"It's not like that …," Ettel began to protest. "Perhaps we can make enquiries …."

"Why should we? *We* know there's nothing wrong with her." Mrs. Redner looked huffily at Ettel. "Frankly, I wouldn't agree to this *shidduch* now if you begged me on bended knees!"

At a loss for words, Ettel shrugged helplessly.

"And don't think *you'll* easily find someone for your son!" Mrs. Redner went on, mercilessly. "He's also an unknown quantity …."

"No, he's not!" Ettel protested, stung. "I knew his parents! They were wonderful people. They were named—"

"I'm not in the least bit interested!" Mrs. Redner interrupted her. "And no one else will be, either. Mark my words! A name means nothing when it comes to *shidduchim*. People like to know more about a boy's family than that! See if I'm not right!"

Ettel had heard enough. She stood up, mumbling, "I guess there's nothing more to say ...," and left.

She went straight to Golda Mirel's house to lick her wounds, repeating the whole upsetting conversation into her older sister's sympathetic ears.

"Is it true?" she asked her finally. "Will it be hard to find him a *shidduch*?"

"I don't see why," Golda Mirel said comfortingly.

"Well, would *you* consider such a *shidduch*, for instance? Supposing someone suggested a war orphan for your Mindy, how would you feel about it?"

"If I knew he came from a good Jewish family, I wouldn't be bothered.

"Thank you, Golda Mirel," Ettel said, standing up. "You've made me feel better ...." Golda Mirel could suddenly see the young, vulnerable little sister Ettel had once been!

"Now, don't worry, Ettel," she said soothingly. "I'm sure he'll find his right *zivug* soon!"

After that, the subject was closed. Ari went back to his yeshiva in Eretz Yisroel, and life carried on as normal.

Two weeks before Pesach, Golda Mirel was hanging up her newly-washed dining room curtains when she spotted Ettel coming up her garden path. Knowing how busy her sister was in the shop before *Yom Tov*, she could hardly conceal her surprise as she hurriedly climbed down from the ladder and ran to the door.

"Ettel! What's up? Aren't you madly busy just now?"

"I am," Ettel told her, "but I had to speak to you before Mindy gets home. Golda Mirel, do you remember our conversation after my confrontation with Mrs. Redner?"

Golda Mirel screwed up her eyes in concentration. "Oh, yes. You wanted to know if I would ever consider someone who—"

"Exactly!" Ettel interrupted. "At the time, it was just a rhetorical question. But this afternoon, it suddenly struck me! Why not? It would be the ideal *shidduch*!"

"You mean your Ari and my Mindy?" Golda Mirel stared at her. "But they're cousins!"

"Not really!" Ettel said, sounding triumphant.

"No, you're right. They're not." Golda Mirel agreed.

"Well, then … ?"

"But … Mindy isn't ready for a *shidduch* yet!" Golda Mirel protested. "We've decided to wait a bit with her."

Ettel looked away. "I see," she said dejectedly. "That's the standard excuse!"

"Not at all!" Golda Mirel objected. "We couldn't wish for a better son-in-law than Ari, if we thought Mindy was ready for it. You know how much trouble we had with her …."

"But she's changed a lot!" Ettel insisted. "She's a different girl these days."

"Yes, that's true," Golda Mirel conceded, glad to hear her sister say it. Mindy really had improved a lot. She was still headstrong by nature and liked to get her own way, but her values had changed. She had been a diligent seminary student and now she took her teaching job seriously. She had also become meticulous regarding *mitzvos*—to the point of being dubbed "the little Rebbitzen" by her siblings. Perhaps, after all, Golda Mirel mused, there was no reason to wait ….

"Let me talk it over with Moshe Leib," she told her sister.

"And I'll discuss it with Kalman. Ari will be home for Pesach in two days. Let me sound him out when he's here, and I'll let you know his reaction."

"Right! I won't say a word to Mindy till I hear from you," Golda Mirel said, feeling a flutter of excitement inside her. The idea was beginning to grow on her, and over the next two days, she found herself building castles in the air.

When Ettel telephoned, she felt the thrill rising up again.

"Golda Mirel, have you spoken to Mindy yet?" Ettel asked.

"No, she's not home yet. Shall I do it when she comes?"

"No, hold it for a while," Ettel said, her voice sounding strange. "Something's cropped up …."

"What?" Golda Mirel asked, her heart sinking.

"I've just had a visit from Mrs. Redner," Ettel told her, sounding bemused. "Let me tell you about it …. I was so amazed to see her on my doorstep! She told me how frightened she had been for Esther when she realized how difficult *shidduchim* were going to be, after our incident. They had decided they had better try to discover more about her origins. They had contacted the Agudah office and procured the name of the woman who had turned her in to them.

"Apparently, it was a young woman, a Freda Beckman, who had been newly married at the start of the war and whose husband had been killed before her eyes, poor thing! *Baruch Hashem*, she managed to survive the concentration camp and ended up in a Displaced Persons camp, where she met a woman with a young baby girl. This woman told her it was not her child, but her mother had died and she had been looking after her. She told Mrs. Beckman that she did not think she had long to live, and Mrs. Beckman took the baby. But, since she was going to America, Mrs. Beckman contacted the Agudah to take charge of the child.

"Now, hear this piece of *Hashgochoh Protis*! The Agudah official found a letter from Mrs. Beckman in the child's file, telling them she had married a diamond merchant named Firman and now lived in Antwerp. She had written because she felt she had abandoned the child and wanted to know what had happened to her. So the Redners contacted Mrs. Firman, but unfortunately, the woman in the DP camp hadn't told her anything about the baby's family."

Golda Mirel was beginning to wonder what all this was leading to, but Ettel's voice sounded very excited, and she continued. "Just today, Mrs. Firman telephoned them! Apparently, she belongs to a *bikur cholim* organization in Antwerp that brings kosher food to people in hospitals, and she was at a nursing home in Brussels and met a woman who had been in Auschwitz with Esther's mother! She remembers her very clearly!

"Now Mrs. Redner wants me to accompany her to Brussels to speak to this woman. So you see, Golda Mirel, everything depends on this trip to Brussels." Ettel continued apologetically, "I hope you understand. I'm very fond of Mindy and I didn't really want this to happen. But I feel that I've got to do this for Ari's sake. There seemed to have been some sort of bond ..." She broke off, embarrassed. "I know it sounds strange, for a *chassidishe* boy, but there it is."

"I understand," Golda Mirel said, hoping Ettel could not detect her disappointment. Her one thought was, *I'm glad I didn't tell Mindy anything about it after all!*

Chapter 26

A modern three-story building, surrounded by well-kept lawns and conifer trees, housed the Brussels nursing home that Ettel and Mrs. Redner visited. The atmosphere inside the home was one of orderliness and efficiency, yet without the clinical air of a hospital.

The two women, led by Mrs. Firman, were ushered into an airy, bright room, with sunlight streaming through a wide picture window. In sharp contrast, the woman in the bed looked pale and listless, propped up on her pillows, her hands resting limply on the covers.

"Good afternoon, Mrs. Reimer," Mrs. Firman said, going up to the bed and placing a hand gently over one of the woman's hands. "I've brought the two ladies I told you about. You said you wouldn't mind telling them about the baby in the camp … and her poor mother …"

Mrs. Reimer nodded weakly, eyeing her visitors with interest. "Of course," she said, speaking in Yiddish, "I'll answer their questions as well as I remember."

"Good," Mrs. Firman said, patting Mrs. Reimer's hand. "I'll leave you to it, then. I'll be back later on with your supper …."

With a nod toward Ettel and her companion and a cheerful wave to Mrs. Reimer, she left the room.

Ettel regarded the woman in the bed apprehensively. She looked so frail and ill, how could they bombard her with questions about a painful period in her life? Tentatively, the two women approached the bed and sat down on the two chairs beside it.

Ettel began, a little uncertainly, "Mrs. Firman said you have a lot to tell us ...."

"About the baby and her mother ...," Mrs. Redner prompted, taking up the lead.

"Yes," Mrs. Reimer said. "I can remember it all so clearly ...."

Her voice was faint and her breathing labored. They had to lean over closely to catch every word, but they managed to get the gist of Mrs. Reimer's narrative as she recounted how a terrified young woman was brought in, clutching a blanket with something inside. It did not take long for the other women in the dank, musty barrack to realize it was a baby.

"She was so afraid the baby would be taken away from her and harmed," Mrs. Reimer said, going on to describe how they had all instinctively rallied round looking for a good hiding place, which they eventually found with some difficulty.

"When we were alone at night, she would nurse the baby and cuddle her, but in the early hours of the morning, when we were roughly driven out to work, she had to leave the child hidden. It was so hard for her to tear herself away, and she was often brutally beaten before she would go.

"Poor thing! She was young and healthy when she first came in, but within a few weeks she became thin and weak. She would give her baby the small amount of water we were allowed and she refused to eat the meager meals we were offered, declaring that nothing would induce her to eat *treife* food.

"We begged her, telling her that we would also not eat meat, if they ever gave us any, but she should at least eat the soup—if you could call it soup! She refused, insisting that it was just as *treife!*"

Tears stood in Mrs. Reimer's eyes. "It was not long before her strength gave out. Before she was *niftar*, she begged Masha Liebenthal to look after her little Esty. Masha promised and she tried so hard, but it was terribly difficult! She could hardly find anything to feed her with, even though we all gave her a bit of our rations …."

"It puzzles me," Mrs. Redner interrupted, "how such a small baby managed to survive at all in a place like that!"

"Yes, indeed!" Mrs. Reimer agreed. "I still think it was a miracle! The *Eibershter* must have sent a *malach* to look after her while she was left hidden and alone, because she never seemed to cry. As long as her mother was there to nurse her, she seemed to thrive. But once the poor little mite was left motherless, she began to look pale and thin. And then, the strangest thing happened!"

The sick woman's audience sat rapt as she continued. "The Kommandant in charge of our unit was a cruel, hard woman named Ulrike, *yemach shemah*. She drove us relentlessly, beating and kicking us if we dared to slack a bit from our work. We tried our hardest to keep little Esty hidden from her, dreading to think what she would do to her if she discovered her! Then one day, she came in unexpectedly, while Masha was trying to get some of the revolting soup into Esty.

"'Whose baby is that?' Ulrike snapped.

"Nobody answered her and she immediately picked up her whip and advanced toward Masha and the baby. Fearing she would strike the baby, Masha quickly told her the truth.

"'Aha! A motherless baby! Give her to me!' She snatched the baby out of Masha's arms and looked down at her with a strange sort of smile. 'I like this infant, even if she is rather skinny! From now on, she belongs to me!'

"We were appalled! We had been afraid that she would kill the child, but this was even worse! She would bring her up as a *goy*! We looked on silently, knowing there was nothing we could do. 'I can't take her now,' Ulrike went on. 'I have to stay here and make sure all you lazy, good-for-nothings do your work properly, but in a few months, my time of service ends, and I will take her home with me. Meanwhile, you …,' she pointed to Masha, 'will have to look after her. I will bring you some milk to give her every day … and I warn you, if any of you try to drink some of it, you will be shot!'

"Masha looked after the baby, with Ulrike coming in from time to time to see how she was doing. If the child as much as whimpered, Ulrike would whip Masha, saying she was neglecting her. Poor Masha! She soon began to look weak and ill. I was so afraid she was going to die and I would be left alone with the baby. All the other women had either died or been moved and we were the only two left. I was only a young girl at the time and I was afraid of the responsibility.

"Then, one morning, we heard a bit of a commotion and all of a sudden Ulrike rushed in, looking pale, a large travel-bag in her hand.

"'Quick! Give me the child!' she cried. For some inexplicable reason, Masha refused to obey and Ulrike reached for her gun. Before she had a chance to raise it, an American soldier rushed in and grabbed hold of her, pulling her hands behind her back. We were so stunned, we didn't know whether to laugh or cry! Then more soldiers arrived and they gave us food, which we were told to take very slowly. They told us that they had come to rescue us and were taking us to a safe place. Masha and I never saw each other again after that. Being ill and having a baby with her, Masha was taken to one Displaced Persons camp and I, being young, went to another one. I often wondered what had happened to her and the baby. When Freda Firman told me that Masha had died in the DP camp," there was deep sadness in Mrs. Reimer's voice, "and that little Esty had been adopted by a family in London, I was relieved."

"Namely, us ...," Mrs. Redner said softly.

Ettel then remembered to ask the most important question. "Mrs. Reimer," she said, "do you know the baby's mother's name?"

"Of course I do. I have a good memory for names. It was Rifka ... Rifka Altstein."

"*Altstein!!*" The shriek escaped from Ettel before she could stop herself. The room began to spin round. She sank into her chair, looking white.

"Mrs. Davinsky!" Mrs. Redner cried, jumping up. "Ettel! What's the matter? Are you all right?" Her voice full of alarm, she bent over Ettel solicitously. "Y-yes ...," Ettel said slowly, making an effort to pull herself together. "It was the shock ... Rifka Altstein!"

Mrs. Reimer eyed Ettel with curiosity. "You knew Rifka?" she whispered.

Still looking dazed, Ettel said in a whisper, "Rifka Altstein was Ari's mother!"

"You mean ... ?" Mrs. Redner exclaimed in shock. "You mean Esther's mother and Ari's mother were one and the same person? But that makes them—"

"Exactly! They are brother and sister!"

"And they nearly got married!" Mrs. Redner commented in an awed, hushed voice.

Their conversation was suddenly cut short by the squeaky sound of wheels as the nurse entered the room. She regarded the two women disapprovingly.

"I am very worried about Mrs. Reimer," she said, speaking in French, which Ettel, having lived in Paris, easily understood. "You have made her too excited, and you have been here too long. Please leave now!"

As she turned to plump up her patient's pillows, Mrs. Reimer tugged urgently at her sleeve. She did, indeed, feel completely drained and exhausted, but she didn't want her visitors to go away without her knowing what all the drama was about.

"Please, nurse," she said imploringly, "let them stay a little longer."

The nurse frowned and shook her head, but, "Very well," she said, relenting. "Another five minutes, then." She began to wheel the trolley to the door. "And no more than that!" she added sternly, going out.

"Mrs. Reimer," Ettel said, "did Rifka talk about any other children?"

"Yes, she had a little boy named Ari, and she was terribly worried about him. She told us that when they were being taken away, a *goy* whom she knew and had always trusted ... Vidor something-or-other ... grabbed hold of him and took him away. She hoped it was to save his life ... Oh!" Mrs. Reimer gasped suddenly. "Oh, no!" All at once, without warning, she began to cry. "I didn't do as she asked!" she wailed, between sobs. "Why didn't I? I was the only one left ... and she trusted me! And now the *Ribono Shel Olam* is punishing me!" She dissolved in a flood of tears.

Ettel and Mrs. Redner bent over her, unable to bear her distress and wondering what had brought it on.

"Mrs. Reimer ... please!" Mrs. Redner begged, "This isn't good for you! Please tell us why you are so upset!"

"There is something I neglected to do," Mrs. Reimer said, making a great effort to calm down, "and now I am getting punished!"

"Tell us," Ettel prompted.

"Before Rifka died, she begged us to go to Budapest when the war was over to find her Ari. If this Vidor *had* done this to save him, he would probably keep him and look after him, but she didn't want him to be brought up as a *goy*—not even knowing he was a *Yid*! Oh, why didn't I do it? I was the only one who could!" She began to become agitated again. "Oh, Rifka, forgive me!"

"Mrs. Reimer, please don't be distressed!" Ettel cried. "You have no reason to be! Ari has been brought up as a fine *yiddishe* boy, just as Rifka would have wanted …."

"W-what do you mean?" There was a hopeful look in Mrs. Reimer's eyes.

"It was just as Rifka thought. Vidor Koják did rescue Ari, but he handed him straight over to me and he's my adopted son!"

Tears began to course down Mrs. Reimer's cheeks, but this time they were tears of relief. "*Baruch Hashem! Baruch Hashem!*" she cried. "Thank you so much for telling me! I would have had it on my conscience forever!"

Realizing that their time was almost up, Ettel quickly put Mrs. Reimer in the picture, explaining why the information she had given them was so important. She had just finished when the nurse returned, looking at her watch and eyeing them sternly.

"Yes, yes, we're going," Ettel told her, standing up. "Well, good-bye, Mrs. Reimer. I know this has been very tiring for you and we're really sorry, but we can't thank you enough …."

"Thank me? I should be thanking you! You've taken a great weight off my mind!" Her voice, though very feeble, had a more positive ring to it. "Could I ask you a favor?"

"Of course!" Mrs. Redner said emphatically, "Anything you want!"

"Would you both *daven* for me … Yehudis *bas* Freidel … that a donor is found soon, so I can have the kidney transplant I badly need."

"Most definitely we will!" they both promised and, wishing her a *refuah sheleimah*, they took their leave. At the door, they turned to wave and saw that, her energy spent, she was lying back with her eyes closed, but her breathing was even and there was a gentle smile of contentment hovering about her lips.

"Imagine if they'd have gotten married!" exclaimed Mrs. Redner on the way back to London. "Ari's Rebbi certainly saved him from disaster!"

"Indeed, he did!" Ettel agreed triumphantly, resisting the urge to voice the comment that was on the tip of her tongue.

"I really owe Ari an apology," Mrs. Redner said, as if reading her thoughts. "I wonder what they'll say when they hear!"

"So do I. Ari's coming home from yeshiva tomorrow. I just can't wait to tell him—and my husband and children, too."

It occurred to Ettel suddenly that there was someone else who would be excited at the news. Her sister Golda Mirel!

Ari's first reaction was enormous gratitude to his Rebbe. The cryptic message in the Rebbe's telegram had not only prevented him from entering into a forbidden marriage—it had led to the discovery of a genuine sister of his own! Although he felt affection for his adoptive siblings, he had always known they were not really his flesh-and-blood, and the knowledge that there *was* someone who was gave him tremendous joy! Although his sister was part of the Redner family, he was nevertheless determined to play the role of protective older brother as much as he could.

Esther, however, reacted quite differently. Raised as an only child, she had never experienced a sibling relationship and didn't know what sisterly feelings meant. She only knew she had felt drawn toward Ari, unaware that this was because of the blood-tie between them. When her mother and Ettel had gone to Brussels, she had secretly cherished a hope that something would come to light enabling them to get married. Now that this was completely unrealistic, she couldn't identify her feelings for him, and felt a pang of jealousy when he became engaged to Mindy Steiner. Worst of all was when he'd come to visit her. He tried to engage her in personal discussions, acting in a free and easy manner, which embarrassed her acutely. She was quite relieved when he went back to yeshiva. His letters, too, were written in a frank and open style, and Esther barely skimmed through them before crumpling them up and throwing them away.

Mrs. Redner began to worry about her. Her pleasant, carefree daughter had become withdrawn and moody. She couldn't even get the girl interested in looking for an outfit to wear at Ari's *chassunah*! She also appeared to be avoiding Mindy, who went out of her way to befriend her future sister-in-law.

"I don't know what's gotten into her," Mrs. Redner confided to Ettel one day. "It's so unlike her!"

"It's probably still shock reaction," Ettel suggested understandingly. "Give her time, Charna Leah. I'm sure she'll adjust to it soon."

However, as the weeks went by, no change was noticeable.

At the kindergarten where Esther worked, it became obvious that something was wrong. Rebbitzen Melnik, the principal, decided to tackle her about it. At first Esther denied any problem, but when the Rebbitzen held her gaze with solemn eyes, her reserve broke down and she suddenly burst into tears, pouring her heart out to her sympathetic employer. The principal listened with astonishment, realizing this was a delicate matter requiring the utmost diplomacy.

"We can't really discuss this here," she told Esther. "Come to my house tonight at eight-o'clock and we'll have a good talk about it, then."

When Esther arrived at her house, Rebbitzen Melnik was busy clearing the supper dishes. Piling them into the sink, she said, "I'll do these later. My husband is out, so we can go into his study." She selected a key as she spoke, and led Esther to a room across the hall. "The children are doing their homework in the dining room," she explained.

In the study they sat together, talking of this and that, and the Rebbitzen gently steered the conversation around to the matter in hand. Tactfully, she described her own thrilled amazement at the remarkable *Hashgochoh Protis* that had led to Esther's discovering she had a brother! This led to a discussion of the value of family closeness, expounding the concept of "blood being thicker than water." Although Esther listened intently, she still found it difficult to relate to this sort of relationship. Knowing her reaction was strange and unwarranted made her feel guilty, adding to her shame and frustration. However, recognizing that her behavior was causing distress to others, she promised to pull herself together and stop walking about with a long face.

As Rebbitzen Melnik walked her out the door, Esther was suddenly startled by wild shrieks and screams coming from the dining room. Turning pale, she whirled to face the Rebbitzen, who looked perfectly calm.

"Nothing to worry about," she said, smiling. "It's just Shmuli and Suri fighting!"

"Fighting?" Esther exclaimed. "But they're brother and sister!"

"It's not unusual for siblings to fight," the Rebbitzen smiled, "but because they really love each other they make up quickly and never bear grudges."

Over the next few months, Esther seemed to come out from behind her defensive wall and was almost like her old self, except in relation to Mindy, whom she still held at arm's length. Also, she had still made no move to find something to wear for her brother's wedding, which caused Mrs. Redner much anxiety. In truth, she had not really come to terms with the situation, and as the wedding day drew near, she dreaded the day Ari would return for his *chassunah*. When he finally arrived and came running over to see his little sister, her withdrawn, defensive attitude had returned.

Somewhat deflated by her half-hearted greeting, Ari felt prompted to ask, "Esther, aren't you glad to see me? Aren't you looking forward to my *chassunah*?"

"Yes, of course," Esther replied politely. Her noticeable lack of enthusiasm disappointed her brother, who became annoyed, remembering something his mother had said about his sister's attitude toward Mindy. Now, convinced it was true, he decided he was not going to stand for it!

"Esther! Why are you doing this?" he said angrily.

"Doing what?" Esther asked, in a small frightened voice.

"Going out of your way to spoil the *chassunah*! Aren't you glad your brother is getting married? Don't you want me to be happy? I never thought you could be so selfish!"

Stung by his words, Esther's face flamed, and tears started in her eyes. How dare he shout at her like that! He obviously didn't care about her as much as he claimed!

About to fling her accusation at him, she suddenly heard Rebbitzen Melnik's voice. *"It's not unusual for siblings to fight—but because they love each other they soon make up …."* Her mouth snapped shut, and she stared at Ari. This was her brother, her own annoying brother, who expected her to do everything his way!

It dawned on her that she and Ari were no different than those two quarrelling children in the Rebbitzen's house, even though they were still relatively unfamiliar with each other. If circumstances had been different, she realized, they, too, would have played as children—and fought!—and probably told each other their secrets. Her anger dissipating immediately, she blinked back her tears and said remorsefully, "Oh, Ari! I'm sorry! Please don't be angry with me!

I don't know what got into me. I wish I could understand it myself! It's just all been so strange for me ...."

Ari looked tenderly at his distressed sister. "You're right, it's hard. I forgot," he continued softly, "because I found my sister almost at the same time as I found Mindy!" He smiled. "I'm sorry, too, for not being understanding."

He looked as if he would say more, but changed his mind. For actually, when he had come to see her that afternoon, he'd had the intention of broaching a certain subject. He had already discussed it with the Redners and they had agreed, suggesting that he should put it to her himself. Now he decided it would be better to wait a while. There was plenty of time, as his best friend and *chavrusa*, Bezalel Weintraub, would be coming in two weeks' time for the *chassunah*.

He had asked Bezalel to come not only because he wanted him to be at his *chassunah*, but also because it had occurred to him that his friend would be the perfect match for his sister Esther!

Chapter 27

The band played a lively melody, and Golda Mirel sat at the side watching the dancing. She marveled how, in just two months, she was again at another family *chassunah*. After two world wars, which had caused so much loss and destruction, it was heart-warming to see this rapidly growing next generation celebrating one *simcha* after another!

Her healthy foot tapped to the catchy tune, but Golda Mirel repressed her urge to join, knowing her weak leg would surely give out on her. A couple of months ago, she *had* danced a little at her daughter Mindy's *chassunah*, but there she was the mother of the *kallah*, and besides, it was a family affair, with her sister Ettel as the *mechuteniste*. These Weintraubs, a family from New York, were relative strangers, and tripping on the dance floor was not her idea of being *mesameach* a *kallah*!

Ettel detached herself from the dancers and came to sit next to Golda Mirel.

"Whew!" she said, fanning herself with a table-napkin. "*Lebedig*, isn't it!"

"Yes," Golda Mirel agreed, her eyes focused on the radiant bride as she drew her guests, one by one, into the center of the circle to dance with her. "Esther looks absolutely gorgeous! And seems really happy."

"*Baruch Hashem!*" Ettel said with feeling "She had us all worried for a while, but she adjusted to the situation at last, especially after she got engaged …."

"Yes, he seems a nice boy," Golda Mirel remarked.

"Well, he would be!" Ettel declared. "He's Ari's friend!"

Looking around the crowded hall, Ettel suddenly caught sight of Mrs. Redner bearing down on them, accompanied by a fairly tall, thin woman who clung to her arm, walking with slow, measured steps.

"Who's that with Charna Leah?" she whispered to Golda Mirel.

"Probably someone from the *chosson's* family."

"She reminds me of someone," Ettel mused, "but I don't know who …."

"Ettel!" Mrs. Redner gushed, reaching their table. "Look who's made us a surprise and come to the *chassunah!*"

Up close, Ettel recognized her immediately as the woman in the Brussels nursing home.

"Mrs. Reimer!" she cried, jumping up and clasping the woman's hand. "How are you? We had heard from Mrs. Firman that you'd had the operation. Did you get our card, by the way?"

"Yes, I did. Thank you so much. I really appreciated it!"

"It's so good to see you well enough to come all the way to England!" Ettel cried.

"Well, my doctor wasn't too happy about it!" Mrs. Reimer said, smiling. "He still thinks I should take things easy. But as soon as I got the invitation, I knew I just had to come! How could I miss the opportunity to witness the marriage of that little baby from the camp!"

"Of course!" Ettel exclaimed. "It must be something really special for you!"

"It's nothing short of a *nes!*" Mrs. Reimer declared vehemently.

"Well, come along," Mrs. Redner said, tucking Mrs. Reimer's

arm back in hers. "Let me introduce you to Esther." She steered her toward the dancing crowd, forcibly pushing her way forward.

"This I must see!" Ettel declared, following them.

Left alone at the table, Golda Mirel watched as Mrs. Redner drew Esther out, taking her by the hand and leading her to where Ettel stood with Mrs. Reimer. The scene was an emotional one, and she dabbed at her eyes with a handkerchief. Mrs. Reimer seemed completely overcome as she kissed Esther, then held her at arm's length to have a good look at her. Ettel and Mrs. Redner watching, too, were obviously extremely moved.

Golda Mirel's eyes moved on, picking out various family members and savoring her *nachas*. Then her gaze fixed on one person in particular. Involuntarily, she pursed her lips as she watched her daughter-in-law, Avigayil, who danced with gusto. Not that there was anything wrong with that. Golda Mirel was not one to begrudge her daughters-in-law any enjoyment, but if only Avigayil could exhibit such enjoyment in her marriage!

For Golda Mirel had had an uneasy feeling about her youngest son's marriage for a while now. Reticent as ever, Menachem Dovid never discussed his personal life, but during the last few weeks he had seemed more withdrawn than usual. There was also a noticeable change in Avigayil's attitude toward the family. At first, she had come often, and been quite friendly and chatty. Lately, she hardly visited at all, often refusing invitations to the Shabbos meals for no apparent reason. When she did come, she was distant, and always seemed in a hurry to get away.

Even now, though they had been in this hall for the best part of two hours, Avigayil had not once come up to Golda Mirel to exchange a few words, unlike her other daughter-in-law, Tzivia, and her daughters Elkie and Mindy, who all stopped by for a little chat every now and then. In fact, Tzivia was wending her way over now, having gone to telephone the babysitter and check up on her children.

"They're all fast asleep ...," she began, and stopped suddenly staring at her mother-in-law's face. "What's wrong?" she asked. "You look upset."

In reply, Golda Mirel jerked her head in Avigayil's direction, almost afraid to say a word. If she had hoped Tzivia would wave away her concerns with a reassuring comment, she was disappointed. Tzivia just sighed and said, "Yes, it's a problem."

"What's gone wrong?" Golda Mirel said despondently, although she actually knew the answer.

"It's obvious, really," Tzivia wasted no time putting the situation into words. "All she's interested in is going out and having a good time, and she expects Menachem Dovid to do the same, which is just contrary to his nature."

"Well, he's partly to blame then," Golda Mirel mused. "If it means so much to her, he ought to give in a bit and try to please her ...."

"Yes, you're right in principle," Tzivia agreed. "But I happen to know that Menachem Dovid *has* tried. Yankel managed to get that much out of him. The trouble is, Avigayil isn't satisfied with a little finger. She wants the whole hand! Some of the places she wants to go to—and some of the people she socializes with—are just not for Menachem Dovid! He's a serious person and can't waste his time indulging in superficial, idle gossip for hours on end. She ought to understand that!"

Golda Mirel nodded, her worried frown deepening. "Can't someone explain that to her?" she asked.

"Believe me, we've tried! Menachem Dovid tried to explain his point of view, but she just called him an 'old stick-in-the-mud' and complained that she was being buried alive! We called on them once and heard the whole thing!"

Golda Mirel sighed heavily. Tzivia, though aware of her distress, continued. "On top of that, she always has her record-player blaring away at full blast, disturbing Menachem Dovid when he's trying to work on the *sefer* he's compiling ...."

"Oh, dear!" Golda Mirel groaned. "It's a pity he has to work at home ...."

"Yes, but what else *can* he do? He's got his typewriter there and all his reference books. He can't very well *schlep* them around with him all over the place." Tzivia eyed her mother-in-law with concern. The poor woman looked devastated. "I've upset you!" she said apologetically. "I'm so sorry! I really hate doing it! It sounds like a lot of *loshon hora*, but Yankel and I have discussed it and we had just decided to let you know the facts ...."

"Yes, it's true. I do have to know everything," Golda Mirel said, "however painful it is. There must be something we can do about it, though. What do you suggest?"

"I don't know ...." Tzivia was thoughtful for a moment. "They need someone—an outsider—to talk to them. Maybe a Rov and Rebbitzen ... ?"

Just then, some of her table companions, including Ettel, began to drift back to their seats, and Golda Mirel, about to make a comment, was silenced. The conversation, too private to be overheard, came to an abrupt end.

"I'm going to try to peep through the *mechitzah* to see what's doing by the men," Tzivia announced. "Coming with me?"

Nodding, Golda Mirel stood up and limped across the hall with her daughter-in-law. Suddenly, she felt a gentle tap on her shoulder. A tentative voice said, "Is it Golda Mirel?"

Swinging around, she faced a woman she had seen at the *chuppah*. "Y-yes ...," she said cautiously, "that is my name. Who are you?"

The woman, middle-aged and wearing a fair *sheitel* and a long black gown, smiled at Golda Mirel and said, "I'm not surprised you don't recognize me. It's over thirty years since we saw each other. I'm your cousin, Malli Tilzow ... formerly Malli Danziger. My father was your mother's older brother, Hershel ....."

"Malli! Of course I remember you!" Golda Mirel cried excitedly, unable to believe this elegant woman was the lively, frizzy-haired girl, two years her senior, with whom she used to play. "I would never have recognized you!"

"Well, I can't say I'd have known *you*, except——" the long-lost cousin broke off suddenly, looking embarrassed.

"If not for my limp—and the clumsy shoe!" Golda Mirel finished for her, with a twinkle in her eye. "It has its uses then!"

The tension released, the two cousins laughed and embraced each other warmly, then began to bombard each other with questions. Golda Mirel explained her connections to the *kallah*, while Malli said she and the Weintraubs were *mechutonim*, her youngest son being married to Sarah Weintraub's daughter.

"Look," she said, "there's my daughter-in-law Tzippy, in the lilac and white dress. Come meet her."

Golda Mirel introduced Tzivia, who was still with her, then followed Malli.

As most of the guests were seated for the main course, they threaded their way between the tables to make their introductions. After meeting Tzippy, Golda Mirel led her cousin straight over to Ettel. Malli could hardly contain her surprise when she saw her. She remembered Ettel as a pretty young girl with ribbons in her hair.

"I should have recognized you," she said, "you're so like your mother!"

Golda Mirel sought out her two daughters and introduced them, then made her way over to Avigayil.

"Avigayil," she said, "this is a cousin of mine whom I haven't seen for over thirty years!"

"Really? Pleased to meet you," Avigayil said perfunctorily, heaping salad onto her plate. Irritated and embarrassed by her daughter-in-law's off-hand manner, Golda Mirel quickly steered her cousin away from the table, some of her evening's pleasure diminished by the encounter.

While Malli remained in England, Golda Mirel couldn't focus on her newest problem with her son and daughter-in-law, and shelved that issue while she renewed her friendship with this dear cousin. They took in some of London's historic sights, but mostly, they just sat in Golda Mirel's kitchen and exchanged war experiences. Golda Mirel recounted the tale of her family's escape to England and how they had fared during the war. Malli, in her turn, described how she, her husband and children had been deported to Siberia, where conditions had been exceedingly harsh. Many had not survived the hardships, but Malli's family was among the fortunate ones. Later, when they learned how lucky they had been, they were grateful, despite their suffering. Had they remained in Poland, they would certainly have perished!

"Do you remember Sheindel … our aunt, although she and I were in the same class in school … ?"

"Of course I remember Sheindel!" Golda Mirel cried. She would never forget her mother's sister, whom she had resented so much for bossing her around and always knowing everything better than her! "What happened to her?"

"She was in Siberia, too, though we never met there. Now, she's in America, too. We don't live very near each other, but we get together often … for *simchos* and so on."

"Oh, please, give her my best regards!" Golda Mirel cried, suddenly overcome with nostalgia.

"I will," Malli promised. "She'll be delighted to hear from you. Not long ago she mentioned you, wondering what had become of you."

At the end of a week, they said their goodbyes, with promises to keep in touch, and Golda Mirel knew it was time to confront Menachem Dovid's marital issues. She brought the topic up to Moshe Leib that very evening at the dinner table. He agreed with Tzivia that an impartial outsider was needed to tackle the problem.

"We can't be the ones to suggest someone to deal with this," he warned his over-eager wife. "We're Menachem Dovid's parents, and parents mustn't get involved. I think Yankel could, though, since Menachem Dovid obviously confides in him."

"Yes, that's true," Golda Mirel agreed. "I'll phone Tzivia first thing in the morning."

However, the matter was brought to the forefront without her intervention. Late that evening, Yankel and Tzivia paid them an unexpected visit. Their parents immediately detected grave expressions on their faces and grew alarmed.

"W-what's happened?" asked Golda Mirel. "Is everyone all right?"

"Yes, yes," Yankel hastened to assure her. "Nobody's ill, *baruch Hashem*. We have some not very pleasant news to tell you."

"Avigayil's left," Tzivia announced, not beating around the bush. "She's left Menachem Dovid!"

"But she can't do that!" Golda Mirel exclaimed, aghast. "She's married to him!"

"Well, that doesn't seem to have stopped her," Tzivia remarked tartly.

The senior Steiners stared in shock. Such a situation was unheard of! Marriage was binding, after all; not something one just walked out of.

"Where has she gone? Did she go abroad?" Moshe Leib asked quietly.

"No," Yankel said. "She hasn't gone far at all, just back to her parents."

"Oh," Golda Mirel said, a tinge of relief in her voice. "They'll surely send her straight back to her husband!"

"I wouldn't bank on it," Tzivia said in contempt. "They've indulged and spoiled her all her life. They're hardly likely to come all heavy-handed on her now! Not dear Mama Fischberg, definitely!" Her tone was scathing.

"It's ridiculous!" Golda Mirel cried, suddenly becoming angry. "Do they think they're doing their daughter a favor, giving in to all her whims? *I'm* going to have a word with that woman! I'd like to go around right now, but I think it's a bit late. In any case, maybe they *will* send her back. I'll wait and see. If she's not back home by mid-day tomorrow, Madam Fischberg is going to get a piece of my mind!"

"Mamme! You're not really going to!" Yankel cried in disbelief, "You can't do that sort of thing!"

"Of course I can!" his mother retorted. "Why shouldn't I?"

"Because ..." Yankel found himself unable to put forward a good reason. "Tatte! You tell her not to do it!"

Moshe Leib shook his head, a faint smile on his lips. Frankly, he agreed with his wife and admired her pluck.

"You know your mother," he told his son. "Once she's made up her mind to do something, there's no stopping her!"

Golda Mirel gazed across the road at the "Fischberg Residence"— as the Steiner family secretly called the large, imposing house in the affluent area of Stamford Hill—and wondered why she had always thought it attractive. Now the sight of it, with its well-tended front garden and polished-oak front door, flanked by marble pillars, merely irritated her.

However, unintimidated by this display of opulence, she limped purposefully up the path and rang the bell. After a few moments, a maid opened the door.

"Is Mrs. Fischberg in?" Golda Mirel asked immediately.

"Who shall I say it is?"

"It's Mrs. Steiner," she replied.

"One moment, please," the maid said, closing the door in Golda Mirel's face. After a few moments, the door opened again, and the maid, her face expressionless, said, "Mrs. Fischberg is resting and can't be disturbed." She was about to close the door again, but Golda Mirel, her hand firmly clasping the highly-polished brass doorknob, prevented her.

"Tell her it's extremely urgent!" she said, assertively. "I refuse to leave without seeing her!"

Taken by surprise, the maid backed away, and Golda Mirel gave the door a shove and stepped inside, limping into the hall. Terrified, the maid left her and hurried away, turning by an archway and disappearing. Golda Mirel had no idea where she'd gone, but she stood and waited. After a few moments, Mrs. Fischberg appeared around the same archway, trailing a long, floral silk robe and looking extremely cross.

Bracing herself for the angry tirade that was sure to follow, Golda Mirel determined to stand her ground. Mrs. Fischberg, however, did not shout at her. She stood for a moment eyeing her visitor with pursed lips. Then she said curtly, "You had better come in."

She led Golda Mirel into the expensively furnished dining room and motioned to her to sit down. Golda Mirel ignored the gesture, making it necessary for her hostess to remain standing, too.

"Is Avigayil here?" Golda Mirel demanded at once.

There was a pause before Mrs. Fischberg replied. "Yes, she is. Where else would she be?"

"I don't know where she *would* be," Golda Mirel retorted. "I only know where she *should* be. At home with her husband!"

"But she isn't happy!" Mrs. Fischberg protested plaintively. "You can't blame her …."

"I don't blame her as much as I blame *you*, Mrs. Fischberg!" Golda Mirel cut in. "You should have sent her straight back home! Encouraging her to run away won't help save her marriage!"

"As far as my daughter is concerned, the marriage is over!" Mrs. Fischberg declared brusquely. "And I must say, I agree with her!"

"Rubbish!" Golda Mirel snapped. "A marriage is binding! One can't just walk out of it whenever one wants. If there are difficulties, one is supposed to work on them …."

"That's an old-fashioned idea!" Mrs. Fischberg interrupted her.

"I don't see where fashion comes into it! Getting married isn't quite the same as buying a new dress. You can't just throw it out if you don't like it! If Avigayil has got that attitude, it's because you have always spoiled her!"

"How dare you speak to me like that, Mrs. Steiner!" Mrs. Fischberg's said, affronted. "Kindly leave my house!"

"I certainly shall!" Golda Mirel retorted angrily, her voice rising. "After I have spoken to Avigayil!"

"You will do no such thing! I will not have you upsetting her! And please keep your voice down. There is no reason my maid should hear everything that's going on!"

Golda Mirel saw she was banging her head against a brick wall. Her energy suddenly spent, she sighed. "Very well," she said dully, "I will go now. But,"—her eyes flashed again—"don't think I will leave it at that. Something has to be done to put things right between them."

"There is no point, Mrs. Steiner." The belligerence had left Mrs. Fischberg, too, and she sounded weary. "If my daughter wants a *get*, we will do whatever we can to see that she gets one!"

The battle raged fiercely for a few months, both sides refusing to give in. If the Steiners secretly felt that Menachem Dovid was better off without Avigayil, they never admitted it, adhering steadfastly to their belief that marriage was sacred and could only be discarded in drastic circumstances.

Some of the involved *rabbonim* in the *kehillah* tried to pour oil on the troubled waters, but to no avail. The Fischbergs remained adamant, and eventually Menachem Dovid decided he preferred to give Avigayil a *get*. Once the formalities were over, he moved his belongings out of the house his father-in-law had bought for them, planning to find a small flat to live in. However, his parents wouldn't hear of it and, rather than hurt their feelings, he agreed to move back to their house.

Mechel Fischberg had actually wanted him to keep the house. He liked and respected his son-in-law and was disappointed with his daughter and her mother. Refusing his offer, Menachem Dovid adamantly insisted that the house belonged to Avigayil.

The divorce, a rare occurrence in the close-knit Stamford Hill *kehillah*, caused quite a stir and set many a gossipy tongue wagging. Golda Mirel felt the shame of it and could hardly bring herself to go out, finding it difficult to face people who were probably whispering behind her back when she walked away from them. On top of that, she had to put up with the "I-told-you-so" expression on Tante Fanny's face!

But what hurt most was the leaden ache in her heart for her child who had been hurt! *A mother can't really protect her child from every ill*, she thought disconsolately. *They eventually have to go it on their own.*

Chapter 28

Golda Mirel gripped the arm of her seat in panic as the plane lurched wildly. She looked around in terror, and was surprised to see no one else was alarmed. A stewardess suddenly appeared at her side. "Are you all right, Mrs. Steiner?" she asked the elderly lady in a solicitous voice.

Golda Mirel swallowed nervously. "Yes, thank you," she said, getting a grip on herself. "Why does the plane rock about like that?"

"Just a bit of turbulence," the stewardess said reassuringly. She checked that Golda Mirel's seat belt was fastened properly and moved on.

Embarrassed that her fear had been so obvious, Golda Mirel turned her face to the window. Why couldn't she remain calm like everybody else? But then, she told herself, the others were probably experienced air travelers by now, whereas this was only her second flight.

Last year, she and Moshe Leib had traveled by air to Eretz Yisroel. It had been a wonderful experience. They had spent a delightful two weeks with Chuni and Roisy, getting to know the grandchildren they rarely saw. And most exciting of all was going to daven at the *Kosel Hama'aravi*! Who could have dreamed such a thing would occur in their lifetime! The Six Day War had occurred just a few weeks before, and everyone was still reeling from this *nes*!

Having Moshe Leib with her on that flight, she had been quite calm. Now she was alone, on a longer flight—all the way to America—and the going was rough. Trying to relax, she leaned back and let her mind wander as she reminisced about the circumstances that had gotten her onto this plane.

Shortly after her cousin Malli's visit, Golda Mirel had received an excited telephone call from Sheindel, her mother's youngest sister. A few letters passed to and fro between them, and then, six weeks ago, Golda Mirel had received an invitation from Sheindel's oldest son Mendel to his daughter's *chassunah*! Sheindel had scribbled a note on the back, begging her to come.

"Why don't you go?" Moshe Leib had suggested. "It will be good for you to meet members of your family again."

"Without you?" Golda Mirel had exclaimed. "Oh, no! I'm not going alone!"

Moshe Leib shook his head, saying he couldn't leave at a time when his pupils were taking exams. He suggested she ask Ettel to go with her.

Ettel, too, had received an invitation, but declared she could not possibly go away just then, as she had too many orders to complete for *chassunahs* in town.

Deciding she would not go, either, Golda Mirel was unprepared for the urging of her children. Tzivia and Elkie waved away her excuses, promising to have Moshe Leib and Menachem Dovid over for meals, while Mindy offered to look after Tante Fanny, who, at ninety-eight, insisted on being independent, yet needed a discreet eye kept on her.

Golda Mirel could not decide what to do. However, when Sheindel telephoned a week later, she heard herself say she would be coming!

"Good. I'll send you a ticket by express post!" Sheindel announced, turning a deaf ear to Golda Mirel's protests.

Sure enough, a ticket arrived by post eight days later, and Moshe Leib suggested she use it and sort it out with Sheindel when she got there.

Golda Mirel thought about their approaching reunion with some apprehension. *What was Sheindel like these days?* she wondered. Her memory of her aunt, only eighteen months her senior, was of a bossy, overbearing girl, who had always manipulated her niece into doing things her way! Thinking about it now, Golda Mirel realized the impression was mostly born out of her resentment that Sheindel could do the things *she* had been prevented from doing, due to her disability. *Childish rivalry can certainly damage a relationship*, Golda Mirel reflected, smiling to herself. Things would be quite different now. A lot of water had flowed under the bridge since those days, and when they got together, they would surely enjoy themselves, indulging in old memories as they covered the years between, making up for lost time!

She came out of her reverie to hear the captain announcing preparations for landing, and she sat bolt upright, clutching her purse. A half hour later, Golda Mirel stood in the vast airport, with its hustling, bustling activity, somewhat daunted by its size. She remembered how she had traveled alone to England before the war. She smiled grimly to herself, thinking, *I coped then and I can surely cope now!* Especially since there wasn't even a language barrier.

Once she had passed through Passport Control, she summoned a porter to retrieve her luggage for her and made her way toward the exit, wondering whether she and Sheindel would recognize one another.

Scanning the sea of faces in front of her, one woman caught her eye. Golda Mirel felt instinctively that this was Sheindel, though she had no definite resemblance to any member of the Danziger family. About average height, she was elegantly dressed in a summer outfit, a snakeskin bag hanging from her shoulder. Her *sheitel* was immaculately styled, and even from the distance, Golda Mirel could see earrings dangling from her ears.

As Golda Mirel limped forward, the woman broke into a smile and began to wave. As soon as Golda Mirel reached the barrier, she ran toward her, enveloping her in a tight hug.

"Oh, Golda Mirel, it's so good to see you again after all these years!" she cried emotionally.

"It's good to see you, too, Sheindel!" Golda Mirel cried, equally overcome.

After a few moments, Sheindel tucked her arm into Golda Mirel's and pulled her away from the people surging forward with their trolleys. "Come. Let's go to the parking lot, where Mendel's waiting in the car. It's a long drive, so we've got plenty of time to talk on the way."

They walked across to the car park, arm in arm, with the porter wheeling the luggage trolley dutifully behind them. As soon as Sheindel's son Mendel saw them, he got out of the car and, greeting Golda Mirel with a warm "*sholom aleichem,*" opened the passenger door for her. Golda Mirel could hardly believe that this was the small boy she remembered, albeit somewhat vaguely. Now a fairly tall forty-five-year-old with telltale gray hairs showing in his black beard, he was another reminder of the world of her youth—a world that she had once feared was completely obliterated!

The porter loaded her luggage into the boot and Golda Mirel drew her purse out of her handbag to give him a tip, but Sheindel forestalled her, handing him a few bills.

"Oh, no!" Golda Mirel began to protest, but Sheindel gently pushed her hand away, shaking her head. "You're my guest!" she declared. Judging by the porter's broad grin as he touched his cap and walked away, Golda Mirel realized that Sheindel's tip was far larger than anything she could have given him.

Before they had driven out of the airport, Golda Mirel began to argue about the ticket her aunt had sent her.

"You must let me pay you back!" she insisted. "Why should you pay my fare?"

"Why shouldn't I? You don't know what it means to me that you came all the way to be at my granddaughter's *chassunah*! It's my way of showing my pleasure!"

"Well, it's an expensive way of showing it!" Golda Mirel answered. "In any case, it's a pleasure for me, too, so I insist on paying for my own ticket!"

"Look, Golda Mirel, for you it's a lot of money, but for me it's peanuts! I can easily afford it!"

"I'm glad to hear it! But still—" Golda Mirel began.

"When we first came here, we had nothing," Sheindel told her, interrupting her, "but since Shia's business began to flourish, he hasn't looked back. I tell you, Golda Mirel, we're *baruch Hashem* very comfortably off!"

Golda Mirel could see there was no point in arguing with her. It was clear Sheindel derived great satisfaction in treating her long-lost relative, and nothing was going to stop her from doing it!

It struck Golda Mirel that, after all, Sheindel *was* quite like the person she remembered, forceful and strong-minded. When she had been young and sensitive it had aggravated her, but now it didn't bother her any more. Sheindel might be rather domineering, but she certainly had a big heart!

As soon as they arrived at the house in Boro Park, Golda Mirel could see that Sheindel's description of her financial state was no exaggeration. Everything about the place oozed elegance. The furniture, the carpets, the luxurious velvet curtains—everything was obviously "the best." Golda Mirel found herself comparing it to another grand house she had been in some time ago. Both equally extravagant and impressive, there was a vast difference between the two homes. The style and furniture of the Fischbergs' huge mansion had an air of austerity about it. Sheindel's home, in contrast, gave a warm, welcoming appearance.

When she was taken to her room, Golda Mirel felt she had entered a dream world. Everything was as perfect as a glossy magazine photograph! A fleeting wave of homesickness swept over her for the familiar coziness of her own little home in England.

The evening went by pleasantly. Sheindel had prepared a light, tasty meal, after which they sat in comfortable leather armchairs chatting, first about the war, and eventually steering the conversation around to the subject of their children.

"*Baruch Hashem*, we also have a lot of *nachas*," Sheindel said, when Golda Mirel finished telling her about her family. "Mendel has eleven children, *k'ein eiyin hora*, and he's also doing well. Shia wanted to take him into his knitwear business, but Mendel preferred to be independent and opened a travel agency, which is very successful, *baruch Hashem*. I can't believe he's making his first *chassunah! How time passes!* I suppose you've realized that Gitty, the *kallah*, is named after my mother, *aleha hasholom* ... your grandmother ...." A look of sorrow crossed her face, and was reflected in Golda Mirel's as she thought with sadness of her beloved Babbe Danziger.

Sheindel pushed away her grief and continued the saga of her other five children and their families, with pride in her voice as she talked about her various grandchildren. Her ramblings came to an abrupt halt when she noticed Golda Mirel's eyes dropping shut. Suddenly, remembering the time difference and realizing it was about three-thirty in the morning for her guest, she sent her off to bed.

Utterly exhausted, Golda Mirel slept well that night, which was fortunate because the next day turned out to be hectic. Malli came over, eager to see her cousin again and was roped in by Sheindel to take Golda Mirel shopping for a new outfit to wear at the *chassunah*. Golda Mirel had no choice but to agree, admitting to herself that the dress she wore for every *simcha* was looking shabby. She hadn't been surprised at the disapproving look Sheindel gave it when she saw it. However, when Malli produced money that Sheindel had unobtrusively pressed into her hand before they left, Golda Mirel adamantly insisted on paying for her purchase.

The *chassunah* was a lavish affair. Golda Mirel had expected it to be grand, yet as she entered the hall she was dazzled by the sparkling crystal chandeliers and the pomp and glitter of the place. Once again she felt like a fish out of water and found herself almost wishing she had stayed at home!

However, the atmosphere was warm and friendly, and she soon forgot her reservations and started enjoying herself. Malli took her under wing, introducing her to people and making her feel at home. Occasionally, Sheindel would take her to meet some friend or relative.

"I must introduce you to another Golda Mirel," she said, leading her toward the center of the hall. "My granddaughter … Libby's sixteen-year-old daughter. Ah, there she is!" She pointed to a group of girls standing together, talking and laughing. To Golda Mirel they looked a strange bunch, dressed in outlandish clothes, with hairdos to match. One girl, whose back was to them, had her hair piled up on her head with ringlets cascading down her back.

"Zahava," called Sheindel, "come here a minute!"

This girl turned, pushing long bangs away from her eyes to peer at them. "Oh, hullo, Bobby," she said, smiling sweetly at her grandmother as she came up.

"Zahava, this is Golda Mirel from London," her grandmother said. "Her mother was my older sister."

"Pleased to meet you," Zahava said politely. "My name is Golda Mirel, too, but no one ever calls me that!" Her tone implied that the idea was quite preposterous. It occurred to Golda Mirel that *she* would feel the same at the idea of being called Zahava!

Zahava turned back to her friends, who had been watching them with amused expressions, and the group moved away to join the dancing crowd, twisting and swaying as they went. Golda Mirel suddenly thought of Mindy and felt overwhelmingly grateful that *her* daughter had turned out well in the end!

The next few days were a whirl of activity. Golda Mirel was taken out to places of interest by various members of the family. Sometimes Sheindel or Malli would whisk her off for a shopping trip. Then, in the evenings, there were *sheva brochos* to attend, some of which finished quite late. Golda Mirel was beginning to feel like a limp rag, but she made an effort not to let her exhaustion show, for Sheindel, so full of energy, would just not understand.

Toward the end of the week, tramping around the shops on Thirteenth Avenue with Malli, Golda Mirel noticed a poster announcing a *shiur* to be given by a certain Rebbitzen Shayna Leibowsky, who was visiting Boro Park. Her interest piqued, Golda Mirel thought she could really do with something spiritual to counteract her materialistic surroundings. A *shiur* by a Rebbitzen would give her that bit of *ruchniyus* she needed. She pointed out the notice to Malli.

"Oh, yes," Malli said, peering at it. "She's a brilliant speaker. I've heard her a few times."

"When is it?" Golda Mirel asked, going closer to look. "If it's while I'm still here, I'd love to go."

"Why not? I'll take you," Malli said enthusiastically, running her finger down the poster in search of the date. "It's tomorrow night," she announced. "What a pity! I've got a *bar mitzvah*. Maybe Sheindel will go …."

"No, she can't. It's the last *sheva brochos* and it's in Monsey. She's expecting me to go, too … but, to tell the truth, I'd rather go to this *shiur*!"

"Well, you could always make the excuse that you're too tired to go schlepping off to Monsey," Malli suggested. "But who can take you to the *shiur*? All of Sheindel's family will be at the *sheva brochos* and all of mine are going to the *bar mitzvah*."

"So, I'll go by myself," Golda Mirel said simply. "Just tell me how to get there."

"Oh, it's quite easy. You shouldn't have any trouble finding it," Malli said, eying her cousin with admiration as she pointed out the way.

The next night, Golda Mirel joined the huge crowd of women at the entrance of the school hall for the *shiur*. She inched her way forward, hoping to get a good seat. Relieved that her enjoyment would not be marred by a guilty conscience, she recalled her surprise at Sheindel's reaction. Instead of protesting strongly, as Golda Mirel had expected, Sheindel had nodded and said that although she was disappointed not to have her niece's company at the *sheva brochos*, she quite understood.

"As a matter of fact, I'm quite jealous," she had confessed, with a conspiratorial wink. "She's such a good speaker. Believe me, I'd much rather come and hear her than go to Monsey! But what can I do?" She threw up her hands with a resigned air.

Before setting off, Sheindel had prepared a meal for her guest and given her a key, telling her not to wait up as they would probably be home in the early hours of the morning.

Golda Mirel found a place in one of the central rows and settled herself down.

Suddenly, a hush came over the hall and everyone stood up as the Rebbitzen entered and began to climb the steps to the platform.

Golda Mirel regarded her with interest. Of average height, she had an aura of dignity about her that commanded respect.

The audience sat in absolute silence as she began to speak. Her English was impeccable, yet she had a faint accent that intrigued Golda Mirel. *Where was she from?* she wondered. All Malli knew, when she had asked about her, was that her husband was *Rosh haYeshiva* at a yeshiva near Philadelphia. Sheindel, a little more informative, said she had heard that Rabbi Leibowsky had been a widower with young children when she had married him.

As she listened, enthralled, to the Rebbitzen, Golda Mirel was conscious of a feeling of familiarity. She tried to shake it off, telling herself it was ridiculous. But the uncanny notion persisted, distracting her concentration from the speaker's words.

The human brain sometimes has a habit of transporting one to a place deep in the recesses of one's memory. For a fleeting moment, Golda Mirel saw herself sitting at a table, bending over some books. Someone was next to her, teaching her. The sensation passed as quickly as it came, but it cleared her mind. She knew, without a doubt, who this woman was.

Sonja!

Just managing to stop herself from crying out loud, Golda Mirel sat back tensely, studying her beloved erstwhile teacher with renewed interest. Although her present appearance was a far cry from the young, fair-haired girl she had known fifty-six years ago, Golda Mirel caught a few telltale signs in her gestures that convinced her she was not mistaken.

So, Sonja's wish had been realized. She *had* married a *talmid chochom*, after all! Golda Mirel was pleased. She longed to know more about Sonja's life and wondered if she dared approach her now that she was a well-known personality. After the *shiur*, as people began to make their way out, she hovered around, watching the Rebbitzen chatting to the women who had accompanied her. All at once she knew that she could not go away without speaking to her and introducing herself.

She drew closer, fervently hoping Sonja would remember her, too, and be pleased to see her! As she stood hesitating, about to turn away, the Rebbitzen looked up and met her eyes. With instant recognition, she moved quickly toward the shy-faced woman, and the others parted, turning to see who it was.

"This is my first pupil," she explained, looking back at them, and then the two women met in a warm embrace. After the heartfelt hellos were over, Sonja—or Shayna, as she was now called—invited Golda Mirel to accompany her to her stepdaughter Bayla's house, where she was staying for the night. They walked along amicably until they came to the apartment building.

"It's such a lovely night," Shayna had said, "and we've still got so much to talk about. Let's sit here on this bench for a while before going up."

Golda Mirel readily agreed, eager to hear her companion's story, and they sat together on the bench catching up on old times. Before giving her account, Shayna asked her about Berel. Golda Mirel, realizing there was no point in cushioning the truth, told her everything. Shayna nodded. "I couldn't have married him," she said earnestly, "and I've always been grateful to you for putting me in the picture in time."

She told Golda Mirel how Rebbitzen Reisbard had sent her to stay with her sister, also a rebbitzen, and how she had later gone on to become a teacher in one of Sarah Schenirer's *Bais Yaakov* schools.

In 1936, at the age of forty-three, she had married Reb Elisha Leibowsky, a *melamed* in the local *cheder*, whose wife had died, leaving him with five young children. Shayna had become a devoted mother to the children and a deep love had developed between them.

"Bayla, the oldest, took a bit longer to accept me, but we eventually established a strong and lasting bond."

A year after their marriage, Reb Elisha had been offered a post as a *maggid shiur* in a yeshiva in America, which he accepted. The move had not been easy, but later, when they heard about the carnage taking place in Poland, they realized what *nissim* they had experienced. Now, many years later, Rabbi Leibowsky had become a prominent *Rosh Yeshiva*.

In her turn, Golda Mirel told Shayna her entire story, ending up with the latest significant incident in her life—Menachem Dovid's divorce.

"I know just how you feel," Shayna said. "Bayla is going through a similar experience with her daughter, Shifra."

"Oh, *nebach*! What happened?" Golda Mirel asked in sympathy.

"Shifra is such a lovely girl," Shayna told her, "and, of course, her parents wanted the best for her. They thought they had found it … a fine young man who could learn well. However, not long after the *chassunah*, he started to mix with a bad crowd, making him stray further and further from the path. He eventually was *mechallel* Shabbos. Shifra tried to keep him back, but one day he just disappeared, leaving her high and dry. For two years no one knew where he was. When, at last, he was discovered, he refused to give her a *get*. He was quite happy to go through a civil divorce because he wanted to marry a non-Jewish woman, but he doesn't see why he should give Shifra a *get* if it means nothing to him. The *Rabbonim* are trying to put pressure on him, but they don't seem to be having much success. It's really so hard for Shifra! This situation could go on indefinitely, and as long as it does, there's no chance of her getting married again."

"Poor thing!" Golda Mirel said in pity. "You must be devastated! I hope it will soon get sorted out, with the *Eibershter's* help, and she'll find the right *shidduch*!"

"*Amein*!" Shayna declared. She stood up. "Come, let's go up now, so you can meet some of my family." Taking Golda Mirel's arm, she gave a contented sigh. "Oh, Golda Mirel, it's so wonderful that we've met again, after all these years! What amazing *Hashgochoh Protis*!"

Golda Mirel heartily agreed, reflecting that her trip—one that she had very nearly not made!—had certainly been worthwhile!

Chapter 29

festive air permeated the Steiners' living room as the family gathered to celebrate Tante Fanny's hundredth birthday. Bunches of colored balloons were pinned to the walls and a banner, made by two of Golda Mirel's grandchildren, with "MAZEL TOV TANTE FANNY! 1870–1970/5630–5730" painted in elaborate lettering, stretched across the room. The table, laden with a variety of cakes and delicacies, also displayed an array of birthday cards sent by family and friends. In pride of place among them was a telegram from the Queen! Tante Fanny, sitting in an armchair at the head of the table, frail but alert, proudly pointed out the telegram to everyone who came in.

"I hope she doesn't decide to phone the Queen and thank her for it!" Elkie had laughingly remarked when the telegram arrived, giving her mother a moment of panic!

Now, watching her aunt happily show off her prize, Golda Mirel had to smile. Dear Tante Fanny! She had been so proud when she had been granted British citizenship, shortly after the war.

With some amusement, Golda Mirel remembered an incident that had occurred soon after that. All through the war—and for some years afterwards—there were no bananas to be had in the country. Indeed, the younger children didn't even know what a banana looked like. Then, one day, Golda Mirel heard that a shipment of bananas had arrived and that the fruit would soon be available in the shops.

A day later, word spread around that a stall in Ridley Road Market had started selling them.

"I'm going to get some," Tante Fanny announced. "I just fancy a nice banana after all this time!"

"Me, too," Golda Mirel said. "And I'm sure the children will love them, too!"

They made their way to the market and were dismayed at the long queue in front of the stall. However, having come all the way, they were determined not to go home empty-handed, and they joined the line of patient people queuing in true English fashion.

After about twenty minutes, while they moved slowly forward, Tante Fanny asked her niece to keep her spot in the queue as she was just going to another stall for some apples. "I'll be back soon."

Ten minutes later she returned and took her place next to Golda Mirel.

"'Ere!" a woman called out belligerently behind her, tapping her on the shoulder. "What d'you think you're doing—pushin' in?"

"Excuse me," Tante Fanny said in her strong German accent, turning around. "I have not pushed in! Together with this lady all the time I have been." And without waiting for a comment from the woman, she nodded her head vigorously and turned back. The woman said nothing for a few moments, then mumbled, "... foreigners!" preceded by an unrepeatable adjective.

This was too much for Tante Fanny! She whirled around and glared at the woman. "What do you mean ... 'foreigners'?" she shouted indignantly, her accent even more pronounced. "Let me tell you, *I* was chosen by the government to be British! *You* are only

British by accident!" And, with a toss of her head as if to say "so there!" she turned away again.

A titter ran through the queue, mortifying Golda Mirel, who would have dearly loved to get away from there ... never mind the bananas ... but Tante Fanny's wrath would surely have turned on *her* if she'd tried!

Now, many years later, the memory of that incident only made her laugh as she regarded Tante Fanny with affection.

Elkie's fourteen-year-old daughter Pessie had thought of this party, and the idea had been greeted with enthusiasm by the rest of the family. Since Tante Fanny now lived with the Steiners, having given in to Golda Mirel's persistence, it was decided to hold the affair in their house. In spite of her age, Tante Fanny did not miss much. Thus, it had not been easy to make the preparations without her knowledge, but when she had been taken into the livingroom at last, she had been genuinely surprised. Although pretending to be annoyed about all the fuss, it was obvious she was pleased.

The room soon filled up with members of the family and a few friends, everyone, including the children, bearing some little gift. Golda Mirel surveyed the scene with pleasure. She loved it when her children—complete with their own children—all gathered together. The only ones missing were Chuni and Roisy, who, unable to make the long journey, had sent a huge card and a beautiful crocheted shawl, which Tante Fanny wore now, draped over her shoulders.

The others were all there; Yankel, Elkie and Mindy, along with spouses and children, and best of all Menachem Dovid, with his wife Shifra and their baby son. They had come from Eretz Yisroel, not only to attend the party but also to introduce Golda Mirel and Moshe Leib to little Avrumi, just four months old.

Golda Mirel had awaited their arrival with mixed feelings. She had been excited to see them, yet dreaded the possibility that her son might again have an unhappy look about him. The *shidduch* had seemed like a miracle, a match made to order, but a recent letter from Roisy had caused her to have misgivings. In the letter, Roisy sang Shifra's praises, describing what a lively person her new sister-in-law was.

She's just put on a little play with the class that she teaches, Roisy had written, *and it was a great success! Now she's organizing a show for older girls, to raise money for* tzedaka. *They all say she's a good actress and a brilliant producer!*

Roisy went on to say how much she enjoyed Shifra's company and how Shifra had a knack of making people laugh. Golda Mirel read the letter with utter disbelief. Shifra had seemed quiet and reserved when she had met her. On reflection, she realized that it was understandable, considering what she was going through at the time. Even at the *chassunah* she had been quiet and quite serious. Could Roisy be talking about the same person?

It was difficult to believe that all this had occurred only fifteen months ago!

It had started one afternoon when Menachem Dovid came home unexpectedly early from *Kollel,* going straight to his room and emerging minutes later with a large folder under his arm. Not being one to pry, Golda Mirel had nevertheless looked inquiring, and he had hastened to explain. A prominent *Rosh Yeshiva* from America, who had come to London to attend a *talmid's chassunah,* was visiting the *kollel,* and Reb Boruch Silberstein, the *Rosh haKollel,* had told him about the *sefer* Menachem Dovid had just finished compiling.

"The *Rosh Yeshiva* seems very interested," Menachem Dovid told his mother, "and he wants to see it. He said he might be able to help me get it published in America."

"Oh, that would be wonderful!" Golda Mirel exclaimed enthusiastically.

"Don't be too hopeful yet," Menachem Dovid told her cautiously. "He might not like it."

Nevertheless, his step seemed a little jauntier as he left with his manuscript. It didn't occur to Golda Mirel to ask who this important *Rosh Yeshiva* was. Her one thought was a fervent hope that something would go well for him at last!

A week later, Moshe Leib received a visit from Rabbi Silberstein, and as they talked behind the closed door of the livingroom, Golda Mirel sat in the kitchen, wondering what it was all about. *Surely, it must mean some good news about Menachem Dovid's* sefer, she thought hopefully.

As soon as Moshe Leib had seen his visitor out, she asked him if her assumption had been correct.

"Oh, it's something more interesting than that!" her husband replied. "Reb Boruch has just a suggested a *shidduch* for Menachem Dovid."

"A *shidduch*? Who is it?" There was eagerness in Golda Mirel's tone.

"Apparently, this *Rosh Yeshiva* who was here, Rabbi Elisha Leibowsky, has a granddaughter who was recently divorced—"

"Leibowsky?" Golda Mirel cried, interrupting him. "That's Sonja's husband! You don't mean … ? Is it the one that I met? … Shifra, I think she's called. But it can't be! Her husband won't give her a *get*!"

"Well, it seems he has capitulated at last, and she's free now. Rabbi Leibowsky was very impressed by Menachem Dovid … and by his work as well … and he's asked Reb Boruch to suggest the *shidduch* to us."

Golda Mirel could hardly believe her ears! She had met Shifra when Sonja had taken her up to her stepdaughter's apartment, and had liked her instantly. The idea of a possible *shidduch* had not occurred to her at the time, yet now it seemed perfectly fitting!

Things had moved quickly after that. The couple had become engaged and were married three months later. They had settled in Eretz Yisroel and Golda Mirel had breathed a sigh of relief.

Now, worrying over Roisy's information, Golda Mirel braced herself. Roisy, of course, had meant well, thinking her letter would make her mother-in-law happy, but Golda Mirel couldn't help fearing a repeat of the "Avigayil" situation.

However, as she watched her son and his wife together, her tension began to ease. Shifra was, indeed, friendly and cheerful, displaying a lively sense of humor, but her manner was decidedly more refined than her predecessor's. Menachem Dovid, although serious as ever, seemed more relaxed than he had been for a long time.

Later that evening, when the party was over and cleared away and Shifra was settling the baby in his cot for the night, Golda Mirel, alone in the kitchen with Menachem Dovid, could not resist asking him about it.

"Shifra has a bit of a social life outside the home," Menachem Dovid explained proudly, "and I'm all for it. She enjoys it and she does a lot of good with it. The thing is, she doesn't expect me to take part in her activities. And what's more, she accepts me as I am and doesn't try to change me."

His confident, matter-of-fact tone reassured Golda Mirel. She was convinced she could stop worrying about her youngest son at last!

"It's unbelievable," she commented to Moshe Leib later that night. "I always thought Menachem Dovid needed a wife who was quiet and serious like him!"

"Well, it just goes to show," her husband smiled, "how we think we know what's good for our children, but the *Ribono Shel Olam* knows better!"

The kitchen clock gave its usual half-hour chime, telling Golda Mirel that it was one-thirty. Hearing Moshe Leib's key in the lock, she placed a loaf of bread on the table and, calling "hullo" to him, turned to the stove, where a vegetable soup was simmering, ready to be served. Lifting the lid, she took out a few vegetables to mash up for Tante Fanny, who, by now, could only eat puréed food.

"Go and wash," she told Moshe Leib. "I'm just going to fetch Tante Fanny, then I'll dish out the soup. I won't be long."

Humming, she went into the livingroom. "Dinnertime, Tante Fanny," she sang out cheerfully. There was no reply from the armchair where Tante Fanny was sitting, her head lolling to one side. It did not surprise Golda Mirel. Tante Fanny spent most of her time sleeping these days.

"Wake up, Tante Fanny," Golda Mirel said softly, going up to her. "Moshe Leib is home and it's time to eat."

There was still no reaction from Tante Fanny, which puzzled Golda Mirel a little. The old lady was not a heavy sleeper. She usually woke as soon as she was called. Golda Mirel didn't like shaking her, but now she automatically put her hand out to tap her aunt gently on the shoulder. All at once she froze, her hand suspended in mid-air. Something did not look right! Golda Mirel suddenly realized that Tante Fanny was—was no longer alive!

Panic-stricken, she ran to the door and called Moshe Leib. He came in at once. "I'll call the doctor," he said solemnly, "though I don't think there's anything he can do. Poor Tante Fanny. At least she went peacefully."

"Yes …," Golda Mirel said softly. "*Baruch Hashem*, she didn't suffer at all." Her lip began to quiver. "I just can't believe it!" she said, brokenly, a tremor in her voice.

Suddenly she sank into a chair, sobbing broken-heartedly. She hadn't known, till that moment, how much she had loved Tante

Fanny. The old lady had become so much a part of her life that it was difficult to imagine how she would go on without her.

She remembered that first day she had met Tante Fanny. Brusque and business-like, Herr Steiner's sister had marched into the house and in her outspoken, patronizing manner, had proceeded to put everyone in their place. Martha and Ilse had cringed visibly at her sharp words, but Golda Mirel had earned Tante Fanny's respect by refusing to be intimidated, and answering back, and from then on an unspoken bond had developed between them. Tante Fanny, although still forthright, had always softened where Golda Mirel was concerned. They had been very close for years. Besides acting as a buffer between Golda Mirel and her disapproving mother-in-law and sister-in-law, Tante Fanny had always been on hand when Golda Mirel needed help.

When she came with them to England, her spirit was undaunted by the unfamiliarity of a strange country. She had thrown herself into community life with gusto. In no time at all, she was on various charitable committees, and had even started a Women's Group for older women, which flourished under her leadership.

There were times when Tante Fanny's outspoken manner had caused the Steiner family some embarrassment, but in general all regarded her with affection. And now, just like that, she was gone!

Quite a large crowd attended the *levayah*, an indication of the high regard the community had for this indomitable old lady. Moshe Leib, as her only living relative, recited *kaddish* and, although no one was sitting *shiva*, many people crowded around the Steiners to console them, making comments such as "she certainly had a long and active life!" or "at least she wasn't ill and was alert till the end!" Golda Mirel and her family knew it was true and they were grateful for that, but it didn't fill the void that Tante Fanny's passing had left.

The legacy Tante Fanny left Golda Mirel was not one she

relished, she thought wryly. Though too frail toward the end to take an active part in the Women's Group, Tante Fanny had still maintained a keen interest in it and kept in touch with its activities. Now, deprived of its founder chairman, the group was in danger of falling apart, until one of the committee members had the idea of asking Golda Mirel to step into her aunt's place. Reluctant to agree—chairing committees was not really her line—Golda Mirel couldn't deny the lady's argument that it was what Tante Fanny would have wanted. Put like that, Golda Mirel found it hard to refuse.

She tried her best but found she could not feel the enthusiasm that Tante Fanny had displayed, and she was tempted many times to resign. It was only the feeling that she was letting Tante Fanny down that stopped her. Eventually, circumstances beyond her control made her relinquish the position.

For some time, Moshe Leib had been giving Golda Mirel cause for concern. He seemed to tire very easily, and was often short of breath after walking a little while. Golda Mirel suspected he was suffering some pain, too, though he never complained to her about it. Time and again she begged him to see a doctor, only to be told he felt perfectly well. Finally, unable to bear the worry any longer, Golda Mirel made an appointment herself, and to her surprise Moshe Leib did not protest.

Dr. Brackner, their family doctor, also thought there was cause for concern and arranged for Moshe Leib to see a specialist. After sending him for various tests, the consultant confirmed what Golda Mirel already suspected. Moshe Leib, he told them, was suffering from a heart condition. Prescribing some pills, he warned Moshe Leib that he would have to take things easy and avoid physical exertion as much as possible.

Knowing what her husband was like, Golda Mirel realized it would be up to her to make sure he didn't overdo things. From now on, he would have her undivided attention. She resigned from the Women's group and cut down on some of her other activities. She made it clear to her children that, though she would still be there to help them if they needed her, their father was her first priority.

Life continued smoothly, albeit at a slower pace. Golda Mirel, herself, found her movements more restricted, due to the onset of arthritis, which was becoming progressively worse as time went by.

One afternoon, as Golda Mirel and Moshe Leib were sitting in the livingroom, she doing her mending and Moshe Leib engrossed in his gemara, she put down her work and tried to flex her painful fingers. It was no use trying to get the mending done. She was having a bad day today and would have to leave it for another time.

She gave a deep sigh. There was no denying it. She was getting old! All at once, she experienced that feeling that one has—usually in mid-November—when one realizes that summer has gone by all too quickly, and that winter is just around the corner.

The winter of her life was fast approaching, she thought with a feeling of melancholy. She sat brooding a few moments, then shook herself vigorously. What a negative way of thinking! *What's wrong with being old?* she asked herself. *We* daven *for* arichas yomim, *don't we? So why do we grumble when we get it?*

Putting away her mending, she snapped her workbasket shut, telling herself resolutely that tomorrow was another day!

PART IV:

Winter

Chapter 30

ourteen years after Tante Fanny's hundredth birthday party, the Steiners were gathered, once again, to celebrate a birthday. The guest of honor this time was the matriarch of the family, Golda Mirel herself.

Strictly speaking, it was not the actual day of her birthday. She had been born on *erev Pesach*—hardly a time to hold a birthday party! It had been decided to postpone the event until two weeks after *Pesach*, giving her children time to make all the necessary preparations. Since the considerably increased family could certainly not fit into the living room of someone's house, the venue chosen was the Assembly Hall of a local school that was often hired out for small *simchos*.

Golda Mirel surveyed the lively scene of happy relatives—men with gray or graying beards; matronly, comfortable-looking women; young men, young women and children of all ages—with an overwhelming sense of gratitude to the *Ribono Shel Olam*. Everyone was there: her five children—including Chuni and Menachem Dovid, who had come from Eretz Yisroel with their wives and children—as well as all her grandchildren in England, not to mention five great-grandchildren!

This whole tribe are my *offspring,* she thought, tears of pride springing to her eyes. She beamed around at them, nodding as she caught someone's eye. At the same time, she felt a twinge of sadness that Moshe Leib wasn't with her to share her *nachas!*

Ten years ago, he had suffered the fatal heart attack that had taken him from her, and she felt the loss keenly. Outwardly, she was full of vivacity and *joie de vivre,* always busy, always lending a sympathetic ear to those in need, but her brave face hid a painful loneliness that made it hard to go on without her life's partner by her side.

Her wandering eye paused at her son-in-law, Elkie's husband Ezriel. He looked so much better now, she noted in relief, glad her advice in that quarter had done the trick. *I still have my uses,* she thought, cheering up again.

She remembered when she had first noticed something strange about Ezriel. Normally friendly and outgoing, he seemed withdrawn, hardly answering when spoken to. His ruddy complexion, too, had faded, giving him a pale sunken look.

"Is Ezriel feeling all right?" Golda Mirel had casually asked her daughter one day. To her great surprise, Elkie suddenly burst into tears.

"Oh, Mummy, you don't know what I've been going through the last few weeks!" Between sobs, she gave her mother a rundown. It seemed that Ezriel, a Jewish and secular history teacher for thirty years, had received a shocking letter from the school's headmaster informing him that his contract was terminating at the end of term, "to make room for younger teachers on the staff."

"But he's not even sixty!" Golda Mirel cried.

"Exactly!" Elkie said indignantly, wiping her eyes. "Apparently, fifty-seven is considered old! 'Young teachers are more in touch with their pupils,'" she quoted in an affected voice. "That's what it said in the letter. I ask you! Why does one have to be 'in touch' to teach ancient history?"

"I'm sure he'll find another job," Golda Mirel said, trying to console her.

"Hardly likely," Elkie replied. "But that's not the real problem. I wouldn't mind him retiring. It's Ezriel himself. He's taken it so badly!" Her voice faltered and she seemed about to cry again. "And now he's suffering from depression!" She looked at her bewildered mother with haunted eyes. "It's horrible, Mummy! At first, he simply refused to speak. I couldn't get a word out of him. Then he stopped eating and just sat in his chair, staring into space all the time. He started having hysterical outbursts ... and ... and sometimes he would go to the window, and I thought ... you can imagine what I thought ... !" The tears began to flow again. "I was petrified!"

"Why didn't you make him go to the doctor?"

"I tried, but he wouldn't go! At the end, I went to the doctor myself and told him the problem. He was sympathetic and pre-scribed some pills, saying he couldn't guarantee they would help but were worth a try.

"I thought Ezriel would never take them, but somehow I man-aged to persuade him. He's a bit calmer now, but still totally depressed. He keeps saying his life is over!"

"What about his work?" Golda Mirel wanted to know. "It's not the end of the term yet, is it?"

"He continued teaching at the beginning, but when the head-master saw what a state he was in, he drove him home himself one day and told me not to let him come back for the rest of the term. He was very kind and offered to write him a sick note for disability. I suppose one can't blame him, not wanting him in the classroom the way he is." Elkie gripped her hands together in her lap. "Oh, Mummy, what am I going to do? Ezriel's a different person, and I can't cope with it. I want to help him, but he won't let me!"

She broke into uncontrollable weeping again, tearing at Golda

Mirel's heartstrings. "My poor Elkeleh," she murmured, her arm sliding around her daughter, "and poor Ezriel, too! But why have you kept it to yourself all this while? Why didn't you tell me sooner?"

"What could you have done?" Elkie said, heaving a sigh. "What can anyone do?"

Golda Mirel sat brooding at the window after Elkie had gone home, thinking, *it's true, there is nothing I can do. I never heard of this depression. In my day, a* Yid *didn't lose himself when he lost his* parnossoh … *Anyway, I can't interfere. But it is so hard to sit back and watch my daughter suffer!* And she shed a few tears.

A few days later she called on them, and when Elkie went into the kitchen to make tea, she tried to make conversation with her son-in-law. It was hard going, and the sight of him staring into space and hardly answering upset and irritated her.

"Ezriel!" she said sternly, forgetting not to interfere. "What's all this about? I don't know you like this!"

"Yes, you do," he said bitterly. "This is me … a useless person …"

"You're nothing of the sort!" Golda Mirel retorted. "What makes you say that?"

"I have no purpose in life," Ezriel replied, in the same flat voice.

"Nonsense! You've got children to be proud of! And look at your grandchildren … Gitty and Yossi, and little Moshe Leib? They look up to their grandfather."

"Not any more …," Ezriel said sadly. "I'll soon be just an aimless old man to them …."

"Don't talk rubbish! You're a long way from being old," Golda Mirel forged on relentlessly, "and you've got no reason to feel aimless! Apart from being a *talmid chochom*, you've got a vast knowledge of history, and no one can take that away from you!"

"A lot of use that is now," Ezriel said dejectedly. "It's all one big waste!"

"It doesn't have to be a waste!" Golda Mirel persisted. "So you're not teaching any more. You can still put your knowledge to use. You could write a history book, for instance."

"Who needs another history book? There are loads of them around." He got up and lumbered over to the bookshelf. "Here you are. World history ... Jewish history ..." He pulled out two books randomly and dumped them on the table, making Golda Mirel jump. She wasn't sure which was worse—his lethargy or this strange belligerence.

"Here! Here, you see them?" he shouted. "Boring old books, full of just plain facts! My pupils hated the textbooks. *I* had to make historical facts seem interesting to them! So why would I add another boring book to the collection?"

"You could write a book on the same lines as you teach ... making it seem interesting," Golda Mirel suggested, not sure she knew what she was talking about. "The schools would snap it up!"

Was she imagining it, she wondered, or did she detect a brief glimmer of interest in his eyes? It was gone a moment later, and he slumped back into his chair, the glum expression back on his face.

But weeks later, Golda Mirel found her idea had taken root. Elkie's voice on the telephone had a different quality, lilting and cheery.

"Mummy, Ezriel's so much better lately! He's talking of writing a Jewish history book ... one that will make learning history more interesting for schoolchildren. I can't help wondering if you said something to him that triggered it off."

"Why would that be?" asked Golda Mirel in a sweetly innocent tone.

"Well, I remember that day you came over, and I went out and left you talking to Ezriel. There was something slightly different about him after you left. It was hardly noticeable at the time, but since then he's been gradually coming out of his depression ...."

"Oh, Elkie, I'm so glad to hear it!" Golda Mirel cried. "I'm sure everything will soon be back to normal!"

"I hope so!" Elkie said fervently. "If it *was* you who started it off, then thanks a million, Mummy!"

Now, observing her son-in-law holding his grandson Moshe Leibele, on his lap, and chatting with his young nephews in pure relaxation, she felt gratified. She reflected on her family, one nucleus comprised of separate units, each with its own pleasures and problems, and she, the solitary link between them all! How she wished she could help them solve all their problems! But she had learned that some things were beyond her control.

Golda Mirel continued smiling benignly, though the noise and constant activity of the crowd were making her tired. *All this is not really healthy for an old woman of eighty*, she thought. Still, it was so sweet of the children and grandchildren to arrange this in her honor, she didn't want them to think she was ungrateful.

To her relief, her son Yankel rapped loudly on the table, and the hubbub died down. Though she knew this meant he was going to make a speech—which made her cringe with embarrassment—she was glad, hoping it would not be long now, and she would soon be in her warm bed.

Clearing his throat, Yankel began. "Ladies and gentlemen ... brothers, sisters, brothers-in-law, sisters-in-law, children, grandchildren, nieces, nephews, great-nieces, great-nephews, *kein yirbu*, relatives, friends and neighbors—whew! That's quite an address, *k'ein ayin hora*! ..." (Laughter and applause followed as he pretended to flop down, exhausted.) "... we're all gathered here today to pay tribute to a wonderful lady, our mother, grandmother ... et cetera, et cetera ..." (Enthusiastic applause filled the hall and Yankel waited for it to subside.) "... You all know and love her, so I don't need to tell you what a great person she is!"

"Yankel! Do you mind!" Golda Mirel interrupted, blushing. "It sounds like a *hesped*!"

"*Chas v'sholom!*" Yankel exclaimed. "It's nothing of the sort! With Hashem's help you'll be with us until a hundred and twenty! Can I just tell you how much we all appreciate you?" He smiled at his mother and turned back to his audience. "As I said, I don't have to point out what a dedicated, selfless mother and grandmother she is and what a tower of strength she has always been in times of crisis. All the same, as the eldest of the next generation, I can tell you a few things most of you don't even know about!

"If not for Mamme's courage and determination, we would probably not have escaped from Vienna, and you can imagine what fate would have befallen us then! She traveled to England all by herself and secured the necessary papers for us, just in time! All through the war years she and Tatte, *alav hasholom*, gave us *chizuk* and instilled *bitochon* in us, making sure we had a happy childhood in spite of the hardships.

"Even as a young married woman, Mamme displayed all the qualities of an *eishes chayil*. Tatte told me how she picked herself up and left her native Poland to join her husband in Vienna so that he could be *mekayem* the *mitzvah* of *kibbud ov v'eym* ...."

Golda Mirel tugged at her son's sleeve, and he bent down to her. "Yankel! Please stop it!" she whispered urgently. "You're making me very embarrassed!"

"Sorry, Mamme," Yankel whispered back. "I didn't mean to do that! I just want to give these next generations a sense of gratitude for all you've done for us!" Straightening up, he resumed his address. "A moment ago I mentioned *kibbud ov v'eym*, a *mitzvah* I, too, try to fulfill; and since my mother has asked me to stop, I must do as she says ... even though I really have much more to say!" There was more laughter and applause at his words. "Now," he went on, "we will get on with the most important part of the evening, which is to present our dear mother with a gift in honor of her eightieth birthday, may she be blessed with *arichas yomim*, in good health!"

A loud "*Amein*" reverberated through the hall and tumultuous applause followed for a full five minutes, while a rosy-faced Golda Mirel kept her eyes lowered. Yankel held up his hand for attention. "I now call on Mamme's oldest great-grandchild to present the gift. Come along, Gitty!"

Pessie's eight-year-old daughter marched proudly up to the table, her beribboned plaits swinging, and placed a beautifully wrapped parcel on her great-grandmother's lap.

"Thank you, Gittele," Golda Mirel said, bending forward and kissing her. "I wonder what it is!"

"You won't know till you open it!" Gitty said, her blue eyes twinkling. She looked so sweet that Golda Mirel kissed her again.

Everyone watched in hushed silence as Golda Mirel undid the green satin bow, then unwrapped the shiny gold paper. Her arthritis made her hands tremble, but with help from Elkie, sitting next to her, the paper soon lay on the table, revealing an enormous, leather-bound volume embossed with gold lettering.

With Yankel's help, Golda Mirel held it up for all to see. For the benefit of those who were not involved in its production, and, indeed, for Golda Mirel herself, Yankel explained.

"I suppose you could call this an album," he said, "but it's more than that. You could say it's a biography in pictures. On the front page, as you can see," he held it up with the cover open, "is a family tree ... expertly compiled and drawn by four of the grandchildren. They have left plenty of space to add to it, as, *b'ezras Hashem Yisborach*, it's by no means complete! The rest of the pages have photos, taken over the years, interspersed with letters, poems and articles written by various members of the family." He turned to face his mother. "Mamme, I'm sure you're eager to read it, and I think you'll enjoy it best if you browse through it in the privacy of your home. A lot of love and appreciation went into putting this together, but ..." Suddenly overcome with emotion, Yankel's voice broke, and he cleared his throat, then continued, thickly, "There are not enough words to express what we feel for you ... !" His voice trailed off, and he whispered, "*Mazel tov*, Mamme, *biz a hundred und tzvantzik!*"

As Golda Mirel wiped tears from her cheeks, shouts began of "Speech! Speech!" She stood up shakily.

"I'm no good at making speeches," she said, her voice somewhat waterlogged, "but, from the bottom of my heart, I thank you all for coming, and for your gifts and good wishes. I don't know how to thank my wonderful family for this lovely party and for this beautiful gift .... I shall treasure this as long as I live.

"May the *Eibershter* bless you all with long, good, happy lives and may we all be *zocheh* to *yemos Hamoshiach, bimheirah b'yomeinu!*"

A vehement cry of "*Amein!*" rang out.

Yankel and Elkie drove their mother home, and after Elkie had made her a cup of cocoa and sat her down in and armchair, they had wished her a good night's sleep and left. The house was quiet and restful, but Golda Mirel, who had felt utterly exhausted at the party, suddenly wasn't tired anymore. She had wanted Chuni and Menachem Dovid to stay here with their families, but they had felt it would be too much for her, with all the children, and had rented a house together for the week. Disappointed at first, she was now glad to be alone.

It had been an emotional day—a mixture of sadness and pleasure. She looked down at the album on the sidetable next to her. It was really beautiful. She ran her finger along the raised gold lettering with her name and date of birth. Opening to the first page, she studied the intricate family tree, so attractively drawn by four of her granddaughters, two of Yankel's, one, Elkie's, and one, Mindy's. They had obviously put a lot of love and care into their work. Her heart was full as she looked at the numerous branches, and she suddenly felt a desire to take her *sefer Tehillim* and say "*mizmor lesodah.*" But first she wanted to look at some more of this remarkable record. She turned to the next page. There was Moshe Leib gazing up at her, looking so lifelike that, caught unawares, she suddenly began to cry.

She wept solidly for a long while, pouring her heart out in her tears. At last it was over, and she sat up, feeling drained but relieved. This was something she should have done long ago. After the first few weeks of grieving for her husband, she had pulled herself together and hadn't allowed herself to wallow. Now, she could almost feel Moshe Leib beside her, and sensing he had been with her in spirit all the time, grew strangely calm. While she would always miss him, she sensed that as long as his offspring lived *b'derech haTorah*, his *neshomoh* would be uplifted, and that somehow he was leaving this up to her. Closing the album, she went upstairs to bed with a feeling of peacefulness.

Chapter 31

The telephone rang while Golda Mirel was washing her
breakfast dishes. Hastily wiping her hands on the tea towel,
she began looking for the phone, the persistent ringing adding to her
frustration. Where had she put it? It wasn't on the table, or on its
base. In fact, it didn't seem to be in the kitchen at all! *Why did they
have to buy me that cordless phone?* she thought, irritated. *I can never
remember where I left it!*

Her children had bought the phone because her arthritic hips
and knees restricted her movements, and she would get upset when
the phone stopped ringing just as she managed to reach it. While
pretending to be grateful, Golda Mirel hadn't been impressed by
what she called "these modern inventions." A telephone, to her way
of thinking, belonged near its socket. How could one possibly talk
on it if it wasn't even connected?

At first, she had carefully returned it to its base after each call,
but with her family always arguing that she was defeating its purpose, she eventually learned to carry it about. However, since she
hardly ever remembered where she had last left it, she was convinced
that this newfangled article was not for her!

Hobbling into the dining room, she spotted it on the table,

ringing for all it was worth. She snatched it up, losing her balance in her haste, and steadying herself on the table.

"H-hullo?" she panted breathlessly.

"Golda Mirel? Are you all right? I didn't wake you up, did I?" It was her cousin, Uncle Berel's daughter, Hindy Moscovsky.

"Hindy! How nice to hear from you!" Golda Mirel cried. Hindy still wrote her from time to time, but the last time they had spoken was at her eightieth birthday party, three years ago.

"I was getting a bit worried when you didn't answer the phone," Hindy said, "so I let it ring for quite long. Are you sure you're all right? You sound out of breath."

"I'm fine," Golda Mirel assured her, having no wish to have her younger cousin know her stupidity in mislaying her phone! "Are you calling from Gateshead?"

"No, I'm in London actually, in Golders Green. Golda Mirel, I'm so excited! Dovi … my youngest … got engaged last night!"

"Hindy! *Mazel tov!* Who to?"

"A girl named Tirtza Zelbstein. Her mother is a Schuller, from Golders Green, and her father is originally from Switzerland. They're such nice people and Tirtza is a lovely girl!"

"Oh, Hindy, I'm so glad for you!" Golda Mirel cried enthusiastically.

"I'm phoning you so early in the morning," Hindy told her, "because I want you to come to the *vort* tonight."

"What? All the way to Golders Green? I'm an old lady, Hindy! I can't go gadding about any more! And I wouldn't know how to get there! I don't like asking any of the children or grandchildren to drive me down. They all have *shiurim* they don't like to miss—"

"Well, that's why I'm phoning now," Hindy cut in quickly. "My *mechuteniste's* sister in Stamford Hill is coming, and they will be only too happy to take you in their car. They're leaving early, so you'll be able to come to us and have a rest before the *vort*. We're staying at an old yeshiva friend of Shimon's, Rabbi Zechariah Levy."

"That's very kind of them … and of you for arranging it …" There was a doubtful note in Golda Mirel's voice. It was a long drive to Golders Green and she was not quite sure she felt up to it.

"Oh, please come!" Hindy begged, detecting her hesitancy. "It won't be the same without you!"

"Sweet of you to say so!" Golda Mirel said, laughing. "Very well, then, I'll come! What time should I be ready?"

The reception rooms at the Zelbsteins were divided by two large glass doors, separating the men and women. As they grew crowded with well-wishers, Hindy took Golda Mirel's arm and led her over to the *kallah* and her mother, and introduced her. They greeted her warmly, and Golda Mirel liked them both instantly. Tirtza, she noted, seemed a sweet girl, just right for Hindy.

As Hindy began to mingle with the guests coming over to wish her *mazel tov*, Golda Mirel gingerly made her way around the clusters of people and retreated to a chair in the corner, content to sit and watch everyone. Hindy stopped by a little while later, explaining, "We've not broken the plate yet, as we're waiting for Mr. Zelbstein's mother to arrive from Zurich. Her plane was delayed, but she should be here soon."

Not long after that, there was a slight commotion in the hall, and Mrs. Zelbstein ushered in a good-looking woman in a neat auburn *sheitel*. Golda Mirel guessed her to be in her early sixties, reasoning that, though she looked quite young, she couldn't be much less if she was the *kallah*'s grandmother.

After the *tenaim* ceremony, people moved about, socializing with old friends and new acquaintances. During the course of the evening, the *Kallah's* maternal grandmother, Mrs. Schuller, sat down near Golda Mirel, making polite conversation for a few moments. Then, some time later, the grandmother from Zurich sat next to her, and began to converse in Yiddish.

"I believe you are the *mechuteniste's* cousin," she said. "A first cousin?"

"Yes," Golda Mirel replied. "Hindy's father was my father's brother ... a much younger brother," she explained.

"I see. Are you also from Germany?"

"No." Golda Mirel wondered how much she knew of Hindy's background. "I was born in Poland, actually, but lived in Vienna after my marriage. We came to England shortly before the war."

"Really? I'm originally from Vienna, too!" There was excitement in Mrs. Zelbstein's voice. "In which part of Vienna did you live?"

"In the *Zweiten Bezirk*," Golda Mirel told her, naming the street she had lived in.

Mrs. Zelbstein straightened up abruptly in her chair, a look of utter shock on her face.

"But that's the street we lived in," she cried, "and we also left just before the war ... just in the nick of time! Then we must know each other!"

Recognition suddenly dawning, she stared intently at Golda Mirel. "One minute. Are you, by any chance, Mrs. Steiner?"

"Yes, that's me! Golda Mirel Steiner."

Mrs. Zelbstein jumped up and took Golda Mirel's hands in her own. "I'm not surprised you don't recognize me. I was only a young girl at the time, but you may remember me. I was Naomi Gradman!"

"Naomi Gradman!" Golda Mirel cried, her face lighting up in joy at finding another face from her past. "I don't believe it! It must be fifty years since we saw each other!" Suddenly, she turned sober.

"And your mother? Your granddaughter's name is Tirtza ... does that mean ... ?"

Naomi Zelbstein nodded, sighing. "Yes, I'm afraid so," she replied sadly. "She was *niftar* eighteen years ago, after a long illness, just before Tirtza was born. She wanted so much to see her first great-grandchild, but it wasn't to be." There were tears in her eyes as she spoke.

Golda Mirel felt tears pricking her eyes, too. "We were such good friends!" she said quietly. "I wish now that we'd kept in touch somehow."

"Yes, Mama talked about you sometimes and wondered how you were getting along. But you know what it was like. First, there was the war, and then we all had to get adjusted to a new place and a different life. It must have been the same for you."

Golda Mirel nodded, glad her companion understood.

"Tell me about your family," Naomi said. "How are ... let me see if I remember ... Yanky ... and Elkie? And the baby? I can't remember his name."

"Chuni," Golda Mirel smiled. The two women sat talking together for quite a while until Golda Mirel, suddenly feeling guilty for monopolizing her time when she had come for a family *simcha*, apologized profusely.

"Oh, think nothing of it!" Naomi assured her. "In some ways, meeting you again was more exciting!"

After the guests were gone and the immediate family were helping clean up, Hindy had a chance to ask Golda Mirel how she knew Tirtza's grandmother.

"Hindy, I must tell you all about it!" Golda Mirel said urgently. "Is there somewhere we can speak privately?"

"Let's go outside in the garden," Hindy suggested, agog with curiosity. "It's a warm night and we won't be disturbed. I don't think Chava Zelbstein's sister is ready to go back yet, so we've got a bit of time."

They found a bench in the pleasant, floodlit garden, and sat down. Golda Mirel told Hindy about her former "best friend" and neighbor, Tirtza Gradman.

"What a surprise to suddenly find you're connected!" Hindy enthused.

"Yes. But what fills me most with wonder is how life goes around in circles!" Golda Mirel answered enigmatically.

"What do you mean?" Hindy asked, puzzled.

Golda Mirel then told her how Naomi had broken her arm, and how she had gone to Munich to see a specialist ... who turned out to be none other than Hindy's own father—Berel!

"So you see, it's through her breaking her arm that I found out about your father ... where he was, and so on. If not for that, I would never have known he was in England, and I wouldn't have gone to see him about my parents. Then you and I would not have met, and you might never have learned that you were Jewish!

"And now your son is engaged to the granddaughter of the woman whose broken arm started it all off! See what I mean about circles?"

Hindy stared into space for a while, a bemused look on her face. "Wow!" she said presently, shaking her head slowly. "I have seen and heard many incidents of *Hashgachah Protis*, but this beats them all!"

That night in bed, Golda Mirel started brooding again. She seemed to do a lot of that lately, she reflected, but that was one of the problems of being old and living alone. And after tonight's shock it was hardly surprising.

Her thoughts dwelled on Tirtza. How she regretted not having tried to contact her ... indeed, not even giving her much thought over the years. The harrowing war years, it seemed, had destroyed many a good relationship. Tirtza had been such a good, supportive friend! It was upsetting to think she had missed the birth of a great-grandchild. But she *had* survived the war, *baruch Hashem*, and been *zocheh* to further generations of *ehrliche* children, one who would soon become a relation of hers! *How lucky I am!* she thought. *I have children, grandchildren and great-grandchildren, all* yarei Shomayim! *Nothing, not loneliness, not aches and pains and the restrictions of my activities, can take these away from me!*

With these peaceful thoughts, Golda Mirel drifted off to sleep.

Chapter 32

Turning her key in the lock, Golda Mirel had to brace herself to step inside her house. *What sort of state will it be in today?* she wondered. During the past few weeks, workmen had been busy "turning her house upside down," as she put it.

Since she had great difficulty climbing stairs, they were converting the house into two flats, giving her the entire ground floor to live in. The rent from the new upstairs flat would also help her financially.

Although she had expected to stay during the renovation, she was glad her children had persuaded her to leave for the interim, as she found the mess intolerable. At first, she had gone every day to watch the work until the foreman, a hefty, rough-and-ready type named Stan, complained to Yankel that she was forever getting in the way, and it made him nervous.

"She'll 'ave something fallin' on 'er 'ead, if she don't look out!" he declared, in his broad cockney accent.

Yankel had begged his mother not to visit while they were working, and Golda Mirel agreed to go only after the workmen had left. Yankel had to accept that, but warned her to take care that she didn't trip over anything. She promised to be careful, and on Sunday mornings, she went to spend some time alone in her house.

Entering now, she was relieved to see the hall was neat. They were tidy workers in general, and always swept up before they left the house. She didn't go into the dining room, where they had just removed an antiquated gas-fire that had been in the house before the Steiners had moved in. Since central heating had been installed, they didn't use it any more, but had never bothered to remove it.

The kitchen was still the same, though she knew it was also scheduled for an upheaval soon. She went in and settled herself down at the table with a pen and writing pad. Although it was reasonably quiet at Elkie's, where she was staying, Golda Mirel found it too distracting to manage her letter-writing to her children in Eretz Yisroel. Today, she didn't have very much time, since her granddaughter Pessie was coming to take her to a *hachnosas sefer Torah*. Yankel had told her last night that his wife Tzivia's cousins, the Mittelstein brothers, were giving a *sefer Torah* in memory of their parents.

Golda Mirel, about to tell him that although she loved a *hachnosas sefer Torah* she really needed that day at home to do her letter-writing, suddenly had given a start! The Mittelsteins! Of course she must go! After all, if not for Reuven and Rosa Mittelstein, her family would not have made it to England. And when the Steiners had arrived, the Mittelsteins had put a roof over their heads and given Moshe Leib his job. She certainly owed them this little bit of honor!

Golda Mirel reflected about past friendships, realizing how many of her friends had passed on. True, she had three generations of loving children around her, but one needed a person outside the family to talk to and confide in. Whom did she have now? Even her sister Ettel was not on hand anymore, having moved to Manchester to be near her children since being widowed a few years previously. Not in the best of health, Ettel couldn't travel down to London, and Golda Mirel only saw her on the rare occasions when Mindy and Ari took her up to Manchester with them. Even then, her sister's mind was become somewhat befuddled and she couldn't converse easily anymore.

Pessie's arrival pulled her out of her reverie, and they left the house together, Golda Mirel leaning heavily on Pessie's arm as they went up the street toward the sound of lively music. When they arrived at the place, Golda Mirel gasped, overawed at the scene. She gazed longingly at the majestic *chuppah* as it moved along in the center of the road. Men sang and danced in a circle before the Mittelstein's eldest son, who held the *sefer Torah* high in its velvet *begged* and glittering silver crown. As the *chuppah* passed her, Golda Mirel caught a glimpse of his joyous face, reverent with ecstasy.

Reuven and Rosa's neshomos must be uplifted by this scene, she mused. *What an appropriate tribute to two such wonderful people!* She was suddenly gripped with a desire to do this in Moshe Leib's memory, too. The idea thrilled her! Her eagerness evaporated a moment later as she watched the *chuppah* enter the wide doors of the *beis hamedrash.* It was all very well for the Mittelstein boys, who *baruch Hashem* could easily afford it. But neither she nor her children could ever raise such a sum. *Moshe Leib surely would deplore their running into debt for such a grand gesture,* she thought resignedly. However, the notion had taken hold of her, and she wished there were some way to make it possible.

"Are you coming back with me to Mummy, Babbe?" Pessie asked when the *sefer Torah* was finally settled in its new home, and people were making their way back home. Her grandmother looked worn out, she thought.

Golda Mirel still stood gazing at the closed doors of the *beis hamedrash*, lost in thought "Yes, soon, Pessie dear," she said absently. Then she blinked, and looked up at her waiting granddaughter. "I'm sorry. I just want to fetch the letters I've written at home and post them."

"I'll come with you, then," Pessie said, knowing her mother was relying on her to bring her grandmother back.

When they returned to her grandmother's home and entered the kitchen, her grandmother sighed. "I wish I could make you a cup of tea," she said, "but all my dishes have been packed safely away."

"Oh, don't worry, Babbe," Pessie said kindly, noting her grandmother's rueful tone "Once you've moved back in, I'll come in for tea and some of your delicious biscuits!"

Golda Mirel smiled at her, looking pleased. "Well, I hope that won't be too long!" she said with feeling. "Right! Here are my letters. Let me put stamps on them so I can post them on the way." She opened a drawer and peered into it. "Oh, dear. There are no stamps left in here. I think there are some in the dining room sideboard. I'll go and get them." She began to hobble toward the door. "I hope there isn't a dreadful mess in there!"

"Oh, Babbe, let me get them!" Pessie cried, jumping up. "It's not safe for you to go!"

"You won't know where to find them. Come, we'll go in together."

Bessie took Golda Mirel's arm and as they crossed the threshold they stopped and stared. The dining room was certainly a mess! Everything was covered in soot, and there was a large hole where the gas-fire had been. A jumble of rubbish was piled near the far wall, chunks of the smashed-up gas-fire mingling with broken planks of wood and fragmented tiles from the fire-surround and the hearth.

Tut-tutting in disapproval, Golda Mirel steered her granddaughter toward the sideboard. She lifted the dust-sheet covering it and took a book of stamps out of the drawer. As they left the room, she stopped by the pile of rubbish and surveyed it.

"All this was once part of my dining room," she said, somewhat sadly. "Look at it now! I think they're bringing a skip tomorrow, so the lot will be thrown out."

"Look at all those beer cans!" Pessie commented. "The men seem to have a good time while they're working!"

"Well, they'd better not get *shikker* on the job," Golda Mirel remarked, "or they'll put things in crooked!" She eyed the tins with distaste, her eye falling on one that didn't look like a beer can. It protruded from under the pile of broken tiles. She bent down and pulled it out. Her hand was immediately covered in soot, and she dropped the tin in disgust. It rolled a few inches across the floor, and as Pessie hurried to pick it up, the lid came off.

Taking a paper tissue from her pocket, Pessie wiped off some of the soot and read, "BENSON'S COFFEE BEANS." "Whoever uses coffee beans these days?" she asked.

"It *is* a bit old," Golda Mirel said. "We had them during the war."

Curious, Pessie peered into the tin. "There's some newspaper inside," she said in surprise.

"Let's take it into the kitchen and have a look."

Pessie put the tin on the countertop and stuck her fingers inside, pulling out a package of yellowed newspaper. She unfolded it carefully, revealing a brown canvas bundle. With slightly trembling hands, she untied the canvas and spread it out, gasping at the sight in front of her eyes!

Golda Mirel leaned forward to see and let out an exclamation of astonishment. Together, they stared down at a mound of jewelry! The pieces were jumbled together, and though some of the stones sparkled a little, the collection had a lackluster appearance, slightly dusty and tarnished with age.

"W-whose are they?" Golda Mirel asked in an awed voice.

"I wish I knew!" Pessie remarked. "It must be someone who lived here before. Do you think they're valuable?"

"I don't know," Golda Mirel said> "I'm not an expert on jewelry. But they've obviously been hidden, probably somewhere in that fireplace, and why would someone hide them if they're only trinkets. What shall I do with them?"

"Well, you can't leave them here! We'd better take them with us to Mummy's."

"I don't know …," Golda Mirel said uncertainly. "Maybe we shouldn't walk in the street with them." She pondered for a moment. "Better phone Yankel. I hope he's home from the *hachnosas sefer Torah* already. If not, I'll wait here till he comes!"

Pessie looked at her watch. "He should be back by now," she said, fervently hoping she was right. There was no chance of persuading her grandmother to come with her now! "The service might be over by now and the *seudah* doesn't start till seven-thirty. I'll ring him right away! And then I'll phone Mummy and tell her not to worry. You might be home a bit later."

Yankel came rushing over as soon as he got Pessie's message, although his niece had told Tzivia there was nothing to worry about.

"What's up?" he asked anxiously. "Are you all right, Mamme?"

"Yes, I'm fine, *baruch Hashem*," his mother assured him. "It's just that we've found something *extremely* interesting … and we don't know what to do with it!" She clearly was enjoying the mystery. She brought him over to the table where the package lay under its wrapping and threw back the canvas with a flourish, reveling in her son's look of amazement.

He listened to their account of the discovery of this "treasure," looking skeptical about its value. But reasoning, as his mother had done, that it would hardly have been necessary to hide them if they were worthless, he made no comment.

"Yankel, what shall I do with them? I surely can't keep them!"

"I don't know," Yankel said dubiously. "It might be a case of 'finders keepers.' We'll have to check up on the law ... and ask a *shailah*."

"But I don't want them!" Golda Mirel protested. "I'd rather get them back to their rightful owner. Perhaps it's a *Yid*. I don't often get the chance to fulfill the *mitzvah* of *hashovas aveidah*."

"You've got a point," Yankel said, smiling. "But it won't be easy to trace the owner." He picked up the crumbly newspaper wrapper, peering at it closely. "July, 1915," he read in amazement. "It *has* been there a long time! Look, Mamme, with your permission, I'll take these home and lock them in my safe until we find out what to do next." He pondered for a moment. "I'll get Shloime Glass, my secretary, to work on it. He can go to the Town Hall and check the deeds to see who all the previous owners were. From whom did you buy the house, by the way?"

"It was a Council house," Golda Mirel told him. "We bought it direct from the Council."

"Well, that's a start. Judging by the date, it's someone who lived there during the First World War. I hope there'll be records that far back. Anyway, I've got a *seudah* to go to and you'd better get back to Elkie. She must be worried by now!"

True to his word, Yankel's secretary visited the Town Hall the next day to inspect the deeds of the house on Fairholt Road and brought back whatever information was available. Yankel reported the finding to his mother.

"The house was the property of the Hackney Borough Council from 1939 until you bought it in 1949," he explained. "Before that it was owned by a Mr. Samuel Green and his wife Sadie. After the widowed Mrs. Green's death in 1938, their daughter Edith Green inherited the property, which was later acquired by the Council under a Compulsory Purchase Order."

"So, we need to contact this Edith Green."

"Exactly! But finding her is easier said than done. We know she was born in Hackney Hospital in 1912—Shloime checked the records—and if she's living in England she must still be alive, as there's no death record in her name.

"She might have got married," Golda Mirel suggested. "She'd have a different name, then. There must be records of marriages, too!"

"Yes, Shloime's going to check that out, but it isn't going to be easy and may take a long time. Don't worry, Mamme," he said appeasingly, seeing her disappointed face, "if anyone can find her, Shloime can! He's a regular bloodhound. I always tell him he's missed his vocation. He would have made a good private detective!"

It did indeed take a long time. Golda Mirel, with little to do while she was living in her daughter's house, brooded over it most of the time, growing impatient.

Meanwhile, the alterations to her house were completed, and the upheaval of moving back and organizing herself in her new flat occupied most of her thoughts. Yankel came in regularly to keep her informed of his secretary's investigations, but Golda Mirel's interest had waned, which was just as well, because most of their leads came to dead ends.

Then, one day, Yankel had something more concrete to report. There had been no trace of Miss Green's whereabouts because, after selling the house, she had gone abroad to America, where she had lived right through the war. Now Shloime's research was directed toward the United States.

"I don't suppose he'll find out much there," Golda Mirel said pessimistically. "It's such a big country."

A month later, however, Yankel came around and jubilantly announced that his diligent secretary had struck gold!

"We're nearly there!" he told his mother. "First of all, Shloime found out that the Greens were, in fact, *Yidden*! Mr. Green's parents, then called Grunowitz, came from Russia in 1885, and Samuel was born here a year later. Mrs. Green, whose maiden name was Katzovsky, was also born here, to Polish immigrants …."

"Were they *frum*?" Golda Mirel asked, interrupting.

"I don't think so. At least their daughter doesn't seem to be. As I told you, she went to America, and in 1948 she married Marcus B. Rafaelson, a wealthy business tycoon from a Liberal synagogue in Los Angeles, where they settled down. After her husband's death, Edith returned to England, a rich widow. Shloime has even found out where she lives. It's in Hampstead Garden Suburb. He's got the address written down. How's that for efficiency?" he finished with a note of pride.

"Wonderful!" Golda Mirel exclaimed, her enthusiasm returning. "I think you should raise your secretary's wages!"

Oh, well," he laughed. "*Der Eibershter wert helfen*. Anyway, the thing now is to contact this Mrs. Rafaelson. I think you should call on her, Mamme. Do you think you're up to it?"

"Of course I am!" Golda Mirel declared, resenting any insinuation that things were too much for her. "When can I go?"

"As soon as we've arranged an appointment," Yankel said, amused by her eagerness. "I hope she's approachable. I don't think we'll mention what it's about. We'll just say it's to do with the house on Fairholt Road. That should pique her interest!"

"Please take a seat, Mrs. Steiner." The frail old woman in the rocking chair waved a heavily bejeweled hand toward one of the high-backed leather chairs in the room.

For the third time in her life, Golda Mirel found herself in the opulent surroundings of a luxurious mansion. Although this one spelled affluence, too, it differed from the other two, in an over-furnished, cluttered style. The room she was ushered into contained various sofas and chairs, placed anywhere as if by guess, several elaborately carved mirrors and paintings, a collection of antiques randomly set on sidetables, an ornate grandfather clock, and a number of oriental lamps, urns and free-standing vases that were scattered about haphazardly.

Huddled in a hand-painted rocking chair, a paisley shawl over her shoulders and a rug across her knees, the woman looked old and feeble and had a kind of shriveled appearance. Golda Mirel could hardly believe that, according to the records Yankel's secretary had unearthed, this person was younger than herself!

One slender hand stroked a Persian cat that purred contentedly on her lap, and a half-filled decanter of whiskey with an empty glass beside it stood at her elbow.

"Excuse my not getting up," Mrs. Rafaelson said. "My legs have become too weak to support me. Might I offer you a drink?"

"No thank you. I don't drink," Golda Mirel replied in disgust.

"Very sensible. I wish I didn't! I notice you, too, have walking difficulties. You were limping, and you use a walking-stick."

Golda Mirel explained how she had been born with the limp, and that the stick supported her arthritic joints.

"Well, at least you *can* walk," the woman said enviously. "Now, I understand you have come to see me about something to do with the house on Fairholt Road. I don't own it anymore, you know."

"I know that," Golda Mirel told her. "I am the present owner. And I found something there that I believe belongs to you."

"You found the jewelry!" Mrs. Rafaelson cried incredulously, suddenly sitting up straight. "So Mother *was* telling the truth! But I searched the whole house! I couldn't find it!"

"You know about it?" Golda Mirel asked, astounded.

"Oh, yes! I'll tell you the story … as much as I know of it." Mrs. Rafaelson refilled her glass and, between sips, began her account. "My parents were both born in England from immigrant parents. My father's parents were not religious, while my mother's were, and when she married my father, they refused to have anything more to do with her. I was only two when my father was called to serve in the army, so I don't really remember him. There was a war on, you understand. My mother never talked about what happened, but I gathered he had been killed in action.

"Before the war, Father was a successful antique-dealer, and my mother once told me that he used to give her pieces of valuable antique jewelry from the collections he acquired. We lived in your house on Fairholt Road—though I don't remember it. I grew up in Cardiff, South Wales, and never knew of another home. I only learned years later, that left alone with a small child, she had fled to my father's parents in Cardiff, having been rejected by her own. In 1935, my mother suffered some kind of mental breakdown and only lived another few years after that. She was only forty-five. Not long before she died, she told me she'd hidden her jewelry in the Fairholt Road house, not wanting to bring them to her mother-in-law. She said she had always intended to go back and retrieve them, but couldn't bring herself to return there. When I asked her where they were hidden, she said she couldn't remember. After her death, *I* went and searched that house from top to bottom, but found nothing. I concluded that it had all been a figment of Mother's imagination! And it was true, after all! Where *was* it hidden?"

"I'm not sure," Golda Mirel replied. "Workmen removed a gas-fire from the dining room and I found it among the rubble."

"There was no gas-fire there when I went to look," Mrs.

Rafaelson said, screwing up her eyes in concentration. "It must have been somewhere in the fireplace. I suppose I should have made a better search of it. Well, soon after, the Council asked me to sell it to them as they were acquiring some other properties there. They offered me a mere pittance, but the house was so dilapidated, I was only too happy to be rid of it. In any case, I was about to leave for America at the time and didn't want to be held up."

"Well!" Golda Mirel took a long breath. "Here is your jewelry." She drew the package from her bag. "I'm so glad to be able to return it to you!"

"Whatever for?" Mrs. Rafaelson looked puzzled. "You found it in your house. Why didn't you keep it?"

"Because," Golda Mirel explained, "there's a Jewish law that says we must return anything belonging to another Jew to its rightful owner. We are happy to do it!"

Mrs. Rafaelson raised her eyebrows curiously. "Is that so?" she asked. "I'm afraid I don't know much about Jewish laws. My mother never adhered to them. My late husband was also not religious … so what can you expect from me?" The cat suddenly jumped off her lap, making Golda Mirel shrink back. She eyed it mistrustfully, but it merely settled itself in a velvet-cushioned cat-basket, giving an enormous yawn.

"But, I do say, I'm really impressed," Mrs. Rafaelson went on. "I always thought religious people … oh, well, never mind …" She began to unwrap the package as she spoke. "So this is Mother's jewelry collection! I think it must be worth quite a lot!" She began to finger the pieces, studying them with interest. "As you can probably see, I'm not exactly short of valuable jewelry … or items of luxury … but these have sentimental value. I'm extremely grateful to you for bringing them to me. You must let me pay you something by way of a reward …."

"Oh no!" Golda Mirel protested. "I don't want anything!"

"Well, of course you do! You deserve it!"

Unsure how to describe a *mitzvah* to this woman who knew nothing of *Yiddishkeit*, she said simply, "Not at all! It was my pleasure to return it."

Mrs. Rafaelson continued to press her, and Golda Mirel persistently refused. Presently, Mrs. Rafaelson selected an item from the pile, and leaning forward, pressed it into Golda Mirel's hand, holding hers clasped over it.

"Please," she begged, a pained look on her face. "Don't do this to me! Don't refuse this small token of appreciation! I'll always feel bad if you don't take it! I don't want to be left feeling I owe someone something!" There was such a pleading expression in her eyes that Golda Mirel saw she could not refuse.

"All right," she said. "If that's how you feel, I will take it. And thank you very much."

The maid entered, saying, "Mrs. Steiner, you son has just knocked on the door. He said to tell you he's waiting in the car whenever you're ready."

Golda Mirel stood up, shook Mrs. Rafaelson's hand, and wished her all the best. Edith Rafaelson squeezed her guest's hand warmly.

"Thank you, Mrs. Steiner," she said, her voice shaking a little. "If we were both younger, I would have suggested we get together from time to time so you could tell me a bit more about Jewish law. But there it is. We live too far away from one another ... and we're both not spring chickens anymore! Goodbye!"

Back in her Yankel's car, Golda Mirel showed him the brooch, an attractive gold piece with a diamond in its center encircled by small rubies. She repeated her conversation with Mrs. Rafaelson to him, and he agreed that she had had to accept it.

"I don't know what I'm going to do with it," Golda Mirel

declared. "I certainly will never wear it! That sort of thing is not for me!"

"Well, in that case," Yankel said, understanding her, "you shouldn't keep it in your house. If you want, I'll lock it in my safe till you decide what to do with it."

Golda Mirel was relieved to give it into his safekeeping. Curious to know its value, Yankel, with his mother's permission, brought it to a client of his who was a jeweler.

"Leave it with me," the jeweler said. "I'll assess it as soon as I can."

That very evening, he telephoned Yankel in excitement. "I don't want to raise your hopes," he said cautiously, "but I think that's a very valuable piece you've got there. I'll have to consult an expert on antique jewelry before I say anything, though."

Two days later, Yankel received another call. "I'd rather not discuss this over the phone," he said. "Could you possibly come around straight away?"

"I'll come at once," Yankel said, wondering what the cloak-and-dagger manner was about. Could it possibly be a stolen article?

When he arrived, the jeweler told him that the expert had confirmed his suspicions. "He saw at once that it was a rare piece, so he took it to Sotheby's and they were very excited to see it. Apparently it is part of a set known as the 'Angleton Collection,' which had belonged to a duchess in the nineteenth century. The duke had fallen into debt and been forced to sell some of the contents of his home, Angleton Towers, including some of his wife's jewelry. The brooch is part of that collection. Sotheby's valued it at twenty thousand pounds."

"Twenty thousand!" Yankel was flabbergasted. "I think I'll advise my mother to sell it!"

Golda Mirel was completely taken aback at the news. She hadn't even considered selling it. On the other hand, she wasn't going to wear it, either. She could, perhaps, give it to one of her granddaughters, but how could she single out one of them for something so valuable. It wouldn't be right.

Pondering, she suddenly remembered how she had wished to donate a *sefer Torah* in Moshe Leib's memory. Her eyes lit up at once! Out of the blue, she could fulfill her heart's desire at last! Bursting with excitement, she telephoned Yankel to come over so that she could put her idea to him. He would be delighted, too!

However, while she waited for him, a thought struck her, and her elation plummeted down at once. Surely, Mrs. Rafaelson could not have been aware of the full value of the brooch. How could she keep it now? Tears of disappointment coursed down her cheeks, but she brushed them away hastily and washed her eyes. Yankel must not see that she had been crying.

When he arrived, she told him that she intended to send the brooch back, explaining her reasons. His first reaction was to protest, but after considering the matter for a few moments, he saw her point of view and offered to have his secretary deliver it.

It was a great struggle, but Golda Mirel made a joke of the whole affair so no one would know about her shattered dream.

A week later, a letter arrived from Mrs. Rafaelson. Golda Mirel opened it with trembling hands, a strange hope rising within her.

Dear Mrs. Steiner, the woman had written, her handwriting thin and shaky,

> *I am at a loss for words! I must admit I was very hurt when the little gift I gave you came back, but after reading your letter I was extremely impressed by your honesty! In truth, I was not aware of its true value, but since I gave it to you it belonged to you, and you were not obliged to return it.*
>
> *I hesitate to send you something else as you seem determined*

not to be rewarded for what you call a "mitzvah." All I can do is express my sincere gratitude to you.

It is a pity that we did not meet years ago. Your attitude has made me see religious people in a different light. Were I younger, I might change a few things about my life. Now I am too old and frail for any changes, so please don't come along and try to reform me!

I wish you well and hope that you will reap a heavenly reward for your good deeds!

Sincerely Yours,

Edith Rafaelson

Golda Mirel was greatly moved by the letter and was glad she had caused a *kiddush Hashem*. All the same, she could not shake her disappointment regarding the *sefer Torah*. After brooding about it for a few days, she argued herself out of it. *It just wasn't bashert,* she told herself philosophically. *In any case, aren't three generations of wonderful children living memorials to Moshe Leib? And who knows, maybe one day, some of them will donate a* sefer Torah *in his memory after all.*

Chapter 33

"Is that you, Elkie?" Golda Mirel called, hearing keys jangling and the front door opening. She put her magnifying-glass down on her book as her daughter entered the room.

"I've brought you the shopping you wanted," Elkie told her. She began unloading packages. "How are you today, Mummy?"

"Could be worse," Golda Mirel said simply, giving her standard reply. "*Nu*, have they fixed the date for Gitty's *chassunah*?"

"No, not yet," Elkie replied, sitting down beside her mother. "But they're talking about some time in *Teves* or *Shevat*."

"What? That's months away!" Golda Mirel exclaimed, looking disappointed. "Why are they waiting so long? It's already three months since she got engaged!"

"I know," Elkie threw her mother a look of sympathy. She understood. She, too, would have liked her granddaughter's *chassunah* to be sooner, but she knew for her, the time would pass quickly. For an old lady of ninety, however, half a year must seem like an eternity.

Poor Mummy, she reflected. *It must be so hard for her. She has always been so active, and now with her movements more restricted, she can't do as much as she used to. Time must drag for her!*

"They didn't want to make it in *Elul*," she continued, "because Ben-Zion's father's butcher shop is busier before the *Yomim Tovim* And after *Succos*, Ezriel is booked for his American tour. He can't very well miss his granddaughter's *chassunah*, can he?"

"American tour?" Golda Mirel looked vague. "You did tell me, but I've forgotten what it's all about."

"Mummy! How could you forget, when it's all thanks to you!" Elkie cried in mock indignation. "He's been invited by this Jewish Literary Society in New York to tour America, promoting his Jewish History book. It's selling so well, it's becoming a hit!"

"Well, it ought to be good," Golda Mirel commented. "He's been working on it for about ten years!"

"Yes, he's really put a lot into it!" Elkie said proudly. "I've always been grateful to you, Mummy, for putting the idea into his head!"

"My main aim was to get him out of his depression," Golda Mirel said, "but I see it's done even more than that. I'm so glad!"

"He's just like he used to be!" Elkie said. "And he always jokes that it's because of his outspoken mother-in-law!" She winked at her mother, who took it in the spirit it was meant and laughed heartily.

Elkie stood up. "I'll just heat up the pea soup I brought for you today, and then I'll be on my way." She moved to the stove. "I know it's your favorite, and besides, I've made such a big potful, it'll only go to waste if you don't have some of it!" she said, persuasively. Elkie had to tread carefully, knowing how much her mother valued her independence. Golda Mirel generally did her own cooking, but the family tended to worry, not sure how much nourishment she was getting. A person living on her own did not always bother much about nutritional value.

Elkie put the last carton into the cupboard, turned down the heat under the simmering soup and, picking up her keys, leaned down to kiss her mother before leaving.

Alone again, Golda Mirel couldn't relax or resume her reading. She was happy for her son-in-law, who really deserved the acclaim for his knowledge and hard work, but why did this tour have to be just now, when it meant pushing off Gitty's *chassunah*? She wanted so much to see her first great-grandchild married! Why did she have to wait so long?

I'm growing impatient in my old age, she thought. She ignored her lurking fear that now that she was in her nineties, she might not make it to some particular occasion.

A few years after her great-granddaughter's *chassunah*, Golda Mirel finally faced the fact that she could not live alone, and allowed Elkie to persuade her to move in with them. She remembered how Tante Fanny's obstinate refusal to leave her own flat had caused problems, and wasn't going to subject her family to that. Once she had accepted the situation, she was happy there. Walking had become difficult, and now that she had taken the advice of Dr. Simms, the rheumatologist, and stopped wearing her built-up shoe, her limp had become so pronounced that she tended to topple over when she walked.

Dr. Simms had actually made the suggestion a few years earlier, telling her the shoe was too heavy for her ankle, increasing the pain from her arthritis. At that time, Golda Mirel had adamantly refused to comply. She was determined to dance at her great-granddaughter's *chassunah*, however difficult it would be. But after plodding on in great pain for a few years, she finally gave in. It meant, of course, that she had to use a walker, and consequently she hardly went out.

Now, sitting in the comfortable recliner her children had bought her, she was pleased to see Pessie's daughter Gitty come into the room. She wanted some company to chat with about this exciting day. Today was the first of January, 2000, and Golda Mirel could hardly believe they had entered a new millennium! When she had been young, the year 2000 had seemed like the end of time! She had never imagined she would actually reach it, and here she was, almost ninety-six years old, watching a new century begin!

"Hullo, Babsy," Gitty said, calling her by the affectionate name she coined to differentiate between her and Elkie, whom she called Bubby. "Here's a cup of tea. How are you today?"

"It could be worse," came the usual answer. She smiled indulgently at her great-granddaughter. "Thank you, darling," she said, taking the tea and sipping it. "That's lovely! Come sit down and talk to me a bit."

As Gitty took a seat next to her, Golda Mirel eyed her closely for a moment. "You're looking tired, Gitty. Have the millennium celebrations kept you awake, too? The *goyim* two doors away made such a noise all night, letting off fireworks and singing and dancing in the street."

"I don't know what there is to celebrate," Gitty said gloomily. "It's only another century. So what?"

Golda Mirel stared at her quizzically. That doleful tone was not like Gitty at all. What had got into her?

"Gitty, you sound so cross! What's wrong with that? It's quite interesting, really."

"Yes, for some," Gitty said dully, then pressed her lips together as if she had said too much. A minute later, however, she seemed to change her mind. Looking at her great-grandmother with tears glistening in her eyes, she burst out, "It makes me realize how quickly time is passing!" She sounded almost desperate.

"So why should that worry you? You're so young. You've got your whole life ahead of you. What should *I* say ... at *my* age?"

"I know, Babsy, you're right, really," Gitty replied sounding contrite, "but you've got children and grandchildren—even great-grandchildren—to show for it, *Boruch Hashem*. The way things are going for me I don't know if I'll ever have that!"

Aha, so that's what it was! Golda Mirel regarded Gitty with compassion.

"Gittele," she said tenderly, placing a wrinkled hand on the young woman's arm. "You mustn't get despondent. It's not even five years! That's not a long time."

"It is to me!" Gitty declared vehemently. "How do I know it's ever going to be?"

"Now, have a bit of *bitochon*," her great-grandmother said soothingly. "Let me tell you something. My mother was married five years before I was born. She also felt desperate and thought it would never happen. The only person who understood and instilled a bit of hope in her was her grandmother, Babbe Golda Mirel, who kept telling her the time would come. And, as you can see, it did!"

"Did you say 'Golda Mirel'?" Gitty asked with interest. "So you must be named after her! But then—" She broke off, looking thoughtful.

"Yes, I am named after her. She was *niftar* the year before I was born. That was the only thing that marred Mamme's happiness–that her grandmother never saw the result of all her *brochos*!"

Gitty sighed. "Your story does give me hope, Babsy. But when will my time come? I'm running out of patience!"

Golda Mirel shook her head, tut-tutting softly. "Impatience won't get you anywhere, *sheffela*," she said kindly. A sudden thought struck her. "Have you and Ben-Zion ever thought of going to a Rebbe?"

"A Rebbe?" Gitty looked surprised. "Whatever for? Ben-Zion's not a *chossid*."

"You don't have to be a *chossid* to get a *brochoh* from a Rebbe," Golda Mirel chided her.

"I know," Gitty said, "but Ben-Zion doesn't really believe in that kind of thing. And anyway, which Rebbe? We haven't got one that we know whom we can go to."

Golda Mirel thought for a moment. She then told Gitty Ari's story with his sister Esther, and how his Rebbe had saved them from disaster. "He certainly had *ruach hakodesh*! And his son, whom Ari now follows, is a great man, too!"

Gitty was impressed, but shrugged her shoulders. "I'll tell Ben-Zion," she said skeptically, "but I doubt he'll take your advice."

Just as she suspected, Ben-Zion was not interested. He agreed that, of course, a Rebbe's *brochoh* can have an effect, but he was not the type to go to Rebbes. "I'd be too ashamed," he admitted, half joking and half serious. "A Rebbe would take one look at me and see all my faults!"

But the more he resisted the idea, the more Gitty persisted. Many a tearful argument followed, until unable to bear his wife's unhappiness, Ben-Zion agreed.

Golda Mirel was delighted when she heard that the young couple were taking a trip to Eretz Yisroel. She fervently prayed their trip would be successful. Ari had given them the Rebbe's address and offered a letter of introduction, which they had politely refused, not wanting to feel committed.

When they returned two weeks later, Gitty came straight to her grandmother's house to see her great-grandmother.

"You wouldn't believe this, Babsy," she said, "but Ben-Zion was absolutely taken with this Rebbe! After the Rebbe gave us a *brochoh*, he asked me to go out of the room and he talked to Ben-Zion for almost an hour. When Ben-Zion came out, he looked sort of overwhelmed. He told me that, although he had no intention of becoming *chassidish*, with a *shtreimel* and *bekeshe* and all that, he would always look to this Rebbe for guidance in matters of importance."

"But Gitty, that's wonderful!" Golda Mirel cried enthusiastically.

"It is—and it isn't," Gitty said, reservation in her tone.

"What do you mean?"

"Well, I'm not too happy with what the Rebbe told us to do."

"Which is … ?" Golda Mirel prompted.

"He said we should come to live in Eretz Yisroel. But I don't know that I *want* to! I'd miss my friends and my work—and all of you!"

"Well, much as I would miss you, too, I think the Rebbe's given you some sound advice!" Golda Mirel declared emphatically. "*Meshaneh makom, meshaneh mazel.* If you change your place, you change your *mazel*," she translated.

"Yes, that's what the Rebbe said. Oh, Babsy! What shall I do?"

"If you think less of what you are losing and more of what you could gain, you'd know what to do!" Golda Mirel commented sagely.

After that conversation, Gitty avoided the subject whenever she came to visit her great-grandmother. Golda Mirel, too, was careful not to mention it, understanding Gitty's conflict and not wishing to put pressure on her. A few weeks later, she heard about the decision, but not from Gitty. Elkie told her the news one afternoon, shortly after *Purim*.

"Gitty and Ben-Zion are moving to Eretz Yisroel," she said, wondering how much her mother knew about the situation.

"Oh, so she's finally decided! I think she's doing the right thing … even though I'll miss her very much."

"You won't be the only one," Elkie said with a sigh. Although she knew it was for a good reason, she couldn't pretend she was glad about the move. She was very attached to her oldest grandchild, and hated the thought of not seeing her every day. Still, if it had the desired result, she was certainly willing to make the sacrifice.

"When are they going?" Golda Mirel wanted to know.

"Straight after *Pesach*," her daughter told her. "Ben-Zion found a *kollel* he liked while he was there, and he's applied and been accepted."

"Very good," Golda Mirel said approvingly. "You know, I have a feeling in my bones that it won't be too long before we hear good news from them!"

The "good news" Golda Mirel had predicted did become a reality, and it reached her one hot, sunny day in August as she rested in a deck-chair under the tree in the garden. Her granddaughter Pessie came up to her, a tray of cool drinks on her arm and a huge smile on her face.

"Hullo, Babbe," she said. "Isn't it a glorious day! Are you sure you're not too hot?"

"No, no. I'm fine," Golda Mirel assured her. "This shade is very pleasant. You're looking very cheerful this morning, Pessie. Have you won a lottery or something?"

"Oh, no, something even better than that!" Pessie said with excitement. "I've just had a phone call from Gitty ..."

"Oh?" Golda Mirel said eagerly, a gleam in her eye. She could guess what was coming. "What does she say?"

"She's settling down well, *baruch Hashem*. And so is Ben-Zion. She likes her flat and she's made quite a few friends ...."

"Come on, Pessie!" Golda Mirel interrupted impatiently. "That's not what you're so excited about! You don't have to prepare me slowly for good news. Is it what I think it is?"

"Yes! It is! Gitty and Ben-Zion are over the moon! Oh, Babbe, so am I! Can you imagine? I'm going to be a grandmother!"

"Oh, Pessie, I'm so happy for you!" Golda Mirel cried, wishing she could jump up and hug and kiss her. She reached up a feeble arm and took her granddaughter's hand, squeezing it tightly. "And what about the rest of us? This makes your mother a great-grandmother and me a great-*great*-grandmother!"

"That's right!" Pessie cried enthusiastically.

Golda Mirel leaned back contentedly. "I knew it would happen," she said simply.

Pessie handed her a cold drink and Golda Mirel sat sipping and thinking. She remembered how Gitty had come to say goodbye, her eyes red with tears. Even the *brochos* Golda Mirel had heaped on her hadn't made her smile. How good to know she was happy now, and that her dearest wish had been fulfilled. Golda Mirel's heart gave a thump with happiness and gratitude to *Hashem Yisborach* for His goodness!

She sent up a prayer that she would live to enjoy her first great-great-grandchild!

The days grew shorter, and summer gave way to autumn with its changeable weather. The *Yomim Tovim* were soon upon them, during which Golda Mirel was kept busy with a constant flow of visitors. Later that autumn, Chuni and Roisy came from Eretz Yisroel, bringing an enormous pile of photos of their children and grandchildren for her to pore over. And not long after they left, Menachem Dovid and Shifra paid her a surprise visit. They, too, brought pictures of their family, but these were all neatly arranged in albums.

It did Golda Mirel good to see that her youngest son, now middle-aged, had mellowed with time. Even his smile was more spontaneous. He told her he was working on another *sefer*, and that his oldest son, Avraham, was a *menahel* in a popular *yeshiva ketana*. But what delighted Golda Mirel most was the pride with which Menachem Dovid spoke about his wife.

"She's headmistress of a girls' school called *Beis Devorah*, and they're all crazy about her there! Well, they ought to be! She puts so much into it ... and that's with looking after her family at home!"

Autumn turned to icy winter, and Golda Mirel was housebound with the short, dark days. She was sleeping more and becoming weaker and frailer. She tired quickly, and found the perpetual stream of grandchildren and great-grandchildren overwhelming, even while they gave her such joy. The knowledge that she was getting too old for the children upset her, but what could she do? At her age, what could one expect?

By December, frosty weather had set in, and like most of the people around her, Golda Mirel came down with a cold, which soon turned into a cough. In spite of Elkie's careful nursing, she could not shake it off. After two weeks of her persistent coughing, Elkie telephoned the doctor, insisting he come to see her mother.

After the doctor examined Golda Mirel, he spoke seriously to Elkie.

"She has a bad chest infection," he said. "I will give her antibiotics and something for her to inhale. If she's not better in three days, let me know and I will come again."

At the end of three days, there was no improvement. The antibiotics had made Golda Mirel weak, and she was barely able to lift her head. The doctor came again and shook his head gravely at her condition.

"I'm not happy that she still has a fever," he said. "She will have to be admitted to the hospital."

"Oh, no!" Elkie cried in dismay. "I can look after her, Doctor! Just give her the right medicine! I'm sure it isn't good for her to go to the hospital!"

"I would be inclined to agree with you," the doctor said, kindly, "but unfortunately she is not responding to the antibiotics. I don't think she can take anything stronger orally. She appears to have developed pneumonia and needs intravenous antibiotics immediately!"

"You mean she'll be on a drip?" Elkie asked, the thought filling her with horror.

The doctor nodded. "Where is your telephone?" he asked. "I will ring for an ambulance. Try not to worry," he said, regarding Elkie sympathetically. "I'm sure they'll do their best for her!"

Golda Mirel lay in the hospital bed, seeming to be in a sort of haze, with nurses and doctors hovering around and members of the family coming in and out. Most of the time she felt too weak to make conversation and just lay listening to them. Occasionally, when she felt a little stronger, she would show a bit of interest and enquire after the children.

On one of those "better" days, Pessie came to see her. "Babbe, I've come to say goodbye, " she said. "I'm off to Eretz Yisroel this afternoon."

"Oh, Gitty's time has come?" Golda Mirel asked, suddenly more alert.

"Yes, any day now," Pessie told her. "Oh, Babbe, I feel so bad going away. But Gitty needs me now!"

"Of course she does!" Golda Mirel nodded in agreement. "Don't worry about it. Your first duty is to your daughter! *Gei gezunterheit.*"

"Thank you, Babbe!" Pessie said, bending down and kissing her grandmother gently. "I'll let you know when there's good news. Now get well quickly, Babbe, and I'll see you, *im yirtzeh Hashem*, when I get back."

Golda Mirel smiled wanly, making no reply.

The atmosphere in the hospital room was somber. All five of Golda Mirel's children were there, their faces grave. The consultant entered, took a look at the patient and withdrew.

"I can't understand it," he remarked to the house doctor as they walked down the corridor. "Her strength has completely ebbed away, yet she seems to be hanging on. It's almost as if she was waiting for something ...."

Elkie sat near the bed, watching her mother anxiously, while the others sat a little farther away, equally apprehensive. Golda Mirel's shallow breathing and a monitor ticking quietly beside her made rhythmic, lulling sounds in the silent room.

Suddenly, she raised her frail hand slightly and Elkie leaned closer. Her mother asked in a weak whisper, "Is the child born yet?"

"No, Mummy," Elkie said gently, "but we'll tell you as soon as we hear."

Silence filled the room again, and the vigil resumed. About an hour later a nurse came in on soft rubber soles, motioning to Elkie. She whispered something in her ear.

"*Baruch Hashem!*" Elkie breathed. Then she turned to the bed and announced, loud enough for all to hear, "*Mazel tov*, Mummy! Gitty has given birth to a little girl!"

"*Baruch Hashem!*" Golda Mirel mouthed faintly, a smile playing about her mouth. Her children drew nearer, but only Elkie, bending over her mother, heard her say in an almost inaudible whisper, "Another Golda Mirel."

Then, with a look of serene contentment on her face and *Shema Yisroel* on her lips, Golda Mirel closed her eyes ... forever.

The date was *chamishah asar B'Shvat* ... when winter ends and spring—bringing with it new life—begins.

Glossary

All terms are Hebrew unless indicated as Yiddish (Yidd.) or Aramaic (Aram.).

Agmas nefesh—aggravation

Agudah—short for Agudath Israel, an international Jewish communal organization

Alav hasholom—may he rest in peace

Aleha hasholom—may she rest in peace

Aleichem sholom—peace be upon you

Alle maalos (Yidd.)—every good quality

Amein—Amen

Anschluss (Germ.)—the annexation of Austria to Germany

Arichas yomim—long life

Aveilus—mourning

B'derech haTorah—in the path of the Torah

Baal habosta (Yidd.)—a housewife

Baal teshuva—one who repents and returns to observing the Torah's commandments

Babbe (Yidd.)—grandmother

Baruch Hashem—thank G-d

Bashert (Yidd.)—heavenly-ordained marriage partner

Beis Din Shel Maalah—the Court of Heaven

Beis hamedrash—Torah study hall

Bekeshe (Yidd.)—rabbinic frock

Bentch (Yidd.)—to recite Birchas Hamazon, Grace after Meals

B'ezras Hashem—with G-d's help

Bikur cholim—attending to the needs of the sick

Bitochon—trust in G-d

Bochur, bochurim—unmarried yeshiva student(s)

Bris—circumcision

Brochoh, brochos—blessing(s)

Bubbe meiseh (Yidd.)—fictional story, fairy tale

Chas v'sholom—G-d forbid

Chassidic, chassidish, chassidishe—characteristic of Chassidim
(see *Chossid*)

Chassunah—wedding

Chavrusa (Aram.)—Torah study partner

Cheder—Jewish elementary school

Cheshvan—the second month in the Jewish year

Chessed—kindness

Chevra kadisha (Aram.)— lit., "holy society"; burial society, a
loosely structured but generally closed organization of Jewish
men and women who see to it that the bodies of Jews are prepared for burial according to halacha (Jewish law)

Chillul Hashem—desecration of G-d's name

Chinuch—education

Chizuk—support

Chometz—leavened bread or other leavened products, which are
forbidden to be eaten on Passover

Chossid—member of a sect of Orthodox Jews that arose out of a
pietistic movement originating in eastern Europe in the second
half of the 18th century

Chosson—groom

Chuppah—wedding canopy

Daven (Yidd.)—pray

Derech eretz—appropriate behavior and good character

Don lekav zechus—to judge a person favorably

Dreidel (Yidd.)—spinning top used in traditional Chanukah game

Ehrlich, ehrliche (Yidd.)—honest

Eibershter (Yidd.)—G-d

Einikel, einiklach (Yidd.)—grandchild(ren)

Eiruv—enclosure around a community, created according to the dictates of halacha (Jewish law), in order to allow residents to carry things from house to house or place to place on the Sabbath

Eishes chayil—woman of valor

Emes—truth

Entshuldigt (Yidd.)—excuse me

Eretz Yisroel—the Land of Israel

Erev Shabbos—Friday

Farherr (Yidd.)—exam

Frum (Yidd.)—religiously observant

Gam zu l'tovah—this is also for the good

Gemara (Aram.)—Talmud

Golus—exile

Goyim—gentiles

Goyishe—characteristic of gentiles

Hachnosas orchim—welcoming guests

Hachnosas sefer Torah—inauguration of a new Torah scroll

Halevai—if only

Hashem yisborach—G-d, may He be blessed

Hashgochoh Protis—Divine providence

Hashovas aveidah—returning a lost object

Haskomoh—approbation

Hatzlochoh—success

Hefker—ownerless

Heilig (Yidd.)—holy

Heimishe (Yidd.)—homey

Hesped—eulogy

Im yirtzeh Hashem—G-d-willing

K'ein ayin hora (Yidd.)—against the evil eye

Kallah—bride

Kedusha—holiness

Kehillah—congregation

Keilim—utensils

Kein yirbu—may they continue to multiply

Kibbud ov v'eym—respect for one's father and mother

Kindertransport (Germ.)—The movement to evacuate children to Britain from Nazi Germany. The first transport was in 1938. By the outbreak of war 9,354 children had arrived, 7,482 of them Jewish.

Kollel—full-time or intensive Torah study program, usually for married men

Kosel Hama'aravi—the Western Wall in Jerusalem, the last standing remnant of the Second Temple

Lebedig (Yidd.)—lively

Lechayim—lit., "to life," a traditional toast

Levayah—funeral

Limudei chol—secular studies

Limudei kodesh—religious studies

Loshon hora—lit., "evil speech," generally referring to gossip, slander, talebearing, etc.

Loshon kodesh—the holy tongue, Hebrew

Maariv—the evening prayer

Maggid—a person who would give sermons on moral subjects

Mammele (Yidd.)—lit., "little mother," an endearing name for a child or grandchild

Maskim—agree

Mazel—luck

Mechallel Shabbos—to desecrate the Sabbath

Mechilah—forgiveness

Mechitzah—divider that separates between men and women in the synagogue

Mechuteniste (Yidd.)—the mother of one's son-in-law or daughter-in-law

Mechutonim (Yidd.)—the parents of one's son-in-law or daughter-in-law

Mein (Yidd.)—mine

Mekarev—to attract, bring close

Mekayem—fulfill

Melamed—teacher

Menachem oveil—to comfort a mourner

Menahel—school principal

Mensch (Yidd.)—an upstanding man

Mesameach—to make happy

Meshugene (Yidd.)—crazy person

Midah, midos—character trait(s)

Mikveh—ritual bath

Minhag—custom

Mishloach manos—gifts of food sent to fellow Jews on the holiday of Purim

Mitzvos—Torah-based commandments

Nachas—satisfaction

Nebach (Yidd.)—a pity

Nechdige tug (Yidd.)—lit., "a yesterday day," a preposterous idea

Nes, nissim—miracle(s)

Neshomoh, neshomos—soul(s)

Niftar—died

Nisayon—test

Olam habah—the World to Come, heaven

Olam Ha-emes—the World of Truth, heaven

Parnossoh—a livelihood

Petirah—death

Peyos—sidelocks

Rabbonim—rabbis

Rachmonus—mercy

Rebbe—leader of a Chassidic group

Rebbitzen (Yidd.)—wife of a Rebbe or rabbi

Refaeinu—prayer for healing

Refuah sheleimah—a complete recovery

Reiss kriyah (Yidd.)—to tear one's garment in grief over the death
   of a close relative

Ribono shel Olam—Master of the Universe, G-d

Rishus—wickedness

Rosh Chodesh—the beginning of a new month in the Jewish calendar

Rosh Hakollel—head of a kollel (see *Kollel*)

Rosh haYeshiva—head of a yeshiva

Rov—rabbi

Ruach Hakodesh—Divine guidance

Ruchniyus—spirituality

Sefer—holy book

Seudah—festive meal

Shaalah—a question of halacha (Jewish law)

Shabbos—the Sabbath

Shacharis—the morning prayer

Shadchan, shadchanim—matchmaker(s)

Sheffela (Yidd.)—a term of endearment

Sh'eiris hapleitah—lit., "the remainder of the escapees," referring to
   Jews who survived the Holocaust

Sheitel (Yidd.)—wig

Shema—the prayer recited each morning and night affirming G-d's singular existence and by which Jews accept the yoke of Divine sovereignty

Shepping nachas (Yidd.)—deriving satisfaction

Sheva brochos—festive meals that take place during the seven days following a Jewish wedding

Shidduch, shidduchim—potential marriage partner(s)

Shikker (Yidd.)—drunk

Shiur, shiurim—Torah lecture(s)

Shiva—the seven-day mourning period that follows the death of a close relative

Shloshim—the thirty-day mourning period that follows the death of a close relative

Shochtim—trained animal slaughterers

Shomayim—Heaven

Shteiblech (Yidd.)—little synagogues

Shtetl, shtetlach (Yidd.)—Jewish village(s)

Shtickel (Yidd.)—a little bit

Shtreimel (Yidd.)—fur hat worn by some Chassidim

Shul (Yidd.)—synagogue

Shvigger, Shwieger-Mama (Yidd., Austr.)—mother-in-law

Simcha, simchos—happy occasion(s)

Simchas Torah—holiday immediately following Succos, which celebrates the completion of the yearly Torah-reading cycle

Succos—Festival of Tabernacles, commemorating the huts the Jews dwelled in during the forty years they wandered in the desert, and celebrated by eating and living in the sukkah, a temporary hut

Tachlis—purpose

Tachlisdik (Yidd.)—having a purpose

Tallis—prayer shawl

Talmid chochom, Talmidei chachomim—Torah scholar(s)

Tante (Yidd.)—aunt

Tehillim—Psalms

Tenaim—engagement contract

Teshuva—repentance

Teves—the fourth month in the Jewish year

Tisch (Yidd.)—lit., "table," referring to the table of a Chassidic Rebbe, which is likened to a royal court

Toivel—to ritually immerse

Torahdik (Yidd.)—exhibiting Torah ideals

Treife—non-kosher

Tzniusdik (Yidd.)—modest

Upsheren (Yidd.)—Chassidic custom of cutting a Jewish boy's hair for the first time at the age of three

Vort (Yidd.)—engagement party

Y'mos Hamoshiach—the era of the Messiah

Yahrzeit (Yidd.)—anniversary of a death

Yarei shomayim—a G-d-fearing person

Yemach shemom—may their names be blotted out

Yeshiva ketana—elementary school

Yichus—pedigree

Yidden (Yidd.)—Jews

Yiddishkeit (Yidd.)—Judaism

Yiras Hashem—fear of G-d

Yomim Noraim—the High Holidays

Zechus—merit

Zeesele (Yidd.)—sweetie

Zeide (Yidd.)—grandfather

Zivug—Divinely-ordained marriage partner

Zocheh—to merit